A Distinguished Collection of Contemporary Fiction

Here are twenty American short stories written since the end of World War II.

All have been selected by the noted critic Orville Prescott for their display of fine writing style and inherent interest. Diverse in subject and presentation, they all possess the virtues of the classic short story—a distinct foundation of plot, action, and surprise, or a strong revelation of character and emotional atmosphere, and frequently both.

Mid-Century

AN ANTHOLOGY OF DISTINGUISHED CONTEMPORARY AMERICAN SHORT STORIES

Selected and with an Introduction by
ORVILLE PRESCOTT

WASHINGTON SQUARE PRESS
POCKET BOOKS • NEW YORK

MID-CENTURY:

An Anthology of Distinguished
Contemporary American Short Stories

WASHINGTON SQUARE PRESS edition published January, 1958
9th printing........................March, 1973

Published by   **L**
POCKET BOOKS, a division of Simon & Schuster, Inc.,
630 Fifth Avenue, New York, N.Y. 10020

WASHINGTON SQUARE PRESS editions are distributed
in the U.S. by Simon & Schuster, Inc., 630 Fifth Avenue,
New York, N.Y. 10020 and in Canada by Simon & Schuster of Canada, Ltd., Richmond Hill, Ontario, Canada.

ACKNOWLEDGMENTS

For permission to reprint copyright material controlled by them, the editor
thanks the following authors, publishers and agents:

BRANDT & BRANDT for "Cyclists' Raid" by Frank Rooney, from the January,
1951, issue of *Harper's Magazine*. Copyright, 1951, by Frank Rooney.

JAMES BROWN ASSOCIATES for "The Trial of Mr. M" by Louis Auchincloss, from the October, 1956, issue of *Harper's Magazine*. Copyright, 1956, by
Louis Auchincloss.

WM. COLLINS SONS & CO., LTD. (London) for "The Cave" from *Tales of
the South Pacific* by James A. Michener.

DODD, MEAD & COMPANY for "The *Terrible* Miss Dove" from *Good Morning, Miss Dove* by Frances Gray Patton. Copyright, 1946, by The Curtis Pub-
lishing Company. Copyright, 1954, by Frances Gray Patton.

FARRAR, STRAUS & GIROUX, INC. for "The Lottery" from *The Lottery*
by Shirley Jackson; copyright, 1948, by The New Yorker Magazine, Inc.; published, 1949, by Farrar, Straus & Giroux, Inc. For "Bad Characters" by Jean
Stafford; copyright, 1954, by The New Yorker Magazine, Inc., from *Stories*,
published, 1956, by Farrar, Straus & Giroux, Inc.

VICTOR GOLLANCZ, LTD. (London) for "The *Terrible* Miss Dove" from *Good Morning, Miss Dove* by Frances Gray Patton. Permission granted by A. M. Heath & Co., Ltd.

HAMISH HAMILTON, LTD. (London) for "The Hour of Letdown" from *The Second Tree from the Corner* by E. B. White.

HARCOURT, BRACE AND COMPANY, INC. for "When the Bough Breaks," copyright, 1947, by Elizabeth Enright; reprinted from *The Moment Before the Rain* by Elizabeth Enright by permission of Harcourt, Brace and Company, Inc. For "The River," copyright, 1953, by Flannery O'Connor; reprinted from *A Good Man Is Hard to Find* by Flannery O'Connor by permission of Harcourt, Brace and Company, Inc. For "A Little Collar for the Monkey," copyright, 1948, by Jessamyn West; reprinted from *Love, Death, and the Ladies' Drill Team* by Jessamyn West by permission of Harcourt, Brace and Company, Inc.

HARPER & BROTHERS for "The Hour of Letdown" from *The Second Tree from the Corner* by E. B. White. Copyright, 1951, by E. B. White. First published in *The New Yorker.*

WILLIAM HEINEMANN, LTD. (London) for "In Greenwich There Are Many Gravelled Walks" from *In the Absence of Angels* by Hortense Calisher and "When the Bough Breaks" from *The Moment Before the Rain* by Elizabeth Enright.

HODDER & STOUGHTON, LTD. (London) for "A Little Collar for the Monkey" from *Love, Death, and the Ladies' Drill Team* by Jessamyn West. Permission granted by A. M. Heath & Co., Ltd.

ALFRED A. KNOPF, INC. for "The Black Prince" by Shirley Ann Grau. Reprinted from *The Black Prince and Other Stories* by permission of the publisher, Alfred A. Knopf, Inc. Copyright, 1953, 1954, by Shirley Ann Grau.

LITTLE, BROWN & COMPANY for "The Day of the Last Rock Fight" from *Able Baker and Others* by Joseph Whitehill; copyright, ©, 1954, by Joseph Whitehill. For "Lunch at Honolulu" from *Thirty Years* by John P. Marquand; copyright, 1945, by John P. Marquand. This story first appeared in *Harper's Magazine.* For "A Cold Potato" from *No But I Saw the Movie* by Peter De Vries; copyright, 1950, by Peter De Vries. This story first appeared in *The New Yorker.* For "In Greenwich There Are Many Gravelled Walks" from *In the Absence of Angels* by Hortense Calisher; copyright, 1950, by Hortense Calisher. This story first appeared in *The New Yorker.*

McGRAW-HILL BOOK COMPANY, INC. for "Land of Our Enemies" from *Clearing in the Sky* by Jesse Stuart, published by McGraw-Hill Book Company, Inc. Copyright, 1945, 1950, by Jesse Stuart.

McINTOSH & OTIS, INC. for "Lost Sister" from *The Hanging Tree* by Dorothy M. Johnson. Copyright, 1956, by Dorothy M. Johnson. This story appeared originally in *Collier's.* Permission granted by the author.

CORD MEYER, JR. for "Waves of Darkness" from the January, 1946, issue of *The Atlantic Monthly.* Copyright, 1945, by The Atlantic Monthly Company.

WILLIAM MORRIS AGENCY for "The Cave" from *Tales of the South Pacific* by James A. Michener. Copyright, 1947, by James A. Michener.

HAROLD OBER ASSOCIATES for "The Shining Thing" by Sidney Carroll, from the May, 1956, issue of *Good Housekeeping*. ©, 1956, The Hearst Corporation.

PEARN, POLLINGER & HIGHAM, LTD. (London) for "A Cold Potato" from *No But I Saw the Movie* by Peter De Vries, published in England by Victor Gollancz, Ltd.

MAX REINHARDT, LTD. (London) for "The Day of the Last Rock Fight" from *Able Baker and Others* by Joseph Whitehill.

CYNTHIA MARSHALL RICH for "My Sister's Marriage." Reprinted from *Mademoiselle*. ©, Street & Smith Publications, Inc., 1955.

NEVILLE SPEARMAN, LTD. (London) for "The River" from *A Good Man Is Hard to Find* by Flannery O'Connor. Permission granted by A. M. Heath & Co., Ltd.

CONTENTS

INTRODUCTION

The twenty stories gathered here have all been published since the end of the Second World War. They demonstrate, it seems to me, that in quality and variety the American short story continues to excel. And this is gratifying, because during the last thirteen years a number of important magazines which regularly printed short fiction have ceased publication. Several of the writers whose brilliant stories appeared in the long armistice between world wars are dead—Stephen Vincent Benét, Ring Lardner, F. Scott Fitzgerald, and John P. Marquand, and Ernest Hemingway. One Master of the short story, Wilbur Daniel Steele, is no longer writing them. But others have taken their places, and not unworthily.

Like all anthologies, this one represents the personal preferences of its editor and his literary convictions about what kinds of work should be represented. My preferences are for stories which are both well written and entertaining. I think that all these are. I believe that a good story must be about something definite; if not a conflict with guns, then at least a conflict within somebody's mind with a decision reached. I prefer stories in which something happens, some revelation about character is made or some comment on life is recorded.

I don't like stories which are ambiguous for ambiguity's sake; which create a mood of defeat and frustration about persons who do not seem real or worthy of attention; which explore the depths of degeneracy and vice merely to shock. You will find none of these here.

But you will find stories which stem from one or the other of the two great traditions in the art of the short story, and stories in which elements of both traditions are mixed. The first of these is the story of plot, action and surprise. Maupassant, Kipling, O. Henry and Jack London all wrote this kind of story and often used it to portray typical kinds of human beings, to satirize them or to glorify them.

The other tradition is the story of character, of emotional atmosphere, of meaning rather than of narrative. Chekhov and Katherine Mansfield pioneered on this frontier and hundreds of able writers have followed them. Such stories can be intellectually stimulating, deeply moving and highly amusing. Most of the stories in this collection are mixtures of both traditions.

A good example is Jesse Stuart's "Land of Our Enemies," which is a superb story about a Kentucky mountain feud. But instead of telling about the various murders in the feud, Mr. Stuart has summed up the essence of feuding emotion in one episode. Typical of the story of pure plot and thoroughly refreshing in its romantic and old-fashioned way is Sidney Carroll's "The Shining Thing." Typical of the character-and-emotion story is "The Trial of Mr. M" by Louis Auchincloss. It contains a dramatic situation, but its chief interest lies in Mr. Auchincloss' wonderfully affectionate and yet gently satirical portrait of a lovable and crotchety schoolmaster.

In this collection are authors as distinguished and popular as James A. Michener and as little known as Joseph Whitehill and Frank Rooney. The subject matter is as various as I could make it. There are stories about war, children, schoolteachers, Negroes, happy people and unhappy people. Two of these stories—"The Lottery," by Shirley Jackson, and "Cyclists' Raid," by Frank Rooney—reflect the violence and fear of our grim modern world. Two are delightfully funny—"A Cold Potato," by Peter De Vries, and "The Hour of Letdown," by E. B. White.

But several kinds of stories are not here because I am tired of them: stories about the corruption of immoral adults as seen through the eyes of a sensitive child and stories about race prejudice. Good stories of both kinds are common, but there have been too many.

Several distinguished short-story writers are not here because I found stories on similar subjects I like better than theirs, or because I have let one story represent a whole school of writing. Thus, *The New Yorker* magazine, which is well represented here, is particularly famous for ironic studies of ineffectual and miserable persons in moments of defeat and despair. Hortense Calisher's "In Greenwich There Are Many Gravelled Walks" is a brilliant example of this kind of story and I greatly admire it; but I think one of its kind is enough.

There is a good reason why no story by William Faulkner is included. Our budget was not large enough to meet the price his representatives asked.

—ORVILLE PRESCOTT

Mid-Century:
An Anthology of Distinguished
Contemporary American Short Stories

What happens when a girl kidnaped by Indians returns to her family in middle age? Not what you would expect in this fine and poignant story of the Old West as it really was.

Lost Sister

IIIIIIIIIIIIIIIII D O R O T H Y   M.   J O H N S O N IIIIIIIIIIIIIIIII

Our household was full of women, who overwhelmed my Uncle Charlie and sometimes confused me with their bustle and chatter. We were the only men on the place. I was nine years old when still another woman came—Aunt Bessie, who had been living with the Indians.

When my mother told me about her, I couldn't believe it. The savages had killed my father, a cavalry lieutenant, two years before. I hated Indians and looked forward to wiping them out when I got older. (But when I was grown, they were no menace any more.)

"What did she live with the hostiles for?" I demanded.

"They captured her when she was a little girl," Ma said. "She was three years younger than you are. Now she's coming home."

High time she came home, I thought. I said so, promising, "If they was ever to get me, I wouldn't stay with 'em long."

Ma put her arms around me. "Don't talk like that. They won't get you. They'll never get you."

I was my mother's only real tie with her husband's family. She was not happy with those masterful women, my Aunts Margaret, Hannah and Sabina, but she would not go back East where she came from. Uncle Charlie managed the store the aunts owned, but he wasn't really a member of the family

1

—he was just Aunt Margaret's husband. The only man who had belonged was my father, the aunts' younger brother. And I belonged, and someday the store would be mine. My mother stayed to protect my heritage.

None of the three sisters, my aunts, had ever seen Aunt Bessie. She had been taken by the Indians before they were born. Aunt Mary had known her—Aunt Mary was two years older—but she lived a thousand miles away now and was not well.

There was no picture of the little girl who had become a legend. When the family had first settled here, there was enough struggle to feed and clothe the children without having pictures made of them.

Even after Army officers had come to our house several times and there had been many letters about Aunt Bessie's delivery from the savages, it was a long time before she came. Major Harris, who made the final arrangements, warned my aunts that they would have problems, that Aunt Bessie might not be able to settle down easily into family life.

This was only a challenge to Aunt Margaret, who welcomed challenges. "She's our own flesh and blood," Aunt Margaret trumpeted. "Of course she must come to us. My poor, dear sister Bessie, torn from her home forty years ago!"

The major was earnest but not tactful. "She's been with the savages all those years," he insisted. "And she was only a little girl when she was taken. I haven't seen her myself, but it's reasonable to assume that she'll be like an Indian woman."

My stately Aunt Margaret arose to show that the audience was ended. "Major Harris," she intoned, "I cannot permit anyone to criticize my own dear sister. She will live in my home, and if I do not receive official word that she is coming within a month, I shall take steps."

Aunt Bessie came before the month was up.

The aunts in residence made valiant preparations. They bustled and swept and mopped and polished. They moved me from my own room to my mother's—as she had been begging them to do because I was troubled with nightmares. They prepared my old room for Aunt Bessie with many small comforts—fresh doilies everywhere, hairpins, a matching pitcher and bowl, the best towels and two new nightgowns in case hers might be old. (The fact was that she didn't have any.)

"Perhaps we should have some dresses made," Hannah suggested. "We don't know what she'll have with her."

"We don't know what size she'll take, either," Margaret pointed out. "There'll be time enough for her to go to the store after she settles down and rests for a day or two. Then she can shop to her heart's content."

Ladies of the town came to call almost every afternoon while the preparations were going on. Margaret promised them that, as soon as Bessie had recovered sufficiently from her ordeal, they should all meet her at tea.

Margaret warned her anxious sisters, "Now, girls, we mustn't ask her too many questions at first. She must rest for a while. She's been through a terrible experience." Margaret's voice dropped way down with those last two words, as if only she could be expected to understand.

Indeed Bessie had been through a terrible experience, but it wasn't what the sisters thought. The experience from which she was suffering, when she arrived, was that she had been wrenched from her people, the Indians, and turned over to strangers. She had not been freed. She had been made a captive.

Aunt Bessie came with Major Harris and an interpreter, a half-blood with greasy black hair hanging down to his shoulders. His costume was half Army and half primitive. Aunt Margaret swung the door open wide when she saw them coming. She ran out with her sisters following, while my mother and I watched from a window. Margaret's arms were outstretched, but when she saw the woman closer, her arms dropped and her glad cry died.

She did not cringe, my Aunt Bessie who had been an Indian for forty years, but she stopped walking and stood staring, helpless among her captors.

The sisters had described her often as a little girl. Not that they had ever seen her, but she was a legend, the captive child. Beautiful blond curls, they said she had, and big blue eyes—she was a fairy child, a pale-haired little angel who ran on dancing feet.

The Bessie who came back was an aging woman who

plodded in moccasins, whose dark dress did not belong on her bulging body. Her brown hair hung just below her ears. It was growing out; when she was first taken from the Indians, her hair had been cut short to clean out the vermin.

Aunt Margaret recovered herself and, instead of embracing this silent stolid woman, satisfied herself by patting an arm and crying, "Poor dear Bessie, I am your sister Margaret. And here are our sisters Hannah and Sabina. We do hope you're not all tired out from your journey!"

Aunt Margaret was all graciousness, because she had been assured beyond doubt that this was truly a member of the family. She must have believed—Aunt Margaret could believe anything—that all Bessie needed was to have a nice nap and wash her face. Then she would be as talkative as any of them.

The other aunts were quick-moving and sharp of tongue. But this one moved as if her sorrows were a burden on her bowed shoulders, and when she spoke briefly in answer to the interpreter, you could not understand a word of it.

Aunt Margaret ignored these peculiarities. She took the party into the front parlor—even the interpreter, when she understood there was no avoiding it. She might have gone on battling with the major about him, but she was in a hurry to talk to her lost sister.

"You won't be able to converse with her unless the interpreter is present," Major Harris said. "Not," he explained hastily, "because of any regulation, but because she has forgotten English."

Aunt Margaret gave the half-blood interpreter a look of frowning doubt and let him enter. She coaxed Bessie. "Come, dear, sit down."

The interpreter mumbled, and my Indian aunt sat cautiously on a needlepoint chair. For most of her life she had been living with people who sat comfortably on the ground.

The visit in the parlor was brief. Bessie had had her instructions before she came. But Major Harris had a few warnings for the family. "Technically, your sister is still a prisoner," he explained, ignoring Margaret's start of horror. "She will be in your custody. She may walk in your fenced yard, but she must not leave it without official permission.

"Mrs. Raleigh, this may be a heavy burden for you all. But she has been told all this and has expressed willingness to conform to these restrictions. I don't think you will have any trouble keeping her here." Major Harris hesitated, remembered that he was a soldier and a brave man, and added, "If I did, I wouldn't have brought her."

There was the making of a sharp little battle, but Aunt Margaret chose to overlook the challenge. She could not overlook the fact that Bessie was not what she had expected.

Bessie certainly knew that this was her lost white family, but she didn't seem to care. She was infinitely sad, infinitely removed. She asked one question: "Ma-ry?" and Aunt Margaret almost wept with joy.

"Sister Mary lives a long way from here," she explained, "and she isn't well, but she will come as soon as she's able. Dear sister Mary!"

The interpreter translated this, and Bessie had no more to say. That was the only understandable word she ever did say in our house, the remembered name of her older sister.

When the aunts, all chattering, took Bessie to her room, one of them asked, "But where are her things?"

Bessie had no things, no baggage. She had nothing at all but the clothes she stood in. While the sisters scurried to bring a comb and other oddments, she stood like a stooped monument, silent and watchful. This was her prison. Very well, she would endure it.

"Maybe tomorrow we can take her to the store and see what she would like," Aunt Hannah suggested.

"There's no hurry," Aunt Margaret declared thoughtfully. She was getting the idea that this sister was going to be a problem. But I don't think Aunt Margaret ever really stopped hoping that one day Bessie would cease to be different, that she would end her stubborn silence and begin to relate the events of her life among the savages, in the parlor over a cup of tea.

My Indian aunt accustomed herself, finally, to sitting on the chair in her room. She seldom came out, which was a relief to her sisters. She preferred to stand, hour after hour, looking out the window—which was open only about a foot, in spite of all Uncle Charlie's efforts to budge it higher. And she always wore moccasins. She never was able to wear shoes from the store, but seemed to treasure the shoes brought to her.

The aunts did not, of course, take her shopping after all. They made her a couple of dresses; and when they told her, with signs and voluble explanations, to change her dress, she did.

After I found that she was usually at the window, looking across the flat land to the blue mountains, I played in the yard so I could stare at her. She never smiled, as an aunt should, but she looked at me sometimes, thoughtfully, as if measuring my worth. By performing athletic feats, such as walking on my hands, I could get her attention. For some reason, I valued it.

She didn't often change expression, but twice I saw her scowl with disapproval. Once was when one of the aunts slapped me in a casual way. I had earned the slap, but the Indians did not punish children with blows. Aunt Bessie was shocked, I think, to see that white people did. The other time was when I talked back to someone with spoiled, small-boy insolence—and that time the scowl was for me.

The sisters and my mother took turns, as was their Christian duty, in visiting her for half an hour each day. Bessie didn't eat at the table with us—not after the first meal.

The first time my mother took her turn, it was under protest. "I'm afraid I'd start crying in front of her," she argued, but Aunt Margaret insisted.

I was lurking in the hall when Ma went in. Bessie said something, then said it again, peremptorily, until my mother guessed what she wanted. She called me and put her arm around me as I stood beside her chair. Aunt Bessie nodded, and that was all there was to it.

Afterward, my mother said, "She likes you. And so do I." She kissed me.

"I don't like her," I complained. "She's queer."

"She's a sad old lady," my mother explained. "She had a little boy once, you know."

"What happened to him?"

"He grew up and became a warrior. I suppose she was

proud of him. Now the Army has him in prison somewhere. He's half Indian. He was a dangerous man."

He was indeed a dangerous man, and a proud man, a chief, a bird of prey whose wings the Army had clipped after bitter years of trying.

However, my mother and my Indian aunt had that one thing in common: they both had sons. The other aunts were childless.

There was a great to-do about having Aunt Bessie's photograph taken. The aunts who were stubbornly and valiantly trying to make her one of the family wanted a picture of her for the family album. The government wanted one too, for some reason—perhaps because someone realized that a thing of historic importance had been accomplished by recovering the captive child.

Major Harris sent a young lieutenant with the greasy-haired interpreter to discuss the matter in the parlor. (Margaret, with great foresight, put a clean towel on a chair and saw to it the interpreter sat there.) Bessie spoke very little during that meeting, and of course we understood only what the half-blood *said* she was saying.

No, she did not want her picture made. No.

But your son had his picture made. Do you want to see it? They teased her with that offer, and she nodded.

If we let you see his picture, then will you have yours made?

She nodded doubtfully. Then she demanded more than had been offered: If you let me keep his picture, then you can make mine.

No, you can only look at it. We have to keep his picture. It belongs to us.

My Indian aunt gambled for high stakes. She shrugged and spoke, and the interpreter said, "She not want to look. She will keep or nothing."

My mother shivered, understanding as the aunts could not understand what Bessie was gambling—all or nothing.

Bessie won. Perhaps they had intended that she should. She was allowed to keep the photograph that had been made of her son. It has been in history books many times—the half-

white chief, the valiant leader who was not quite great enough
to keep his Indian people free.

His photograph was taken after he was captured, but
you would never guess it. His head is high, his eyes stare
with boldness but not with scorn, his long hair is arranged
with care—dark hair braided on one side and with a tendency
to curl where the other side hangs loose—and his hands hold
the pipe like a royal scepter.

That photograph of the captive but unconquered warrior
had its effect on me. Remembering him, I began to control
my temper and my tongue, to cultivate reserve as I grew
older, to stare with boldness but not scorn at people who
annoyed or offended me. I never met him, but I took silent
pride in him—Eagle Head, my Indian cousin.

Bessie kept his picture on her dresser when she was not
holding it in her hands. And she went like a docile, silent
child to the photograph studio, in a carriage with Aunt Margaret early one morning, when there would be few people
on the street to stare.

Bessie's photograph is not proud but pitiful. She looks out
with no expression. There is no emotion there, no challenge,
only the face of an aging woman with short hair, only endurance and patience. The aunts put a copy in the family
album.

But they were nearing the end of their tether. The Indian
aunt was a solid ghost in the house. She did nothing because
there was nothing for her to do. Her gnarled hands must have
been skilled at squaws' work, at butchering meat and scraping
and tanning hides, at making tepees and beading ceremonial
clothes. But her skills were useless and unwanted in a civilized
home. She did not even sew when my mother gave her cloth
and needles and thread. She kept the sewing things beside her
son's picture.

She ate (in her room) and slept (on the floor) and stood
looking out the window. That was all, and it could not go
on. But it had to go on, at least until my sick Aunt Mary was
well enough to travel—Aunt Mary who was her older sister,
the only one who had known her when they were children.

The sisters' duty visits to Aunt Bessie became less and
less visits and more and more duty. They settled into a bear-

able routine. Margaret had taken upon herself the responsibility of trying to make Bessie talk. Make, I said, not teach. She firmly believed that her stubborn and unfortunate sister needed only encouragement from a strong-willed person. So Margaret talked, as to a child, when she bustled in:

"Now there you stand, just looking, dear. What in the world is there to see out there? The birds—are you watching the birds? Why don't you try sewing? Or you could go for a little walk in the yard. Don't you want to go out for a nice little walk?"

Bessie listened and blinked.

Margaret could have understood an Indian woman's not being able to converse in a civilized tongue, but her own sister was not an Indian. Bessie was white, therefore she should talk the language her sisters did—the language she had not heard since early childhood.

Hannah, the put-upon aunt, talked to Bessie too, but she was delighted not to get any answers and not to be interrupted. She bent over her embroidery when it was her turn to sit with Bessie and told her troubles in an unending flow. Bessie stood looking out the window the whole time.

Sabina, who had just as many troubles, most of them emanating from Margaret and Hannah, went in like a martyr, firmly clutching her Bible, and read aloud from it until her time was up. She took a small clock along so that she would not, because of annoyance, be tempted to cheat.

After several weeks Aunt Mary came, white and trembling and exhausted from her illness and the long, hard journey. The sisters tried to get the interpreter in but were not successful. (Aunt Margaret took that failure pretty hard.) They briefed Aunt Mary, after she had rested, so the shock of seeing Bessie would not be too terrible. I saw them meet, those two.

Margaret went to the Indian woman's door and explained volubly who had come, a useless but brave attempt. Then she stood aside, and Aunt Mary was there, her lined white face aglow, her arms outstretched. "Bessie! Sister Bessie!" she cried.

And after one brief moment's hesitation, Bessie went into her arms and Mary kissed her sun-dark, weathered cheek.

Bessie spoke. "Ma-ry," she said. "Ma-ry." She stood with tears running down her face and her mouth working. So much to tell, so much suffering and fear—and joy and triumph, too—and the sister there at last who might legitimately hear it all and understand.

But the only English word that Bessie remembered was "Mary," and she had not cared to learn any others. She turned to the dresser, took her son's picture in her work-hardened hands, reverently, and held it so her sister could see. Her eyes pleaded.

Mary looked on the calm, noble, savage face of her half-blood nephew and said the right thing: "My, isn't he handsome!" She put her head on one side and then the other. "A fine boy, sister," she approved. "You must"—she stopped, but she finished—"be awfully proud of him, dear!"

Bessie understood the tone if not the words. The tone was admiration. Her son was accepted by the sister who mattered. Bessie looked at the picture and nodded, murmuring. Then she put it back on the dresser.

Aunt Mary did not try to make Bessie talk. She sat with her every day for hours, and Bessie did talk—but not in English. They sat holding hands for mutual comfort while the captive child, grown old and a grandmother, told what had happened in forty years. Aunt Mary said that was what Bessie was talking about. But she didn't understand a word of it and didn't need to.

"There is time enough for her to learn English again," Aunt Mary said. "I think she understands more than she lets on. I asked her if she'd like to come and live with me, and she nodded. We'll have the rest of our lives for her to learn English. But what she has been telling me—she can't wait to tell that. About her life, and her son."

"Are you sure, Mary dear, that you should take the responsibility of having her?" Margaret asked dutifully, no doubt shaking in her shoes for fear Mary would change her mind now that deliverance was in sight. "I do believe she'd be happier with you, though we've done all we could."

Margaret and the other sisters would certainly be happier with Bessie somewhere else. And so, it developed, would the United States government.

Major Harris came with the interpreter to discuss details, and they told Bessie she could go, if she wished, to live with Mary a thousand miles away. Bessie was patient and willing, stolidly agreeable. She talked a great deal more to the interpreter than she had ever done before. He answered at length and then explained to the others that she had wanted to know how she and Mary would travel to this far country. It was hard, he said, for her to understand just how far they were going.

Later we knew that the interpreter and Bessie had talked about much more than that.

Next morning, when Sabina took breakfast to Bessie's room, we heard a cry of dismay. Sabina stood holding the tray, repeating, "She's gone out the window! She's gone out the window!"

And so she had. The window that had always stuck so that it would not raise more than a foot was open wider now. And the photograph of Bessie's son was gone from the dresser. Nothing else was missing except Bessie and the decent dark dress she had worn the day before.

My Uncle Charlie got no breakfast that morning. With Margaret shrieking orders, he leaped on a horse and rode to the telegraph station.

Before Major Harris got there with half a dozen cavalry-men, civilian scouts were out searching for the missing woman. They were expert trackers. Their lives had depended, at various times, on their ability to read the meaning of a turned stone, a broken twig, a bruised leaf. They found that Bessie had gone south. They tracked her for ten miles. And then they lost the trail, for Bessie was as skilled as they were. Her life had sometimes depended on leaving no stone or twig or leaf marked by her passage. She traveled fast at first. Then, with time to be careful, she evaded the followers she knew would come.

The aunts were stricken with grief—at least Aunt Mary was—and bowed with humiliation about what Bessie had done. The blinds were drawn, and voices were low in the house. We had been pitied because of Bessie's tragic folly in having let the Indians make a savage of her. But now we were traitors because we had let her get away.

Aunt Mary kept saying pitifully, "Oh, why did she go? I thought she would be contented with me!"

The others said that it was, perhaps, all for the best.

Aunt Margaret proclaimed, "She has gone back to her own." That was what they honestly believed, and so did Major Harris.

My mother told me why she had gone. "You know that picture she had of the Indian chief, her son? He's escaped from the jail he was in. The fort got word of it, and they think Bessie may be going to where he's hiding. That's why they're trying so hard to find her. They think," my mother explained, "that she knew of his escape before they did. They think the interpreter told her when he was here. There was no other way she could have found out."

They scoured the mountains to the south for Eagle Head and Bessie. They never found her, and they did not get him until a year later, far to the north. They could not capture him that time. He died fighting.

After I grew up, I operated the family store, disliking storekeeping a little more every day. When I was free to sell it, I did, and went to raising cattle. And one day, riding in a canyon after strayed steers, I found—I think—Aunt Bessie. A cowboy who worked for me was along, or I would never have let anybody know.

We found weathered bones near a little spring. They had a mystery on them, those nameless human bones suddenly come upon. I could feel old death brushing my back.

"Some prospector," suggested my riding partner.

I thought so too until I found, protected by a log, sodden scraps of fabric that might have been a dark, respectable dress. And wrapped in them was a sodden something that might have once been a picture.

The man with me was young, but he had heard the story of the captive child. He had been telling me about it, in fact. In the passing years it had acquired some details that surprised me. Aunt Bessie had become once more a fair-haired beauty, in this legend that he had heard, but utterly sad and silent. Well, sad and silent she really was.

I tried to push the sodden scrap of fabric back under the log, but he was too quick for me. "That ain't no shirt, that's a dress!" he announced. "This here was no prospector—it was a woman!" He paused and then announced with awe, "I bet you it was your Indian aunt!"

I scowled and said, "Nonsense. It could be anybody."

He got all worked up about it. "If it was *my* aunt," he declared, "I'd bury her in the family plot."

"No," I said, and shook my head.

We left the bones there in the canyon, where they had been for forty-odd years if they were Aunt Bessie's. And I think they were. But I would not make her a captive again. She's in the family album. She doesn't need to be in the family plot.

If my guess about why she left us is wrong, nobody can prove it. She never intended to join her son in hiding. She went in the opposite direction to lure pursuit away.

What happened to her in the canyon doesn't concern me, or anyone. My Aunt Bessie accomplished what she set out to do. It was not her life that mattered, but his. She bought him another year.

John P. Marquand was one of the most distinguished of American novelists and a master of social satire. The satire in this story is clever and the double-barreled ending is brilliant, a surprise punch which shocks the reader into awareness of his own insensibility.

Lunch at Honolulu

|||||||||||||||| J O H N   P.   M A R Q U A N D ||||||||||||||||

The house was off Nuannu, beyond the cemetery where Hawaiian royalty lay with symbolic tabu sticks at the corners of their burial plots. It was a fine clear day by the sea, but rain was falling up by the jagged skyline of the mountains. Mr. Huntley knew that in Honolulu they called it liquid sunshine.

The house where he was invited for lunch was built of coral stone and redwood, and a porte-cochere covered the drive. The house might have been in Redlands, California, except for the ornamental planting. It was said that almost anything could grow on the Hawaiian Islands. By the time the taxicab had stopped beneath the porte-cochere, Mr. Huntley had identified upon the lawns a traveler's palm, an Alexandra palm, a Norfolk Island pine, ginger flowers, hibiscus, and a bed of calla lilies, snapdragons and forget-me-nots. There were also some bamboo and banana. This dizzying combination gave its own horticultural evidence that Honolulu was the melting pot of races and the crossroads of the Pacific.

Even before Mr. Huntley had climbed the steps, a middle-aged Japanese maid had opened the door. Her hair was done in Japanese convention. She wore the kimono and the obi. When she bowed and took his hat, she looked like a part of the chorus of *Madame Butterfly*. Inside, the long living room was cool and shadowy, paneled with some polished darkish wood. There were reed mats on the dark, highly polished floor. There were comfortable American upholstered chairs and Chinese lacquered tables. There were Hawaiian calabashes filled with ginger flowers. There was a large Capehart phonograph, and on the walls were Chinese ancestral portraits, an oblong of old tapa cloth, and some Malay weapons.

The Japanese maid smiled. Before she put her hand in front of her mouth, she revealed three black teeth and one brilliant gold one. She drew in her breath politely.

"Mr. Wintertree, he waits, on the back lanai, please," she said. "This way, please."

As Mr. Huntley followed her, he had a glimpse of himself in a cloudy ornate Italian mirror. His image was disturbing in that shadowy room that was heavy with the scent of tuberoses. He was a moist, dumpy, middle-aged interloper in a wrinkled Palm Beach suit.

Mr. Wintertree was on the back veranda. The veranda, furnished with wicker chairs, potted ferns and hanging air plants, looked over a deep-green tropical gorge to the darker jagged mountains. To the left, far below, were the streets and houses of Honolulu, and the docks and the Aloha Tower, and the harbor and the sea. Mr. Wintertree was a cadaverous man. He was dressed in an immaculate linen suit. His face was deeply tanned. His hair was as white and as smooth as his coat.

"Aloha, Mr. Huntley," he said. "It's very kind of you to come and take pot luck. Mrs. Wintertree was dreadfully sorry she couldn't be here. It's her day at the Red Cross, so it will be a stag party—just five of us. Admiral Smedley is coming with Captain Rotch of his staff. Henry D. Smedley—you know the admiral?"

"No, I have never met him," Mr. Huntley answered. "I hope I'm not too early."

"Oh, no, no," Mr. Wintertree said. "They'll be here any minute now. Just the admiral and Captain Rotch, and Lieutenant—" A slight frown appeared on Mr. Wintertree's face. "What the devil is his name? Oh yes, Wright. A Lieutenant Wright. He's just off a carrier. Walter Jones wrote me about him, too. He's a naval aviator. Did you ever hear Walt mention him?"

"No, not that I remember," Mr. Huntley said. "It's very kind of you to have me here."

"It's always a pleasure to see a friend of old Walt's," Mr. Wintertree said. "Maybe he told you, we were together in the class of '08 at Yale. When did you last see Walt?"

"In New York last month," Mr. Huntley told him. "Walt told me to be sure to look you up."

"I wish you could see this place the way it used to be before the war," Mr. Wintertree said. "It's the duty of kamaainas to make malihinis like the islands, but Honolulu is a madhouse now. Army, Navy—they're into everything. They'll be taking over the golf club next."

"What's a kamaaina?" Mr. Huntley asked.

Mr. Wintertree smiled.

"That's a Hawaiian word. Roughly translated it means 'old-timer,'" Mr. Wintertree said. "I'm an old-timer and you're a malihini. This is a kamaaina house. Father built it in 1880. Honolulu was just a small town on a small Pacific island then. My God, how it's changed!"

"You have a beautiful view from this porch," Mr. Huntley said.

"Lanai, not porch," Mr. Wintertree told him. "I suppose we're eccentric the way we cling to Hawaiian words. This is a lanai, and that couch over there is called a hikkiai. It's a real Hawaiian hikkiai, not just a couple of mattresses the way they make them now. You can see it is made out of lahala mats, the woven leaves of the pandanus tree."

"Hikkiai," Mr. Huntley repeated.

"Good," Mr. Wintertree said. "That's the way to say it."

"What do you do with it?" Mr. Huntley asked.

"Why, you lie on it," Mr. Wintertree said. "Do you want to lie on it?"

"No thanks, not now," Mr. Huntley answered. "You do have a beautiful view from here."

"Those light-colored trees that you see on the side of the mountain are kukui trees," said Mr. Wintertree. "They have small round nuts called kukui nuts. In old times the Hawaiians would string those nuts on a reed and use them for candles.

My father used to say when he was a child that his father—
we come of missionary stock—used to say, 'Children, one more
kukui nut and it's bedtime.'"

Mr. Huntley glanced at a low table, hoping to find a
cigarette.

"When my father was a boy," Mr. Wintertree said, "he
spoke of seeing a little crowd of native Hawaiians on the
docks, about where the Aloha Tower is now. We were all
friends in those days. Those Polynesian boys were looking at
something and laughing—two bluebottle flies. Yes, they had
never seen a fly, and now we have everything—flies, marines,
planes, battleships. I suppose you're out here for the government, Mr. Huntley."

"Yes," said Mr. Huntley. "I'm out for the OWI."

"What's the OWI?" Mr. Wintertree asked.

"That's a native American expression," Mr. Huntley said.

"Now, now," Mr. Wintertree told him. "Don't forget that
we're just as native American here as any other part of
America." He looked at his wrist watch. "I've never known
Admiral Smedley to be so late. Wait—I'm wrong, I think I
hear him now."

Brisk and somewhat heavy steps sounded on the floor of
the living room. It was Admiral Smedley, followed by Captain
Rotch. The admiral's glance was sharp and direct. His face
was set in tranquil lines, like the bust of a Roman emperor.
His gray hair was cut very short. He was dressed in fresh
khaki. He wore two tiny silver stars in his shirt collar. On his
finger was a Naval Academy ring.

"We're just waiting for one other guest," Mr. Wintertree
said. "A friend of a friend of mine. He is just off a carrier—
Lieutenant Wright."

"That must be the *Great Lick*," the admiral said. "She ran
into a little difficulty. What did you say the officer's name
was?"

"Wright," Mr. Wintertree answered.

"I don't know him," the admiral said. "Rotch, did you ever
hear of anybody named Wright?"

"No, sir," the captain said.

"Well, it's a big navy," the admiral said. "And the Pacific's
a big ocean."

"We might have something to drink while we're waiting," Mr. Wintertree said. "Would you care for something, Admiral? Sherry or a Martini?—or a little of our island drink, Okulehau?"

"Okulehau, I haven't had any of that since I was stationed here in '32," the admiral said. "We used to call it Oke. How about you, Rotch?"

"If the boss falls off the wagon, I guess I can fall, too," the captain said, and he laughed.

"I hope you'll excuse me if I don't join you," Mr. Wintertree said. "I very seldom indulge in the middle of the day, but Taka and Togo will give you anything you want. Would you care for a Martini, Mr. Huntley?"

"Thank you," Mr. Huntley said.

The Japanese maid came through the door on the far end of the porch, which evidently led to the dining room. She carried a large tray of dark wood, upon which were small plates of olives and other appetizers. Behind her came an old Japanese in a white coat, with bottles, ice and glasses.

"Taka and Togo have been with us for thirty years," Mr. Wintertree said, and he lowered his voice. "They were very unhappy on December 7th."

"So was I," the admiral said. "Do you live out here too, Mr. Huntley?"

"Oh, no," Mr. Huntley said. "I'm with the OWI. I've only been here about a week."

"Oh, a writer, are you?" the admiral asked. "Well, there's a lot to write about."

"You have a beautiful view from this veranda," Mr. Huntley heard Captain Rotch say to Mr. Wintertree.

"Yes, we think it's a very pleasant lanai," he heard Mr. Wintertree answer. "You see it faces both Mauka and Makai. Those are the old Hawaiian words for the sea and the mountains, Captain Rotch. They form two of the cardinal points on our island's compass. Those light-colored trees on the mountainside are called kukui trees."

"Let's see," the admiral said to Mr. Huntley. "I think I have read something that you have written. Didn't you write an article for the *Saturday Evening Post* about trailers?"

"No, sir, that must have been someone else."

"Yes, maybe it was someone else. Did you fly out, or come by boat?" the admiral asked.

"I flew out," Mr. Huntley told him.

"You can get places flying—anywhere in the world in two days' flying," the admiral said. "It's a great place, Honolulu. We're certainly lifting its face for it. Give us another year and we'll make it look like Pittsburgh. No one's ever going to say again that America can't fight a war. Thank you." He took a glass from the tray the old Japanese was passing.

The Japanese houseman bowed and smiled. He was a very polite old-time Japanese.

"This is like old times," the admiral called. "This is real Oke, Wintertree."

"It comes from the big island," Mr. Wintertree answered. "They used to make it in the old days—that was during prohibition—but there were only two kinds of Okulehau, the right kind and the wrong kind. This is the right kind. It was made from the root of the ti plant. You've seen its leaves on dinner tables, Admiral. In the old days the Hawaiians would break off a ti plant and sit on it and slide down a mountain slope. It was one of the old royal sports."

"Yes, I've heard they did," the admiral said. "In my spare time I've been making a little study of the Polynesians. I've got a dictionary of Hawaiian words."

"It will be useful to you," Mr. Wintertree said. "Hawaiian words still crop up in kamaainas' conversations."

"Some of the words are very expressive," the admiral said. "Do you know the word for cat?" But Mr. Wintertree did not answer. He was moving to the living-room door, to shake hands with the last of his guests, Lieutenant Wright. Lieutenant Wright had a piece of adhesive tape above his left eye, but even so he looked very fresh and young. His voice was loud and mellow.

"And how do you do, sir," Lieutenant Wright said. "Thanks for letting me aboard. I hope I'm not too late to snap onto a drink."

"Oh—not too late at all. I am very glad you could come, Lieutenant," Mr. Wintertree told him. "As soon as I heard from your Uncle Walt . . ."

Lieutenant Wright laughed so loudly that Mr. Huntley saw the admiral's forehead wrinkle.

"Uncle Walt would have given me hell if I had passed you up," Lieutenant Wright said. "Uncle Walt told me if I ever hit this rock to look you up, sir, and now I've hit it." He looked at Mr. Huntley's glass. "Is that a Martini I see him drinking?"

"Yes, that's a Martini," Mr. Wintertree said. "And this is Admiral Smedley, Captain Rotch, and Mr. Huntley."

"How do you do, Admiral," Lieutenant Wright said. "Sorry I'm late, but I don't mind catching up." He took a Martini from the tray. "Make me another one, boy," he added gently. "Maybe you better make me two. This is really a nice place you've got here, Mr. Wintertree."

The conversation had died. There was a silence while Lieutenant Wright picked up another Martini. The admiral cleared his throat.

"I hear you're off the *Great Lick*," the admiral said.

Lieutenant Wright laughed loudly, although there appeared to be no reason for his laughing.

"Yes, sir, the old *Lick* and promise. That's what the kids call her, Admiral, sir," Lieutenant Wright answered. "And she's mostly *Lick*." Lieutenant Wright laughed again. "She really is, sir. She really took them aboard, sir, but we knocked off one of their BBs."

The admiral turned to Captain Rotch. "How many did you say she took?"

"Three of them, sir," the captain said.

"She really took them," Lieutenant Wright laughed again. "Oh, boy! she really took them."

The admiral glanced at Mr. Huntley and then at Mr. Wintertree. He seemed to feel that the occasion compelled him to say something but not too much.

"Occasionally," he said, "in the course of an air battle a Japanese plane crashes on the deck or superstructure of one of our ships—a suicide plane. It naturally causes considerable damage."

Lieutenant Wright whistled. He was on his third Martini, and as far as Mr. Huntley could see, rank did not disturb him.

"Did you say damage, sir?" he asked.

The wrinkles deepened on the admiral's forehead.

"Just one minute, please," he began, but the lieutenant raised his voice.

"It's really rugged when one of them comes in at you," the lieutenant said. "Now this first that hit us—it was about eighteen hundred and thirty hours—he came in from the port side. We gave him everything we had. You could see the 40s going into him like red-hot rivets."

"Just a minute," the admiral said. "Just a minute, son—" but the lieutenant's voice was louder.

"That kid must have been dead, but he still kept coming in. You got the idea there was nothing you could do but stand and take it. It was a very rugged feeling."

"Rotch," the admiral said to the captain. Captain Rotch's manner reminded Huntley of that of a kindly policeman. He rested his hand on Lieutenant Wright's shoulder and whispered something. As he listened, the lieutenant's face looked blank and his thoughts seemed to drift away from him and he was back again where he had started, right on Mr. Wintertree's lanai.

"I'm sorry, sir," he said. "I didn't know it was restricted."

"That's all right, son," the admiral told him. "That's all right."

"Down in Numea we had a song about it," the lieutenant said. "Some of the kids made it up at the club. 'I'm forever whispering secrets.'"

Mr. Wintertree's voice interrupted.

"I think luncheon is ready now," Mr. Wintertree was saying.

"Well, let's skip it," Lieutenant Wright said. "As long as pop here says luncheon's ready."

"If you'll just lead the way, Admiral," Mr. Wintertree said.

In the dining room a narrow dark table was set for lunch. There was a center decoration of breadfruit and green leaves. There were Chinese plates and small wooden bowls filled with a gray pastelike substance, that Mr. Huntley knew was a native food called poi. The admiral was at Mr. Wintertree's right, Mr. Huntley at his left. Captain Rotch was beside Mr. Huntley and the lieutenant was beside the admiral.

"I'm forever whispering secrets," the lieutenant was singing beneath his breath. He lifted up his plate very carefully and set it down. Then Mr. Huntley saw him staring at his bowl of poi. The servants were passing plates of clear consommé.

"I'm sorry there isn't a sixth to balance the table," Mr. Wintertree said. "This is Mrs. Wintertree's day at the Red Cross. I see you looking at the table, Admiral. Do you know what wood it's made from?"

"Yes," the admiral said, "koa wood."

"No, no," Mr. Wintertree said. "It's made from the monkey-pod tree."

"Have they got monkeys on this rock?" the lieutenant asked.

Mr. Wintertree went on without answering.

"Now, the chairs we are sitting on are koa. They are our best wood, very close to mahogany. The koa is a very hand-some tree, Mr. Huntley, long, graceful, curving leaves. You still find specimens in the mountains, but our most beautiful wood came from the kou tree."

"I never heard of the kou tree," the admiral said.

"As long as it isn't the cuckoo tree," Lieutenant Wright said and he began to laugh.

"The old calabashes were all made from the kou," Mr. Wintertree said. "You can see one of them—a very handsome one—on the sideboard, but the kou is nearly extinct. When ants appeared on the island, they ate the kou."

"What did they want to eat it for, pop?" Lieutenant Wright asked.

"They ate the leaves," Mr. Wintertree answered.

"Well, bugs do eat the damnedest things on islands," Lieu-tenant Wright said. "At Hollandia something ate the seat right out of my pants. Maybe it was ants. Ants in my pants, pop."

"Mr. Wintertree," the admiral asked, "do you know the Hawaiian word for cat?"

"Why, yes," Mr. Wintertree said. "Poopooki."

"I suppose you know how the word was derived?" the admiral asked.

The soup was finished. Mr. Wintertree glanced at the servants and they began to take away the plates.

"Oh, yes," he said. "Of course I know." But the admiral went on telling him.

"Well, Huntley ought to hear it," the admiral said. "Mr. Huntley can write it down sometime. It seems that there didn't use to be any cats in the Hawaiian Islands."

"No cats, no ants," Lieutenant Wright said. The admiral glanced at him sideways.

"And no Naval Reserve officers," the admiral said. "It seems the missionaries brought the cats."

Lieutenant Wright smiled.

"And the Navy brought in the reserve officers, Admiral, sir. They had to, to win this war."

Captain Rotch cleared his throat.

"Perhaps the admiral would like to finish what he is saying," he said gently.

"Sorry, sir," Lieutenant Wright said quickly. "Aye, aye, sir. The missionaries brought the cats . . ."

"You see, none of the kanakas had ever seen a cat. They didn't have a name for it," the admiral went on. Mr. Huntley saw that Mr. Wintertree winced when the admiral used the word 'kanaka.' "Then they must have heard one of the white missionary women call her cat 'poor pussy' and that's how you get it—poor pussy—poopooki."

"By God, what do you know," the lieutenant said, and he whistled. "You come to an island and it's like every other island and all the native Joes and Marys are just alike. Coral, palm trees, a lagoon, and then out come the canoes—and there you are, like that." He snapped his fingers. "Pretty soon you beat a drum and start singing."

"You have never been to Honolulu before, have you?" It seemed to Mr. Huntley that Mr. Wintertree's voice was sharp. "I think you'll find it different. These fish are mullet. The old kings used to keep them in the royal fish ponds."

"There's nothing better than good mullet," Captain Rotch said.

"Back out there"—the lieutenant waved his hand to illustrate back out there—"we used to chuck a stick of dynamite in a lagoon and get mullet, and did the natives go for those fish? You ought to have seen them go for them. Once when I was out with a sub over in the Zulu Sea—all right, Admiral, sir, security."

"I'm sorry we can't hear about it," the admiral said.

"This is one-finger poi," Mr. Wintertree told the table. "There's a shortage of good poi, like everything else, but some of my native friends help me."

Mr. Wintertree stopped, because Lieutenant Wright had begun to laugh for no apparent reason.

"You know, they tell a story about me out there, pop," the lieutenant said, and he waved his hand again, to illustrate out there, "and I guess I can tell it to you without breaking security. It's rather a funny story." He laughed again as he remembered it and pushed his plate away. "One of the CPOs who was working with me came up to me one day and he said—'Lieutenant, sir, I ought to get a little leave. This country here is getting me queer.' Well, I didn't blame him. So I just told him to relax and tell me what was the matter. And he said: 'It's this way, sir. All these dark women begin to look to me as though they were white.' And do you know what I said to him? At least, it's what they say I said to him." The lieutenant paused and beamed at everyone. "I said to him—'Kid, what dark women?'" The admiral smiled. Mr. Huntley laughed, although he had heard the story several times before.

"We are having papaya for dessert," Mr. Wintertree said. "It isn't quite the season, but I'm proud of my papayas."

They had small cups of very black coffee out on the lanai. Mr. Wintertree explained that it was kona coffee, so named because it was grown on the slopes of the Kona coast on the big island of Hawaii. There was an island too big to be spoiled, Mr. Wintertree said. The ghosts of the past still lingered over the Kona coast. You could still see the old burial caves in the cliffs that fringe the bay where Captain Cook was killed. You could still see the black walls of lava rock that marked the compounds of the native villages.

As Mr. Huntley sat listening, he was thinking of the irrational accidents that threw people together. In a few moments this party on the lanai would be breaking up. The admiral would return to his office. Mr. Huntley would return to his hotel. He wondered what the lieutenant would find to do.

Very little, he imagined, now that Honolulu was a garrison
town.

"They still sing the old meles on Hawaii," Mr. Wintertree
was saying. "Those old word-of-mouth songs have been passed
on for centuries."

The lieutenant looked at his small cup of coffee.

"Would it be out of order to turn this in for something
else?" he asked.

"Turn it in?" Mr. Wintertree repeated.

"For a Scotch and soda," the lieutenant said. "If you
wouldn't mind, pop."

"Oh, certainly," Mr. Wintertree answered. "A Scotch and
soda, Togo."

"Double," the lieutenant said. "If you wouldn't mind."

"Sometime you should hear an old Hawaiian chant—a
mele," Mr. Wintertree told the admiral. "It's a living page of
history."

The lieutenant clapped his hands together and drummed
his foot on the floor.

"Boom-boom," he said. "Yai, yai, boom-boom. One night at
Tanga those Joes began singing—Oh, thanks."

Togo was back with a double Scotch and soda, but the
lieutenant had grown restless. He prowled back and forth
across the lanai, withdrawn from the conversation, but Mr.
Huntley could still hear him, muttering beneath his breath,
"Yai, yai, boom-boom." This must have gone on for several
minutes while the rest of them were talking before the
Japanese maid appeared. She said some officers in an automobile were calling for Lieutenant Wright. Lieutenant Wright
looked very much relieved.

"I thought those boys could wrangle some transportation,"
he said. "You've got to see these rocks when you hit them.
Well, I'd better be shoving. Thank you, Mr. Wintertree. Good-
by, Admiral, sir. So long, Captain. So long, Mister."

There was a moment's silence when Lieutenant Wright left.
They could hear him cross the living room.

"Boom-boom, boom-boom," he was still chanting. "Yai, yai,
boom-boom."

The admiral looked at his empty cup, and then he looked
at the captain.

"That was a pretty fresh kid," the captain said.

"Yes," the admiral answered. "It's quiet, now he's gone."

"You never can tell about a new guest," Mr. Wintertree said. "I'm sorry."

The wicker chair in which the admiral was sitting creaked as he leaned forward to set down his cup on a little table.

"That's all right," he said. "Every now and then they act that way. You and I would, too." The chair creaked again as the admiral rose. "Will you see if the car is outside, Rotch? It's only that boy was glad—and that's natural—just glad he is still alive."

The agony of adolescence is an old subject, but the
fresh originality with which Mr. Whitehill reveals
both the brutality and the courageous loyalty of
schoolboys is outstanding.

The Day of the Last Rock Fight

IIIIIIIIIIIIII J O S E P H   W H I T E H I L L IIIIIIIIIIIIII

FALLBROOK ACADEMY

May 16, 195—

DEAR DAD,

I expect this will be a very long letter, so I am sending it
to your office marked *Personal*. I know you don't like to do
family business at the office, but I wanted you to have a
chance to read this all by yourself, and I didn't want Mother
or Sue reading it before you did.

Thank you for sending my allowance, and also for the
subscription to the home paper. Thank you also for the nice
new wallet for my birthday. I really needed it, as my old one
was afflicted with rot and falling apart.

I apologize for not having written sooner. As you said in
your last letter, "*Something* must have happened in the last
two months worth writing down." I have been very busy with
things here at school, but mainly I haven't written because I
didn't know how to say what I wanted to say. I hope this
letter will make up for the long delay.

You keep asking me what I think of Fallbrook Academy
and if I'm happy here, and so on. Well, I don't like it here,
and I want to come home. That's what this letter is for—to
tell you that now it's all right for me to come back home. I
guess I know why you sent me here, and I admit that I wanted
very much to come when I did. It's not that the people here

27

aren't nice or anything. They are. They're so nice it's phony. In all the catalogues of the school they call it a *Special School*, but the boys here call it *Goodbar*. (Mr. Goodbar is a chocolate bar full of nuts.) They all kid about it, and pretend they don't care about being put in a school for misfits and boys with emotional problems. I guess most of them like it here. Most of them say they hate their parents, one or both, and are really glad to get away from them. All the faculty are so sweet and kind and sympathetic that a lot of the boys get away with murder. (That last word was sort of a poor choice, I suppose, but I'll leave it there anyway.) But I don't feel like I belong here any more.

It is going to be very complicated to explain everything in just one letter, because there are lots of different ways of looking at that mess that happened there at home, and I suppose I am the only one who knows the whole story. I guess you sent me here because you thought I was terribly upset by Gene Hanlon getting killed out there at Manning Day School at home, and seeing his body lying in the creek, and so on. Well, that was part of it, but only a little part. The rest of it I couldn't tell anybody until Detective Sergeant Gorman put the story in the paper last week. I got that paper in the mail yesterday and I have been reading the story over and over, and feeling relieved and awful at the same time.

I'm sure you read the same story, so you already know that Gene Hanlon was murdered, instead of getting killed accidentally as they said at first. But neither you nor anybody else knows that I saw the murder done, and knew all the time who did it. I guess if I acted upset afterwards it was from knowing all this and not being able to tell anyone about it. I'm going to work on this letter all night, if it takes that long, because I have to get all this out of my system. (When you stay up after curfew around here they don't actually *make* you go to bed, but the doctor who is on duty looks in on you every half hour or so to see what you're doing, and to try to make you *want* to go to bed.)

I suppose the beginning is the best place to start, so I will tell you first about Gene Hanlon, the boy who got killed. He came to Manning Day School last fall as a senior. They said he was fired from his last school, but I don't know about

that. I didn't like him just from looking at him. I know you
hate judgments that way on first impressions, but I couldn't
help it. I wouldn't ever bring him over to our house, but if I
had, you might have seen what I was talking about. He was
big and beefy, and he played on the first string last fall. He
was also blond, and the girls thought he was cute and from
what I heard they fought over him for dates. But he was a
bully, and he cheated in the classroom and he borrowed your
stuff without asking you and then left it some place where you
had to go hunt it up for yourself.

In a school like Manning Day there are always a number
of tight little groups—cliques, I guess you call them—that move
around independently and generally stay out of the way of
the others. I mean there is a football group, and a group of
boys who drink beer, and a group who studies hard, and a
group who loafs and tries to avoid everything that looks like
work, and a group that meets in the locker room to talk about
sex and tell dirty jokes. It was probably the same way when
you yourself went to school, but you may have forgotten.
When you go to a school like that, you pretty soon find the
group that suits you best, and you stay there and don't try
to mix with any of the others, because if you do you won't
be let in.

What I am getting at in this long explanation is that Gene
Hanlon was the Big Man in all the groups I wouldn't be
seen dead in. He was tops among the football players and
their fans. He could tell filthier stories and, he said, hold
more liquor than anybody else. And he told stories about
the things he had done to girls that you wouldn't believe
if anybody else had told them, but with him telling them, you
knew they were all possible. I guess he was feared more than
he was liked, but one thing sure, he never went anywhere
alone. There was always a loud bunch along with him horse-
laughing and beating him on the shoulders.

I stayed out of his way. There is something about me
that brings out the worst in bullies. That's what Peter Irish
used to say. I guess it's because I'm slightly built, and because of those glasses I have to wear. Once, I was going
upstairs to lab, and Gene Hanlon was coming down and we
met halfway, and for no reason I could see, he belted me as

hard as he could on my shoulder. My glasses flew off and bounced halfway down the stairs along with a whole arm-load of books and papers. I had to grab the bannister to keep from following them down myself. Two other guys with him saw him do it and didn't say anything at first, but then they looked at Gene and knew they'd better laugh, so they did. So I sat there on the stairs all confused inside, holding my shoulder to make it stop hurting. Gene Hanlon and the others went on down the stairs laughing to beat all at how I looked there with everything scattered around me. On the way down, Gene kicked my physics book ahead of him, bouncing it all the way to the bottom. When I could stand up all right I went down and got it. When I picked it up it fell apart in my hands with its binding broken and I guess I started to cry. I hate to see books treated that way.

When I had about got everything picked up, Peter Irish came up to where I was and wanted to know what had happened. Peter being my best friend, I told him all about it. Probably there were still tears in my eyes about the physics book because Peter said, "Do you want me to get him for you?"

I thought for a minute how swell that would be, but then I said no. It was almost yes because Peter was the only one in school who could have whipped Gene under any rules, and it was a very satisfying thing to think about. But then I thought about afterwards, when Gene would have gotten over his beating and would begin to wonder why Peter had done it, and he would remember that Peter was my best friend. Then he would put one and one together and start out after me seriously. So I said no.

Peter Irish was a good friend to have. I suppose he was the strongest kid in school, but he didn't ever use his strength to bully people, but just for things that were fun, like squashing a beer can in one hand. You knew him pretty well because of all the times he came over to the house to study with me. I remember the time he beat you at Indian hand wrestling on the dining-room table, and you were a real good sport about it because Mother was watching and laughing at your expression. But anyway, you know how strong Peter was, and you can feature what he would have done to Gene if I'd told him to. Peter always stayed out of fights unless they were for fun, and if they ever got serious he'd quit because he didn't want to hurt anybody. But he would have torn Gene Hanlon apart if I had asked him to.

That was something I don't think you understood—Peter and me, I mean, and why we hung around together. The simplest way to say it is that we swapped talents. I used to write a lot of his themes for him, and help him in labs so he'd finish when the rest of us did, and he'd show me judo holds and how to skin a squirrel, and such things. You would call it a good working agreement.

Now, there are just two more things you have to know about to see the whole picture. The first one is Peter Irish and Angela Pine. Peter and Angela went together all last year and the year before, and neither of them wanted anybody else. Both their folks made them date other kids because they didn't like to see them going steady, but everybody knew that Angela belonged to Peter, and Peter belonged to Angela, and that's all there was to it. He used to talk to me a lot about her, and how they were going to get married and run a riding stable together. And he told me that he would never touch her that way until they were married. They used to kiss good night and that was all, because Peter said that when the great thing happened, he wanted it to happen just right, and it could never be really right while they were both kids in high school. A lot of the fellows thought that more went on between them than I know did, but that's because they didn't understand Peter really. He had a simple set of rules he operated under, and they suited him very well. He was good to Angela and good to animals, and all he asked was to be let alone to do things his own way.

The other thing you have to know about is the noontime rock fights. From the papers and the inquest and all, you know something about them, but not everything. I guess most of the parents were pretty shocked to learn that their little Johnny was in a mob rock fight every day at school, but that's the way it was. The fights started over a year ago, as near as I can recollect, and went on all that time without the faculty ever finding out. The papers made a big scandal out of them and conducted what they called an

"exposé of vicious practices at select Manning Day School."
It was comical, actually, the way everybody got all steamed
up over the things we knew went on all the time, not only
at Manning but in all the other schools in town. Of course,
we all knew the rock fights were wrong, but they were more
fun than they seemed wrong, so we kept them up. (That
time I came home with the mouse under my eye, I didn't get
it by falling in the locker room. I just forgot to duck.)

We had a strict set of rules in the fights so that nobody
would really get hurt or anything, and so the little guys
could get into them too without fear of being killed. All
sixty of us, the whole school, were divided into two teams,
the Union Army and the Confederates, and after lunch in
the cafeteria we'd all get our blue or gray caps and head
out into the woods behind the school. The faculty thought
we played Kick the Can and never followed us out to check
up on us.

Each team had a fort we'd built out of sapling logs—
really just pens about waist high. The forts were about
two hundred yards apart, invisible to each other through
the trees and scrub. You weren't allowed to use rocks any
bigger than a hazelnut, and before you pegged one at a guy
in the opposite army, you had to go *chk, chk* with your
mouth so the guy would have a chance to find where it was
coming from and duck in time. We had scouting parties and
assault teams and patrols, and all the rest of the military
things we could think up. The object was to storm the
enemy's fort and take it before recess was up and we had to
quit.

These rock fights weren't like the papers said at all. I
remember the *Morning Star* called them "pitched battles
of unrelenting fury, where injuries were frequent." That was
silly. If the injuries had been frequent, it wouldn't have been
fun any more, and nobody would have wanted to keep
doing it. You *could* get hurt, of course, but you could get
hurt a lot worse in a football game with the grandstand full
of newspaper reporters and faculty and parents all cheering
you on.

Now I guess you know everything that was important

before the day Gene Hanlon got killed, and I can tell you how it happened so that you'll know why.

After our last morning class, Peter Irish and I went down to the washroom in the basement to clean up for lunch. All morning Peter had acted funny—silent and sort of tied up inside—and it was worrying me some. At first I thought I had done something he didn't like, but if I had, he'd have told me. He'd hardly said two words all morning, and he had missed two recitations in English that I had coached him on myself. But you couldn't pry trouble out of Peter, so I just kept quiet and waited for him to let me in on it.

While he was washing his hands I had to go into one of the stalls. I went in and shut the door and was hanging up my jacket when I heard somebody else come into the washroom. I don't know why, but I sat down—being real careful not to make any noise.

Somebody said, "Hi, Pete, boy." It was Gene Hanlon, and he was alone for once.

"Hi, Gene." That was Peter. (I am trying to put this down as near as I can just the way they said it.)

"Oh, man!" Gene said. "Today I am exhaust pipe!"

"Tired?"

"You said the word, man. Real beat under."

"Why so?"

"Big date last night. Friend of yours, Angela Pine." Just as if that stall door hadn't been there, I could see Gene grinning at Peter and waiting for a rise out of him. Peter didn't say anything, so Gene tried again. "You're pretty sly, Pete."

"What do you mean?"

"I mean about Angela. You've done a real fine job of keeping her in drydock all this time."

"She dates other guys," Peter said, sounding like he ought to clear his throat.

"Aaaah. She goes out with those meatballs and then comes home and shakes hands at the door. What kind of a date is that?"

"Well, that's *her* business."

Gene said, giggling. "I don't know what her business is, but I got a few suggestions for her if she ever asks me."

"What are you getting at?"

"Real coy, boy. She's crazy for it. Just crazy. Real crazy hungry chick, yeah."

"Are you through?"

"What? . . . Oh, sure. *Hey!* You sore or something?"

Peter said, "It's time for you to go eat lunch."

"All right already. Jesus! You don't have to get *that* way about it. A guy gives you a compliment and you go and get sore. You *are* an odd ball. You and your screwy horses too. See you around." And Gene went out scuffing his feet along the floor.

When I came out of the stall Peter was hunched stiff-armed over the washbasin. He didn't even know I was around. I wished right then that I could have gone back and unlived the last five minutes. I wished they had never happened, and that everything was back just the way it was before. I was hurt and mad, and my mind was whirling around full of all the stuff Gene Hanlon had said. Just to be doing something, I got busy combing my hair, wetting and shaking the comb and all, trying to find a way to say what I was feeling. Peter was very busy turning both faucets on and off again in a kind of splashy rhythm.

Finally I said, "If you believe all that crap, you're pretty silly. That guy's a bragging liar and you know it."

Peter looked up at me as though he had just noticed I was there. "I've got to believe it," he said.

I jumped on him for that. "Oh, come on," I said. "Give Angela a little credit. She wouldn't give that pile of you-know-what the right time."

Peter was looking down the basin drain. "I called her this morning to say hello. She wouldn't talk to me, Ronnie. She wouldn't even come to the phone."

Now I knew what had been eating him all morning. There wasn't any more a friend could say to Peter, so I made him let go of the faucets and come with me to eat lunch in the cafeteria. All through lunch he just pushed dishes around on his tray and didn't say anything. As we scraped our plates I asked him if he was going out to the fight in the woods, and he surprised me by saying yes, so we got our caps and hiked out to the Confederate fort.

Almost everybody, Gene Hanlon too, was there before us, and they'd already chosen today's generals. Smitty Rice was General of the Armies of the Confederacy, and Gene Hanlon was the Union commander. Gene took all his boys off to the Union fort to wait for the starting whistle, and Smitty outlined his strategy to us.

There was to be a feint at the south side of the Union fort, and then a noisy second feint from the north to pull the defenders out of position. Then Smitty and Peter Irish were to lead the real massed assault from the south, under the lip of the hill where the first feint had come from. When five minutes had gone by on my watch, we all got up and Smitty blew the starting whistle and we piled out of the fort, leaving only five inside as a garrison, and a couple of alarm guards a little way out on each side of the fort.

I got the job I usually got—advance observation post. I was to note enemy movements and remember concentrations and directions and elapsed times between sightings. Even though you couldn't see more than a hundred feet through the woods, you could always get a fair idea of the enemy strategy by the way they moved their troops around. So all I had to do was stay in one place and watch and listen and remember, and every so often Smitty would send a runner over from field headquarters to check up on what had happened lately. I had three or four good posts picked out where I could hide and not be seen, and I never used the same one twice running.

Today's was my favorite—Baker Post, we called it. It was a dense thicket of young blackjack oak on a low hill on the inside of a bend in the creek, and because nothing grew on the gravel bars of the creek, you could see a long way to each side. The creek ran generally south, cutting the fighting area between the forts right in two, and it made a good defense line because there were only a few places you could cross it in one jump and not get your shoes wet. The east bank of the creek, directly across from Baker Post, is a vertical bluff about ten feet high so that the ground up there is right on eye level with Baker, and the creek and the gravel bars are spread out between you and the bluff bank. I always knew that Baker Post was good, because

every time I took it up I had to flush out a covey of quail
or a cottontail.

It was always quiet in the woods during the first few
minutes of those fights. Even the birds shut up, it seemed
like, waiting for the first troop contacts. Out of the corner of my eye I saw somebody jump the creek at the North
Ford, and I rolled over to watch. Because of the brush up
there I couldn't see who it was, but I knew he was there
because once in a while a bush would stir, or his foot would
slide a little on the gravel. Pretty soon he came out to the
edge of the underbrush and crouched there looking around
and listening. It was Gene Hanlon. His eyes crossed right
over me, without finding me, and after a minute he came
out and ran low along the creek. When he got even with
Baker Post, he went down to his knees and began filling
his cap with rocks. I had to laugh to myself at how stupid
that was. He should have collected his ammunition earlier,
when he and his army were on their way over to their fort.
He was wasting maneuvering time and exposing himself
for no good reason. It makes you feel good when a guy you
hate does something dumb like that.

I got ready to go *chk, chk* with my mouth just to scare
him and see him run. But then I looked up at the bluff above
him and my heart flopped over inside me. Peter Irish was
there, down on one knee, looking over at Gene Hanlon.
Gene never looked up. Peter moves like that—floating in and
out of the brush as quietly as if he didn't weigh anything.
Peter was a good woods fighter.

So instead of going *chk, chk* I hunkered down lower in
my thicket and thought to myself that now it wasn't a game
any more. Peter looked a long time over at where I was
hiding, then he looked up and down the creek bed, and
then he moved back a little from the edge of the bluff. He
put all his weight pulling on a half-buried boulder beside
him until it turned over in its socket and he could get a good
grip on it. Even from where I was I could see the cords
come out in his neck when he raised it up in his arms and
stood up. I hadn't heard a sound except the creek gurgling
a little, and Gene Hanlon scratching around in the gravel.
And also the blood roaring in my own ears. Watching this

was like being in a movie and seeing the story happen on the screen. Nothing you can do or say will change what is going to happen because it's all there in the unwinding reel.

Peter held the heavy stone like a medicine ball and walked to the edge of the bluff and looked down at Gene Hanlon. Gene had moved a few feet south along the creek, so Peter above him moved south too, until he was even with Gene. Peter made a little grunt when he pushed the rock out and away and it fell. Gene heard the grunt and lifted his head to look up, and the rock hit him full in the face and bent his head away back and made his arms fly out. He sat right down in the water with his red and dirty face turned up to the sky and his hands holding him up behind. Then he got himself up with his head still twisted back like that, so he was looking straight up, and he wandered a little way downstream with the water up to his knees, and then he fell out on a gravel bar on his stomach. His legs and arms spread out like he was asleep, but his head was up rigid and his mouth was open. I couldn't look any more.

Peter hadn't made a sound leaving, but when I looked up, the bluff above was empty. As soon as I could move without getting sick I faded out of there and went up north a ways to Able Post and lay down in the foxhole there and held myself around the knees and just shook. I couldn't have felt more upset if I had dropped that rock myself. Just like the movie reel had the ends tied together, the whole scene kept rolling over and over in front of my eyes, and I couldn't stop the film or even turn off the light in the projector.

I lay there with my head down waiting for someone to find the body and start hollering. It was little Marvin Herold, Smitty's courier, who started screaming in his high voice, "Safety! . . . Oh, God! . . . Safetysafetysafety! . . . Help! . . . Help!" "Safety" was the call we used to stop the fights if anyone saw a master coming or somebody got hurt. I lay there for several minutes listening to guys running past me through the brush heading for Baker Post, then I got up and followed them. I couldn't move very fast because my knees kept trying to bend the wrong way.

When I came out of the brush onto the gravel bank, I was

surprised that everything looked so different. When I had left
just five minutes before, the whole clearing and the creek
were empty and lying bright in the sun, and Gene Hanlon
was there all alone on the gravel bar. Now, with all the guys
standing around and talking at once with their backs to the
body, the whole place was different, and it wasn't so bad
being there. I saw little Marvin Herold go over and try to
take the pulse of Gene Hanlon's body. Marvin is a Boy Scout
with lots of merit badges, and I expected him to try artificial respiration or a tourniquet, but he didn't find any pulse
so he stood up and shook his head and wobbled over to
where we were. He looked terribly blank, as though the
Scout Manual had let him down.

The assumption going around was that Gene had run
off the bluff and landed on his head and broken his neck.
I couldn't see Peter anywhere, so I finally had to ask
Smitty where he was. Smitty said he had sent Peter in to
the school to tell somebody what had happened, and to
get the ambulance. Smitty was still being the General, I
guess, because there was nothing less for him to do. I
tried to think to myself what Peter must be feeling like
now, sent off to do an errand like that, but I couldn't get
anywhere. My head was too full of what *I* was feeling
like, standing with the fellows on the gravel bar looking
at Gene Hanlon spread out half in the water like a dropped
doll, knowing just how he had gotten there, and not being
able to say anything.

Then Smitty got an idea, and he said, "Ronnie, weren't
you here at Baker Post all the time?"

I made myself look at him, and then I said, "No, damn
it. I got to thinking their army might try a crossing up by
Able Post, so I went up there instead."

He said, "Oh," and forgot it.

Not long after, we heard a siren. We all knew what it
was, and everybody stopped talking to listen to it as it got
nearer. It was the first time I ever heard a siren and knew
while hearing it why it had been called, and where it was
going. It was sort of creepy, like it was saying to us over the
trees, "Wait right there, boys. Don't anybody leave. I'll be
there in a minute, and then we'll see just what's going on."

I wanted to run and keep on running, until I got away from all the things swarming around inside me. You always wish afterward you had never joggled the wasp ball.

Pretty soon we heard somebody moving in the woods on the bluff and then two big men in white pants, carrying a folded-up stretcher, and another man in a suit, carrying a black bag, came out to the lip of the bluff. They stood there looking at us a minute without saying anything until one of the stretcher-bearers saw Gene Hanlon lying there all alone on the gravel bar. The man said something to the other two, and they all three looked where he pointed. Then the doctor looked at us all bunched up where we were and said, "Well, how do we get down?" He sounded sore. None of us moved or said anything, and in a minute the doctor got tired of waiting and blasted us. "Wake up over there! How do we go to get down?" Smitty came unstuck and gave them directions, and they went back into the brush heading north.

From then on things got pretty crowded in the woods. Two uniformed policemen and a photographer and a plain-clothes man showed up, and then Peter Irish came back leading almost the whole school faculty, and later a reporter and another photographer arrived. Nobody paid any attention to us for a while, so we just sat there in a clump, not moving or saying much. I managed to get right in the middle, and I kept down, hiding behind the guys around me and looking between them to see what was going on. After the police photographer was through taking pictures of Gene Hanlon from all sides, the two ambulance men raised him onto the stretcher and covered him with a piece of canvas or something and carried him away. The photographer took pictures all around by the creek and then went up onto the bluff and took pictures of the ground up there too. The plain-clothes man poking around on the gravel bar found Gene Hanlon's blue cap half full of rocks and gave it, with the rocks still in it, to one of the policemen to save.

I finally got up nerve enough to look for Peter Irish. He was standing with Smitty and Mr. Kelly, the math teacher, and they were talking. Peter didn't look any different. I didn't see how he could do it. I mean, stand right out there in plain sight of everyone, looking natural, with all that in his head. He looked around slowly as though he felt me watching him, and he found me there in the middle of the bunch. I couldn't have looked away if I had tried. He gave me a little smile, and I nodded my head to show him I'd seen it, then he went back to his talking with the other two.

Then the plain-clothes man went over to the three of them, and I got all wild inside and wanted to jump up and say that Peter couldn't possibly have done it, so please go away and let him alone. I could see the plain-clothes man doing most of the talking, and Peter and Smitty saying something once in a while, as though they were answering questions. After a little the plain-clothes man stopped talking and nodded, and the other three nodded back, and then he led them over to where the rest of us were. Smitty and Peter sat down with us and Mr. Kelly collected all the other faculty men and brought them over.

The plain-clothes man tipped his hat back and put his hands in his pockets and said, "My name is Gorman. Sergeant Gorman. We know all about the rock fight now, so don't get nervous that you'll let on something that'll get you into trouble. You're already *in* trouble, but that's not my business. You can settle that with your instructors and your parents. Uh . . . you might think some about this, though. It's my feeling that every one of you here has a share in the responsibility for this boy's death. You all know rock fighting is dangerous, but you went ahead and did it anyway. But that's not what I'm after right now. I want to know if any of you boys actually saw this (what's his name?), this Hanlon boy run over the bluff." I was looking straight at Sergeant Gorman, but in the side of my eye I saw Peter Irish turn his head around and look at me. I didn't peep.

Then Sergeant Gorman said, "Which one of you is Ronnie Quiller?"

I almost fainted.

Somebody poked me and I said, "Me." It didn't sound like my voice at all.

Sergeant Gorman said, "Which?"

I said, "Me," again.

This time he found me and said, "Weren't you supposed to be lying here in this thicket all the time?"

"Yes," I said. All the kids were looking at me. "But there wasn't anything doing here so I moved up there a ways."

"I see," he said. "Do you always disobey orders?"

"No," I said, "but after all, it was only a game."

"Some game," said Sergeant Gorman. "Good clean fun."

Then he let me alone. There was only one person there who knew I would never have deserted the post assigned to me. That was Peter Irish. I guess, Dad, that's when I began to get really scared. The worst of it was not knowing how much Peter knew, and not daring to ask. He might have been waiting out of sight in the brush after he dropped that rock, and seen me take out for Able Post. I had always been his friend, but what was I now to him? I wanted to tell him everything was okay and I wouldn't for the world squeal on him, but that would have told him I knew he did it. Maybe he knew without my telling him. I didn't know what to do.

Sergeant Gorman finished up, "Let's all go back to the school now. I want to talk to each of you alone." We all got up and started back through the woods in a bunch. I figured Peter would think it was funny if I avoided him, so I walked with him.

I said, "Lousy damn day."

He said, "Real lousy."

I said, "It seems like a hundred years since lunch."

We didn't say any more all the way back.

It took all afternoon to get the individual interviews over. They took us from Assembly Hall in alphabetical order, and we had to go in and sit across from Sergeant Gorman while he asked the questions. He must have asked us all the same questions because by the time he got to me he was saying the words like they were tired. A girl stenographer sat by him and took down the answers.

"Name?"

"Ronnie Quiller." I had to spell it.

"Were you at the rock fight this afternoon?"

"Yes, I was."

"What side were you on?"

"The Confederates."

"What were you supposed to do?"

"Watch the guys on the other side."

"After this whistle, did you see anyone?"

"No."

"You sure?"

"No, I didn't. That's why I moved from Baker Post up to Able Post. There wasn't anything doing where I was hiding."

"In rock fights before, have you ever changed position without telling somebody?"

"Sure, I guess. You can't run clear back to the field headquarters to tell anyone anything. It's up to them to find *you*."

Sergeant Gorman squinted at me with his eyebrows pulled down. "You know that if you had stayed where you were supposed to be you would have seen him fall over that bluff there?"

"Yes," I said.

"I wish you had."

Afterwards I ran into Smitty out in the hall and I asked him why all this fuss with the police and all. I asked him who called them.

"It was Peter, I think. He told Mr. Kelly to, and Mr. Kelly did."

"What do you suppose they're after?" I asked Smitty.

"Oh, I guess they're trying to get a straight story to tell Gene's parents and the newspapers. From what I get from Mr. Kelly, the school is all for it. They want everybody to know they weren't responsible."

"Do *you* think Gene fell over that bluff?" I couldn't help asking that one.

"I don't know. I suppose so." He cocked his head to one side and grinned a little at me. "Like they say in the papers, 'fell or was pushed,' huh?"

I said, "I guess nobody'd have nerve enough to do that to Gene—push him, I mean." All of a sudden I was thinking about something I had seen. Going back in my mind I remembered seeing Sergeant Gorman pick up Gene's cap half full of rocks. Gravel rocks taken from the low bank of the creek. Now, I figured that Sergeant Gorman wouldn't have been a sergeant if he was stupid, and unless he was stupid he wouldn't go on for long thinking that Gene had fallen from above—*when the cap half full of rocks said he'd been down below all the time!*

I got my bike and rode home the long way to give me time to think about Peter and what he had done, and what I should do. You were real swell that night, and I guess I should have told you the whole story right then, but I just couldn't. I put myself in Peter's place, and I knew he would never have told on me. That's the way he was. He hated squealers. I couldn't think about his ever learning I had squealed on him. That would put me right alongside Angela Pine in his book. To him, I would have been the second person he trusted who let him down.

I felt like a rat in a cage with no place to go and no way out. When you kept me home nights after that, I didn't mind, because I wouldn't have gone out after dark if I'd been paid to. I don't blame you and Mother for thinking I had gone loony over the whole thing. Every noon recess for two whole weeks they pulled us into Assembly Hall and one of the masters would give a speech about group responsibility or public conscience or something awful like that, and then, worst of all, they made us bow our heads for five minutes in memory of Gene Hanlon. And there I'd be, sitting next to Peter Irish on the Assembly Hall bench, thinking back to the day of the last rock fight, and how Peter had looked up there on the bluff with the cords of his neck pulled tight, holding that big rock like it was a medicine ball. I had the crawliest feeling that if anybody in the hall had raised up his head and looked over at us together there on the bench, he would have seen two great fiery arrows pointing down at us. I was always afraid even to look up myself for fear I would have seen my own arrow and passed out on the spot.

It was my nightmares that got you worried, I guess. They always started out with Peter and me on a hike on a dusty country road. It was so hot you could hardly breathe. We would walk along without saying anything, with me lagging a little behind Peter so I could always keep an eye on him. And then the road would come out on the football field there at school, and he would go over to the woodpile and pick up a thin log and hold it in one hand, beckoning to me with the other and smiling. "Let's go over to the drugstore," he'd say, and then I'd start running.

I would follow the quarter-mile track around the football field and I'd know that everything would be all right if I could only get around it four times for a full mile. Every time I turned around to look, there he'd be right behind me, carrying that log and running easily, just like he used to pace me when I was out for the 880. I would make the first quarter mile all right, but then my wind would give out and my throat would dry up and my legs would get heavy, and I'd know that Peter was about to catch me, and I'd never make that full mile.

Then I would jar awake and be sweating and hanging on tight to the mattress, and in a minute you'd come in to see why I'd screamed. Your face was always kind of sad over me, and there in my bed in the dark, with you standing beside, I would *almost* let go and tell you why things were so bad with me. But then as I'd come awake, and the hammering in my heart would slow up, and the sweat would begin to dry, all the things I owed Peter Irish would stand out again and look at me, and I would know that I could never tell you about it until my telling could no longer get Peter Irish into trouble.

I'm tired now, Dad—tired in so many ways and in so many places that I don't know where to begin resting. This letter took all night, as I thought it would. It's beginning to get light outside and the birds are starting up. I just reread the story in the paper where it says that Sergeant Gorman knew all along that Gene Hanlon had been murdered. I told you he wasn't stupid. He knew what that cap half full of rocks meant, and he knew what it meant to find a big damp socket in the earth on top of the bluff, and the rock which had been *in* the socket down below in the creek. And after he had talked to each of us alphabetically there in the school office, he knew the name of the only boy in school strong enough to lift up a seventy-pound rock and throw it like a medicine ball. He knew all of these things before the sun went down on the day of the last rock fight, but he was two months putting the rest of the story together so he could use it in his business.

As I read it in the paper, Sergeant Gorman went over to Peter's house last Monday night and talked to him about the things he had learned, and Peter listened respectfully, and then, when Sergeant Gorman was through and was ready to take Peter along with him, Peter excused himself to go up-stairs and get his toilet articles. He got his four-ten shotgun instead and shot himself. I suppose it was the same four-ten he and I hunted squirrels with.

There's only one good thing about this whole stinking lousy mess, Dad. Because Sergeant Gorman talked to Peter and Peter listened, there in the living room; when Peter Irish climbed up those stairs he did it knowing that I, Ronnie Quiller, had not squealed on him. That may have made it easier. I don't know.

Now please, Dad—please may I come home again?

RONNIE

One of the most accomplished writers of short stories
now at work, Jessamyn West demonstrates here that
the selfishness and malice of an old woman can be
dramatized with charming humor and irony.

A Little Collar for the Monkey

JESSAMYN WEST

It was Thursday, the day the fish wagon came by, so
old Mrs. Prosper shouted from her bed to her daughter in the
room next to hers, "Thursday, Lily, fish day!"

The strength of her shouting lifted her momentarily above
her pillows, and she sank back pleasurably, awaiting a reply.
The sun was just up but it was not rising on a world in any
way strange to it. It was rolling back into its own heat, heat
left over from the day before. It was moving across the sky
in a blaze of its own redness, mounting a streak of crimson
spread out above it like a length of welcoming carpet. Outside in the growing light the birds, who for two hours had
been whetting and sharpening their already thin, sharp little
voices, now cut the air with razor strokes of sound.

"Poor fools," wise old Mrs. Prosper addressed them, "poor
fools."

Two more hours and sparrow and linnet, towhee and
mockingbird would be sitting in the umbrella tree's deepest
shadow, wings extended, mouths gaping, and tongues—dry
from singing and heat—shrunk to the size of little black bast-
ing threads. They would then drop down to the hydrant, dripping inside the circle of ferns, to lick up a warm drop or two.

"Poor fools," said Mrs. Prosper. "Not the least idea in the
world what's good for you. Screeching now because the sun's
up—and in two hours it will have you parched to the bone.

Poached like eggs, and willing to pay money to be rid of your feathers."

Mrs. Prosper, herself old, thin, and unfeathered, enjoyed the heat. She let one foot dangle out from under the single sheet which covered her until it touched the uncarpeted floor boards. The floor boards were still warm from yesterday's heat, and the feel of that lingering warmth excited Mrs. Prosper. A small ripple shook her, as if she had been some variety of electrical mechanism suddenly enjoying the shock of a propulsive voltage. Be a scorcher today, she thought, be a record breaker—but probably not, she concluded. Nature continually disappointed Mrs. Prosper. It seemed capable of so much variety and actually was so repetitious. Mrs. Prosper was always searching for a wildness, a violence, nature never provided. A strangeness which any day might by very simple means provide: let only the sun reverse itself, or flowers fly; let fish sing or rain fall upward. That would do it. The possibilities were endless. Life might easily be exciting, strange, and awesome; as it was, everything was in a rut. Spring, summer, winter, fall. First the bud and then the blossom. First the egg and then the bird. And then the song at sunup. "Poor fools," said Mrs. Prosper, listening.

Mrs. Prosper wasted very little time wondering about who was at the helm of the world, who ordered matters thus tamely. That someone was there she took for granted; she wasn't a fool, only imaginative. But she had long ago concluded that it was someone either dozing or unaware of the possibilities; someone, at least, totally unlike herself.

She herself, limited as she was, had gone out one spring, when the apricot trees were smaller, and had broken from one of the sturdiest trees every single bud and blossom. Painstakingly, every one. Then, when the trees all about it had been heavy with fruit, she had been pleased to stand beside it noting its peculiarity and bareness: full of heart-shaped, shining leaves, a perfect bower of greenness, but no fruit. Looking at it, she had felt full of power and accomplishment.

"What do *you* make of it?" she would inquire, addressing it, her tree, her handiwork, turned in a direction quite opposite from what nature had intended.

Her husband, then alive, had also looked at her tree, though
with no notion it was hers. "An odd business," he had said.
"Gopher at the roots, maybe. Possibly gum disease."

"Possibly," Mrs. Prosper, not then old, had replied. "But it
looks healthy, doesn't it? Green and flourishing."

Mr. Prosper had laid a hand on the puce-colored bark, like
a father testing his child's temperature. "It does," he agreed.
"It does for a fact. I can't figure it out."

"Can't you, Enos?" asked Mrs. Prosper.

"It's a mystery to me," he said, feeling and touching.

"A mystery," said Mrs. Prosper.

She liked her husband well enough, considering she despised him. But then, whom did she not despise? She could
have respected only a man capable of looking at her and
saying, "You don't for a minute fool me." And there had
never been anyone to say that. And for her, a woman alive in
a world in a rut and among men without insight, Enos Prosper was as good a man as any other and better than many.

They had walked back to the house together. "Next year
I'll make it bloom and bear," she had said.

Her husband took her hand. He kissed the fingers that had
broken off the buds. "I believe you could," he said. For Mrs.
Prosper, who lived on irony, that was a dainty mouthful.

"Fool, fool," she said now, coming near enough the edge
of her bed to rest the whole of her foot upon the floor boards,
whose warmth, retained from yesterday, promised still greater
heat for the coming day. The words she spoke recalled her
to the present, and she listened for a sound from her daughter's room. There was none.

"Thursday, Lily," she shouted again. "Fish day. Time to
curl and primp." Again there was no answer, but there were
now other sounds. A car down the road. A cock crowing. A
faraway tractor. Bees in the Gold of Ophir rose which had
laced itself among the limbs of the umbrella tree at the
corner of the house.

"Get up," shouted Mrs. Prosper. "Rouse yourself, Lily, and
make yourself pretty for the fishmonger."

Mrs. Prosper got out of her own bed and walked to the
front window. She unlatched the hinged screen, swung it
open, and leaned out into the morning air. "Be a furnace by

noon," she speculated; but the rest of the world was disappointing. With the help of a half dollar and a matchbox a child could draw it: rounds, squares, and rectangles, that was the whole of it. Round sun, round sky, and apricots and their leaves nearly round. The road itself, in front of the house, a half circle, a tunnel of green under the wholly round umbrella trees: trees round as upturned green basins and chinked only enough to let sufficient light to travel through. The ranches she looked out on were squares or rectangles, separated by a road or a row of standpipes. A world for a child to draw. But she herself, she thought, too complex for any such picturing.

She spread her unbleached muslin gown across the foot of the bed to air, walked to the old bureau, and saw herself in the mirror which was blurred with constellations and sunspots, pocked with moonlike craters. Gone sallow, gone stringy, but not flabby; tight in buttock and neat in breast; no one with a matchbox and a half dollar could draw her. She gave herself a smart slap and put on her wrapper. She lived inside herself as precisely as a walnut in its shell, nothing rattling, nothing wasting, rich and orderly, too tough a nut for time to crack.

"Get up, Lily," she called again in the hall, on her way to the bathroom. "Get up and slick yourself up for your fish peddler." But as she waited for a reply she heard Lily, already downstairs, bustling about in the kitchen.

Mrs. Prosper went down to breakfast, smooth and shiny as a beetle in her coal black; her gold brooch and earrings as many-faceted as a beetle's eye in the morning light. She found the table already set in the breakfast room, and curtains already partly drawn against the heat. From beneath the curtains, bars of yellow light slanted down onto the rag rugs; but this light was only ankle deep: above the ankles the room was dusky. Hodge, the cat, lay on a window sill, one ear cocked to follow the buzzings of a fly, self-conscious with being watched. Hodge was a fly trap more certain than Tanglefoot, more deadly than a Daisy Fly-Killer; and this lone survivor, having witnessed since sunup the engulfment of all his kind in the breakfast room, buzzed now a nervous swan song.

"Good morning, Hodge," said Mrs. Prosper. The mar-
malade-colored tom closed his yellow eyes.

In the dusk of the upper room Mrs. Prosper saw white
sweet peas in a glass bowl on the center of the table, coffee
already poured, dishes of strawberries, and a fringed napkin,
covering, she knew, a plate of Lily's fine-grained scones.

Mrs. Prosper appreciated the scene, all of it, even the
buzzing fly. It looks like a home, she thought. She imagined
herself a stranger standing outside the windows and peering
through the glass with a stranger's eyes. She saw how pleasant
the surface was. It does look like a home, she thought, it
looks like a nice breakfast, I look like a nice old lady come
down to eat my breakfast; and Lily, there, pulling out my
chair, looks like a daughter.

Only Mrs. Prosper had never been able to think of Lily
as a daughter at all. She thought of her as a female relation,
connected, but distantly, through Mrs. Prosper's mother's
people. A niece or possibly a cousin of her mother's. Indeed,
Lily looked so like Mrs. Prosper's mother that Mrs. Prosper
sometimes had the feeling that she had spent her entire life
with her mother, knowing her first as a mature woman and
then, in Lily, as a child and girl. Now, at forty, Lily was her
mother as Mrs. Prosper best remembered her: the same soft,
dun-colored hair looped back in the same aimless way; the
same light brown eyes, faintly pink lips, and teeth that,
curving inward, gave the mouth its peculiarly childlike look.
Well-fleshed, as her mother had been, but no muscles beneath the flesh, so that she was as soft to the touch as a
handful of yarn. Always neat, always the same flowered
dresses, white aprons, and black oxfords; shoes sensible of
heel but so fancifully cut about the vamp that they contra-
dicted everything else Lily wore.

"Good morning, Lily," said Mrs. Prosper, seating herself
in the chair that Lily pushed carefully in for her.

"Good morning, Mother," said Lily.

"I called you early this morning, Lily," said Mrs. Prosper.
"Several times. At the top of my voice. No answer."

"I didn't hear you, Mother," said Lily. "I came downstairs
early this morning."

"Then you did remember," said Mrs. Prosper. "Good. I didn't want you to oversleep."

Lily said nothing, but took the napkin from the scones and held the plate for her mother.

"Courted by a fish peddler," said Mrs. Prosper, helping herself. "How does that seem?"

Lily put the napkin back over the scones and said nothing.

"Ah, well," said Mrs. Prosper, "it's an intimate subject. I don't blame you for not wanting to talk of it. What's his name again, by the way? I know, but I keep forgetting it."

"Olav," said Lily. "Olav Duun."

"Sounds like an owl hooting," observed Mrs. Prosper. "An old owl in the dead of night. He a foreigner?"

"He's Swedish," said Lily.

"He don't look it. Black. Black as soot and long mustaches like a catfish. I've heard that people who live a long time in China begin finally to look like Chinamen and that people in charge of the crazy begin after a while to look crazy themselves. Do you reckon if you sell fish long enough, you begin to look like a fish?" asked Mrs. Prosper.

"Olav hasn't sold fish for so very long," said Lily.

"He's made progress, then," declared Mrs. Prosper. "Whiskered like an old catfish already."

Lily, undisturbed, insofar as Mrs. Prosper could see, buttered a scone. "Courted by a Swedish fish peddler, name like an owl in the night! Has Hodge been fed this morning?" she asked, suddenly tiring of Lily's unresponsiveness.

"No," said Lily.

Mrs. Prosper took the saucer from under her coffee cup and half filled it with yellow cream. She handed the saucer to her daughter and Lily placed it on the sill beside the cat.

"Kit, kit, kit," said Mrs. Prosper. "Cream for breakfast."

Hodge turned his eyes for a moment away from the bemused fly, buzzing just now against the hot windowpane above his head.

"Cream," said Mrs. Prosper. "Thick cream!"

Hodge turned back to the window, with a sudden soft slap killed the sun-struck fly, and, negligently chewing it down, settled himself for sleep beside the untasted cream.

Mrs. Prosper laughed and struck her hands together. "Won-

derful animals," she said, "wonderful Hodge." She glanced
up at Lily and it was her mother who regarded her.

"The sugar, please, Lily," she said. She sprinkled sugar
thickly over the big, deep-red berries. "I remember picking
strawberries once, when a girl. A day about like this."

"Yes, mother," said Lily.

"I and a friend, a hulk of a girl, twice my size and a year
or two older. Her name was Rose. Rose Vawters. Our mothers
sent us over to a Jap's who had berries for sale. The berries
were cheaper if you picked them yourself. It was a hot
muggy day with gnats and the ground had been newly ir-
rigated and wasn't nice to kneel on. 'You'll pick mine, too,' I
told Rose. 'Why?' she asked. 'My mother only wants . . .'
'Don't talk,' I said. 'Pick.' She began to pick. 'Faster,' I said,
and she picked faster. I only nudged her with my toe now and
then, never kicked her or really hurt her. She was twice my
size and considerably older, but she picked all my berries. A
bucket for each of us. And she carried them home. 'Walk
in a ditch,' I would say, and she walked there. 'Hide,' I
would say, 'you've stolen the berries,' and she would hide. 'Lie
flat on your stomach, they'll see you,' and she would flatten
herself in the slime of an empty irrigation ditch. 'Run,' I
would tell her, 'run, you're being chased,' and she would run.
Pretty fast too, though the berries were heavy and she wasn't
slim herself. I can still see her pounding down the road ahead
of me, a berry jolting now and then out of the two full buckets
she carried."

Mrs. Prosper finished her berries. "I never eat berries but
I remember that morning. I've forgotten a lot of things that
happened when I was a girl . . . not that morning and how
I felt. But I've told you before, haven't I, Lily?"

"Yes, mother," said Lily.

Mrs. Prosper noticed that her daughter had pushed her
own berries aside and was looking at nothing, or possibly a
crack in the floor boards or a spot on the wallpaper. "But you
don't listen, do you, Lily?" she asked.

After the breakfast work was finished Lily and her mother
sat in the shadowy, still-cool living room. Tightly closed as
it was against the heat, it smelled of furniture polish, of the
acacia branches which Lily put in the fireplace in summer to

hide its reminder of heat and burning, and of Hodge, the cat. The smell of Hodge was remarkably like that of the Shasta daisies which, like spokes from a wheel, rayed out from a bowl on the center table: a smell Mrs. Prosper had been sampling since her youth, unable to decide whether it was good or bad. On each side of the daisies were candles, which were not reminders of heat or burning since they had never been intended for lighting. They were candles by reason of their being placed in candlesticks. Actually, encrusted as they were with deep swirls of blue and green paint, they more nearly resembled stalagmites rising upward from the gloom of the center table.

In this pleasant darkness Lily sat tatting, Mrs. Prosper buffing her nails, Hodge watching the pendulum of the clock on the mantelpiece, with its movement so like that of something which might be crushed and eaten. Lily's bobbin, as the thread left it, made a very light tick, the clock echoed it on a deeper note, Mrs. Prosper's buffer went over the ridges of her old nails with a dry swish. Only Hodge was silent, his eyes following the pendulum, which he believed would sooner or later forget he was there, fly out from behind the glass that housed it, and finally slide, a round juicy mouthful, down his throat.

As the clock struck ten, Mrs. Prosper put down her buffer and listened. Within a few minutes, so faint that any other sound would have drowned it, came the tootle of a horn blown three times.

"There he is," said Mrs. Prosper. "The fishman. Right on time."

Lily paused for a minute in her tatting. Then her bobbin flew again.

"Ladies a quarter-mile in each direction freshening themselves up," said Mrs. Prosper, "in order to be ready to buy a half-pound of halibut."

"He blows it so they can have their money ready," Lily said, "and a pan to put the fish in."

"He tell you?" asked Mrs. Prosper.

"Yes," said Lily.

"Money and pan ready don't seem to speed him any here."

"He's polite," said Lily. "He thinks of more than selling. He likes to pass the time of day. He don't rush."

"No, he don't," said Mrs. Prosper. "Why don't you walk down a ways to meet him, Lily? He goes clear round the section before he gets here. You could ask him which fish were most tasty this week. Inquire if the sand dabs are up to par."

Lily's shuttle went perhaps a little faster but she said nothing.

"I will, then," said Mrs. Prosper. "I'd like a little ride. I'll catch him at the corner, ride round the section with him, ask him about his wares."

Mrs. Prosper put her buffer on the center table. "How is it exactly you say his name, Lily?"

"Duun," said Lily, "Olav Duun."

"Mr. Duun, I'll say, I've come to ride a ways with you."

That was what she did. She walked down the tunnel of green under the umbrella trees and caught Mr. Duun at the Burneys'. Mrs. Burney had just departed with her change and fish for the house. Mr. Duun stood at the back of his wagon, wiping out his scales.

"Mr. Duun," said Mrs. Prosper, "I've come to ride a ways with you."

"Duun's the name," said Mr. Duun without turning about.

"Duun," repeated Mrs. Prosper.

Mr. Duun gave his cleaver a final swipe, placed it in its rack, and closed the heavy doors of the truck upon his stock of fish.

"Hop in," he said.

Mrs. Prosper walked around to the right side of Mr. Duun's fish truck, climbed up and in, and closed the door behind her.

Mr. Duun, for whom the height of the running board had been less of an impediment than for Mrs. Prosper, was already in the cab, writing down his sales, when she got there. Without looking up he said, "Slam your door, otherwise it rattles."

"Slam it yourself," said Mrs. Prosper, settling comfortably back.

Mr. Duun did so. He reached across Mrs. Prosper, pencil

still in hand, and banged the door. Then he went back to
his totting up.

Mrs. Prosper watched him as he worked. In age, he was
a man halfway between Lily and herself. It was untrue, what
she had said about his mustache. The hairs about the mouth
of a catfish are sparse, gray, and stiff. The hairs about Mr.
Duun's mouth were thick, soft, and black. There was only
something in the angle of their growth, their curve being long
and downward, which had put her in mind of a catfish. There
was no gray in either his mustache or his hair, which he wore
roached back in an unstylish pompadour. From its bridge his
nose ran along straight enough for two-thirds of its length,
then splayed out, became thumb shaped. His eyes, Mrs.
Prosper knew, were black; now, because he was looking
downward and because they scarcely bulged his eyelids,
they seemed very flat. He was olive skinned and smooth con-
toured, the smoothness being broken only by his high cheekbones and full Adam's apple. He looked a good, craggy man
to Mrs. Prosper, wearing a white apron and woven straw
gauntlets on his wrists, as a fish peddler ought. His hands,
busy with his writing, were perfectly clean except for a splash
or two of fish blood.

"You wouldn't think fish peddling would take so much book
work," said Mrs. Prosper.

"You know much about fish peddling, Mrs. Prosper?" asked
Mr. Duun, closing his book and placing it in a little rack above
his left shoulder.

"I know what I think," said Mrs. Prosper.

"Ah," stepping on the starter.

"Do you write down, five cents for a quarter of a pound
of smelts sold to Mrs. Butts's cat on Thursday?" asked Mrs.
Prosper.

"Sometimes less, sometimes more," said Mr. Duun swinging out onto the road.

"More?"

"A word about Mrs. Butts herself, and now and again a
word about the cat."

"Have you ever put down a word about—us?"

"About your daughter."

"What did you say?"

Mr. Duun looked full at Mrs. Prosper, and she saw that his eyes were less flat than she had thought. "It slips my mind," he said.

Mr. Dunn then picked up his horn, an ordinary cow horn it looked to Mrs. Prosper, silver tipped at the blowing end. Neatly parting his mustache with the tip, he blew three blasts, two short and one long.

"That like to burst my drums," said Mrs. Prosper.

"They tell me it'll carry a mile if the wind's right," Mr. Duun agreed.

While Mr. Duun sold fish at his next stop to the O'Toole sisters—two plump maiden ladies who brought him iced lemonade and warm spongecake to stay his mid-morning hunger—Mrs. Prosper took a look at the cab of Mr. Duun's truck. It was thoroughly decorated. There were flowers painted on the glass of the dome light and a little vase in a bracket, the vase now filled with some wilting lop-headed fuchsias. There were tacked-up picture post cards, mostly of boats and harbors, and some oddments, unfamiliar to Mrs. Prosper but connected, she supposed, either with fishing or fish selling. There was even a motto of some kind, in a language Mrs. Prosper could not read, above the rear-view mirror.

When Mr. Duun and the O'Toole sisters had concluded their considerable visit, and after Mr. Duun had written down whatever it was he did write down after such sales, Mrs. Prosper asked him about the motto.

"What language is that?" she asked.

"Swedish," replied Mr. Duun, putting his account book in its rack and his pencil behind his ear.

"It's a peculiar-looking language," said Mrs. Prosper.

"Not to Swedes," said Mr. Duun.

"So you're Swedish," said Mrs. Prosper.

Mr. Duun, busy backing his truck out of the O'Toole driveway, nodded.

"You don't look it."

Mr. Duun, now in the clear, replied, "The Lord must've thought so, otherwise he wouldn't've set me down among Swedes."

"The Lord makes mistakes."

Mr. Duun did not contradict this.

"How did you happen to come to America?"

"My ship put in here at a time when I'd decided I'd had enough of the sea. Time to learn something about the land."

"You a sailor?"

"I was."

"How'd you come to take to fish peddling?"

"Nearest there is to sailing. You move about and you move with fish. Nothing lacking but water and that was what I wanted to get away from."

Mr. Duun turned into the Smedleys' palm-lined driveway. Mrs. Prosper, looking at the drawn blinds, the closed garage door, said, "No one home here."

"Home or not," said Mr. Duun, "every Thursday I put a lobster in the Smedley icebox."

When Mr. Duun returned from delivering this lobster, Mrs. Prosper handed him a silver-inlaid leather circlet, which she had lifted from a hook that also held a calendar, a good luck medal on a chain, and two brown shoelaces braided together.

"A nice piece of work," she said, "a pretty bracelet for a plump arm."

Mr. Duun turned the leather circlet about in his hands a time or two; then, lifting up his apron, he vigorously polished the silver work on his pants leg.

"It's a collar," said he.

"It'd take a skinny neck to fit that little circle."

"I made it for a skinny neck," said Mr. Duun, "and it fit to a T."

"You a silversmith, too?" Mrs. Prosper asked. While Mr. Duun's hands looked skillful enough to handle a fish knife, the silver work on the collar was fine and intricate—something beyond a mere fish carver.

"My father did the silver work. He was a farmer, and in the winters, when work was slack, he made collars—first for his own dogs and then for the dogs of all his neighbors, until finally he was as much a maker of dog collars as a farmer."

Mrs. Prosper took the collar from Mr. Duun and ran her fingers around its circumference. "Tiny little dogs you have in Sweden," she said.

"That was never made for a dog—it was made for a monkey."

"Where's the monkey?" asked Mrs. Prosper.

"You're ahead of the story," said Mr. Duun. "When I was twelve I got a piece of leather—that piece of leather," he said touching the collar Mrs. Prosper now held. "And I cut it just that size. When my father saw it he was just like you. 'Well boy,' he said, 'what toy neck you planning to span with this collar, what lady's lap dog?' 'It's not for a dog,' I told him, 'it's for a monkey, a little collar for a monkey.' 'A monkey!' said my father. 'So you're going to sea,' for every sailor who came home to Göteborg, which was a port town, had his monkey with him."

"You were forehanded," said Mrs. Prosper. "A monkey collar at twelve."

"So my father said. But he helped me with the collar, set in all the silver work himself, though he was against my going and needed another hand on the farm. And when the day came for leaving—I was seventeen then—I was so excited I forgot all about my little collar. My father went up to my room, and fetched it down. He opened my bag, already strapped shut for my journey, and laid the collar inside. 'There's your little collar, son,' he said, 'and I hope you find a good little monkey to wear it.' "

"Did you?" asked Mrs. Prosper.

"No," said Mr. Duun. "I found a bitch of a monkey, a regular she-devil, the devil in monkey form maybe."

Mr. Duun reached over, took the collar out of Mrs. Prosper's hands, and hung it once again on its peg. Then he started his motor and backed out of the Smedleys' palm-lined driveway.

The fish truck, because of the amount of ice Mr. Duun carried, was cooler than the air outside, but even so it was hot. Mrs. Prosper could no more sweat than a stone, but she saw that Mr. Duun's olive skin had become ruddy and that among the black hairs of his mustache fine beads of sweat glistened like little brilliants.

He turned left and right, and then into the green tunnel under the umbrella trees. The little monkey collar swung back and forth with the momentum of his turning.

"It doesn't appear to have been much used," observed Mrs. Prosper, watching it swing.

"Two weeks," said Mr. Duun. "We were two weeks out of Montevideo when I took the collar off her neck and tossed her into the sea."

"Drowned?" said Mrs. Prosper.

"She asked for it," said Mr. Duun. "She was vicious. She had bad habits."

"So you drowned her," said Mrs. Prosper. A monkey's dying by drowning seemed somehow stranger than if it had come to its death from a blow on the head or a knife thrust.

"She drowned herself, I reckon," said Mr. Duun. "I only tossed her over the rail. She clung to the rail, she clung to me. She knew what was coming and she was suddenly loving. I threw her over and she looked like a big black spider there on top of the water. She cried out, too. Pitiful to hear, I suppose, if you hadn't known how she had asked for it."

Mr. Duun's recital was calm enough, like that of a law-respecting judge summing up a case, but Mrs. Prosper's heart was beating faster. She could see it all, very clearly. Mr. Duun, large, young then, handsome; though he was handsome now, for that matter. She could see him take the collar from the monkey's neck and hand it to a fellow sailor. And she could see the look in the monkey's eyes as he did that, the foreknowledge, and the thin black hands on the rail, and the little hands torn off, and the unbelief in the eyes as it fell, and the desperate flailing as it tried for a time to regain the ship.

"Did you ever get another?" asked Mrs. Prosper.

"One was enough," said Mr. Duun.

Mrs. Prosper reached out and touched the collar. "But you kept the collar."

"So far I have," said Mr. Duun. "To remind me."

"Did you think as you watched it drowning," asked Mrs. Prosper, "your monkey—did you think—monkey, you were born to live in a tree, but I've changed all that for you?"

"I did not," said Mr. Duun, who was now turning into the Prosper driveway.

"It would have been an interesting thing to see," Mrs. Prosper said as Mr. Duun brought his truck to a stop at the back steps of the Prosper house, "a monkey drowning in mid-ocean. I wish I had been there."

Mr. Duun took his hands from the wheel and turned side-ways so that he squarely confronted Mrs. Prosper. Sitting thus, he gave Mrs. Prosper the glance she had never before encountered, but which, now that she had received it, she felt she had spent a lifetime looking for. It was a glance of recognition. It took her all in. It missed nothing. Mr. Duun sat for quite some time in this way, gazing at Mrs. Prosper; then, slowly, he turned away, and after a few seconds or a few minutes—Mrs. Prosper was too shaken by the complete reflection and recognition she had seen in Mr. Duun's eyes to keep track of time—he spoke.

"What will you have today?" he asked in the same matter-of-fact tone he had used to describe the drowning of the monkey.

"Have?" repeated Mrs. Prosper, somewhat bewildered.

"What fish?" asked Mr. Duun. "I've got some nice halibut. Sea bass. Salmon. Barracuda."

Mrs. Prosper recalled herself. "No fish today, Mr. Duun," she said.

"No fish! Don't tell me, Mrs. Prosper, you ladies have lost your taste for fish!"

"Not I," declared Mrs. Prosper. "Not I. But Lily's never cared for them and she's finicky. She says that in this hot weather the smell of so much as a fish frying would turn her stomach."

Mrs. Prosper unlatched the door on her side of the cab.

"You might ask your daughter, when you go in," said Mr. Duun, "if she'd like a little ride with me out San Jacinto way. She'd find it cooling, I think."

Mrs. Prosper let the door—which she had been holding open—come to, but not latch. "It would be better not," she said. "Lily's my daughter, Mr. Duun, but it's my duty to tell you she's at the age an old maid's likely to reach. The age when it's her pleasure to think every man has his eye on her. For harm, you understand. The milkman, a Mexican come to clean out the hen house, an agent with magazines, it's all one to Lily, so he wears pants. She's going to make trouble for some man someday. And I wouldn't want it to be you."

Mrs. Prosper looked upward, once again searching Mr. Duun's glance for that shock of recognition—for that reflection of her whole self.

It was there. It was fully there. While Mrs. Prosper was using it, making up for what she felt to be a lifetime's lack, Mr. Duun suddenly opened his own door and stepped out.

"It would be better, I see, for me to ask her myself," he said, and went into the house without a knock at the door or even a pause. Mrs. Prosper climbed slowly down out of the fish truck—and stood for a minute in the driveway, enjoying the sun, now almost at its height, and thinking about what might be going on in the house. Whatever it was, it was soon over. Before she had turned about the screen door slammed, and there was Lily—her white apron off, her Milan straw hat on, Mr. Duun with his hand on her elbow, and, at Mr. Duun's heels, Hodge.

"I'm going for a little ride with Mr. Duun, Mother," said Lily, and Mrs. Prosper watched Mr. Duun hand her up into the truck like an honored guest. When he had done that and closed the door he walked on around to the back of the truck and got out a smelt for Hodge. Then he climbed up into the cab with Lily, and slammed the door after him. He didn't at once start his engine, however, but sat leaning out of his window, looking at Mrs. Prosper. Mrs. Prosper thought he intended speech. Instead he reached across Lily, took down the little collar, and tossed it at Mrs. Prosper's feet.

"A gift from the groom," he said.

"Groom?" asked Mrs. Prosper.

"Groom-to-be," said Mr. Duun.

Mrs. Prosper stooped and picked up the collar. "A gift to the bride's mother in memory of her that wore it," said Mr. Duun; then he started his engine, and he and Lily drove on around the house and out the driveway on the other side.

Mrs. Prosper, who lived on irony, had her cupful then, pressed down and running over: the "bride's mother," and that collar, and known as she was; those three, all together and at one time. Mrs. Prosper stood for some time in the dry, burning sunlight without moving. Then she laughed. Not silently, but loud enough to cause Hodge, busy with his fish, to look up.

"Come, Hodge," said Mrs. Prosper, quickly stooping, "you'll wear the collar." But Hodge was faster than Mrs. Prosper. In one snake-like curve he was out of her arms and under the oleanders, carrying what was left of Mr. Duun's gift. So Mrs. Prosper had to enter the house without him, empty-handed except for the monkey collar.

Although "The Lottery" is probably the most celebrated modern American short story, its chilling
power and sinister suggestiveness are so compelling
it cannot be reprinted too often. Is it a sardonic
comment on the evil of outworn traditions, the cruel-
ty of organized society or the curse of original sin?
This is a story which excites the mind and shocks
the nervous system.

The Lottery

SHIRLEY JACKSON

The morning of June 27th was clear and sunny, with
the fresh warmth of a full-summer day; the flowers were
blossoming profusely and the grass was richly green. The
people of the village began to gather in the square, between
the post office and the bank, around ten o'clock; in some
towns there were so many people that the lottery took two
days and had to be started on June 26th, but in this village,
where there were only about three hundred people, the whole
lottery took less than two hours, so it could begin at ten
o'clock in the morning and still be through in time to allow
the villagers to get home for noon dinner.

The children assembled first, of course. School was recently
over for the summer, and the feeling of liberty sat uneasily on
most of them; they tended to gather together quietly for a
while before they broke into boisterous play, and their talk
was still of the classroom and the teacher, of books and rep-
rimands. Bobby Martin had already stuffed his pockets full
of stones, and the other boys soon followed his example,
selecting the smoothest and roundest stones; Bobby and
Harry Jones and Dickie Delacroix—the villagers pronounced
this name "Dellacroy"—eventually made a great pile of stones

63

in one corner of the square and guarded it against the raids of
the other boys. The girls stood aside, talking among themselves, looking over their shoulders at the boys, and the very
small children rolled in the dust or clung to the hands of their
older brothers or sisters.

Soon the men began to gather, surveying their own children, speaking of planting and rain, tractors and taxes. They
stood together, away from the pile of stones in the corner,
and their jokes were quiet and they smiled rather than
laughed. The women, wearing faded house dresses and
sweaters, came shortly after their menfolk. They greeted one
another and exchanged bits of gossip as they went to join
their husbands. Soon the women, standing by their husbands,
began to call to their children, and the children came reluctantly, having to be called four or five times. Bobby Martin
ducked under his mother's grasping hand and ran, laughing,
back to the pile of stones. His father spoke up sharply, and
Bobby came quickly and took his place between his father
and his oldest brother.

The lottery was conducted—as were the square dances, the
teen-age club, the Halloween program—by Mr. Summers, who
had time and energy to devote to civic activities. He was a
round-faced, jovial man and he ran the coal business, and
people were sorry for him, because he had no children and his
wife was a scold. When he arrived in the square, carrying the
black wooden box, there was a murmur of conversation among
the villagers, and he waved and called, "Little late today,
folks." The postmaster, Mr. Graves, followed him, carrying
a three-legged stool, and the stool was put in the center of the
square and Mr. Summers set the black box down on it. The
villagers kept their distance, leaving a space between themselves and the stool, and when Mr. Summers said, "Some of
you fellows want to give me a hand?" there was a hesitation
before two men, Mr. Martin and his oldest son, Baxter, came
forward to hold the box steady on the stool while Mr. Summers stirred up the papers inside it.

The original paraphernalia for the lottery had been lost
long ago, and the black box now resting on the stool had been
put into use even before Old Man Warner, the oldest man in
town, was born. Mr. Summers spoke frequently to the vil-

lagers about making a new box, but no one liked to upset even as much tradition as was represented by the black box. There was a story that the present box had been made with some pieces of the box that had preceded it, the one that had been constructed when the first people settled down to make a village here. Every year, after the lottery, Mr. Summers began talking again about a new box, but every year the subject was allowed to fade off without anything's being done. The black box grew shabbier each year; by now it was no longer completely black but splintered badly along one side to show the original wood color, and in some places faded or stained.

Mr. Martin and his oldest son, Baxter, held the black box securely on the stool until Mr. Summers had stirred the papers thoroughly with his hand. Because so much of the ritual had been forgotten or discarded, Mr. Summers had been successful in having slips of paper substituted for the chips of wood that had been used for generations. Chips of wood, Mr. Summers had argued, had been all very well when the village was tiny, but now that the population was more than three hundred and likely to keep on growing, it was necessary to use something that would fit more easily into the black box. The night before the lottery, Mr. Summers and Mr. Graves made up the slips of paper and put them in the box, and it was then taken to the safe of Mr. Summers' coal company and locked up until Mr. Summers was ready to take it to the square next morning. The rest of the year, the box was put away, sometimes one place, sometimes another; it had spent one year in Mr. Graves's barn and another year underfoot in the post office, and sometimes it was set on a shelf in the Martin grocery and left there.

There was a great deal of fussing to be done before Mr. Summers declared the lottery open. There were the lists to make up—of heads of families, heads of households in each family, members of each household in each family. There was the proper swearing-in of Mr. Summers by the postmaster, as the official of the lottery; at one time, some people remembered, there had been a recital of some sort, performed by the official of the lottery, a perfunctory, tuneless chant that had been rattled off duly each year; some people believed that the official of the lottery used to stand just so when he said

or sang it, others believed that he was supposed to walk
among the people, but years and years ago this part of the
ritual had been allowed to lapse. There had been, also, a
ritual salute, which the official of the lottery had had to use
in addressing each person who came up to draw from the
box, but this also had changed with time, until now it was
felt necessary only for the official to speak to each person
approaching. Mr. Summers was very good at all this; in his
clean white shirt and blue jeans, with one hand resting care-
lessly on the black box, he seemed very proper and important
as he talked interminably to Mr. Graves and the Martins.

Just as Mr. Summers finally left off talking and turned to
the assembled villagers, Mrs. Hutchinson came hurriedly
along the path to the square, her sweater thrown over her
shoulders, and slid into place in the back of the crowd. "Clean
forgot what day it was," she said to Mrs. Delacroix, who
stood next to her, and they both laughed softly. "Thought my
old man was out back stacking wood," Mrs. Hutchinson went
on, "and then I looked out the window and the kids was gone,
and then I remembered it was the twenty-seventh and came
a-running." She dried her hands on her apron, and Mrs. Delacroix said, "You're in time, though. They're still talking away
up there."

Mrs. Hutchinson craned her neck to see through the crowd
and found her husband and children standing near the front.
She tapped Mrs. Delacroix on the arm as a farewell and began
to make her way through the crowd. The people separated
good-humoredly to let her through; two or three people said,
in voices just loud enough to be heard across the crowd, "Here
comes your Missus, Hutchinson," and "Bill, she made it after
all." Mrs. Hutchinson reached her husband, and Mr. Summers, who had been waiting, said cheerfully, "Thought we
were going to have to get on without you, Tessie." Mrs.
Hutchinson said, grinning, "Wouldn't have me leave m'dishes
in the sink, now, would you, Joe?" and soft laughter ran
through the crowd as the people stirred back into position
after Mrs. Hutchinson's arrival.

"Well, now," Mr. Summers said soberly, "guess we better
get started, get this over with, so's we can go back to work.
Anybody ain't here?"

"Dunbar," several people said. "Dunbar, Dunbar."

Mr. Summers consulted his list. "Clyde Dunbar," he said. "That's right. He's broke his leg, hasn't he? Who's drawing for him?"

"Me, I guess," a woman said, and Mr. Summers turned to look at her. "Wife draws for her husband," Mr. Summers said. "Don't you have a grown boy to do it for you, Janey?" Although Mr. Summers and everyone else in the village knew the answer perfectly well, it was the business of the official of the lottery to ask such questions formally. Mr. Summers waited with an expression of polite interest while Mrs. Dunbar answered.

"Horace's not but sixteen yet," Mrs. Dunbar said regretfully. "Guess I gotta fill in for the old man this year."

"Right," Mr. Summers said. He made a note on the list he was holding. Then he asked, "Watson boy drawing this year?"

A tall boy in the crowd raised his hand. "Here," he said. "I'm drawing for m'mother and me." He blinked his eyes nervously and ducked his head as several voices in the crowd said things like "Good fellow, Jack," and "Glad to see your mother's got a man to do it."

"Well," Mr. Summers said, "guess that's everyone. Old Man Warner make it?"

"Here," a voice said, and Mr. Summers nodded.

A sudden hush fell on the crowd as Mr. Summers cleared his throat and looked at the list. "All ready?" he called. "Now, I'll read the names—heads of families first—and the men come up and take a paper out of the box. Keep the paper folded in your hand without looking at it until everyone has had a turn. Everything clear?"

The people had done it so many times that they only half listened to the directions; most of them were quiet, wetting their lips, not looking around. Then Mr. Summers raised one hand high and said, "Adams." A man disengaged himself from the crowd and came forward. "Hi, Steve," Mr. Summers said, and Mr. Adams said, "Hi, Joe." They grinned at one another humorlessly and nervously. Then Mr. Adams reached into the black box and took out a folded paper. He held it firmly by one corner as he turned and went hastily back to his place in

the crowd, where he stood a little apart from his family, not
looking down at his hand.

"Allen," Mr. Summers said. "Anderson. . . . Bentham."

"Seems like there's no time at all between lotteries any
more," Mrs. Delacroix said to Mrs. Graves in the back row.
"Seems like we got through with the last one only last week."

"Time sure goes fast," Mrs. Graves said.

"Clark. . . . Delacroix."

"There goes my old man," Mrs. Delacroix said. She held
her breath while her husband went forward.

"Dunbar," Mr. Summers said, and Mrs. Dunbar went
steadily to the box while one of the women said, "Go on,
Janey," and another said, "There she goes."

"We're next," Mrs. Graves said. She watched while Mr.
Graves came around from the side of the box, greeted Mr.
Summers gravely, and selected a slip of paper from the box.
By now, all through the crowd there were men holding the
small folded papers in their large hands, turning them over
and over nervously. Mrs. Dunbar and her two sons stood together, Mrs. Dunbar holding the slip of paper.

"Harburt. . . . Hutchinson."

"Get up there, Bill," Mrs. Hutchinson said, and the people
near her laughed.

"Jones."

"They do say," Mr. Adams said to Old Man Warner, who
stood next to him, "that over in the north village they're talking of giving up the lottery."

Old Man Warner snorted. "Pack of crazy fools," he said.
"Listening to the young folks, nothing's good enough for
them. Next thing you know, they'll be wanting to go back to
living in caves, nobody work any more, live *that* way for a
while. Used to be a saying about 'Lottery in June, corn be
heavy soon.' First thing you know, we'd all be eating stewed
chickweed and acorns. There's *always* been a lottery," he added petulantly. "Bad enough to see young Joe Summers up
there joking with everybody."

"Some places have already quit lotteries," Mrs. Adams said.

"Nothing but trouble in *that*," Old Man Warner said stout-
ly. "Pack of young fools."

"Martin." And Bobby Martin watched his father go forward. "Overdyke. . . . Percy."

"I wish they'd hurry," Mrs. Dunbar said to her older son. "I wish they'd hurry."

"They're almost through," her son said.

"You get ready to run tell Dad," Mrs. Dunbar said.

Mr. Summers called his own name and then stepped forward precisely and selected a slip from the box. Then he called, "Warner."

"Seventy-seventh year I been in the lottery," Old Man Warner said as he went through the crowd. "Seventy-seventh time."

"Watson." The tall boy came awkwardly through the crowd. Someone said, "Don't be nervous, Jack," and Mr. Summers said, "Take your time, son."

"Zanini."

After that, there was a long pause, a breathless pause, until Mr. Summers, holding his slip of paper in the air, said, "All right, fellows." For a minute, no one moved, and then all the slips of paper were opened. Suddenly, all the women began to speak at once, saying, "Who is it?" "Who's got it?" "Is it the Dunbars?," "Is it the Watsons?" Then the voices began to say, "It's Hutchinson. It's Bill," "Bill Hutchinson's got it."

"Go tell your father," Mrs. Dunbar said to her older son.

People began to look around to see the Hutchinsons. Bill Hutchinson was standing quiet, staring down at the paper in his hand. Suddenly, Tessie Hutchinson shouted to Mr. Summers, "You didn't give him time enough to take any paper he wanted. I saw you. It wasn't fair!"

"Be a good sport, Tessie," Mrs. Delacroix called, and Mrs. Graves said, "All of us took the same chance."

"Shut up, Tessie," Bill Hutchinson said.

"Well, everyone," Mr. Summers said, "that was done pretty fast, and now we've got to be hurrying a little more to get done in time." He consulted his next list. "Bill," he said, "you draw for the Hutchinson family. You got any other households in the Hutchinsons?"

"There's Don and Eva," Mrs. Hutchinson yelled. "Make *them* take their chance!"

"Daughters draw with their husbands' families, Tessie," Mr. Summers said gently. "You know that as well as anyone else."

"It wasn't *fair*," Tessie said.

"I guess not, Joe," Bill Hutchinson said regretfully. "My daughter draws with her husband's family, that's only fair. And I've got no other family except the kids."

"Then, as far as drawing for families is concerned, it's you," Mr. Summers said in explanation, "and as far as drawing for households is concerned, that's you, too. Right?"

"Right," Bill Hutchinson said.

"How many kids, Bill?" Mr. Summers asked formally.

"Three," Bill Hutchinson said. "There's Bill, Jr., and Nancy, and little Dave. And Tessie and me."

"All right, then," Mr. Summers said. "Harry, you got their tickets back?"

Mr. Graves nodded and held up the slips of paper. "Put them in the box, then," Mr. Summers directed. "Take Bill's and put it in."

"I think we ought to start over," Mrs. Hutchinson said, as quietly as she could. "I tell you it wasn't *fair*. You didn't give him time enough to choose. *Every*body saw that."

Mr. Graves had selected the five slips and put them in the box, and he dropped all the papers but those onto the ground, where the breeze caught them and lifted them off.

"Listen, everybody," Mrs. Hutchinson was saying to the people around her.

"Ready, Bill?" Mr. Summers asked, and Bill Hutchinson, with one quick glance around at his wife and children, nodded.

"Remember," Mr. Summers said, "take the slips and keep them folded until each person has taken one. Harry, you help little Dave." Mr. Graves took the hand of the little boy, who came willingly with him up to the box. "Take a paper out of the box, Davy," Mr. Summers said. Davy put his hand into the box and laughed. "Take just *one* paper," Mr. Summers said. "Harry, you hold it for him." Mr. Graves took the child's hand and removed the folded paper from the tight fist and held it while little Dave stood next to him and looked up at him wonderingly.

"Nancy next," Mr. Summers said. Nancy was twelve, and her school friends breathed heavily as she went forward, switching her skirt, and took a slip daintily from the box. "Bill, Jr.," Mr. Summers said, and Billy, his face red and his feet overlarge, nearly knocked the box over as he got a paper out. "Tessie," Mr. Summers said. She hesitated for a minute, looking around defiantly, and then set her lips and went up to the box. She snatched a paper out and held it behind her.

"Bill," Mr. Summers said, and Bill Hutchinson reached into the box and felt around, bringing his hand out at last with the slip of paper in it.

The crowd was quiet. A girl whispered, "I hope it's not Nancy," and the sound of the whisper reached the edges of the crowd.

"It's not the way it used to be," Old Man Warner said clearly. "People ain't the way they used to be."

"All right," Mr. Summers said. "Open the papers. Harry, you open little Dave's."

Mr. Graves opened the slip of paper and there was a general sigh through the crowd as he held it up and everyone could see that it was blank. Nancy and Bill, Jr., opened theirs at the same time, and both beamed and laughed, turning around to the crowd and holding their slips of paper above their heads.

"Tessie," Mr. Summers said. There was a pause, and then Mr. Summers looked at Bill Hutchinson, and Bill unfolded his paper and showed it. It was blank.

"It's Tessie," Mr. Summers said, and his voice was hushed. "Show us her paper, Bill."

Bill Hutchinson went over to his wife and forced the slip of paper out of her hand. It had a black spot on it, the black spot Mr. Summers had made the night before with the heavy pencil in the coal-company office. Bill Hutchinson held it up, and there was a stir in the crowd.

"All right, folks," Mr. Summers said. "Let's finish quickly."

Although the villagers had forgotten the ritual and lost the original black box, they still remembered to use stones. The pile of stones the boys had made earlier was ready; there were stones on the ground with the blowing scraps of paper that had come out of the box. Mrs. Delacroix selected a stone so large she had to pick it up with both hands and turned to Mrs. Dunbar. "Come on," she said. "Hurry up."

Mrs. Dunbar had small stones in both hands, and she said, gasping for breath, "I can't run at all. You'll have to go ahead and I'll catch up with you."

The children had stones already, and someone gave little Davy Hutchinson a few pebbles.

Tessie Hutchinson was in the center of a cleared space by now, and she held her hands out desperately as the villagers moved in on her. "It isn't fair," she said. A stone hit her on the side of the head.

Old Man Warner was saying, "Come on, come on, everyone." Steve Adams was in the front of the crowd of villagers, with Mrs. Graves beside him.

"It isn't fair, it isn't right," Mrs. Hutchinson screamed, and then they were upon her.

Retirement always has its problems, but when a celebrated schoolmaster retires and then remains on the campus and meddles in the school's affairs, the problems can be both poignant and humorous.

The Trial of Mr. M

IIIIIIIIIIIIIIIIL O U I S   A U C H I N C L O S S IIIIIIIIIIIIIIII

Everyone had agreed that it was a mistake for Mr. Minturn to live so close to Chelton after his retirement. The neat red-brick house which the board of trustees had remodeled for him was almost within the shadow of the Gothic spire of the school chapel and actually within sight of the headmaster's rambling mansion that he had occupied for forty years.

How could Arthur Knox, people asked, ever feel that it was his school if he had to administer it under the penetrating eyes of the small, brisk, silver-haired, round-bodied man who had become to every graduate and boy a living symbol of the school itself? And worse yet, Arthur Knox was a Chelton man; he, too, had been exposed when young to the strange compulsion of that diminutive figure in the pulpit, the arms rising and falling as the full, rich, cadenced voice, in measured tones, held up before three hundred boys the sanitary virtues, clean living, clean talking, clean thinking, until life itself took on the whiteness of a sheet. He had known, too, the tireless pedestrian of the school grounds, inspecting, unrelaxing, with the poking ebony walking stick, the benevolent figure in the headmaster's study, chuckling as he read aloud the Fezziwig chapters of the "Christmas Carol," and, never to be forgotten, the stiff, disciplining magistrate, shaking with the gusts of a terrifying anger. For Mr. Minturn, who breathed the pale,

thin air of an early New England, with a straight code of
what was wholesome and what was not, what was funny and
what merely sophisticated, or, as he put it, "blazzy," could be
terrifying. It was why so many of his graduates, in their
atrophied religious consciences, later in life, thought of him
when they thought of God.

But Mr. Minturn did not think of himself as terrifying, or of
anyone else, much less Arthur Knox, as being afraid of him.
He saw no reason whatsoever to move away from the school.
His wife was dead, and his daughters, large, bony, middle-
aged women of undoubted filial devotion but limited sympathy, had both married Chelton men, one now a trustee of
the school, and had prospered undemonstratively in Boston,
only an hour away. They wanted him, sincerely enough, to
come to them, but he had no more interest in them than in
their lives. His life was the school.

A few, a very few of the older graduates had ventured to
hint that his continued residence on the campus might prove
an embarrassment to the new head, but he could not see it.
He was quite sure that they did not realize the tact of which
he was capable. He had known Arthur Knox since the latter's
boyhood: he had followed his early career in the ministry
and his more recent years as head of a smaller boys' school:
he believed him thoroughly grounded in the ideals of Chelton
and most capable of their efficient promotion. Now it would
be Arthur's school; it was as simple as that. And he, they
asked? Why, didn't he have his correspondence with the
graduates and his sermons to preach? What more did he need
but his daily walk around the school and the playing grounds,
past the long, rambling Elizabethan dormitories with their
coats of ivy, the war memorial fountain, so white and placid,
the chapel with its Gothic tower thrust up sharply against the
lowering sun; ending up, stick in hand and puffing at a pipe,
to watch the football practice on the first squad field?

It was impossible, of course, for him not to notice things.
It was impossible, for example, not to observe that the number
of boys playing tennis on October afternoons was double
what it had been in his day. And there was something silly, in
Mr. Minturn's opinion, about a fifteen-year-old batting a little
white ball across a net on a crisp autumnal day within actual

earshot of the staccato "Signals! Signals!" from the football
field below. However, he supposed it was not fatal.

What was a good deal worse was the appearance of a white
refrigerator truck with soft drinks driving right through the
Eliot Gate and parking by the first squad field. Mr. Minturn
had hardly thought he was interfering when he had ordered
the driver summarily from the grounds, scattering the boys
around the vehicle with a word. What had been his surprise to be told by the driver, and not politely, either, that
authority had come from the headmaster himself! He had
brooded about this and thereafter avoided the first squad field
where the hateful truck squatted brazenly, silhouetted against
the chapel itself. But this was not all. He had even to admit
it was minor compared to what was still to come.

Returning home late one evening when he had walked as
far as the river, he passed the great windows of the dining-
hall as the boys were filing in for supper. Filing, however, was
no longer the appropriate term. They piled in each way, every
way, no longer standing at their places before the long tables
in silence, waiting as an assembled body for grace, but sitting down immediately and grabbing for the bread and butter. And he noticed distinctly, approaching a side window in
the cold, darkening air, seeing but unseen, that they had not
changed to stiff collars.

Well, it was disturbing. It really was. One could argue that
boys had been brought up as Christians without stiff collars
in the evening or that the sale of pop on the campus was not
necessarily fatal to their development, but how many stones
could be pulled out of the foundation before a crack appeared
in the façade itself? And it was just such a crack that he
thought he perceived one Sunday afternoon while walking
past the fields behind the gymnasium. A group of younger
boys was engaged in a game of touch football, and as he
paused, leaning on his stick to watch them, his ears were cut
by a cry.

"Jesus Christ, butterfingers, can't you ever hang on to that
ball!"

He stared, incredulous, at the small, fat, serious boy who
had shouted this. The others, however, seemed to treat it as
entirely normal.

"Boy!" he shouted in his old tone, and now they stopped, and turned to him in astonishment. "You, boy!" he continued, pointing at the offender, "come over here!"

"But I'm playing in the game, sir."

"Come here this minute!" Mr. Minturn thundered, and the boy came quickly over. "What's your name?"

"Sloane, sir."

"Do you know what day it is, Sloane?"

"Yes, sir. It's Sunday, sir."

"And don't you know Whose day Sunday is?"

"I beg your pardon, sir?"

"Isn't Sunday the Lord's Day?"

"Oh. Yes, sir. I expect it is."

"He whose name you were taking in vain?"

The boy's face cleared now. He even smiled.

"Oh, I get it, sir. I was swearing, wasn't I? Sorry, sir. It was the game, you know."

But Mr. Minturn's face became even graver.

"The game!" he exclaimed. "Do you think a game excuses you? We'll have to teach you, Sloane. Yes, indeed, I'm afraid we will. You will go immediately and report to the head-master at his house. If he isn't in, you will wait in the front hall until he comes. You will tell him what I heard you say. I don't wish to repeat it."

He saw the consternation in the troubled face before him and sensed it in the hovering figures of the other boys. Did he have to be obeyed, they were wondering, this testy old man from another world, this legend known to them more through the portrait in the dining-hall and the tales of their fathers than from their own vision of the shuffling little figure who sat in the back of the chapel and sometimes lunched at the head table?

"Well, Sloane, did you hear me?"

The boy turned and walked sulkily off in the direction of Mr. Knox's house. Mr. Minturn nodded to the others. "Continue your game, boys," he said gruffly and proceeded on his tour. His mind, however, was in too much of a turmoil for pleasant walking and after some minutes' debate he turned down Knox's driveway toward the rambling Victorian mansion that he had occupied so long. The maid showed him into the study just as young Sloane, avoiding his eye, slipped by him in the corridor.

"Well, Mr. M!" the headmaster cried heartily, rising as he entered and stretching out his hand. "It's been too long. Much too long! You must know that Sally and I want you to feel this house is yours."

"You're very kind, Arthur."

He sat down and glanced about the huge bare study whose walls had once been covered to the ceiling with his own pictures of crews, of teams, of glee clubs, of countless rows of earnest strong young faces. Over the mantel now was a colored print of a Rouault Christ. Mr. Knox, bare and energetic as his study, long, strong, balding, big-nosed, leaned forward on his elbows.

"This is a sort of a busman's holiday for you, isn't it, Mr. M?" he asked smiling. "Helping the new administration with its disciplinary problems?" He threw his hands in the air. "Not that we don't need it! We do, we do! No doubt of it! I'm grateful for your trouble, sir."

"You mean Sloane," Mr. Minturn answered in a more serious tone. "I was sure you wouldn't regard that as interfering. I thought you'd want to know."

"That's right. You're quite right." Mr. Knox nodded his head several times in brisk succession. "We don't want language like that to become current on the campus. I think Sloane will keep more of a rein on his tongue when he's spent Saturday afternoon washing my new Buick."

Mr. Minturn paused for a moment as he took this in.

"Am I to understand that that will be his punishment?" he asked. "To wash your car?"

"Well, of course, he'll have to miss the game, too. They hate that, you know."

"Do *we* care what they hate and what they don't?" Mr. Minturn demanded, raising his voice in spite of himself. "Isn't it a question of the offense? Washing a master's car is the penalty for skipping assembly or having an untidy cubicle. You know that, Arthur. Not for blasphemy! What do you think you'd have got when you were a boy here?"

"Well, if you'd heard me, Mr. M," Mr. Knox answered,

grinning broadly, "I'd have been lucky if I hadn't been suspended!"

"If I'd heard you!" Mr. Minturn stared, shocked, at his successor. "Do you imply, Arthur, that there were different levels of justice in my day?"

"No, no, nothing like that, sir," Mr. Knox replied hastily, raising his hands to deprecate the suggestion. "It's only that today—well, sir, it's hard for some of these boys. They hear their fathers, even their mothers, I'm afraid, saying the kind of thing that you heard young Sloane say. Some parents are actually proud of it. It makes them feel their children are intimate with them." He shook his head. "Even in some of our best families, sir."

"And why, then, do these 'best families,' as you call them, send their sons here?" Mr. Minturn demanded with a snort. "Isn't it because they want the school to do the job they lack the fortitude to do themselves?"

But he could get nowhere with Knox. The latter simply nodded in a maddening way, conceding every point he made, admitting cheerfully that the situation was complicated, that he, Knox, was undoubtedly making a mistake, probably lots of them, but that, after all, somebody had to make the decision. And all the while Mr. Minturn had the uncomfortable feeling that he was congratulating himself for his amiable toleration of a reactionary and meddlesome old man.

The next morning after chapel he fell in with Mr. Collins behind the long file of boys who walked two by two to the schoolhouse. Collins, the head of the classics department, was a tubby, rather mincing bachelor of fifty-odd who craved gossip and whose company Mr. Minturn ordinarily took some pains to avoid. This morning, however, he was seeking information.

"Tell me, Collins," he began, "is it true that Latin is to be made optional?"

Mr. Collins paused and nodded.

"The mother of languages, Mr. M," he answered in mournful tones, "must veil her features at Chelton."

"What will be put in its place?"

"Cooking, I daresay, or Icelandic sagas!" Collins exclaimed. "Who knows, with *him?*"

Mr. Minturn did not like the suggestion of disloyalty in this use of the pronoun.

"Come now, things can't be that bad."

"Can't they? Can't they indeed, Mr. M?" Collins paused, almost smacking his lips. "You haven't heard, then, about our pickaninny?"

"Your what, man?"

"You haven't heard that he's embraced the cause of racial toleration? That he's opening the school to a Negro boy?"

"You don't mean it!"

"But I do," Collins continued, delighted with his reaction. "You can read about it in the papers tomorrow. Our white knight, needless to say, has not forgotten the reporters. Oh, he'll be cock of the walk now!"

"A colored boy? *One* colored boy?"

Collins shrugged.

"One, I suppose, for a start. I wonder if it won't be something of a shock to the little girls who come up to the Washington's Birthday dance. Or to their mothers, anyway. But I suppose you and I are antediluvian, Mr. M. A good century behind the times."

"I'll speak to him," Mr. Minturn muttered, half to himself. "I'll speak to him this very morning."

He went straight to the classrooms building and to the headmaster's office.

From the waiting room he could hear Mr. Knox talking on the telephone, but the secretary, who was new, seemed not to think it in the least unreasonable that Mr. Minturn should be asked to wait, that two other people, in fact, parents of a prospective student, should be ushered in ahead of him.

When his turn finally came and he brushed indignantly by her into the office, he hadn't planned to say what he did.

"You've kept me waiting! A full half-hour!"

"I'm sorry, sir." The headmaster was on his feet immediately as Mr. Minturn entered.

"You're not sorry! Speak the truth, man! You did it to put me in my place. To let me know you were tired of interference!"

"My dear Mr. M, I beg you to believe me—"

But Mr. Minturn cut him short by raising his hand. He stared down at the carpet, his other hand at his mouth as he repeatedly cleared his throat, desperately fighting down the black, erupting tide of anger.

He sat down, still coughing.

"Let that be," he said finally. "It doesn't signify. I'm sorry. It's about the colored boy that I came to see you. Is it true?"

"That we're taking one in? It is. Next fall." Mr. Knox folded his hands as he sat down again in his chair. "I trust you're not going to side with the unenlightened. You, of all people, Mr. M?"

"You'll take one unhappy child like that and put him in a white boys' school!" Mr. Minturn exploded in a high, tense tone. "To show what a liberal, forward-looking headmaster you are! Is that fair to the boy, Knox?"

"But don't we have to make a start? Somewhere?"

"Then take ten! Twenty!"

Mr. Knox simply smiled.

"I'm afraid it's a bit more complicated than that, Mr. Minturn," he said patiently. "Quite a bit more complicated. I know you ran a great school, sir. One of the greatest. There's no question of that. But it was a school of its time, like others. And it was a highly class-conscious, race-conscious time. That's nobody's fault. It's simply a fact. But what I have to do is what anyone in my place would have to do, and that is to form a bridge, as it were, from that time to this. We can't build Rome in a day, of course. But we can start by making a few changes. I know, of course, that it was your policy to give preference to sons of graduates—"

"But that had nothing to do with class-consciousness or race-consciousness!" Mr. Minturn interrupted.

"Oh?"

"It didn't, I tell you! I wanted the school to be a family. And it was, too! I wanted the boys to have the sense of something handed down, of loving the school their fathers loved, perhaps even sometimes their grandfathers. Not in all cases, of course. I wanted new boys, too. But I cared about preserving a tradition. Of course, you can't do that alone by making football a required sport or saying grace before meals, but those things help."

He broke off, realizing that as on the previous day, he was getting no more than a polite and disbelieving attention. It was too much. It was really and truly too much.

"And we were democratic, too," he went on explosively. "More democratic than you'll ever be, with one homesick Negro boy as a feather in your liberal cap!"

Mr. Knox actually had the nerve to burst into a laugh, an overgenial, good-natured laugh.

"Oh, Mr. M, you're priceless! You really are! Wait till I tell my wife *that* one!" Mr. Knox said. Mr. M, however, was not to be placated. Without another word or so much as a nod he turned and left the office, once again possessed of a fighting purpose in life. Going to the schedule board, he checked to see if Mr. Collins had a class that hour and then climbed the stairway to the second floor. As he paused outside the Latin teacher's room he heard the sound of laughter.

"Collins?" he called.

Collins, his back to the half-opened door, jumped up.

"Why, Mr. Minturn!" he gasped. "How good to see you, sir! You know Mr. Prince, sir, of the English department?"

"Of course, I know him." Hadn't he hired him? He nodded brusquely to the sandy-haired, long-nosed shambling English teacher who had somehow got to his feet and was bowing.

"I'll come back later, Collins. When you're not busy."

"Oh, but I'm not, sir! Mr. Prince and I were just discussing what you and I talked about this morning. Did you see *him?*"

"I saw the headmaster." Mr. Minturn looked suspiciously at Mr. Prince. He had never been entirely sure about Prince, a moody, preoccupied creature with a cerebral, high-church faith that he loved to discuss at the most unsuitable times and places. "You'll let me know, Mr. Collins, when you're free?"

"Oh, but we can talk in front of Bobbie," Collins assured him, hurrying to close the door. "In front of Mr. Prince, I mean. He's one of us!"

Mr. Minturn turned his slow, even gaze from one to the other.

"What do you mean, Collins," he asked, with an ominous mildness, "by 'one of us'?"

"Perhaps I can answer that, sir," Prince volunteered with the unexpected boldness that Mr. Minturn remembered from his off-the-cuff theological discourses. "By 'one of us' Mr. Collins means one of a small group of masters wholeheartedly devoted to the Minturn concept of Chelton." He paused and drew himself up. "A group that happens to be totally convinced that the new headmaster is doing everything in his power to wreck the school!"

Collins clasped and unclasped his hands.

"It's true, sir!" he cried nervously, encouraged by the example of his younger friend. "I don't know why we should be ashamed of caring about the things you taught us!"

Mr. Minturn looked down at the floor for several silent moments. Was this the way it came? He wondered if he had ever really experienced temptation, if this grim moment in Collins' classroom, here on the very boards where the Latin teacher paced daily up and down, clad in imagined purple, before maps of Augustus' empire, was not the moment that he had so often preached about. Once to every man and nation. He looked back up at the two worried faces before him, like anxious puppy dogs waiting to be taken for a walk. Surely, whatever their angularities, and one learned to tolerate such things in schoolmasters, they were round and whole in their love of Chelton. Yet the Devil could use love; had he not preached that himself?

"Gentlemen, I only want one thing, as you do," he said finally, in a sadder tone, "and that is the good of the school. What else matters?" He sighed and rested both hands on his cane. "Let us not make our judgments hastily. Let us gather our facts. That is all I want. Facts. If we could meet together from time to time and tell each other what we've seen? Not as critics, mind you. Not as people who have to *do* anything about what we find. But simply as good old friends of Chelton?"

It was this suggestion that led to their Wednesday night meetings, in Collins' study, a schedule which they maintained for the rest of the term. Here they debated, with a seriousness only briefly interrupted by Collins' flights of fancy and Prince's somber humor, the innovations that continued to erupt on the placid Chelton scene: the abolition of blue suits on Sunday, the weekly movie in the assembly hall, the permitted weekends to New York and Boston.

It sometimes seemed to Mr. Minturn that Collins and Prince actually outdid him in their conservatism. Not, indeed, that he approved of the innovations. Far from it. It was impossible for him even to conceive of the school as otherwise than he had made it, a haven where boys could remain unspotted from the world until they had developed the inner strength which was to be their permanent immunity. But it did occur to him that some of the changes to which his colleagues took such violent exception were a shade trivial, that there was almost an air of juvenile conspiracy to their deliberations, like two schoolboys playing Brutus and Cassius. He even began to wonder if the deference which they accorded him might not be the deference paid an elder statesman lured from his retirement to lend respectability to an act of naked revolt. Once, encountering Mr. Knox in the hall below Collins' study, it struck him that the latter, embarrassed, hurrying on about his duties, had given him just the flash of a smile of timid amiability, one that had seemed to hint:

"Oh, yes, *I* know where you've been, of course, and I'll pretend to know nothing about it, but, oh, Mr. M, do *you?*"

The idea that he might be a dupe, that Collins and Prince might be laughing behind his back, made him peculiarly sensitive to the smallest sign of familiarity. The evening that he came in to discover Prince sipping a glass of sherry, he remained standing in the doorway, eying the decanter with a frosty stare.

"Drinking was not allowed in the masters' studies, Prince," he said gruffly. "Not in my day, anyway. Perhaps that is another of the rules that Mr. Knox has seen fit to change. Is it so, Collins?"

He turned to Collins as the senior and hence the one responsible. The latter became quite ashy with embarrassment.

"No, sir, I don't think so, I guess not," he replied nervously. "Except Bobbie and I, who are practically teetotalers, can't somehow really regard a sip of sherry as *drinking*." His smile was one of desperate appeal. "Can you, sir? Really?"

"I can," Mr. Minturn retorted. "What else is it? Put it

away, Prince. Put it away. I certainly shan't be a party to
breaking a man's rules while I'm criticizing the administration
of his school."

It satisfied him to watch how quickly they scurried to remove the last traces of the incipient sherry party, even to the
inoffensive plate of biscuits beside the decanter.

"Of course, you're quite right, sir," Collins said a bit breath-
lessly as he resumed his seat. "Quite right. But to tell the
truth, sir, I only got out that decanter to drink a little toast."

Mr. Minturn rose above the inconsistency of his excuses.

"A toast? A toast to what?"

Collins looked at Mr. Minturn for a long moment, his eyes
beaming a bright admiration, undimmed, apparently, by his
recent reproof.

"We wanted to drink a toast to the next headmaster of
Chelton." He held up an imaginary glass. "To Mr. M!"

Mr. Minturn stared from one to the other of their smiling,
nervous faces.

"Gentlemen," he said, after clearing his throat, "would you
mind telling me what in blazes you're talking about?"

"It's about Founder's Day, Mr. M," Prince explained in his
dry tone. "When the trustees and so many of the graduates
are here. That's the time to catch them, Mr. M! That's the
time to *tell!*"

Mr. Minturn stared at the long, oval, gray face before him,
so prematurely old, so intensely earnest.

"Tell them?" he echoed. "Tell them to replace Knox? With
me?"

"Oh, good heavens, Mr. M, don't take us that literally,"
Collins intervened hastily. "That would never be necessary.
All you will want to do is to tell them in private your thoughts
on the subject of Mr. Knox. They'll do the rest, don't worry.
They never wanted you to retire, anyway. They *begged* you
not to. Every boy in the school knows that."

"But I *did* retire, man!" Mr. Minturn protested. "One
doesn't come back after that!"

"Why not?" demanded Prince. "Is there a law against it?
It wouldn't have to be permanent, of course. Not if you didn't
want it. You could be the interim head until you'd picked a
new successor."

It was this last that came nearest to convincing him, the idea that he could be given the opportunity to undo the one wrong that he had ever done the school, to take back the reins for a final drive, to restore the damage and hand them over to a worthy successor. Oh, then, what bliss retirement would be, what ecstasy, unlike the first time, to slip back into the shadows and rest with the sense of danger averted! And why not? Was it too great a boon to be given the chance to rectify an error? Were not the trustees with him? And as for the graduates, had he not had letters protesting his retirement, hundreds of them? Literally hundreds?

He would not, however, commit himself to Prince or Collins. He would only agree to think the matter over, and think it over he did, painfully and conscientiously throughout the long winter, until the preparations observed around him in his daily walks gave notice of the advent of the great day itself. The winter boardwalks were being taken up, the handball courts repainted, the memorial fountain was receiving a thorough cleaning, and through the windows of the assembly hall he could see the great blue curtains for the school pageant being laboriously hung. For this was to be no ordinary Founder's Day; it marked the hundredth anniversary of the school, and masses of graduates were expected to overrun the campus and fill the chapel to overflowing on the Sunday service of thanksgiving.

And before he had really made up his mind what to do, before he had truly conceived of a plan of action, while he still, on the Wednesday before that weekend, was thinking that he had another two days for reflection, he returned from his walk to find his study jammed with a cheering throng of early arrivals. The great day was already upon him.

It was not at all as he had visualized. He had taken it for granted that it would be Mr. Knox's day, that he would be able to stand quietly in the periphery and have chats with the older trustees. Instead, he found that the torrent of nostalgia unloosed by the anniversary raged around himself; he felt like a piece of cork tossed and pitched about, grasping as many of the proffered hands as he could, searching valiantly for small boys' names to attach to hard, smiling faces, obliged to remember whole packets of things that he didn't

recall at all. It was touching, it was heart-filling and it
seemed at first encouraging for the project that he still debated, but he began to discover, before the mid-afternoon
of the ensuing Friday, that the center of the graduates' emotional esteem was not necessarily the center of their intellectual attention.

In fact, his very apotheosis seemed to create an odd power-
lessness; his words seemed to be carried away from the ad-
miring multitude by the very clouds of their incense. When
he finally managed to get his own son-in-law, Sam Storey,
off in a corner to tell him about the new system of "cuts" for
chapel, he had the greatest difficulty in making himself heard.
Sam, whom Mr. Minturn even suspected, trustee though he
was, of having had something to drink, finally realized that
he was being asked a question and chose to answer it on the
cozy plane of reminiscence.

"You've got to give the guy a chance, Mr. M," he said,
taking his father-in-law by the elbow for perhaps the first
time in his life. "He's doing his best. Now I know the term
'chapel cut' is offensive to you, but isn't it better than having
boys hiding out in the cellar?"

"In the cellar, Sam? What on earth are you talking about?"

"It's what I used to do as a kid. Half my form did it." Sam's
broad red face broke into a grin. "It was the only time it was
safe to smoke, when all the masters were in chapel!" His grin
vanished as he saw the expression on Mr. Minturn's face.
"But that was thirty years ago, sir! You can't mind now!"

Mr. Minturn shook his head as he turned away.

"You're a trustee, Sam," he protested. "A *trustee!*"

But Sam's reaction, he discovered, was unfortunately typical. It was difficult even to make the men realize that he had
a complaint, and when he did, they minimized it with remarks such as "He can't live up to *you*, Mr. M" or "These are
changing times, you know." Even when they agreed with
him, as Bishop Fisher vociferously did about the chapel cuts,
he would promise no more than to raise the point at the
next meeting of the board of trustees. But worst of all, far the
worst, was his conversation with Mr. Fuller, the school's
financial counsel, a sharp, thin, driving, preoccupied man of

less than forty who confided in Mr. Minturn his reluctant approval of the headmaster's racial policy.

"I know how it must pain you, Mr. M, to have a coon at Chelton," he said, shaking his head. "I know how you've always cared about keeping the school for the good old families. But the fact of the matter is—"

"I never kept Chelton for any good old families!" Mr. Minturn exploded.

"Well, you know what I mean," Mr. Fuller continued, with the shrug of one who has no time for quibbles. "Tradition, *noblesse oblige*, old school tie and all that. Not that I'm against it, mind you." He held up a deprecating hand. "I'm all for it. I think it's terrific. Given my way, Chelton would go on the way you made it forever and ever. But we have to face facts, Mr. M. And this fellow Knox is a smart one. If a private school these days doesn't have a couple of Jew boys and a jigaboo to show the tax people, it stands a chance of losing its tax exemption."

These remarks, delivered to a speechless Mr. Minturn in the lobby by the dining-hall just before the alumni and trustees went in to dinner, the culminating event of the jubilee, left him cold and shaken. When he had recovered himself sufficiently to answer, Fuller had already gone, to be replaced by the Bishop who was telling him something about the doors being open, that they were going in, and would he lead the way, please? He walked slowly ahead, dazed, only dimly aware of the multitude that pressed behind him into the great Jacobean chamber; he made his way mechanically through the long tables gleaming white and silver to the dais where the headmaster's table was laid beneath the portrait of himself in clerical vestments, his own gray eyes staring at him with a confidence that he would never feel again. Once, during the long, jumbled meal he saw his successor's eyes upon him, timidly sympathetic, rapidly averted. For Knox had been watching him. And it suddenly burst on him that Knox knew! It seemed to say, that brief, apologizing glance:

"I'm sorry, Mr. M. I couldn't warn you. You had to find it out, didn't you? For yourself?" And still dazed, he saw the headmaster rise, as main speaker of the evening, and turn in his direction.

"There is certainly no one in this room," Knox was saying, "who has not come under the spell of Mr. M's personality. Much has been said of this personality; often has it been vaunted, and I will not take up your time tonight in idle reiteration. But I should like to point out what to me is the unique quality of Mr. M, which is his power, when we are with him, to make us, well, not as good as he thinks we are, but at least several sizes larger than our usual selves. Mr. M, one might almost say, has created his own world around him, and who would deny that it is a braver, better world than the one in which we would entirely live without him? And if one has been at Chelton, can one ever quite forget his vision, can one ever entirely, however surrounded by compromise and practicality, forget that there *is* another way?"

Mr. Minturn found himself suddenly frozen by a picture that flashed across his mind, remembered from a day, oh, thirty years back, when he had taken his daughters to a vaudeville in Boston, of a small, frightened clown scampering about a darkened stage, unable to get out of the center of a round spotlight that remorselessly and tightly held him. And it broke upon him gradually that this indeed was he, or what he had been, that it was the he who had moved about Chelton for close on half a century, seeing only the lighted circle whose circumference had been his furthest boundary. Oh, true, the circle had shifted, constantly, to follow him, up and down halls and corridors, into darkest corners; there had been no nook or cranny of Chelton life over which it had not cast its brilliant light. It showed things, yes, but not quite as they were. The board, the graduates, the boys themselves could be good, wanted, indeed, to be good, for the brief period in any day or month or year when they found themselves caught in that spotlight with quaint little Mr. M. Now, with retirement, the light had gone out, and he saw the dark. The dark that everyone else had always seen.

The headmaster was ending now; he bowed to Mr. Minturn as he took his seat, but as he did so, he shot him a final, telling look, communicative as only Arthur's glances could be, a look that seemed to say that what Mr. Minturn had believed in, *he* believed in, that his predecessor's image was *his* image, that it was the only image, when all was said and done, that a headmaster could really live by. It was this which in the end seemed to make them strange allies, isolated from the cubic yards of smoke and incomprehension that filled the air of the great hall around them.

Mr. Minturn rose to his feet, and the applause died slowly away, scuttling into silent corners before the reverberating hushes.

"I have only one thing to say," he heard his voice, oddly low, sound out. "May each and every one of you live to have the joy that I have in knowing that his work is carried on."

The applause burst out again, almost frenzied now, and he had only a tumbled sense of the rest of the evening before he returned, accompanied by the whole board of trustees, to his little house. Somewhere in the background, as he left the hall, he caught a glimpse of two frightened faces, but he looked away. Collins and Prince had ceased to exist for him.

This is a sardonic and dramatic story about a neg-
lected child, an ignorant baby sitter and a primitive
faith healer. Miss O'Connor has written more savage
stories than this, but none more disturbing.

The River

||||||||||||||||| FLANNERY O'CONNOR |||||||||||||||||

The child stood glum and limp in the middle of the
dark living room while his father pulled him into a plaid
coat. His right arm was hung in the sleeve but the father buttoned the coat anyway and pushed him forward toward a
pale spotted hand that stuck through the half-open door.

"He ain't fixed right," a loud voice said from the hall.

"Well then for Christ's sake fix him," the father muttered.
"It's six o'clock in the morning." He was in his bathrobe and
barefooted. When he got the child to the door and tried to
shut it, he found her looming in it, a speckled skeleton in a
long pea-green coat and felt helmet.

"And his and my carfare," she said. "It'll be twict we have
to ride the car."

He went in the bedroom again to get the money and when
he came back, she and the boy were both standing in the
middle of the room. She was taking stock. "I couldn't smell
those dead cigarette butts long if I was ever to come sit with
you," she said, shaking him down in his coat.

"Here's the change," the father said. He went to the door
and opened it wide and waited.

After she had counted the money she slipped it somewhere
inside her coat and walked over to a watercolor hanging near
the phonograph. "I know what time it is," she said, peering
closely at the black lines crossing into broken planes of violent
color. "I ought to. My shift goes on at 10 P.M. and don't get

off till 5 and it takes me one hour to ride the Vine Street car."

"Oh, I see," he said; "well, we'll expect him back tonight, about eight or nine?"

"Maybe later," she said. "We're going to the river to a healing. This particular preacher don't get around this way often. I wouldn't have paid for that," she said, nodding at the painting, "I would have drew it myself."

"All right, Mrs. Connin, we'll see you then," he said, drumming on the door.

A toneless voice called from the bedroom, "Bring me an icepack."

"Too bad his mamma's sick," Mrs. Connin said. "What's her trouble?"

"We don't know," he muttered.

"We'll ask the preacher to pray for her. He's healed a lot of folks. The Reverend Bevel Summers. Maybe she ought to see him sometime."

"Maybe so," he said. "We'll see you tonight," and he disappeared into the bedroom and left them to go.

The little boy stared at her silently, his nose and eyes running. He was four or five. He had a long face and bulging chin and half-shut eyes set far apart. He seemed mute and patient, like an old sheep waiting to be let out.

"You'll like this preacher," she said. "The Reverend Bevel Summers. You ought to hear him sing."

The bedroom door opened suddenly and the father stuck his head out and said, "Good-by, old man. Have a good time."

"Good-by," the little boy said and jumped as if he had been shot.

Mrs. Connin gave the watercolor another look. Then they went out into the hall and rang for the elevator. "I wouldn't have drew it," she said.

Outside the gray morning was blocked off on either side by the unlit empty buildings. "It's going to fair up later," she said, "but this is the last time we'll be able to have any preaching at the river this year. Wipe your nose, Sugar Boy."

He began rubbing his sleeve across it but she stopped him. "That ain't nice," she said. "Where's your handkerchief?"

He put his hands in his pockets and pretended to look for it while she waited. "Some people don't care how they send one off," she murmured to her reflection in the coffee shop window. "You pervide." She took a red and blue flowered handkerchief out of her pocket and stooped down and began to work on his nose. "Now blow," she said and he blew. "You can borry it. Put it in your pocket."

He folded it up and put it in his pocket carefully and they walked on to the corner and leaned against the side of a closed drugstore to wait for the car. Mrs. Connin turned up her coat collar so that it met her hat in the back. Her eyelids began to droop and she looked as if she might go to sleep against the wall. The little boy put a slight pressure on her hand.

"What's your name?" she asked in a drowsy voice. "I don't know but only your last name, I should have found out your first name."

His name was Harry Ashfield and he had never thought at any time before of changing it. "Bevel," he said.

Mrs. Connin raised herself from the wall. "Why ain't that a coincident!" she said. "I told you that's the name of this preacher!"

"Bevel," he repeated.

She stood looking down at him as if he had become a marvel to her. "I'll have to see you meet him today," she said. "He's no ordinary preacher. He's a healer. He couldn't do nothing for Mr. Connin though. Mr. Connin didn't have the faith but he said he would try anything once. He had this griping in his gut."

The trolley appeared as a yellow spot at the end of the deserted street.

"He's gone to the government hospital now," she said, "and they taken one-third of his stomach. I tell him he better thank Jesus for what he's got left but he says he ain't thanking nobody. Well I declare," she murmured, "Bevel!"

They walked out to the tracks to wait. "Will he heal me?" Bevel asked.

"What you got?"

"I'm hungry," he decided finally.

"Didn't you have your breakfast?"

"I didn't have time to be hungry yet then," he said.

"Well when we get home we'll both have us something," she said. "I'm ready myself."

They got on the car and sat down a few seats behind the driver and Mrs. Connin took Bevel on her knees. "Now you be a good boy," she said, "and let me get some sleep. Just don't get off my lap." She lay her head back and as he watched, gradually her eyes closed and her mouth fell open to show a few long scattered teeth, some gold and some darker than her face; she began to whistle and blow like a musical skeleton. There was no one in the car but themselves and the driver and when he saw she was asleep, he took out the flowered handkerchief and unfolded it and examined it carefully. Then he folded it up again and unzipped a place in the innerlining of his coat and hid it in there and shortly he went to sleep himself.

Her house was a half-mile from the end of the car line, set back a little from the road. It was tan paper brick with a porch across the front of it and a tin top. On the porch there were three little boys of different sizes with identical speckled faces and one tall girl who had her hair up in so many aluminum curlers that it glared like the roof. The three boys followed them inside and closed in on Bevel. They looked at him silently, not smiling.

"That's Bevel," Mrs. Connin said, taking off her coat. "It's a coincident he's named the same as the preacher. These boys are J. C., Spivey, and Sinclair, and that's Sarah Mildred on the porch. Take off that coat and hang it on the bed post, Bevel."

The three boys watched him while he unbuttoned the coat and took it off. Then they watched him hang it on the bed post and then they stood, watching the coat. They turned abruptly and went out the door and had a conference on the porch.

Bevel stood looking around him at the room. It was part kitchen and part bedroom. The entire house was two rooms and two porches. Close to his foot the tail of a light-colored dog moved up and down between two floor boards as he scratched his back on the underside of the house. Bevel jumped on it but the hound was experienced and had already withdrawn when his feet hit the spot.

The walls were filled with pictures and calendars. There were two round photographs of an old man and woman with collapsed mouths and another picture of a man whose eyebrows dashed out of two bushes of hair and clashed in a heap on the bridge of his nose; the rest of his face stuck out like a bare cliff to fall from. "That's Mr. Connin," Mrs. Connin said, standing back from the stove for a second to admire the face with him, "but it don't favor him any more." Bevel turned from Mr. Connin to a colored picture over the bed of a man wearing a white sheet. He had long hair and a gold circle around his head and he was sawing on a board while some children stood watching him. He was going to ask who that was when the three boys came in again and motioned for him to follow them. He thought of crawling under the bed and hanging onto one of the legs but the three boys only stood there, speckled and silent, waiting, and after a second he followed them at a little distance out on the porch and around the corner of the house. They started off through a field of rough yellow weeds to the hog pen, a five-foot boarded square full of shoats, which they intended to ease him over into. When they reached it, they turned and waited silently, leaning against the side.

He was coming very slowly, deliberately bumping his feet together as if he had trouble walking. Once he had been beaten up in the park by some strange boys when his sitter forgot him, but he hadn't known anything was going to happen that time until it was over. He began to smell a strong odor of garbage and to hear the noises of a wild animal. He stopped a few feet from the pen and waited, pale but dogged.

The three boys didn't move. Something seemed to have happened to them. They stared over his head as if they saw something coming behind him but he was afraid to turn his own head and look. Their speckles were pale and their eyes were still and gray as glass. Only their ears twitched slightly. Nothing happened. Finally, the one in the middle said, "She'd kill us," and turned, dejected and hacked, and climbed up on the pen and hung over, staring in.

Bevel sat down on the ground, dazed with relief, and grinned up at them.

The one sitting on the pen glanced at him severely. "Hey

you," he said after a second, "if you can't climb up and see
these pigs you can lift that bottom board off and look in
thataway." He appeared to offer this as a kindness.

Bevel had never seen a real pig but he had seen a pig in
a book and knew they were small fat pink animals with curly
tails and round grinning faces and bow ties. He leaned forward and pulled eagerly at the board.

"Pull harder," the littlest boy said. "It's nice and rotten. Just
lift out thet nail."

He eased a long reddish nail out of the soft wood.

"Now you can lift up the board and put your face to
the . . ." a quiet voice began.

He had already done it and another face, gray, wet and
sour, was pushing into his, knocking him down and back as
it scraped out under the plank. Something snorted over him
and charged back again, rolling him over and pushing him
up from behind and then sending him forward, screaming
through the yellow field, while it bounded behind.

The three Connins watched from where they were. The
one sitting on the pen held the loose board back with his
dangling foot. Their stern faces didn't brighten any but they
seemed to become less taut, as if some great need had been
partly satisfied. "Maw ain't going to like him lettin out thet
hawg," the smallest one said.

Mrs. Connin was on the back porch and caught Bevel up
as he reached the steps. The hog ran under the house and
subsided, panting, but the child screamed for five minutes.
When she had finally calmed him down, she gave him his
breakfast and let him sit on her lap while he ate it. The shoat
climbed the two steps onto the back porch and stood outside the screen door, looking in with his head lowered sullenly. He was long-legged and humpbacked and part of one
of his ears had been bitten off.

"Git away!" Mrs. Connin shouted. "That one yonder favors
Mr. Paradise that has the gas station," she said. "You'll see
him today at the healing. He's got the cancer over his ear. He
always comes to show he ain't been healed."

The shoat stood squinting a few seconds longer and then
moved off slowly. "I don't want to see him," Bevel said.

They walked to the river, Mrs. Connin in front with him
and the three boys strung out behind and Sarah Mildred, the
tall girl, at the end to holler if one of them ran out on the
road. They looked like the skeleton of an old boat with two
pointed ends, sailing slowly on the edge of the highway. The
white Sunday sun followed at a little distance, climbing fast
through a scum of gray cloud as if it meant to overtake them.
Bevel walked on the outside edge, holding Mrs. Connin's
hand and looking down into the orange and purple gully
that dropped off from the concrete.

It occurred to him that he was lucky this time that they
had found Mrs. Connin who would take you away for the
day instead of an ordinary sitter who only sat where you lived
or went to the park. You found out more when you left where
you lived. He had found out already this morning that he had
been made by a carpenter named Jesus Christ. Before he had
thought it had been a doctor named Sladewall, a fat man
with a yellow mustache who gave him shots and thought his
name was Herbert, but this must have been a joke. They
joked a lot where he lived. If he had thought about it before,
he would have thought Jesus Christ was a word like "oh" or
"damn" or "God," or maybe somebody who had cheated them
out of something sometime. When he had asked Mrs. Connin
who the man in the sheet in the picture over her bed was, she
had looked at him a while with her mouth open. Then she had
said, "That's Jesus," and she had kept on looking at him.

In a few minutes she had got up and got a book out of
the other room. "See here," she said, turning over the cover,
"this belonged to my great grandmamma. I wouldn't part
with it for nothing on earth." She ran her finger under some
brown writing on a spotted page. "Emma Stevens Oakley,
1832," she said. "Ain't that something to have? And every
word of it the gospel truth." She turned the next page and
read him the name: "The Life of Jesus Christ for Readers
Under Twelve." Then she read him the book.

It was a small book, pale brown on the outside with gold
edges and a smell like old putty. It was full of pictures, one
of the carpenter driving a crowd of pigs out of a man. They
were real pigs, gray and sour-looking, and Mrs. Connin said
Jesus had driven them all out of this one man. When she

finished reading, she let him sit on the floor and look at the pictures again.

Just before they left for the healing, he had managed to get the book inside his innerlining without her seeing him. Now it made his coat hang down a little farther on one side than the other. His mind was dreamy and serene as they walked along and when they turned off the highway onto a long red clay road winding between banks of honeysuckle, he began to make wild leaps and pull forward on her hand as if he wanted to dash off and snatch the sun which was rolling away ahead of them now.

They walked on the dirt road for a while and then they crossed a field stippled with purple weeds and entered the shadows of a wood where the ground was covered with thick pine needles. He had never been in woods before and he walked carefully, looking from side to side as if he were entering a strange country. They moved along a bridle path that twisted downhill through crackling red leaves, and once, catching at a branch to keep himself from slipping, he looked into two frozen green-gold eyes enclosed in the darkness of a tree hole. At the bottom of the hill, the woods opened suddenly onto a pasture dotted here and there with black and white cows and sloping down, tier after tier, to a broad orange stream where the reflection of the sun was set like a diamond.

There were people standing on the near bank in a group, singing. Long tables were set up behind them and a few cars and trucks were parked in a road that came up by the river. They crossed the pasture, hurrying, because Mrs. Connin, using her hand for a shed over her eyes, saw the preacher already standing out in the water. She dropped her basket on one of the tables and pushed the three boys in front of her into the knot of people so that they wouldn't linger by the food. She kept Bevel by the hand and eased her way up to the front.

The preacher was standing about ten feet out in the stream where the water came up to his knees. He was a tall youth in khaki trousers that he had rolled up higher than the water. He had on a blue shirt and a red scarf around his neck but no hat and his light-colored hair was cut in sideburns that curved into the hollows of his cheeks. His face was all bone and red light reflected from the river. He looked as if he might have been nineteen years old. He was singing in a high twangy voice, above the singing on the bank, and he kept his hands behind him and his head tilted back.

He ended the hymn on a high note and stood silent, looking down at the water and shifting his feet in it. Then he looked up at the people on the bank. They stood close together, waiting; their faces were solemn but expectant and every eye was on him. He shifted his feet again.

"Maybe I know why you come," he said in the twangy voice, "maybe I don't.

"If you ain't come for Jesus, you ain't come for me. If you just come to see can you leave your pain in the river, you ain't come for Jesus. You can't leave your pain in the river," he said. "I never told nobody that." He stopped and looked down at his knees.

"I seen you cure a woman oncet!" a sudden high voice shouted from the hump of people. "Seen that woman git up and walk out straight where she had limped in!"

The preacher lifted one foot and then the other. He seemed almost but not quite to smile. "You might as well go home if that's what you come for," he said.

Then he lifted his head and arms and shouted, "Listen to what I got to say, you people! There ain't but one river and that's the River of Life, made out of Jesus' Blood. That's the river you have to lay your pain in, in the River of Faith, in the River of Life, in the River of Love, in the rich red river of Jesus' Blood, you people!"

His voice grew soft and musical. "All the rivers come from that one River and go back to it like it was the ocean sea and if you believe, you can lay your pain in that River and get rid of it because that's the River that was made to carry sin. It's a River full of pain itself, pain itself, moving toward the Kingdom of Christ, to be washed away, slow, you people, slow as this here old red water river round my feet.

"Listen," he sang, "I read in Mark about an unclean man, I read in Luke about a blind man, I read in John about a dead man! Oh you people hear! The same blood that makes this River red, made that leper clean, made that blind man stare, made that dead man leap! You people with trouble," he cried, "lay it in that River of Blood, lay it in that River of Pain, and watch it move away toward the Kingdom of Christ."

While he preached, Bevel's eyes followed drowsily the slow circles of two silent birds revolving high in the air. Across the river there was a low red and gold grove of sassafras with hills of dark blue trees behind it and an occasional pine jutting over the skyline. Behind, in the distance, the city rose like a cluster of warts on the side of the mountain. The birds revolved downward and dropped lightly in the top of the highest pine and sat hunch-shouldered as if they were supporting the sky.

"If it's this River of Life you want to lay your pain in, then come up," the preacher said, "and lay your sorrow here. But don't be thinking this is the last of it because this old red river don't end here. This old red suffering stream goes on, you people, slow to the Kingdom of Christ. This old red river is good to Baptize in, good to lay your faith in, good to lay your pain in, but it ain't this muddy water here that saves you. I been all up and down this river this week," he said. "Tuesday I was in Fortune Lake, next day in Ideal, Friday me and my wife drove to Lulawillow to see a sick man there. Them people didn't see no healing," he said and his face burned redder for a second. "I never said they would."

While he was talking a fluttering figure had begun to move forward with a kind of butterfly movement—an old woman with flapping arms whose head wobbled as if it might fall off any second. She managed to lower herself at the edge of the bank and let her arms churn in the water. Then she bent farther and pushed her face down in it and raised herself up finally, streaming wet; and still flapping, she turned a time or two in a blind circle until someone reached out and pulled her back into the group.

"She's been that way for thirteen years," a rough voice shouted. "Pass the hat and give this kid his money. That's what he's here for." The shout, directed out to the boy in the river, came from a huge old man who sat like a humped stone on the bumper of a long ancient gray automobile. He had on a gray hat that was turned down over one ear and up over the other to expose a purple bulge on his left temple. He sat bent forward with his hands hanging between his knees and his small eyes half closed.

Bevel stared at him once and then moved into the folds of Mrs. Connin's coat and hid himself.

The boy in the river glanced at the old man quickly and raised his fist. "Believe Jesus or the devil!" he cried. "Testify to one or the other!"

"I know from my own self-experience," a woman's mysterious voice called from the knot of people, "I know from it that this preacher can heal. My eyes have been opened! I testify to Jesus!"

The preacher lifted his arms quickly and began to repeat all that he had said before about the River and the Kingdom of Christ and the old man sat on the bumper, fixing him with a narrow squint. From time to time Bevel stared at him again from around Mrs. Connin.

A man in overalls and a brown coat leaned forward and dipped his hands in the water quickly and shook it and leaned back, and a woman held a baby over the edge of the bank and splashed its feet with water. One man moved a little distance away and sat down on the bank and took off his shoes and waded out into the stream; he stood there for a few minutes with his face tilted as far back as it would go, then he waded back and put on his shoes. All this time, the preacher sang and did not appear to watch what went on.

As soon as he stopped singing, Mrs. Connin lifted Bevel up and said, "Listen here, preacher, I got a boy from town today that I'm keeping. His mamma's sick and he wants you to pray for her. And this is a coincident—his name is Bevel! Bevel," she said, turning to look at the people behind her, "same as his. Ain't that a coincident, though?"

There were some murmurs and Bevel turned and grinned over her shoulder at the faces looking at him. "Bevel," he said in a loud jaunty voice.

"Listen," Mrs. Connin said, "have you ever been Baptized, Bevel?"

He only grinned.

"I suspect he ain't ever been Baptized," Mrs. Connin said, raising her eyebrows at the preacher.

"Swang him over here," the preacher said and took a stride forward and caught him.

He held him in the crook of his arm and looked at the grinning face. Bevel rolled his eyes in a comical way and thrust his face forward, close to the preacher's. "My name is Bevvvuuuuul," he said in a loud deep voice and let the tip of his tongue slide across his mouth.

The preacher didn't smile. His bony face was rigid and his narrow gray eyes reflected the almost colorless sky. There was a loud laugh from the old man sitting on the car bumper and Bevel grasped the back of the preacher's collar and held it tightly. The grin had already disappeared from his face. He had the sudden feeling that this was not a joke. Where he lived everything was a joke. From the preacher's face, he knew immediately that nothing the preacher said or did was a joke. "My mother named me that," he said quickly.

"Have you ever been Baptized?" the preacher asked.

"What's that?" he murmured.

"If I Baptize you," the preacher said, "you'll be able to go to the Kingdom of Christ. You'll be washed in the river of suffering, son, and you'll go by the deep river of life. Do you want that?"

"Yes," the child said, and thought, I won't go back to the apartment then, I'll go under the river.

"You won't be the same again," the preacher said. "You'll count." Then he turned his face to the people and began to preach and Bevel looked over his shoulder at the pieces of the white sun scattered in the river. Suddenly the preacher said, "All right, I'm going to Baptize you now," and without more warning, he tightened his hold and swung him upside down and plunged his head into the water. He held him under while he said the words of Baptism and then he jerked him up again and looked sternly at the gasping child. Bevel's eyes were dark and dilated. "You count now," the preacher said. "You didn't even count before."

The little boy was too shocked to cry. He spit out the muddy water and rubbed his wet sleeve into his eyes and over his face.

"Don't forget his mamma," Mrs. Connin called. "He wants you to pray for his mamma. She's sick."

"Lord," the preacher said, "we pray for somebody in affliction who isn't here to testify. Is your mother sick in the hospital?" he asked. "Is she in pain?"

The child stared at him. "She hasn't got up yet," he said in a high dazed voice. "She has a hangover." The air was so quiet he could hear the broken pieces of the sun knocking in the water.

The preacher looked angry and startled. The red drained out of his face and the sky appeared to darken in his eyes. There was a loud guffaw from the bank and Mr. Paradise shouted, "Haw! Cure the afflicted woman with the hangover!" and began to beat his knee with his fist.

"He's had a long day," Mrs. Connin said, standing with him in the door of the apartment and looking sharply into the room where the party was going on. "I reckon it's past his regular bedtime." One of Bevel's eyes was closed and the other half closed; his nose was running and he kept his mouth open and breathed through it. The damp plaid coat dragged down on one side.

That would be her, Mrs. Connin decided, in the black britches—long black satin britches and barefoot sandals and red toenails. She was lying on half the sofa, with her knees crossed in the air and her head propped on the arm. She didn't get up.

"Hello Harry," she said. "Did you have a big day?" She had a long pale face, smooth and blank, and straight sweet-potato-colored hair, pulled back.

The father went off to get the money. There were two other couples. One of the men, blond with little violet-blue eyes, leaned out of his chair and said, "Well Harry, old man, have a big day?"

"His name ain't Harry. It's Bevel," Mrs. Connin said.

"His name is Harry," *she* said from the sofa. "Whoever heard of anybody named Bevel?"

The little boy had seemed to be going to sleep on his feet, his head drooping farther and farther forward; he pulled it back suddenly and opened one eye; the other was stuck.

"He told me this morning his name was Bevel," Mrs. Connin said in a shocked voice. "The same as our preacher. We been all day at a preaching and healing at the river. He said his name was Bevel, the same as the preacher's. That's what he told me."

"Bevel!" his mother said. "My God! what a name."

"This preacher is name Bevel and there's no better preacher around," Mrs. Connin said. "And furthermore," she added in a defiant tone, "he Baptized this child this morning!"

His mother sat straight up. "Well the nerve!" she muttered.

"Furthermore," Mrs. Connin said, "he's a healer and he prayed for you to be healed."

"Healed!" she almost shouted. "Healed of what for Christ's sake?"

"Of your affliction," Mrs. Connin said icily.

The father had returned with the money and was standing near Mrs. Connin waiting to give it to her. His eyes were lined with red threads. "Go on, go on," he said, "I want to hear more about her affliction. The exact nature of it has escaped . . ." He waved the bill and his voice trailed off. "Healing by prayer is mighty inexpensive," he murmured.

Mrs. Connin stood a second, staring into the room, with a skeleton's appearance of seeing everything. Then, without taking the money, she turned and shut the door behind her. The father swung around, smiling vaguely, and shrugged. The rest of them were looking at Harry. The little boy began to shamble toward the bedroom.

"Come here, Harry," his mother said. He automatically shifted his direction toward her without opening his eye any farther. "Tell me what happened today," she said when he reached her. She began to pull off his coat.

"I don't know," he muttered.

"Yes you do know," she said, feeling the coat heavier on one side. She unzipped the innerlining and caught the book and a dirty handkerchief as they fell out. "Where did you get these?"

"I don't know," he said and grabbed for them. "They're mine. She gave them to me."

She threw the handkerchief down and held the book too high for him to reach and began to read it, her face after a second assuming an exaggerated comical expression. The

others moved around and looked at it over her shoulder. "My
God," somebody said.

One of the men peered at it sharply from behind a thick
pair of glasses. "That's valuable," he said. "That's a collector's
item," and he took it away from the rest of them and retired
to another chair.

"Don't let George go off with that," his girl said.

"I tell you it's valuable," George said. "1832."

Bevel shifted his direction again toward the room where
he slept. He shut the door behind him and moved slowly
in the darkness to the bed and sat down and took off his
shoes and got under the cover. After a minute a shaft of
light let in the tall silhouette of his mother. She tiptoed
lightly across the room and sat down on the edge of his bed.
"What did that dolt of a preacher say about me?" she whispered. "What lies have you been telling today, honey?"

He shut his eye and heard her voice from a long way away,
as if he were under the river and she on top of it. She shook
his shoulder. "Harry," she said, leaning down and putting her
mouth to his ear, "tell me what he said." She pulled him
into a sitting position and he felt as if he had been drawn up
from under the river. "Tell me," she whispered and her bitter
breath covered his face.

He saw the pale oval close to him in the dark. "He said
I'm not the same now," he muttered. "I count."

After a second, she lowered him by his shirt front onto
the pillow. She hung over him an instant and brushed her
lips against his forehead. Then she got up and moved away,
swaying her hips lightly through the shaft of light.

He didn't wake up early but the apartment was still
dark and close when he did. For a while he lay there, picking his nose and eyes. Then he sat up in bed and looked
out the window. The sun came in palely, stained gray by
the glass. Across the street at the Empire Hotel, a colored
cleaning woman was looking down from an upper window,
resting her face on her folded arms. He got up and put
on his shoes and went to the bathroom and then into the
front room. He ate two crackers spread with anchovy paste,
that he found on the coffee table, and drank some ginger ale

left in a bottle and looked around for his book but it was not there.

The apartment was silent except for the faint humming of the refrigerator. He went into the kitchen and found some raisin bread heels and spread a half jar of peanut butter between them and climbed up on the tall kitchen stool and sat chewing the sandwich slowly, wiping his nose every now and then on his shoulder. When he finished he found some chocolate milk and drank that. He would rather have had the ginger ale he saw but they left the bottle openers where he couldn't reach them. He studied what was left in the refrigerator for a while—some shriveled vegetables that she had forgot were there and a lot of brown oranges that she bought and didn't squeeze; there were three or four kinds of cheese and something fishy in a paper bag; the rest was a pork bone. He left the refrigerator door open and wandered back into the dark living room and sat down on the sofa.

He decided they would be out cold until one o'clock and that they would all have to go to a restaurant for lunch. He wasn't high enough for the table yet and the waiter would bring a highchair and he was too big for a highchair. He sat in the middle of the sofa, kicking it with his heels. Then he got up and wandered around the room, looking into the ashtrays at the butts as if this might be a habit. In his own room he had picture books and blocks but they were for the most part torn up; he found the way to get new ones was to tear up the ones he had. There was very little to do at any time but eat; however, he was not a fat boy.

He decided he would empty a few of the ashtrays on the floor. If he only emptied a few, she would think they had fallen. He emptied two, rubbing the ashes carefully into the rug with his finger. Then he lay on the floor for a while, studying his feet which he held up in the air. His shoes were still damp and he began to think about the river.

Very slowly, his expression changed as if he were gradually seeing appear what he didn't know he'd been looking for. Then all of a sudden he knew what he wanted to do.

He got up and tiptoed into their bedroom and stood in the dim light there, looking for her pocketbook. His glance passed her long pale arm hanging off the edge of the bed down to the floor, and across the white mound his father made, and past the crowded bureau, until it rested on the pocketbook hung on the back of a chair. He took a car-token out of it and half a package of Life Savers. Then he left the apartment and caught the car at the corner. He hadn't taken a suitcase because there was nothing from there he wanted to keep.

He got off the car at the end of the line and started down the road he and Mrs. Connin had taken the day before. He knew there wouldn't be anybody at her house because the three boys and the girl went to school and Mrs. Connin had told him she went out to clean. He passed her yard and walked on the way they had gone to the river. The paper brick houses were far apart and after a while the dirt place to walk on ended and he had to walk on the edge of the highway. The sun was pale yellow and high and hot.

He passed a shack with an orange gas pump in front of it but he didn't see the old man looking out at nothing in particular from the doorway. Mr. Paradise was having an orange drink. He finished it slowly, squinting over the bottle at the small plaid-coated figure disappearing down the road. Then he set the empty bottle on a bench and, still squinting, wiped his sleeve over his mouth. He went in the shack and picked out a peppermint stick, a foot long and two inches thick, from the candy shelf, and stuck it in his hip pocket. Then he got in his car and drove slowly down the highway after the boy.

By the time Bevel came to the field speckled with purple weeds, he was dusty and sweating and he crossed it at a trot to get into the woods as fast as he could. Once inside, he wandered from tree to tree, trying to find the path they had taken yesterday. Finally he found a line worn in the pine needles and followed it until he saw the steep trail twisting down through the trees.

Mr. Paradise had left his automobile back some way on the road and had walked to the place where he was accustomed to sit almost every day, holding an unbaited fishline in the water while he stared at the river passing in front of him. Anyone looking at him from a distance would have seen an old boulder half hidden in the bushes.

Bevel didn't see him at all. He only saw the river, shimmering reddish yellow, and bounded into it with his shoes and his coat on and took a gulp. He swallowed some and spit the rest out and then he stood there in water up to his chest and looked around him. The sky was a clear pale blue, all in one piece—except for the hole the sun made—and fringed around the bottom with treetops. His coat floated to the surface and surrounded him like a strange gay lily pad and he stood grinning in the sun. He intended not to fool with preachers any more but to Baptize himself and to keep on going this time until he found the Kingdom of Christ in the river. He didn't mean to waste any more time. He put his head under the water at once and pushed forward.

In a second he began to gasp and sputter and his head reappeared on the surface; he started under again and the same thing happened. The river wouldn't have him. He tried again and came up, choking. This was the way it had been when the preacher held him under—he had had to fight with something that pushed him back in the face. He stopped and thought suddenly: it's another joke, it's just another joke! He thought how far he had come for nothing and he began to hit and splash and kick the filthy river. His feet were already treading on nothing. He gave one low cry of pain and indignation. Then he heard a shout and turned his head and saw something like a giant pig bounding after him, shaking a red and white club and shouting. He plunged under once and this time, the waiting current caught him like a long gentle hand and pulled him swiftly forward and down. For an instant he was overcome with surprise; then since he was moving quickly and knew that he was getting somewhere, all his fury and his fear left him.

Mr. Paradise's head appeared from time to time on the surface of the water. Finally, far downstream, the old man rose like some ancient water monster and stood empty-handed, staring with his dull eyes as far down the river line as he could see.

Jesse Stuart, who was born in the Kentucky mountains, has written scores of stories about his people. This is my favorite.

Land of Our Enemies

|||||||||||||||||| JESSE STUART ||||||||||||||||||

"Pap will never ride another log raft down this river," Pa said, as he looked from the train window at the Big Sandy River. "I've gone down this river to Gate City with 'im many a time when I was a little shaver. I've seen a big poplar log break loose from the raft and I've seen Pap jump from the raft onto it and the spikes in his boot heels wouldn't ketch and the log would dump 'im in the icy water. Pap would come up a-spittin' water and a-cussin'. But he'd get his log back to the raft. It makes a body have a funny feelin' to remember all of these things."

Our train was lumberin' and creakin' around the curves farther up the twisting Big Sandy. The sun had gone down and twilight was settling over the deep valley. Here and there we could see a light in a shack beside the railroad tracks. Soon the thin-leafed mountain slopes faded into twilight and gradually into darkness, until we could no longer see the outlines of the mountains and the white streams of water. We were riding into darkness, a darkness so thick that it looked like from the train window one could reach out and slice it into black ribbons with a pocketknife.

"Lindsay, Lindsay," the conductor said as he entered our coach. "All out for Lindsay!"

"Do you reckon anybody will be at the station to meet us?" I asked Pa.

"Somebody'll be here," he said. "Somebody'll be at this station to meet every train. Powderjays will be a-comin' back here on every train."

"When will they bury Grandpa?" I asked Pa.

"Shhh! Not so loud," he whispered, as he glanced over his shoulder.

I looked around to see two beardy-faced men with mean-lookin' eyes listening to what we said.

"You never know whether you're a-talkin' before a friend 'r an enemy here," Pa whispered to me.

The two beardy-faced men got up from their seats and followed us from the train.

"Air ye a-goin' to Cousin Mick Powderjay's funeral?" one of the men asked Pa soon as we had stepped off the train.

"That's where we're a-goin'," Pa said. "Is he akin to you?"

"We're brother's children," the man said. "I'm Zack Powderjay. And this is my brother, Dave Powderjay! We're Zack Powderjay's boys."

"I'm Mick Powderjay," Pa told them. "Pap's eleventh child by his first wife!"

"We've heard of ye," Zack Powderjay said. "See, we had to leave the Big Sandy a long time ago."

"When did you leave?" Pa asked.

"In President Hayes's administration," Dave Powderjay said.

"I left in Grover Cleveland's second administration," Pa said.

"Why did you leave?" Dave Powderjay asked Pa.

"Trouble with the Hornbuckles," he said.

"Trouble with th' Hornbuckles and Dangerfields caused us to leave," Dave said.

"Did Cousin Mick die a natural death?" Zack Powderjay asked Pa.

"I ain't heard yet but I know Pap didn't die a natural death," Pa said. "He had more enemies than he had ailments of the body."

"Ye're right, brother," a husky voice sounded in the darkness now that the train had gone. "I'm Keith Powderjay, son of Jimmie Powderjay, oldest son of Mick Powderjay. I've come to meet this train to direct any and all Powderjays and their bloodkin to the right spot."

"Then Pap was killed?" Pa asked Keith Powderjay, who had come close enough for Pa to recognize him.

Keith was a mountain of a man towering above us.

"He was beaten to death with a club," Keith told us. "Wait until ye see 'im."

"Who kilt Cousin Mick?" Dave Powderjay asked.

"We know but we ain't a-sayin' now," Keith said. "Two men done it. And we got men out atter 'em tonight. Ye may hear of two deaths before mornin'."

"It makes my blood bile," Pa said. "But I've been expectin' somethin' to happen to Pap fer many years. He's been a-fightin' a long war."

"We're all riled a-plenty," Keith said. "We'd better git goin'."

"Do you have a lantern?" Pa asked. "I can't see well in the dark."

"But ye can't have a lantern, Uncle Mick," Keith said. "Lanterns air good targets at night."

"I've been away a long time," Pa said. "I jist fergot. Hit's all a-comin' back to me now."

And as we followed Keith Powderjay through the darkness, Pa's words came back to me. I remembered when we used to sit around the fire on winter nights at home how Pa would tell about going to the railroad station or to church and how he would walk in the darkness because he was afraid to carry a lantern. He would tell us how men had waited for him because he was a son of old Mick Powderjay and how he had been shot at many times. Once a bullet came so close he felt the wind from it on the tip of his nose.

"No talkin' here," Cousin Keith told us. "Quiet until I tell ye when to talk."

Everybody got quiet and we had to walk hand in hand with Cousin Keith leadin' us. But he had been over this path so many times he could feel the path with his feet.

I'm glad Grandpa Powderjay moved to the Little Sandy River in Cleveland's second administration, I thought. I'm glad Pa didn't go back with Grandpa when he got homesick for the Big Sandy and moved back to fight with his enemies. I'm glad Pa stayed on the Little Sandy and I was born there.

Grandpa had been a soldier; he had fought in Pennsylvania,

Maryland, and Virginia. Gettysburg was a name to him that he would never forget; Antietam, Bull Run, Cold Harbor, Fredericksburg, Richmond were names that I had heard him talk about since I could remember. He had fought through the war from beginning to end and the only scars he had were around his wrists where he had been hanged by the arms to the joist of an old house. Captured twice and hanged once, he had come out of the war a living man.

But this was not the war that got Grandpa into trouble. When he came home he fought a long war. It was a war that never ended. He waged war on the guerrilla bands, who had captured, killed, and plundered while he and other mountain men were away fighting in Northern and Southern armies. These guerrilla bands didn't belong to either army. Grandpa had fought them since eighteen sixty-five, all but the three years he had lived on the Little Sandy. Now they had gotten 'im in the end as they said they would.

"We're a-past the dangerous places," Cousin Keith said. "We're a-past the Hornbuckles and Dangerfields."

"How much fudder do we haf to go?" Dave Powderjay asked.

"About three miles," Cousin Keith said.

"When will they bury Pap?" Pa asked.

"Two o'clock in the mornin'," Cousin Keith said.

"It's too bad to haf to bury Pap at night," Pa sighed.

"But this is a land of our enemies," Cousin Keith said. "Grandpa died a-fightin' his enemies. He told me two days before he's kilt that if all his bloodkin had stayed with 'im he'd a-winned this war in the end."

"But brother Zack and I were glad to get out'n it," Dave Powderjay said. "Glad to get into the mountains of West Virginia. We left soon as Pap and brother Tom were kilt, and we have lived in West Virginia and raised our famblies in peace."

I had never heard of a funeral at night but I had read in my history book in school where General Braddock was buried at night so the Indians wouldn't find his grave. I guess the reason that we buried Grandpa at night wasn't that his enemies would bother his grave but that his enemies would bother his bloodkin that had gathered to see him buried. I

knew if we couldn't walk from the railroad to the shack where
Grandpa lived and carry a light, we couldn't have a funeral
in the daytime. I knew that we were among our enemies.
Though we had killed many of their people, there wasn't a
family among us but Pa's where one, two, or three men had
not fallen from the ambush shots of our enemies.

Why are we such hated people? I thought.

"I'll tell you where Pap made his mistake," Pa said. "He
made it when he married his second wife, Mattie Henson.
She's a first cousin of Anse Dangerfield and Tobbie Horn-
buckle! I can't understand what made Pap marry an en'my!"

"That's right, Uncle Mick," Cousin Keith said. "Ye hit the
nail on the head. If our men air lucky tonight, ye'll know tomorrow that this is the truth."

I couldn't tell when we reached Grandpa's shack. There
wasn't a light from any window. Cousin Keith knocked three
times on the door; it was opened by Pa's oldest brother,
Uncle Cief. "Come in," he said softly.

And we followed him into the crowd of our people—
beardy-faced men and women with deep-lined faces. There
was silence in the room, and everybody's face was clouded.

"Where's Mattie?" Pa asked.

"She's not here any more," Aunt Arabella said. "Pap and
her's been separated fer some time."

And now I saw assembled for the first time Pa's people—my
bloodkin from the East Kentucky mountains. They were my
bloodkin that I had heard about but didn't know very well;
many of the men had scars on their faces and hands and many
of them limped. I was glad, after I looked at them, that I
had not been through a long guerrilla war.

"Come this way," Cousin Keith said, beckoning to us.

We followed him into the room where Grandpa was in his
homemade coffin.

"Look at this, won't ye!"

Cousin Keith pointed to the wide blue marks across Grandpa's battered face where he had been beaten to death. And
then he bent over and opened his coat and shirt and showed
us the pulp-beats on his chest. I had never seen a man beaten
as he had been beaten—this mountain of a man who had
died in the battle he had been fighting forty-six years. His

face was clean shaven and his mustache neatly trimmed and
his gray hair parted on the side. His mouth was set firmly. I
had seen him in life when his mouth was set as it was now.
His mouth was like this in life when he spoke of his enemies.

Pa turned and walked away. He couldn't stand to look at
Grandpa. He went back into the room where the old crippled
soldiers sat, wearing their tattered uniforms and holding their
rifles in their hands. They had fought with Grandpa. Now
they had come for his funeral. Pa called them by their names
and shook their hands. They were white-haired, white-
bearded, and grisly old warriors who had seen their best days
and had come to see an old comrade buried. They seemed to
have risen from a dim and distant past.

"Your pap wuz as good a soldier as ever lived," one spoke
feebly to Pa. "But one war wuz not enough fer 'im. He outa
quit then. No use fightin' all his life."

"He was the best wrestler in Grant's army," another said.
"I never saw him rode in all the bouts he had."

There were low whispers among my people in the small
crowded, three-room shack. Heavy quilts were hangin' over
the windows so not a ray of light could be seen from the outside. Wind came between the log cracks, and the flames of
oil lamps sputtered and smoked the lamp globes. I remembered while I stood here among my people and these old
soldiers in their faded uniforms what Pa had told Mom. He
had told her how Grandpa wouldn't sleep in a room unless
a lamp was burning. Said he put quilts over the windows so
they wouldn't be a target for his enemies shooting with rifles
from the thickets on the mountain slopes.

We were quiet enough in the shack to hear the roosters
crow for midnight. And as soon as they had finished crowing
from their roosts outside the shack, Uncle Jason came into the
room.

"It's about time fer us to start," he announced.

Six of my cousins, sons of Pa's older brothers, picked up
Grandpa's coffin and stepped out into the darkness. They
were tall beardy men with broad shoulders. The muscles in
their forearms bulged as they carried the big coffin and the
big warrior in it from his shack out into the darkness. Aunt
Emerine blew out the lamps and the crowd of Powderjays,

their in-laws and friends followed the coffin into the darkness.
Cousin Keith led the way up the mountain path and we followed. A moon came from behind a dark bread-loaf-shaped
mountain where jutted rocks were outlined against the misty
sky. There were whispers among us as we walked along slowly. Twice my cousins had to let six more cousins carry the
coffin, since it was such a load in the darkness to carry up a
mountain slope.

"Not one of Pap's eight young'ins by Mattie air here,"
Uncle Cief told Pa. "And hit's good they ain't here. Thar's
too much en'my blood in 'em to suit us."

I didn't know the part-guerrilla Powderjays from the real
Powderjays. But I knew that the real Powderjays didn't have
any use for them even if the same blood did flow through
their veins. I heard Pa and Uncle Cief talking about them as
the crowd moved slowly along. I was with my people and it
seemed like a dream. I didn't know there was a world like
the one I was in.

Suddenly our stumbling, whispering funeral crowd stopped
on a lonely mountaintop. I could see rows of brown sand-
stones that had been chiseled with pickaxes and broad axes
marking the rows of graves. And I saw men standing by a
fresh-dug grave holding their picks, adzes, and long-handled
shovels. An owl flew over us on outspread wings we could
hear fanning the night wind. And on a distant mountaintop
we heard a whippoorwill. But there was not a light nor a
sound among us while my cousins placed Grandpa's coffin
beside his grave. "Tonight, we're a-buryin' a soldier who has
had many fights," an old soldier said after Grandpa's coffin
had been placed beside the grave. "He has fit through a long
war in the land of his enemies and he has fit well."

From among men and women of our silent funeral crowd
two men walked toward the old soldier. As they walked toward him, Uncle Cief put his hand on his pistol until he
recognized them. One whispered something to the old soldier
in charge of Grandpa's funeral.

"And I am glad to tell you Mick Powderjay's death has
been avenged," the old soldier announced. "Eif Dangerfield
and Battle Henson've paid fer thar crime!"

That was all that was said for Grandpa. There wasn't a

preacher to preach his funeral and there weren't any songs. The old soldiers fired a farewell volley across his grave, and the fire from their rifles was the only light we had seen except the moonlight shining dimly through the sheets of white mists rising from the valley below us. Grandpa's coffin was lowered into his grave with leather checklines on a mountaintop where only Powderjays, their bloodkin, and in-laws were buried—a mountain high enough to overlook the rugged land of our people and our enemies.

The tender and touching relationship between a
little girl and an eccentric old maid would make this
charming story notable even without its pathetic and
stunning surprise ending.

When the Bough Breaks

ELIZABETH ENRIGHT

Miss Pruitt Clovelly lived with her mother in the yellow house on the corner of Pine and Van Buren streets; the
one that had been boarded up for so many years before they
moved in. It was a narrow alert-looking house with tall gables
which were trimmed with wooden rickrack, and all the upstairs windows had pointed tops like church windows. It
stood in a perpetual green revery all summer long, for the
maples were close-pressed around it, and the grass grew as
high as the porch steps. Vines spread their fingers across the
shutters and held them closed. When Miss Pruitt and her
mother moved in they did remarkably little to the place; they
pruned the vines and shrubs, of course, or at least Ben Dwyer
did it for them, and he cut a path from the front gate to the
front steps, but that was about all. They seemed to like to
have a tall lake of grass around the house, and when you
passed that corner in summertime the crickets were louder
than anywhere else, and on June nights the fireflies floated
and glimmered there like the lights of a fairy regatta.

Lorna Reckettson and her mother and sisters had watched
from their house across the street when Mrs. Clovelly and
her daughter moved in, though everyone except Lorna pretended to be doing something else; and everyone except
Lorna thought it strange that old Mrs. Clovelly and Ben
Dwyer and the truckmen did all the heavy lifting, while Miss

Pruitt, who looked able-bodied enough in a middle-aged way, just sat on the porch railing and directed, or left the whole project to take care of itself and wandered through the high grass picking twigs of mock orange.

"She may have heart trouble," Mrs. Reckettson murmured to Stella. "Heart conditions often look healthy, you know," and she went back to pretending to tie up the tree peonies.

Lorna pretended nothing. She was seven and a half and at that age it was still all right to stare. She stood on the gate and swung it slowly, grindingly, to and fro, and stared at the couch being warped through the doorway like a ship into port, and at the upright piano, and the chairs and the pictures with gold frames. A large pier glass leaning against a maple gave back her image to her: a fat girl swinging forward on a gate with sunshine behind her.

"Maybe she's just getting over an illness," said Stella. "Maybe she has to guard her strength."

"Maybe she's just bone lazy," said Josephine, who was fourteen and did not like people.

Something was strange about Miss Pruitt Clovelly, certainly, and about her mother, too. They seemed to have no wish for society, no wish for entertainment. Every day or so one of them would go down the street to the stores, carrying a market basket: sometimes it was Miss Pruitt, walking with her tranquil, unhurried pace, and sometimes it was Mrs. Clovelly, head bent forward and feet scuffling hastily as if the wind were at her back; but these were the only occasions on which they left the house. Why they had moved to that town and where they had come from no one knew for many years.

Mrs. Clovelly was a little old parched thing with all different kinds of wrinkles, and a high witch voice. When people called she seemed always half abstracted, more apt to watch her daughter than the guests. And on the front porch as she guided them out she murmured, "Pru is delicate, you know. She's always, from a little girl, been very delicate."

"Doesn't look delicate to *me*," the callers remarked to each other as they walked along the street. "Why, I'd say she was the picture of health, wouldn't you?"

The queer thing was that not one of the calls was ever

returned; and in that town no other hint was needed: the Clovellys were studiously left to their solitude. Except for the children, about the only people who entered the house at all were Ben Dwyer, who worked for the ladies, and Dr. Oliver Purcell, and whether the latter came in a professional or social capacity was never known for certain. But the children! They were welcome there at all times, as Lorna soon found out.

One day as she was swinging on the gate watching Mrs. Clovelly prune the hydrangea bush she saw Miss Pruitt come out on the porch with a plate in her hand which she put down on the front steps. Then she stood up and looked across the street at Lorna and called the word "FUDGE!"

Lorna swung and stared, her mouth blank.

"Little girl, I've just made a plate of fudge!" Miss Pruitt insisted. "Come on over and help me cut it when it cools, and then we can sample it."

Lorna stepped down from the gate.

"Don't ever accept candy from strangers," warned the stern memory of her mother's voice; Lorna listened to it for a moment, appraised it, and pushed it back into the cupboard where many such admonitions were laid away.

She walked to the curbstone, and listening to another admonition, looked once to the left, once to the right, though nothing was in sight but a faraway horse and wagon, and took the plunge across the empty street.

"Good morning, dear," said Mrs. Clovelly, looking up from the hydrangea bush and smiling her crumpled smile, and Miss Pruitt said, "Hello, honey. Come on up here and sit in the hammock while the fudge cools."

Lorna walked up the porch steps which had an empty sound like wooden boxes, never taking her eyes from Miss Pruitt's face. She went over to the hammock and sank her bottom in it, still never taking her eyes away from Miss Pruitt's face. Miss Pruitt smiled at her and rocked her chair back and forth, and took some pink knitting out of a pinned towel. The plate of fudge on the front steps gave off a faint, rare fragrance of chocolate.

"I have a dog home," Lorna suddenly decided to say. "His

name is Sport and he's fourteen years old. Old as my sister Josephine."

After that Lorna spent a lot of her time at Miss Pru's house. In the beginning her mother was inclined to disapprove, but in the end she consented tacitly, saying only: "What in mercy's name do you want to hang around *there* for all the time? I declare it's more than I can understand when you've got your own lovely yard with a swing and a playhouse and all!"

How could Lorna explain that her own lovely yard was tame territory to her; every stone in it as familiar as a family face, while at Miss Pru's there was a feeling of wilderness and wonder as one pressed through the feathery grass of the yard, tall as lion grass on the African plain; or climbed the warped branches of the quince bush at the back of the house, or swung around and around on the arms of the whirligig clothes drier, or hid in the dark, rich-smelling corners of the woodshed. Every child in the neighborhood could be located in the Clovelly place at some time during the day; they sat on the front steps blowing sedum leaves into frogs' tongues, or rocked and sailed, two or three together in the string hammock; they were rooted out of the shrubbery and the back porch by the loud calling of relatives at mealtime, and in the long twilight their voices could be heard shrill and high, in bursts of acrimony or excitement, as they played hide-and-seek, or still-pond-no-more-moving. There were cookies in the Clovelly kitchen always, big oatmeal cookies, and brownies and cinnamon wheels. Often there was a dish of fudge or a special kind of jaw-locking vinegar candy.

But stronger, more magnetic, than any of these interests and enticements was the quality of Miss Pru herself. Mrs. Clovelly was all right, nobody minded her, but Miss Pru was special. For one thing, the most important thing, she was happy all the time. That may not sound like anything, but consider it. Happy *all* the time. Most people are happy now and then, but their state is something which is temporary and foredoomed, something to be appreciated rather frantically; a condition bright and evanescent. There are other people who know how to maintain a passive contentment for months at a time; but Miss Pruitt was not like these.

She was happy in a tranced durable way as though she knew a secret, a wonderful personal secret that never lost its value.

On summer days she sat on the front porch rocking and sewing, rocking and sewing, with that shut-away, faraway, impervious smile on her lips. "See-cret. See-cret. I know a see-cret," croaked the rocking chair interminably. And in the wintertime you could see her in the kitchen window, rocking and sewing, rocking and sewing, with a shawl across her shoulders and smiling that same smile all to herself.

"I think she's a little— Well, a little—*you* know," Lorna's mother said to her father across the supper table, and gave him an adult glance, with her mouth turned down at the corners.

"Harmless, I hope?" said her father.

"Oh, *harmless!* Heavens yes."

What could the thought of harm have to do with Miss Pru, Lorna wondered. Miss Pruitt was good as gold and her kindness was as easy to take as the summer air itself. It was as though from some central love she had a lot of spare love spilled over; for children at least, and for animals. There were always kittens in that house, and all through the winter the cardinals and chickadees found their breakfast on the broad porch railing.

Lorna did not inquire into her mother's comment. She had learned early in life that to protect her loves she must keep them secret, and especially from grownups, from whom there was often apt to be a bald, mirthful, merciless response to a child's confessions of attachment.

So when her mother asked questions she became vague and absent-minded.

"What's Miss Pruitt like, Lorna?"

"Oh I do' know. She's all right I guess. Can I have some bread and sugar?"

"No. What's the house like upstairs?"

"It's—well, it's just plain bedrooms and things. And a bathroom. Can I have some bread and sugar?"

"No. Are there any pictures on the walls?"

"I guess so. Some brownish ones. Can't I just have a little teeny slice with sugar on it?"

"Oh for pitysakes. No. Oh, all right. I don't care."

So Miss Pruitt was protected and she was worth protecting. When Lorna and the others came to her on rainy or dreary days in the unspeakable boredom of childhood she never failed them.

"Miss Pru, what can we *doo-oo*?"

"Do, honey? Well, let's see. How'd you like it if I made us a cake and you-all could lick the bowl?"

Or she might suggest making clothespin dolls. That was fun once in a while and it was the kind of thing you always forgot about between times: drawing the little ink faces on the top of the clothespin and making the clothes from scraps in Miss Pru's piece bag. Little skirts and trousers cut out of silk and crumpled satin, and tiny capes, never coats, for clothespin dolls were armless.

Or she might say, "Why, I tell you what, you can dress up in some of our long skirts and pretend like you're grown-up ladies at a ball. I'll play the piano for you to dance."

The piano was old and it sounded as if there were knives and forks inside it, but Miss Pru got music out of it anyway. She played the "Valse Bleue," Bartlett's "Dream," and "When the Swallows Homeward Fly." She could play for hours on end, but she would never, never dance with them.

"No, honey," she would say, smiling that slow, blissful smile of hers. "I mustn't dance with you. I mustn't tire myself out."

She was very careful of herself, Miss Pru; never lifting anything heavy, never hurrying, always holding onto the railing when she went up the stairs or down. She moved quietly, as if she tiptoed through a world asleep, and she spoke quietly, too, in a very smooth even voice. Sometimes when the children staggered onto the porch worn out with play, red-cheeked, moist-browed and quarreling, she would say, "Come on, you-all, sit down somewhere or other and I'll tell you a story." And then in that peaceful, uneventful voice she spun them long tales about princesses and villains and narrow escapes and virtue's inevitable reward. Sometimes she drew upon her own memory and gave them detailed accounts of childhood exploits with her long-ago chum Anne-Ethel Pritchett.

"Once, when Mama bought the piano Anne-Ethel and I

made a little house out of the piano box. A great big wooden box, it was—"

"The same piano as you have *now*, Miss Pru?"

"The very one. Anne-Ethel's father cut a window in the side of the piano box for us, and he leaned a couple of old doors against the front, so it was a regular little house. We kept our dolls and our doll dishes in it, and sometimes when it rained we'd take our supper out there and eat it; and the rain on the roof—oh, that sound of rain on the roof—" Miss Pru laid her sewing in her lap, leaned back in her chair with her eyes closed as if that remembered sound of raindrops made her almost too happy for endurance.

She and Anne-Ethel had had lots of dolls but Miss Pru had had the most. Lorna knew the names of all of them: Lillian, Heliotrope, Ethel (named for Anne-Ethel), Shirley, Rebecca and Rowena, Roger, Grover Cleveland, and all the others. Billy Boy had been the favorite one, a big baby doll with a soft rag body.

"Honey, I've still got that dolly packed away in a trunk somewhere. I loved him like he was alive. Oh, like he was alive! The paint's all worn off his poor little nose and one of his arms is broken, but I declare I love him still."

Miss Pru's smile of reminiscence forced upon Lorna a faint feeling of guilt. She had never felt tenderness for her dolls; in the end they had all suffered at her hands. Their glue-smelling wigs had been ripped from their heads and their round glass eyeballs plucked out of their empty skulls. Scalped and blind they lay in the cupboard, their limbs dangling from tendons of loose elastic.

"Mine are all girl dolls; all dumb and all pretty," said Lorna. "*Were*," she added with satisfaction. "Miss Pru, is that a doll's dress you're making now?"

Miss Pru held up the tiny thing. "No. That's for a baby I know of, honey. A real live baby."

Miss Pruitt knew a lot of babies, it seemed. She was always knitting pink things or blue things, or stitching the tucks on small yokes. She liked to sew and did it almost without noticing it. When she wasn't sewing or knitting she was in the kitchen baking, or out in the garden taking casual care of her flowers. Flowers grew for her in return for very little, and even they seemed more interesting than other people's flowers. In the two cleared beds beside the porch bloomed pink freckled rubrum lilies and triple-crowned spider plants. In spring there were blue and purple columbines there, and bleeding hearts like strings of lockets; in the fall came crowds of white-stemmed autumn crocuses. Inside the house there were flowers too: round, velvety calceolarias pressed against the windowpane, and a begonia with glittering blood-red flowers.

Sometimes, in the winter, Lorna took her homework to the Clovellys' house. She liked to do it there at the kitchen table with the big coal range rustling and breathing like another person, a huge strong quiet person in the room. The catsup bottle and the pickle jar and a tumbler with a flower in it surveyed her work dispassionately. Old Mrs. Clovelly creaked and scurried about the house, and Miss Pru sat sewing beside the kitchen window never speaking or interrupting. Sometimes she sighed, a full soft sound which seemed the final expression of contentment, as impersonal and involuntary in its peacefulness as the breath of wind on a summer day.

To have her there was wonderful; a comfort. For any other purpose she was nearly useless. "Honey, I can't add two and two," she said complacently, when Lorna applied to her for help. "When it comes to arithmetic I'm just as *helpless* . . ." Her spelling was almost as bad, though not quite, and geography, for her, did not exist. "The things I know about are things I can touch and look at, real things," said Miss Pru. "Real things like cats and children and cooking and making things. Playing a piano, too. That's kind of real. But silly old commas and periods and long division, why those are just a waste of time and good eyesight. Nobody needs them except the old bookkeepers and the old storekeepers and the men in banks."

Lorna agreed with this, and her own sighs were rebellious, but not for long. Presently the peacefulness enveloped her again. Her pencil scratched and paused, the eraser rubbed brusquely, and then the pencil scratched on again. Being in this place made Lorna feel good, it made her feel smooth and loving. At home Stella and Josephine lived in a state of peevish civil war, her mother was constantly being overtaken by her temper, and as a result of these things her father lived nine-tenths below the surface like an iceberg. But here all was placid, untorn, unhurried. Now and then Mrs. Clovelly came in and looked at her daughter, felt of her forehead, and asked questions: "Did you have your glass of milk, Pru? Don't you want to lay down for a while?"

"Yes, I suppose I *ought* to have a little rest," Miss Pru might say, standing up slowly and stretching, and the cat that fell out of her lap stretched too, paw by paw. Lorna closed her book reluctantly; it was time to go home.

The winter that Lorna was twelve years old Mrs. Clovelly died. She died abruptly, with no notice, as if she were in a hurry to let go. The neighbors forgot their grievances and did all they could to help. After all, though living people may be dull, eccentric, irritating, once they die they attain a terrible, immense dignity. They must be placated: who knows what they have become? It is then that we cluster about the bereaved with our kindnesses, trying in vain to improve a memory of ourselves which is now completed. Miss Pruitt's house was suddenly full of grown-up people, tiptoeing through the rooms, whispering in the hallway, arranging flowers, and making cups of tea in the kitchen.

"And she just *let* us," said Lorna's mother the day after the funeral. "I don't mind helping people, never did. When people are in trouble I can't do too much for them, I'm funny that way. I'll just give everything I've got to help them, just wear myself out, but I must say! The way that woman sat back and watched us do *every*thing. Well, honestly! And half the time she was smiling, too, she hardly shed a tear. I wonder if she's got a heart at all!"

Mother doesn't understand anything, Lorna thought; I wish I had a mother like Miss Pru; and after school for those next days she helped her friend pack away old Mrs. Clovelly's old clothes, folding them, and sprinkling them with black pepper to keep out the moths, and wrapping them in newspaper. They ought to see her now, Lorna thought resentfully, watching Miss Pruitt's silent tears drop onto the printed paper where they made dark spreading stars of damp.

"She was a good mother," was all she said.

"You would have been a good mother, too," Lorna told her on impulse.

And suddenly Miss Pruitt smiled again.

That year and the next one went by like the years before. Except for the absence of Mrs. Clovelly everything was the same; but the year she was fourteen the world began to change for Lorna. Both her sisters got married, for one thing, and she went to high school for the first time and fell in love with the sophomore football captain who did not fall in love with her. She then fell in love with the senior football captain who did not know she was on the earth. At the same time she fell in love with the boy at the Idlewild Drug Store soda counter and he seemed to like her, too, since he called her "fish face." The rest of the time she was engaged in deadly combat with Latin declensions and algebra, and in the afternoons she made extra money by wheeling babies on their mothers' bridge afternoons, or sitting with them in the evenings. Nowadays when she went to see Miss Pru she was always in a hurry, gasping and red-cheeked in her haste; and Miss Pru herself was not quite the same, either: Lorna was a little hurt that now and then she mislaid her name, fumbling first with names like Pearl or Barbara or Maureen, before she came to Lorna. Nowadays, too, there was a whole new group of children playing about the place, kid sisters, kid brothers of her own contemporaries; and though she herself no longer used Miss Pruitt's home as headquarters she resented the small new babbling rabble that did, and passed among them without looking at them.

She had regular babies to take care of: little Millicent Quintz, Linda Lesser, and Gary Alan Gellhouse. Gary Alan was her favorite because he never cried and because she had helped look after him from the time he was newborn, with a little red face like a clenched fist, till now when he was a large pale silent baby with a sort of impervious acceptance of life. After school closed in June Lorna planned to take him calling on Miss Pru, but somehow she never got around to it. . . . She seemed to do nothing but wheel Gary Alan along the deep summer streets, along miles of streets, hardly seeing where she was going she was so intent upon her own vision of the future: the mirage of beautiful faces, and successes; of words spoken, and deeds done.

In September she stopped in to see Miss Pruitt one day after school. Something was different, though. There was now an impression of *haste* about Miss Pru. She was not settled down with her sewing, nor was she moving with her ample leisure about the house. She had a handkerchief bound around her head; a broom and dustpan leaned in the doorway, and all the time Lorna was there she kept rising from her chair to straighten the curtains, or adjust the ornaments on the parlor mantel. For the first time in that house Lorna had the feeling that she had not only caused, but was herself, an interruption.

She had never looked at Miss Pru in any way but the same one. Almost daily for seven years she had seen her, if only to wave as she went by; she had been a familiar factor in her life, reliable in her changelessness, always kind. Yet now, as if a searching light penetrated the shadowed house, Lorna saw that her old friend had changed. The face which for so many years had been calm and rosy was now clay-colored, haggard, and its expression of great happiness shone oddly from it. The happiness seemed out of place, as if an inner source of strength had become too powerful, too dominating, and was now able to destroy what it had sustained so long.

She talked a lot, too; and that was not like her: rapid, restless talk about the children, the summer just gone by, the weight of housework; reminiscences of the past in which Lorna shared, and still earlier ones in which she did not, except that she had heard them all before. At last she interrupted.

"Miss Pru, you shouldn't be doing all this house cleaning. You're working too hard."

"I'm in a hurry, honey. I want everything ready, every single thing."

"Ready for what?" Lorna felt strange, a little scared. "Miss Pru, are you feeling all right? You look kind of—tired."

But the bright queer look of joy intensified.

"It's all right, honey. You'll understand some day. All women understand some day."

Understand what? Lorna wondered, and for an instant she

was overwhelmed by a sense of the woman's life ahead of her:
a long, long vista of alternating mystery and revelation, mystery and revelation, forever and ever until the ultimate mystery. And after that the ultimate revelation?

She was worried about her friend, and now and then in
the midst of her school activities, in the midst of fantasies
concerning herself and her heroes, in the midst of eating,
and wheeling babies, and arguing with her mother, she was
suddenly caught by a memory of Miss Pruitt's worn joyful
face.

"You," she said to Gary Alan, thumping him into his carriage one autumn day. "You're going to go calling this afternoon. Try and stay dry for once."

Gary Alan gazed remotely at nothing with his tranced
brown eyes. He summoned a sound from within himself, a
voice sound, wordless, uneven, but filled with an inflection
of assertion. The sound pleased him and he summoned forth
another. As Lorna pushed the carriage along the street these
noises gained in authority, became loud crowings of power.

"Okay, Sinatra," Lorna said, scuffling her feet through the
drifts of maple leaves.

Miss Pruitt was not on her porch, though the day was mild
and golden. In the cleared beds beside the steps the autumn
crocuses bloomed on pale stems; Lorna went up the steps
and turned the winding doorbell handle with a rusty tingle
of sound. Then she opened the door and called "Miss Prue-
oo!" before she saw Dr. Purcell's black bag on the hall table.

She heard his footsteps on the carpetless upstairs floor
and his head looked over the bannisters.

"Oh, Lorna Reckettson. Thank the Lord you came. Get
my office on the phone, please, and tell Miss Findlay to pack
a bag right away. She'll have to spend the night here."

"Is Miss Pru—is anything the matter?"

"Yes, plenty. I just happened to drop in and I found her
in a heap on the kitchen floor. Don't know how long she'd—
but make that call now, like a good girl, and then bring my
bag up here and give me a hand."

Miss Pruitt's telephone grew out of a box on the wall and
wore its two round gongs like a pair of spectacles. Lorna

wound the little handle at the side and took down the receiver with a damp hand.

When she went upstairs Dr. Purcell was bending over the bed. "See if you can find a shawl or a blanket to put over her," he said, without turning.

Lorna pulled open the drawers of the marble-topped old huge bureau and shut them again, one by one. She opened the two chests in the room, one cedar, and one wicker, and shut them again. She opened the door of the wardrobe and looked at the shelves, quite certain, now, of what she would see there.

In every one of the drawers, in every chest, and on every shelf in the wardrobe were orderly piles of tiny dresses: pink, blue, white. There were small folded shawls with fringed edges and nests of moth balls in the centers of them. There were little flannel jackets, and robes trimmed with feather stitching; shirts, socks, petticoats, bonnets, hoods, and hundreds upon hundreds of bird's-eye squares, hand-hemmed. Diapers, dresses, booties for a regiment of infants; perfect to the tiniest embroidered bud, the finest tucked yoke.

Lorna closed the wardrobe door and looked over her shoulder at Dr. Purcell. He had turned and was now looking at her, too, above his eyeglasses. He sighed regretfully.

"I didn't realize—" he said. "I'm sorry, Lorna, I just wasn't thinking that naturally that's what you'd have to find out about if you went looking among her things. . . . Now, of course, you've discovered her secret, haven't you? But try to remember, try to realize, that this was her only aberration. Believing it kept her happy for twenty-seven years, probably a world's record, and it did no one any harm. *You* liked her."

Lorna was thinking of the smiling face, the tranquil, unhurried steps, the hand always holding onto the stair rail. . . .

"Come here, Lorna. Bring some of those baby blankets, anything to keep her warm."

Lorna did not want to obey. Superimposed on all that was well-loved and familiar was something new and strange, and she was afraid of Miss Pru, now, afraid to look at her.

"Please get the blankets, Lorna," said Dr. Purcell sternly. "And then come here and help me. Hold her head up while I try to get her to take this."

And after all, it was all right. At sight of Miss Pru the unfamiliar frightening thing dissolved into nothing: all that was left was her old friend lying on the bed, diminished, dying, but still good, still lovable. She looked shrunken and blue and her breath came hard, but as Lorna bent over her she looked up, a struggling, triumphant, urgent look. A whisper rustled from her.

"What?" Lorna bent closer.

"The baby. The baby."

Above Miss Pruitt's head Lorna saw that Dr. Purcell looked helpless, almost scared; and then she heard her voice, her own calm voice, saying the words: "A fine boy." As if she were a nurse of years' experience.

Miss Pru searched for her voice again. "Let-me-see."

"Now look what you've done," said Dr. Purcell, the words coming out on a great despairing sigh. But Lorna was inspired. I know what I'm doing, she thought, running down the stairs, and out into the fresh evening air.

Gary Alan was heavy when she lifted him out of the buggy, and wet everywhere; he was an inert lump in her arms, smelling of wool and rubber and good health. As she carried him up the stairs she could feel his nose brush against her cheek as he turned his head to look at this new place.

Dr. Purcell, a man aghast, stared as Lorna took the baby to the bed and sat him against the pillow beside Miss Pruitt where he lay passively, with most of one hand in his mouth, drooling around each side of it.

"There," said Lorna, repeating the splendid words. "A fine boy!" She never knew why instinct assured her that Miss Pruitt's wandering intellect would protect her from wonder at having produced a baby seven months old, but this was the case. On the top of Gary Alan's head, under the frail nap of hair, the fontanel stirred with its tiny life-beat. Miss Pruitt laid her finger there to feel it moving.

"His coloring . . ." she whispered. "The Clovelly coloring . . ."

Lorna looked across the bed at Dr. Purcell with a feeling of triumph and competence and saw in his face a sort of irritated awe.

"Just why you knew you could get away with it," he said.

"Just *how* you knew . . ." Then he glanced at Miss Pruitt and laid his fingers on her wrist. "She's tired now, Lorna, take the baby away." He bent close to his patient, and spoke gently. "You must sleep now. Go to sleep."

"Yes—doctor." Weak tears of joy trembled in Miss Pruitt's eyes.

"But tomorrow morning," Lorna said, when Dr. Purcell followed her from the room, "I have to go to school and then she'll find out."

"No she won't, Lorna. For her there's not likely to be any tomorrow." He hesitated. "Go home now and thank God that you know how to tell a lie at the proper time."

Lorna stuffed Gary Alan into his carriage again and wheeled him back along Van Buren Street. She was not yet ready to grieve, and as she walked she felt within herself a great strengthening of pride and hope and promise. The air was still and smelled of autumn; a big clear star stood in the deepening sky. Gary Alan resumed his voice sounds, but this time on a quieter, more thoughtful level; he was getting sleepy.

E. B. White, poet, essayist and master stylist, doesn't write many short stories, but when he does, he is always unpredictable. This is only an anecdote, a clever, original and wryly funny anecdote written with wonderful economy of words.

The Hour of Letdown

IIIIIIIIIIIIIIIII E . B . W H I T E IIIIIIIIIIIIIIIII

When the man came in, carrying the machine, most of us looked up from our drinks, because we had never seen anything like it before. The man set the thing down on top of the bar near the beerpulls. It took up an ungodly amount of room and you could see the bartender didn't like it any too well, having this big, ugly-looking gadget parked right there.

"Two rye-and-water," the man said.

The bartender went on puddling an Old-Fashioned that he was working on, but he was obviously turning over the request in his mind.

"You want a double?" he asked, after a bit.

"No," said the man. "Two rye-and-water, please." He stared straight at the bartender, not exactly unfriendly but on the other hand not affirmatively friendly.

Many years of catering to the kind of people that come into saloons had provided the bartender with an adjustable mind. Nevertheless, he did not adjust readily to this fellow, and he did not like the machine—that was sure. He picked up a live cigarette that was idling on the edge of the cash register, took a drag out of it, and returned it thoughtfully. Then he poured two shots of rye whiskey, drew two glasses of water, and shoved the drinks in front of the man. People were watching.

131

When something a little out of the ordinary takes place at a bar, the sense of it spreads quickly all along the line and pulls the customers together.

The man gave no sign of being the center of attention. He laid a five-dollar bill down on the bar. Then he drank one of the ryes and chased it with water. He picked up the other rye, opened a small vent in the machine (it was like an oil cup) and poured the whiskey in, and then poured the water in.

The bartender watched grimly. "Not funny," he said in an even voice. "And furthermore, your companion takes up too much room. Why'n you put it over on that bench by the door, make more room here."

"There's plenty of room for everyone here," replied the man.

"I ain't amused," said the bartender. "Put the goddam thing over near the door like I say. Nobody will touch it."

The man smiled. "You should have seen it this afternoon," he said. "It was magnificent. Today was the third day of the tournament. Imagine it—three days of continuous brainwork! And against the top players in the country, too. Early in the game it gained an advantage; then for two hours it exploited the advantage brilliantly, ending with the opponent's king backed in a corner. The sudden capture of a knight, the neutralization of a bishop, and it was all over. You know how much money it won, all told, in three days of playing chess?"

"How much?" asked the bartender.

"Five thousand dollars," said the man. "Now it wants to let down, wants to get a little drunk."

The bartender ran his towel vaguely over some wet spots. "Take it somewheres else and get it drunk there!" he said firmly. "I got enough troubles."

The man shook his head and smiled. "No, we like it here." He pointed at the empty glasses. "Do this again, will you, please?"

The bartender slowly shook his head. He seemed dazed but dogged. "You stow the thing away," he ordered. "I'm not ladling out whiskey for jokestersmiths."

" 'Jokesmiths,' " said the machine. "The word is 'joke-smiths.' "

A few feet down the bar, a customer who was on his third highball seemed ready to participate in this conversation to which we had all been listening so attentively. He was a middle-aged man. His necktie was pulled down away from his collar, and he had eased the collar by unbuttoning it. He had pretty nearly finished his third drink, and the alcohol tended to make him throw his support in with the under-privileged and the thirsty.

"If the machine wants another drink, give it another drink," he said to the bartender. "Let's not have haggling."

The fellow with the machine turned to his new-found friend and gravely raised his hand to his temple, giving him a salute of gratitude and fellowship. He addressed his next re-mark to him, as though deliberately snubbing the bartender.

"You know how it is when you're all fagged out mentally, how you want a drink?"

"Certainly do," replied the friend. "Most natural thing in the world."

There was a stir all along the bar, some seeming to side with the bartender, others with the machine group. A tall, gloomy man standing next to me spoke up.

"Another whiskey sour, Bill," he said. "And go easy on the lemon juice."

"Picric acid," said the machine, sullenly. "They don't use lemon juice in these places."

"That does it!" said the bartender, smacking his hand on the bar. "Will you put that thing away or else beat it out of here. I ain't in the mood, I tell you. I got this saloon to run and I don't want lip from a mechanical brain or whatever the hell you've got there."

The man ignored this ultimatum. He addressed his friend, whose glass was now empty.

"It's not just that it's all tuckered out after three days of chess," he said amiably. "You know another reason it wants a drink?"

"No," said the friend. "Why?"

"It cheated," said the man.

At this remark, the machine chuckled. One of its arms dipped slightly, and a light glowed in a dial.

The friend frowned. He looked as though his dignity had

been hurt, as though his trust had been misplaced. "Nobody can cheat at chess," he said. "Simpossible. In chess, everything is open and above the board. The nature of the game of chess is such that cheating is impossible."

"That's what I used to think, too," said the man. "But there *is* a way."

"Well, it doesn't surprise me any," put in the bartender. "The first time I laid my eyes on that crummy thing I spotted it for a crook."

"Two rye-and-water," said the man.

"You can't have the whiskey," said the bartender. He glared at the mechanical brain. "How do I know it ain't drunk already?"

"That's simple. Ask it something," said the man.

The customers shifted and stared into the mirror. We were all in this thing now, up to our necks. We waited. It was the bartender's move.

"Ask it what? Such as?" said the bartender.

"Makes no difference. Pick a couple big figures, ask it to multiply them together. You couldn't multiply big figures together if you were drunk, could you?"

The machine shook slightly, as though making internal preparations.

"Ten thousand eight hundred and sixty-two, multiply it by ninety-nine," said the bartender, viciously. We could tell that he was throwing in the two nines to make it hard.

The machine flickered. One of its tubes spat, and a hand changed position, jerkily.

"One million seventy-five thousand three hundred and thirty-eight," said the machine.

Not a glass was raised all along the bar. People just stared gloomily into the mirror; some of us studied our own faces, others took carom shots at the man and the machine.

Finally, a youngish, mathematically minded customer got out a piece of paper and a pencil and went into retirement. "It works out," he reported, after some minutes of calculating. "You can't say the machine is drunk!"

Everyone now glared at the bartender. Reluctantly he poured two shots of rye, drew two glasses of water. The man drank his drink. Then he fed the machine its drink. The machine's light grew fainter. One of its cranky little arms wilted.

For a while the saloon simmered along like a ship at sea in calm weather. Every one of us seemed to be trying to digest the situation, with the help of liquor. Quite a few glasses were refilled. Most of us sought help in the mirror—the court of last appeal.

The fellow with the unbuttoned collar settled his score. He walked stiffly over and stood between the man and the machine. He put one arm around the man, the other arm around the machine. "Let's get out of here and go to a good place," he said.

The machine glowed slightly. It seemed to be a little drunk now.

"All right," said the man. "That suits me fine. I've got my car outside."

He settled for the drinks and put down a tip. Quietly and a trifle uncertainly he tucked the machine under his arm, and he and his companion of the night walked to the door and out into the street.

The bartender stared fixedly, then resumed his light house-keeping. "So he's got his car outside," he said, with heavy sarcasm. "Now isn't that nice!"

A customer at the end of the bar near the door left his drink, stepped to the window, parted the curtains, and looked out. He watched for a moment, then returned to his place and addressed the bartender. "It's even nicer than you think," he said. "It's a Cadillac. And which one of the three of them d'ya think is doing the driving?"

This is a war story of a different kind—the terrifying ordeal of a young soldier, an idealist and a man of thought, during a night battle on a Pacific island. With skill and power, it shows that what a man thinks and how he feels can be made more interesting than what he does or what happens to him.

Waves of Darkness

IIIIIIIIIIIIIIII CORD MEYER, JR. IIIIIIIIIIIIIIII

They lay in a hole just wide enough to lie in side by side, and not more than a foot deep. They had arranged that one should keep guard while the other rested. Every two hours they changed.

Lying on his stomach the lieutenant was able to prop himself up with his elbows to see over the mound of dirt. He held the Thompson gun in his arms and kept two grenades in readiness by his right hand. The even breathing of his friend comforted him with the knowledge that he was not alone. During the day, physical action and the necessity for decision occupied his mind. Now he had nothing to do but wait and watch. Each minute of waiting made the next more difficult.

He tried to remember the surrounding terrain as it had looked before the light failed. He looked for the broken stump of a coconut tree and the large boulder whose relative position he had deliberately impressed on his memory as he dug his hole. He had memorized the harmless shadows so that he might know the shadows of the real enemy for whom he waited. A heavy layer of clouds obscured the tropic stars and he could see nothing but the formless night, isolating in worlds apart each small hole with its occupants.

He continued to stare into the blackness with wide-open,

unblinking eyes, and found fear crouched menacingly at the end of every corridor of thought. He deliberately attempted to lose his fear, and the hysteria that mounted in his heart, in another emotion, and strove to awaken lust by summoning up pornographic memories. It proved a poor substitute, and he could find hardly a passing interest in the indecent scenes that he paraded before his mind's eye.

Then he attempted to rationalize his fear. What was he afraid of, he asked himself. Death, was the simple answer. He knew that it might come at any moment out of the dark, carried on the bayonets of a banzai charge or dealt skillfully by the well-placed hand grenade of an infiltrating scout. He could not deny this fact on which his fear nourished and grew. It was inevitable that the enemy would attack during the night. They must know how thinly the line was held and that they would never again have such an opportunity. It was merely a question of time.

Most of his companions had a superstitious faith in their own luck. No matter how great the odds, the vast majority of his men always preferred to believe that though others might fall, they would not. It was only on the basis of this conviction that they found the courage for the risks they had to take. He preferred to think death inevitable. By absolving himself of all hope prior to each battle, he had found himself prepared for the most desperate eventualities. Now, with an effort of the will, he urged his mind down this accustomed path of reasoning. He stripped the night of its hideous pretensions to find only death, an old familiar companion. Though his fear remained, it became controllable, and this was all that he asked.

He turned his head sharply toward the sound of a gun fired offshore. An illuminating shell burst overhead with a soft popping sound, like the breaking of a Fourth of July rocket. For fear of being silhouetted against the light, he allowed only his eyes and the top of his helmet to project above the rim of dirt. He knew the shell was fired from a friendly destroyer lying off the beach, but it must have been ordered because of the suspicion of enemy movement. With a scarcely audible hissing the flare settled slowly down.

The blasted coconut trees cast deceptive shadows that

danced in slow rhythm as the flare swayed to and fro in its
descent. The unearthly, pallid light accentuated rather than
dispelled the threat of horror that the night held. It was
impossible to distinguish shadow from substance. Every small
depression in the ground was filled with darkness, and the
line of thick jungle growth some sixty yards ahead presented
an impenetrable question. He could make out nothing for
certain. Each natural object assumed enormous and malevolent
proportions in the shadows that lengthened toward him. He
felt as if he were lost in the evil witch forest of some ancient
folk tale and he shivered involuntarily.

With his finger on the trigger, he longed to let go a
burst of fire in defiance, but restrained the impulse. In the
game he played, the one who first revealed his position
became the hunted and was lucky to escape with his life.
The flare settled on the ground and burned up brightly for
a moment. Then the night surged back. It was as if he sat
in a theater where the scenes are silently shifted in the dark.
Even more than before, the darkness seemed a curtain behind which some fantastic tragedy waited. Again the destroyer fired and a shell burst.

He glanced behind him and saw the village they had
paid for so dearly during the day. It sprawled desolately
beneath the uncertain light. No roof remained, and only a
few of the walls stood upright, like the remnants of a decaying skeleton. It seemed an archaeological curiosity from the
long-vanished past instead of a place where men had lived
forty-eight hours ago. When the naval bombardment began,
the natives had fled to the hills and left their town to the
foreigners who fought in a war the inhabitants could not
understand and the outcome of which could leave them no
different than before. He guessed that there were many who
had fought bravely, on both sides, who understood it all no
better than the natives and had as little stake in eventual
victory. The flare sank to earth behind the village. Ghastly,
still as the dead that lay among its wreckage, he saw it in
the flare's sick light as the symbol of all war.

The ship fired three more shells at irregular intervals. He
waited for the fourth in vain. Each silent minute seemed a

tiny weight added on a scale that slowly tipped toward destruction. He allowed himself to think of the dawn and looked hopefully for the long, thin streak of gray in the east, as if by some special dispensation the sun might rise six hours early. The day appeared infinitely remote, and he thought of it as one dreams of some distant and charming country which one has no real hope of ever seeing.

The small sound of a stick broken near-by focused all his senses. He twisted his body quickly and brought the Thompson gun to bear in the direction from which the sound came. He held his breath and the blood drummed in his ears. His friend felt the movement and inched over onto his stomach. Together they stared fruitlessly into the blackness. Gradually the tension left his limbs, and he allowed his breath to escape softly.

"Guess it was nothing."

"Sand crabs probably. What time is it?"

Cupping his watch in his hands, as if the slightest wind might blow out the light, he made out the tiny green figures. It was four minutes past one.

"Past time. Your turn," he said.

He felt for the two grenades and put them into the hands of his friend. Without words they traded weapons.

He rolled over on his back. Unbuckling his chin strap, he rested his head in the leather harness of the helmet and stretched out his legs. There was hardly room for them, and he pushed his feet into the soft dirt at the end of the shelter trench. His breathing came easier. He was aware that there was just as much danger as ever, but he liked the feeling that he was no longer directly responsible. There was nothing now that he could do to prevent their being surprised, and his eyes closed. He did not attempt to sleep. Perhaps after two or three nights like this one, he thought, he would be tired enough. But not yet.

A cold, thin rain began to fall. He buttoned his dungaree jacket to the throat and hugged his body. There was nothing to do but lie there under the open sky. The earth in the narrow hole turned slowly to a sticky mud, and his clothes clung to him. A long spasm of shivering shook him. He wondered whether it was caused by cold or fear. The rain seemed a wanton addition to his misery. Slanting down, it pinned him to the earth.

For a moment he was overwhelmed by self-pity.

But gradually the rain no longer seemed directed especially against him. He felt its huge indifference and imagined how the tiny drops fell on all that lay without shelter beneath the night. The rain merged with the saltier oblivion of the sea, each drop leaving a transient ripple on its broad impassive face. It seeped down to the roots of the tropic plants and nourished that abundant life. With an equal carelessness it streaked the dirt on the faces of the living and washed the blood from the bodies of the friends he'd lost. He imagined the rain falling through the dark on their upturned, quiet faces.

2

Slowly he went over in his mind the names of the men of his command. Of the platoon of forty-four who had climbed up the steep beach in the morning, thirty remained to dig their holes in the evening. The bodies of the others lay behind to mark the path of the advance.

The lieutenant could form no continuous picture of what had happened. With terrible clarity a particular scene would present itself, only to be replaced by another equally sharp but unrelated vision. It was as if he watched magic-lantern slides whose logical order had been completely disarranged.

He saw himself crossing a rice paddy and signaling his first squad to follow. There was the familiar whistle of an approaching shell and he flattened himself. When he looked up, the three men who had been carrying the machine gun lay sprawled in the open field. He ran back but they were past help. In the awkward attitudes of death, they looked like small boys who had flung themselves down to cry over some little sorrow. He wondered at the brute chance that chose them and left him alive.

He saw again the still body of one of the enemy collapsed against the wall of a trench with his head thrown back. The man was obviously dead, but in a moment of childish bravado he lifted his carbine and fired a bullet through the throat. The body did not move, and the high-cheekboned Oriental face continued lost in its impenetrable dream. A thin fountain of dark blood sprang from the hole in the throat and spilled down over the wrinkled uniform.

He stood staring and ashamed, feeling that he had wantonly violated the defenseless dead. One of his men walked past him and stood over the corpse. Casually and with a half smile he swung his rifle butt against the head, which wobbled from side to side under the impact. Jocularly, as if death were an intimate joke they shared together, his man addressed the corpse. "You old son of a bitch," he said, and there was a note of admiration in the remark.

He remembered standing behind a tank trying to direct its fire. A great bull whip seemed to crack by his ears and he fell to the ground as if some enormous hand had jerked him roughly by the shirt front. Scrambling to cover, he ripped open his dungaree jacket and found only a small welt. With resignation, for he understood that he could not continue to escape, he climbed to his feet. The bullet had torn through his breast pocket and cut the tip of the cigar he carried there. Though his fingers trembled, he lit the cigar with a melodramatic gesture and pretended a courage that he did not feel.

The day came crowding back. Again he was lying beside Everett, the youngest man in his platoon, under the remorseless sun. The boy had been shot through the abdomen and chest. A medical corpsman joined him and together they attempted to stop the flow of blood. Because of the continuous enemy fire, they had to keep close to the ground while they wound the bandage around the body. The flies gathered. The boy's head arched backward. His mouth was wide-open, gasping for air. Both the lieutenant and the corpsman knew in their hearts that there was no hope for the wounded man, but they tightened the bandages mechanically, as one might shut a house at evening to keep the night out.

"I've got to leave," he said to the corpsman, who kept waving the flies away with one hand while he felt the failing pulse in the boy's wrist. "Has he got any chance?"

"Always a chance, Lieutenant," was the cheerful reply.

"Now if we had him on a good clean operating table we'd bring him round in no time." The corpsman smoothed the hair back from the wet forehead with a tender gesture. Then, realizing there was no operating table and no need for professional optimism, he shook his head wordlessly and finally added, "I'll keep the flies away. They bother him."

When some time later the lieutenant returned, the corpsman had gone to other duties and Everett lay dead and alone, the bandages dark with his blood. He had liked Everett best of all his men, and because of the boy's youthfulness felt particularly responsible for him. He remembered a letter he'd had to censor, which Everett had written to his mother just before the landing. It was full of hope and assurances that there was no need to worry. Now the body was covered with flies and already he thought he could detect the odor of decay. He caught the slight form under the armpits and dragged it to where a low bush cast a dark pool of shade. The feet, dragging limply, left two furrows in the sandy soil. Opening the pack, he took out the poncho and wrapped it carefully around the body, and stuck the rifle, bayonet first, into the earth as a marker for the burial detail.

Out on the oil-smooth sea the battleships and transports stood silhouetted against the burning sky. As he stared at them, he was surprised to find his vision blurred with tears. An unreasoning indignation shook him against all who had placed Everett where he lay. For the frightened enemy that shot Everett and was probably already dead he had pity. "But I wish," he thought, "that all those in power, countrymen and enemy alike, who decided for war, all those who profit by it, lay dead with their wealth and their honors and that Everett stood upright again with his life before him."

3

Then the present claimed him. His friend was shaking him gently by the shoulder and whispering, "Listen." The rain had stopped but the earth still smelled of it. Then he heard. Overhead there was the beating of tremendous wings. He twisted quickly onto his belly and pressed his face into the dirt as the night's stillness exploded. The shell landed well to their rear. Then, like pond water gradually rearranging itself after it has been disturbed, the fragments of silence fell back into place.

Quickly he buckled on his helmet. He listened. Sharp and distinct came the sound for which he waited. It was the crack of a gun, but the pitch was higher than that of the destroyer's and the sound came from inland. Slowly he counted the seconds before the shell reached them. Then again the great wings beat overhead, only this time louder and more insistently. "The angel of death passing," he thought. The shell crashed to their rear still, but closer.

"Goddamn them, George. They're walking the stuff in on us."

"Must have somebody spotting for them right near," was the almost inaudible reply.

Because the unknown and imagined were more terrible than the known, he found relief in the certainty that the enemy's plans were no longer a total mystery. After adjusting their artillery fire onto the thinly defended line with a single gun, they obviously intended to open a barrage with all their batteries and probably follow it closely with a banzai charge.

The distant gun fired once again. The enforced inaction became almost intolerable. They must cower in their holes while the invisible enemy deliberately found the mathematical formula for their destruction. Each explosion closer than the last was like the footfalls of some enormous beast. The shell crashed in front of them this time instead of behind. The trap was set. In order to spring it the enemy gunners had only to split the difference between the range settings on the last two shots.

"Bracketed," George said.

It did not enter his head to pray. His mind was washed vacant by fear, and long fits of trembling ran through his body as he clutched the wet earth. The enemy batteries opened fire simultaneously and sent their shells curving through the night. Enough presence of mind remained for him to raise himself just off the ground with his elbows and toes in order to avoid the dangerous shock of a near miss.

The barrage fell on them. It ripped and plowed the earth into smoking craters and lit the night with the hot flash of the explosions. The deep roar of the shell bursts mingled with the high, despairing wail of jagged splinters of steel flung at random against the night. Indiscriminately the shells dropped.

A near miss erupted in a geyser of flame and sound close to their hole. His head rang with the concussion, and the fine earth sifted down over their bodies. The stinging smell of the high explosives lingered in his nostrils for a moment to remind him how tenuous was his hold on life. The casual purposelessness of the destruction appalled him. One moment you lived and the next you were snuffed out like an insect—no courage, no skill, no strength, could make one iota of difference. He pinned his faith on the narrowness of their small hole and endured, helpless and insignificant.

As suddenly as it had begun the barrage lifted. Softly he worked the bolt of his weapon back and forth to assure himself it was ready. "If they're going to come, they'll come now," he thought. By contrast the silence was more profound than ever and stretched like a precarious bridge from minute to minute, until the beating of his heart seemed to fill the world. The darkness pressed down on him, and the air itself seemed too thick to breathe. Tightening his grip on the weapon, he noticed that his hand was wet and slipped along the smooth wood of the stock.

"What in hell are they waiting for?" his friend murmured.

He did not answer. With a detachment that astonished him, he found himself suddenly able to look down on the spectacle as if he were no longer involved in it. On the one side, he saw his countrymen lying in their scooped-out holes with their backs to the sea, each one shivering with fright yet determined to die bravely. On the other, the poor peasantry from which the enemy recruited his soldiers were being herded into position like cattle, to be driven in a headlong charge against the guns. For a moment it appeared impossible to him that what was about to take place could actually occur. Adult human beings of the civilized world did not slaughter one another. There must be some mistake which could be corrected before it was too late.

What if he should get out of his hole and explain the matter reasonably to both sides? "Fellow human beings," he would begin. "There are very few of us here who in private life would kill a man for any reason whatever. The fact that guns have been placed in our hands and some of us wear one uniform and some another is no excuse for the mass murder we are about to commit. There are differences between us, I know, but none of them worth the death of one man. Most of us are not here by our own choice. We were taken from our peaceful lives and told to fight for reasons we cannot understand. Surely we have far more in common than that which temporarily separates us. Fathers, go back to your children, who are in need of you. Husbands, go back to your young wives, who cry in the night and count the anxious days. Farmers, return to your fields, where the grain rots and the house slides into ruin. The only certain fruit of this insanity will be the rotting bodies upon which the sun will impartially shine tomorrow. Let us throw down these guns that we hate. With the morning, we shall go on together and in charity and hope build a new life and a new world."

4

A single rifle shot interrupted his imaginary eloquence. "What a fool I am!" he thought. Suspended in that last moment when the whole black wall of the night seemed a dam about to break and engulf him, he felt utterly helpless. All the events of the past seemed to have marched inevitably toward this point in time and space, where he lay shivering between an implacable enemy and the indifferent sea. To object or to struggle was like shouting into a big wind that tears the words from the corners of one's mouth before even oneself can hear them. He, his friend, his countrymen, the enemy, were all dying leaves cast on the black waters of some mysterious river. Even now the current ran faster and the leaves whirled toward the dark lip of destruction.

The echoes of the rifle shot were lost now, and the wave of silence mounted and hung poised. Catching his tongue between his teeth, he held himself rigid to prevent the trembling. Then, at last, the night was fulfilled, and the listeners had their reward. A long-drawn-out cry of furious exultation rose from the line of jungle growth, wavered, then rose higher in barbaric triumph.

"Now," his friend breathed.

A crescendo of rifle fire swept down the line in answer. The steady rattle of machine guns sounded in his ears. Rocked by conflicting emotions, hoping all, fearing all, confused by the roar of sound, he knew nothing but that he must defend himself. An illuminating shell burst. In its brief light he could make out figures stooped and running. Smoke swirled from his machine guns and obscured the scene with monstrous shapes. Flame from the muzzles leaped against the dark. Holding his weapon ready, he could find nothing to shoot at. The strange foreign voices, high with excitement, seemed all about him.

A bullet snapped overhead. He ducked instinctively. Nearby, a man screamed in the universal language of pain and he could not tell if it was friend or enemy. All human thought and emotion withered and died. Animal-like, he crouched, panting. Like a cornered beast run to earth at last, he awaited the fierce hunters. He could hear them at their savage work, uttering harsh, short cries of triumph, and he imagined them plunging the long bayonets through the twisting bodies of his companions. He could see nothing.

Then a voice began shouting, running the words together in an incomprehensible stream of speech. The firing faded to sporadic rifle shots.

"They're falling back," whispered his friend incredulously.

It was true. The high tide of the attack had rolled to the edge of the foxholes, wavered while a few grappled hand to hand, and then drifted back into the dark. In the battalion combat report long afterward it would read, "In the Battalion's first night ashore, C Company repelled a local counterattack in its sector and suffered minor casualties." For him, there had been such noise, confusion, and terror that he knew nothing for certain except that by some miracle he survived. He had not fired a shot. Gradually the tension left his limbs and he was aware again, almost gratefully, of physical discomforts, the wet clothes and the mud. He would have been

willing to believe the attack a fevered nightmare if it had
not left behind it appalling evidence. The cries of the wounded rose in supplication or diminished to low continuous
moans of incoherent agony.

His watch showed half past one, and his friend shook his
head in disbelief. Settling himself on his back again he could
feel his heart still pounding. It seemed longer than ever to
the dawn. The enemy might well attempt another mass attack,
and the danger of infiltration was continuous. Looking up
into the apex of the night, he noticed that the clouds were
thinning and that a few stars shone with a cold, implacable
brilliance. Full of a sweet regret, gentler times came back
to him when in another land the stars had seemed close and
warm. Now it appeared as far to that land as it was to the
stars, and as improbable a journey.

5

Abruptly, a heavy object bounced in the hole and rested
against his right leg. It lay there and gave off a soft hissing
sound. Though he moved with all the speed in his body, he
felt in a dreamlike trance and seemed to stretch out his hand
as a sleepwalker toward the object. His fingers closed around
the corrugated iron surface of a grenade, and he knew that
it was his own death that he held in his hand. His conscious
mind seemed to be watching his body from a great distance
as with tantalizing slowness his arm raised and threw the
grenade into the dark. In mid-flight it exploded and the
fragments whispered overhead. Another bounced on the edge
of the hole and rolled in. He reached for it tentatively, as a
child reaches out to touch an unfamiliar object.

A great club smashed him in the face. A light grew in his
brain to agonizing brightness and then exploded in a roar
of sound that was itself like a physical blow. He fell backward and an iron door clashed shut against his eyes.

He cried aloud once, as if through the sound the pain that
filled him might find an outlet to overflow and diminish. Once
more a long, rising moan was drawn from him and he lifted
his hands in a futile gesture as though to rip away the mask
of agony that clung to his face. Then, even in that extremity,

the will to survive asserted itself. Through the fire that seemed to consume him, the knowledge that the enemy must be near-by made him stifle the scream that rose in his throat. If he kept quiet they might leave him for dead, and that was his only hope.

There was no time yet to wonder how badly he had been hurt. Like a poor swimmer, he struggled through the successive waves of pain that crashed over him. There would be a respite and then, again, he would be engulfed, until the dim light of consciousness almost went out. He pressed his hands to his temples, as if to hold his disintegrating being together by mere physical effort. His breath came chokingly. He allowed his head to fall to one side and felt the warm blood stream down his neck. There were fragments of teeth in his mouth and he let the blood wash them away.

It did not seem possible that anyone could have done this to him without reason. In a world on the edge of consciousness, he forgot the war and kept thinking that there must be some personal, individual explanation for what had happened. Over and over he repeated to himself, "Why have they done this to me? Why have they done this to me? What have I done? What have I done?" Like an innocent man convicted of some crime, he went on incoherently protesting his innocence, as if hoping that heaven itself might intervene to right so deep a wrong.

At last he became calmer. Hesitantly, he set out to assess the damage done his body. The pain was worst in his face, but to investigate it was more than he yet dared. His right arm moved with difficulty, and blood slipped down his shoulder. It seemed that his ears were stuffed with cotton or that he stood at the end of a long corridor to which the sounds of the outside world barely penetrated.

From a great distance he heard a heavy thud on the ground, as of a fist pounded into the earth. There was another even heavier, followed by silence. He attempted to form the name of his friend with his lips. "George," he tried to whisper, but no sound came. He could see nothing, but in the loneliness of his pain reached out his hand. It seemed that a gradually widening expanse of darkness separated him from everything in the world, but that if he could only make contact with his friend it would be easy to find the way back. His fingers touched a dungaree jacket and felt the warm body beneath it. His hand moved upward, until suddenly he withdrew it. There was no need to search further.

A flood of the kindest memories obliterated momentarily the knowledge of his own misfortune. The empty body beside him had housed the bravest and the simplest heart. Between them there had been an unspoken trust and the complete confidence that comes only after many dangers shared together. If he had met him years later he would have had to say simply, "George." They would have shaken hands and the years between would have been nothing at all. Now, cold and impassable, stronger than time, stood death, and a hopeless, irremediable sense of loss flowed through him. The noise that at first had attracted his attention must have been the last despairing movement of his friend. Gently, he wiped the blood from his hand on his trouser leg. A long spasm of pain recalled him to his own condition.

Gratefully, he noticed that the edge of the pain was dulled. It continued to flow through his body, but his conscious self seemed to be slightly removed from it. The occasional rifle shots appeared to come from further and further away. His right arm had lost almost all power of movement. With care, he rested it across his stomach. While sufficient strength remained, he determined to know the extent of the damage done his face. Truth was never more terrible than at that moment when, fearfully, he raised his left hand to trace the contours of his personal disaster. As delicately as a blind man touches the features of one he loves, he ran his fingers over the lineaments of the face he did not know. Though there was considerable blood, the bones of his chin and nose seemed intact.

Then at last there was no choice. The fear whose existence he had refused to admit grew monstrous and possessed his mind. Tightly he cupped his hand, without touching the eye itself, over his left eye and suddenly withdrew it. He repeated the process with the other eye. There was no change in the even texture of the dark. It remained impenetrable, unrelieved by the slightest glimmer of starlight. One hope

remained and he clung to it as the condemned believe to the
last in the hope of pardon. It might be that the clouds had
returned and that the complete blackness was not his alone,
but shared by all. There was a way of finding out. For a
moment he hesitated, and then with cold fingers touched
his left eye. There was no eye there, only a jelly-like substance peculiarly sensitive to the touch.

A long sigh escaped his lips. The evidence was undeniable
and the sentence pronounced. He did not care to investigate
the other eye. Even the idea of touching again that useless
jelly revolted him. With slow reluctance his mind accepted
the full meaning of his loss. The emotional portion of his
being continually revolted against the real event and kept
asserting the reality of a world where such things do not
happen. It was an almost irresistible temptation to reject the
whole experience as an illusion. He felt that he would almost
welcome madness if it could save him from his empty to-
morrows. But little by little his reason forced him to understand.

"Blind," he whispered at last. "Oh, my God, my God." It
was not a prayer so much as the expression of the bitterest
despair. In all its poverty his life as it would be appeared
before him. All other things, he felt,—the mutilation of his
face, the loss of his limbs,—would have been endurable, but
not this: the dark dragging hours, the mocking blackness of
his nights, the loneliness of a world where people are only
voices which if beautiful are more bitter to hear, the unas-
suageable regret provoked by every memory of the lighted
past, the cheerful self-sacrifice of kind relations to goad the
sense of his own parasitic uselessness, and always the mind
growing more deformed in its crippling attempts to escape
the dark of prison.

6

The memory returned of how as a boy he had almost
drowned. It seemed that again he struggled upward through
the black water. An illusory hope filled him that he could
break the confines of the dark that pressed down on him as
the ocean had so long before, but the excitement passed

quickly. Above this ocean no sunlight flashed on white waves. It was infinite, and extended in blank perspective from that moment to the day of his death, when, he thought, one form of eternal night would be exchanged for another devoid of anguish and regret. Behind the sightless eyes, his mind would burn down like a fire in a room the guests have left until, mercifully, darkness was all.

There was nothing in those weary years that he wished to have, nothing for which he cared to wait. He felt a strange and brotherly companionship with the dead. The fact that such friends as he had known were gone seemed a warm assurance that death could be no terrible disaster. Their presence in that other world into which he drifted lent it a familiarity that the world of the living lacked, and took all fear from the journey he was about to make. Deliberately, he felt for his weapon.

He could not find the gun. Perhaps the explosion had blown it out of reach. The difficulty he had finding it allowed him a moment of indecision. What a spectacle he would make in the morning! The others who had died had done so bravely in the performance of what they had considered to be their duty. Death crowned their boyish honor, but would remain his shame, for he perceived well enough that he wished to die because he could not endure the pain and feared the dark years to come. He guessed that many during the long war had endured a life more unbearable than his. If they had not been happy, they had been admirable by the courage that they brought to their misfortune, and the knowledge of his own weakness was bitter.

A solitary, stubborn pride refused him the oblivion for which he longed, just as so often before, far more than any fear of social disgrace, it had forced upon him the consistent series of decisions that led inevitably to where he lay. Why did he enlist in so dangerous a service? Why did he refuse the job with the artillery or with the regimental staff, where one could afford to hope? Asking himself these questions, he knew there was no logical answer.

Certainly he had always expected this, or something like it. Not because he believed the war was fought for any cause worth dying for. Rather, he saw the war clearly as the finished product of universal ignorance, avarice, and brutality. A little out of adolescent vanity, but more because he had failed to become a conscientious objector, as he ought to have done, he chose to accept the consequences in an effort to redeem by personal valor a lost consistency of purpose. From the monotony and occasional violence, he had saved only his courage intact, and now he stood to lose it in a final ignominious act. Giving up his search for the weapon, he accepted his dark fate.

7

There was no way to tell the passage of time. It might have been hours or minutes since he had been hit. Whenever he tried to move his right arm the blood would start running again. Body and mind seemed to be drifting further apart. It was not the pleasant sensation of slipping gradually off to sleep. He seemed to fight the slow effect of a drug that paralyzed his limbs but left his mind active.

Occasionally he would test himself by raising his left arm. It became heavier, and the translation of wish into action grew more difficult. All sounds reached him from very far away, as if he were listening on a faulty telephone connection. Like one dying of cold, he abandoned himself to the slow change that was taking place, and hoped that death would not be too long in coming. He was sure now that he was dying, and was grateful that nature would accomplish what he had hesitated to do himself.

In the certainty that he would soon leave the world, he looked down from a great height and was glad that he was done with it. With a new severity, he contemplated the few short years of his life to discover some strand of meaning running through the trivial sequence of days and nights stretching back to the earliest memory. There was nothing in those transient joys to interest him, and even the moments of love or insight that he had once valued seemed entirely inconsequential when weighed against the vast extent of the descending night. Life seemed so poor a thing that he smiled to himself at having feared to lose it.

There was no hatred in his heart against anyone, but rather

pity. He considered the shortness of man's days, the pointless-
ness of his best hopes in comparison with the certainty and
conclusiveness of death, and could see him only as a poor
creature struggling for a moment above a forever escaping
stream of time that seemed to run nowhere. It would have
been better for man, he felt, if he had been given no trace
of gentleness, no desire for goodness, no capacity for love.
Those qualities were all he valued, but he could see they were
the pleasant illusions of children. With them men hoped,
struggled pitifully, and were totally defeated by an alien
universe in which they wandered as unwanted strangers.
Without them, an animal, man might happily eat, reproduce,
and die, one with what is.

Above him he imagined the imperturbable stars swinging
on their infinite wanderings to God knows what final destination, and the knowledge of how slight a ripple there would
be when he slipped beneath the surface of reality reconciled
him easily to oblivion. Part of a prayer from his schooldays
returned: "When the shadows lengthen and the evening
comes and the busy world is hushed, and the fever of life is
over, and our work is done, then in thy great mercy, O Lord,
grant us a safe lodging and peace at the last." A safe lodging
he would have as his body decayed to feed the rich jungle
growth, and his mind the peace of nothingness as its precarious balance dissolved like a soap bubble into air.

Without hope or fear, he waited for death. It was a long
time later, he guessed, when he felt a tear run down his
cheek. Where his right eye should be there was a smarting
itch that made him wish to rub it.

Surprise wakened him from the dreamy state into which
he had fallen. There must be more of his right eye left intact
than he thought. In the depths of his consciousness stirred an
indefinite hope. He tried to work the lid but there was no
movement. The beating of his heart echoed the expectation he
hardly dared admit. Starting to raise his arm he let it drop.
What difference could it make? Bereft of all desire and convinced of the futility of existence, he had no cause now to
disturb that profound indifference. It was his strength. Hope
was weakness and could bring only a vain regret and the

despair he had renounced. Reasonably he knew all this, but it did not stem the rising flow of excitement.

With gentle, inquiring fingers he touched the tissues of the right eye. It was swollen shut, but beneath the dried blood on the lid he could feel the rounded form of the eyeball. Hardly aware of the pain, he forced the lid open roughly and searched the blackness above him for a sign. Gone was all indifference. Light was life, and the possibility of hope both intoxicated and appalled. All that he was, hung poised in dreadful suspense on the frail miracle he awaited.

Then down the long corridor of the night it swam into his vision. Out of focus, it trembled for a moment hazily, and then burned steady and unwinking. Fearing that he might have created it out of the intensity of his wish, he let his lid close and then forced it open again. The star still lay in the now soft and friendly dark. It flooded his being like the summer sun. He saw it as the window to Hope. Another appeared, and another, until the whole tropic sky seemed ablaze with an unbearable glory. Joyful tears rose in his heart. Gently, he permitted the torn lid to shut. Warm on his cheek and salty in his mouth were the tears of his salvation.

Unashamedly romantic, popular in matter and manner, with a grand *beau geste* for its climax, "The Shining Thing" is entertainment only, but what expert entertainment!

The Shining Thing

||||||||||||||||||| SIDNEY CARROLL |||||||||||||||||||

My Lord Gerald Wallace Trimmeline was rich beyond rich. My Lord was also inclined to boast that he took good care of what he had. He was right. He was also conscientious about looking for more of the same. Ever since Waterloo he had maintained the best private intelligence service in Europe, a company of dark, hard men who prowled the Continent for him and returned with all sorts of useful information. This one, for example—Crippus. Half Cockney, half Irish, a rough specimen to look at, but inside, behind the pugilistic brow, behind the blunt, black eyes? Smooth as the hunter, shrewd as the fox. Here was Crippus back from France with gossip about the solvency of royal houses and the general shortage of meats and grills in the Low Countries, and trade talk about Russian silver. Good man, thought his Lordship. Earns his money. Deserves a pinch of the best snuff (though it costs a guinea a jar!) instead of the pigtail tobacco he sniffs. Deserves a glass of the old sherry, my Lord decided, leaning over his big belly to pour a short one for Crippus.

"And by the by, your Lordship," said Crippus, after making his proper report, "in Caen last week I saw an old friend of yours."

"Friend of *mine?*" asked my Lord, popping a pecan into his mouth.

"George Brummell, sir."

"Brummell!" exclaimed my Lord.

"Yes, sir," answered Crippus quickly.

"Well, fancy that! What'd old Butterfly have to say?"

"It's not a short tale, sir, if you want all the details—"

"Fire away, Crippus! Brummell. Fancy that."

"Well, sir, first off, I'd never *met* the gentleman before. I was never quite in 'is—his—class, you might say."

Lord Gerald looked hard at his man. That was typical of Crippus. Make a nonsensical remark like that and not a crack in the brute's face. Crippus not *quite* in Brummell's class! By heaven, who was? Who ever *was* in Brummell's class? It was one of Crippus' starchy little Irish jokes. "Help yourself to the sherry, Crippus."

"Thank you, my Lord. Second, I didn't have much 'eart— heart—to speak to him, sir."

"What do you mean?"

"I mean his condition and all."

"What's his condition, for heaven's sake?"

"You haven't heard, sir? I always took it you were one of his friends."

His Lordship jerked his fat round head back just once, then let it rock back into position. "I suppose I was," he said. "I suppose I can make the claim. I lent him money. Twenty-five years ago if Brummell *permitted* you to lend him money, it meant something in society. You could come and watch him dress. Anybody *permitted* to sit and watch while the valet wrapped the cravat around his neck—it always took an hour, Crippus—was *persona grata* at White's or Brooks's or Watier's from then on." My Lord beat a little tune on his fat nose with a fat finger. "Of course he still owed me money when he skipped the country. Skipped because of his debts, you know. I'm not sure I'd still call him a friend, Crippus. I'm not sure. Anyway, what's his condition?"

"Perfectly awful, sir. Hard to believe, my Lord. I didn't *know* the man in his prime, sir. Too young I was. But what I've heard, sir, he must have been grand as the King of Spain."

"Grander," said my Lord. "Grander. Believe me. Well?"

"Well, sir, he's a daft, dirty old man now. Lives in a hole and sleeps on straw."

My Lord thought it over for a long moment. "I don't believe it," he said.

George Bryan Brummell had been in exile 21 years. That splendid man, that mighty lion, had bowed heavily to the years. His upper teeth were gone, he still showed signs of his second paralytic stroke, he took laudanum to ease his pains. Actually, everything about him had been ravaged by time and the long unbreachable distance from home—teeth, face, and now, finally, brain. He had taken to sitting in his tiny room most of the day, combing curls into a black wig and holding imaginary conversations with the Duchesses of Bedford and Devonshire. Everything was threadbare now—teeth, face, brain; shirts, cravats, collars. (Brummell was sewing patches on his own shirts! When this gossip reached old friends in England, they merely laughed. It was too absurd. Too absurd!) Death, possibly, had stepped up behind him a long time before, had raised a finger to tap his shoulder—and death, which should have tapped so long ago, had remained to watch, too amused to tap.

The room he lived in now was a dingy closet in the Hotel Angleterre—a window, a straw mattress, a fireplace he could not fill. A chambermaid stole peat from the cellar to keep him warm. Even the room was on sufferance, for the landlord had not the heart to collect from him or to throw him out. Even then, after 21 years of sliding downhill, beaten, dirty, and toothless, with a worm in his brain, he was Brummell, he was still Brummell. In a lucid moment he could charm a bird off a tree, a laugh from a creditor, a postponement from a landlord. It was his habit to go down to Mme. Rolandais' café in the morning and bend over a glass of coffee and a biscuit. Madame herself would serve him. On those occasions when her good French conscience prompted her to ask him for payment, Mr. Brummell would favor her with the boneless remnant of the most celebrated bow in Christendom, kiss her hand, and say, "You will receive payment at the full moon, Madame, at the full moon." And such was his power, still, that the old woman's heart would flutter.

Madame Rolandais would say, "As you wish, Monsieur," and watch him limp across the street back to the Angleterre, back to his wig and his duchesses. Even the ruin was irresistible. Imagine what he was when the Prince of Wales came to his chambers to watch him dress!

All his pretty things were gone, of course. The Sèvres china he had loved, his famous collection of snuffboxes, the clouded cane, the chased plate, the books in silk bindings, all had gone to pay the insistent tailor, the unreasonable shirtmaker, the obstreperous man from Paris who supplied him with *Vernis de Guiton,* the only blacking, said Brummell, fit for a man's black boot. He hadn't been able to purchase any of the *Vernis* for a long, long time, not since the last piece of Sèvres had been auctioned off at Christie's. In big houses in Grosvenor Square now certain men were pointing with pride to pieces locked under glass, saying, "That box there, that was Brummell's! Picked it up for a song. Beau's been liquidating ever since he slipped off to France, you know. There's not much of the old stuff left by now, I'll warrant."

No, there wasn't. There was the wig, sitting on a wooden form in the center of his room, like a wet cat on a spindle. There was one pair of trousers, one coat, one shirt, one cravat, one pair of boots, all adorning the owner. There were a few sea shells he kept on the mantelpiece. There was an ormolu dragon.

"I followed him," said Crippus. "Saw him in one of those French cafés one morning, drinking coffee. Recognized him, sir. I'd *seen* him once before, when I was a boy, getting out of a carriage at the opera with 'Is—His—Royal Highness. But I recognized him, sir. He's that—well, he can't be mistaken, sir. Not him. Not in a crowd. Not even what he looks like now, sir. Waited for him to finish his coffee. Followed him—with my eyes only, I might say, sir, seeing that he lives straight across the street from the café. Hotel Angleterre is the place. Might have been respectable one time, sir. Dirty and damp enough it is now, sir. I give him five minutes to get to his lodgings. I go in, and I hold what you might call a cozy little conversation with the owner of the hotel."

"Why did you do all this, Crippus? What impelled you to follow George Brummell, of all people?"

"Why—" Mr. Crippus' very black eyebrows rose high over his very black eyes. "It's what you pay me for, sir, isn't it? Sniffing around, you might say. I knew that he was a *friend* of yours, and—"

"Good," said his Lordship. "Very good. If all my ferrets had your sense of smell, I'd be sitting on top of the Bank of England. Go on."

"Thank you, sir. Well, I showed the owner the red side of a ten-shilling note, and glad enough he was to get it. You'll find it, all proper, on the expense account, sir. 'Ten shillings, owner Angleterre Hotel, Caen, France.'"

"You've got something to learn about French hotelkeepers. He would have blabbed for five shillings. Go on."

"He told me lots, sir. Told me Brummell owes everybody in the town. Told me he's half daft, sir. Perfectly sensible at one o'clock, crazy at two—they never know. Told me he was in prison for his debts for three months and come out not quite right in the head, sir."

"In a *French* prison? *Brummell?*"

"Yes, sir."

"Good Lord. Go on."

"Told me he still owes everybody in the town, sir. But nobody collects because"—Mr. Crippus seemed to puzzle himself by his own next utterance—"well, because they *like* him, sir."

My Lord Gerald nodded. "Yes. Of course they would. That was part of it. That was the spell. He could insult you, Crippus. Sneer at the cut of your coat. Laugh out loud at the color of your hat. Borrow the eyes out of your head. Bow to your washerwoman and cut *you* dead. And still you'd like him. Go on."

"The owner told me he owes back room rent for nine months. Told me he does nothing but take walks and talk to himself and make friends with all the dogs in town. Told me I could go right on up to see him if I liked. He wouldn't mind a bit."

"Did you?"

"Yes, sir. That's what I'm paid for, sir. I went up. Knocked on his door. He says—I tell you, it surprised me, sir. You ever talk to anybody that was daft, sir?"

"No. What did he say?"

"Sings out, bright as a bird, 'Come in, your Grace!' Just like that. 'Your Grace!' To *me*, sir. I opened up and walked in, and there he sits, in the middle of the floor, putting a comb to an old wig."

"A great black curly wig?"

"Yes, sir."

"Of course. Go on."

"He stands up, gives me a bow like I was the ambassador from Turkey, my Lord. Says to me, 'Ah, dear Henry! On the dot, as usual! Your promptitude does you honor and me shame. I am not quite ready, as you see. Another twenty minutes with the wig and we'll go arm-in-arm off to Watier's. How's dear Bunny? In the carriage? Good!' " Mr. Crippus almost made a face. "I didn't know what it was all about, sir, but I put it all to memory, figuring you'd like to hear it all, sir."

"I do. Go on."

"Well, sir, the rest of it I don't remember very well. It was all talk way over my head. Something about dinner at Watier's, and then the opera, and how he'd be getting ready, and would I sample the port while he was making his ablutions. Port, sir! He didn't have a bottle of *anything* on the premises. Nothing but that black wig on the stand and the mattress on the floor. Not a bootjack in sight, sir! Not a warming pan! Not even a pipe! And there he was, cock o' the walk, talking sixty to the minute about what he wore at Devonshire House and some bets he was making on the pit bulls and the Prince asking him to sample a barrel of snuff just come in at Rideout's. I didn't understand a word of it, sir. Balmy as a bug he is. Taking me for a duke of something or other, talking as if 'e—he—and me and Bunny was ready to paint the town. It was nice talk, but beyond me, sir, beyond me."

"He could talk," said his Lordship, "so that even Byron had to stop and listen."

"Who, sir?"

"Never mind. Go on."

"Well, sir, I left. I tell you, I'm being very frank and honest, sir, it give me the creeps. I left him standing at the window, looking down at the street, telling me what a fine carriage I'd brought to the door. I turned me back and I left, and he was still talking away. That's all, sir. I thought you'd like to know."

Lord Gerald munched a nut and sipped his sherry. He let the gentle silence fall over his thoughts, his remembrances of his old friend Brummell.

What a life! What a fool!

"You say there was nothing but a mattress and a wig in the room? Nothing but that? No silver spittoon? No large green macaw on a perch? No Arabian slippers?"

"Empty, sir. Empty as an honest man's pocket. There was a few shells on his mantelpiece. In the middle of the mantel a little—what's the stuff called, sir? It looks like gold, but it's not gold, that I know, because I know gold. This is the French stuff, sir, with a funny name. He had this little statue of it. Well, I suppose you'd call it a dragon, sir. Right there in the middle of the mantel."

"What!" cried his Lordship. "He still has *that*? He still owns the ormolu dragon?"

"That's it, sir! That's the word! Ormoloo."

Twenty-four hours later my Lord Gerald, having spent long hours in conference with himself and his sherry bottle, sent for Mr. Crippus.

"Crippus, you're going back to France."

"Yes, sir. As you say, sir."

"To Caen."

"Aha, sir. Something to do with Mr. Brummell?"

"At the moment, Crippus, you'll best earn your keep by listening. Do your guesswork later."

"As you say, sir."

"As a matter of fact, the business *has* to do with Mr. Brummell."

"Yes, sir."

My Lord Gerald was fat and pink and, of course, cherubic. He had the gift of looking most pink, most cherubic, when his intentions were most vile. Crippus knew, from his jolly look now, that the business would be a dirty business. "Crippus, do you happen to know what ormolu is?"

"I know it looks like gold, sir, and the Frenchies make it. It can be expensive, I hear, sir."

"Correct. All correct. An excellent summary. You leave out only one vital fact. Ormolu, Crippus, does more than *look* like gold. It has another quality in common with it. It can turn a sensible man into a raving maniac. I mean to say, it can turn him into a collector."

"Sir?"

"The world is full of ormolu collectors, Crippus. They scoff at your Rembrandts, your Roman stuff, your prints and stamps and morocco books. All they crave is ormolu. They're fanatics, Crippus. Absolute fanatics. Do you know who has the finest collection of ormolu in England?"

"No, sir, I do not."

"I have, Crippus."

"I see, sir."

"I want that dragon, Crippus."

"Yes, sir."

My Lord broke out the snuff and the nuts and the sherry. He rang for a bit of Persian fruit too, just off his charter boat from Salonica. He liked to christen a good plot with a mouthful of the best, just as he liked to baptize a new boat with an old bottle.

"I'd better fill you in a bit, Crippus. Might come in handy to know what this is all about once you get over there. Very well. These are the facts. The dragon was given Brummell by the Duchess of Bedford. It was a famous gift, Crippus. Brummell was notorious, and the Duchess was beautiful, and the dragon belonged to the Duke. Do you follow, Crippus?"

"Quite, my Lord."

"It's a marvelous piece in its own right, Crippus. But when it passes through hands like that, its value grows the greater. And the smell of scandal helps. The Duke, the Duchess, Brummell. And the greatest of these, as the book says, was Brummell. Do you know what he was, Crippus? Do you actually know?"

"I think so, sir."

"You couldn't. You'd have to have known him in the high

days. You'd have to have seen him—shine. Well, leave it at that. The dragon is worth thousands."

"That little thing, sir?"

"Thousands. I am prepared to *pay* thousands."

"I see, sir."

"But he won't sell."

"Sir?"

"You'd have to know him, Crippus. He was a very perfect, gentle knight. He was a gentleman."

"Aha!"

"He's daft, you tell me. And sleeping on straw. And sponging on everybody in the town. But he still keeps the dragon. Of course you see what it means."

"I don't know if I rightly do, sir."

"Oh, Crippus! There he sits in a pesthole, holding on to something that's worth thousands. If I were a sentimentalist, I'd say it was a white plume he's holding on to, the one last feather in his cap. His one last link with the past. I'd say it's the one thing he'll never sell, no matter how desperate he gets. But I'm no romantic, Crippus. You know what I say? I say he's not desperate enough!"

"Yes, sir."

"Low as he is, I will make him sink lower. The way to get the dragon, Crippus, is to squeeze him absolutely dry. *Make* him desperate enough to sell. My experiences with the breed of gentlemen, Crippus, have taught me one thing over and over again. In spite of their puff speeches about a gentleman's code, Crippus, every one of them has his price."

"Very true, sir."

"Here's how we'll do it. First man you see when you get to Caen is Masselon, the banker. Here's what you are to tell him. . . ."

M. Masselon may have had his reservations about my Lord Gerald Wallace Trimmeline's choice of operatives. This one, particularly, with his savage eyebrows and his total absence of any expression but that of the surly beast—he was hardly the type to represent the great house of Trimmeline. Nevertheless, he did—he did, and he must be handled accordingly.

"Welcome, dear Monsieur Crippus. Welcome and good day. I hope you found His Lordship well."

"Very well. It's at 'is—" Mr. Crippus took a deep breath. "It's at *his* request I'm back 'ere, Mr. Masselon."

A little frown hovered over M. Masselon's nose; the tip of the nose seemed to twitch. "But our affairs with Monsieur Trimmeline are all in perfect order! Our payments—"

"Don't worry none," said Crippus. "It's nothing to do with you. Leastways, not with your account with 'is Lordship. 'E's got no complaints there."

It was M. Masselon's turn to breathe easier.

"I'd like to get right down to business, Mr. Masselon. Time is very valuable, you might say."

"Of course!"

"There's an Englishman living 'ere in Caen. Name of Brummell."

"That excellent unfortunate gentleman."

"Unfortunate, eh?"

"Well, my dear sir, I speak of nothing that is not common knowledge here. Monsieur Brummell is the most charming, the most amusing of men. But he is a chronic maker of debts, monsieur. Since the day he came here he has owed—*mon Dieu*, how he has contrived to owe! The man is a genius among debtors. This is interesting, monsieur. When he first came here, do you know to *whom* he owed? To the tailor, the bootmaker, the shirtmaker, the confectioner, the vintner, the tobacconist. That was in the beginning, when he was still *en prince* among us. But nowadays do you know whom he owes, monsieur? Simply the doctor, the landlord, the washerwoman, the butcher, the baker. *Voilà!* The story of the last ten years of his life in the roll call of his creditors."

Mr. Crippus looked hard at a fingernail. "Matter of fact, Mr. Masselon, that's just what I'm here about."

M. Masselon, who was a good man, studied the expressionless face of the man Crippus. Life is strange, thought M. Masselon. Life is very strange. I would say this man is born to bring destruction and bad tidings; born to club us all to death. A born galley master. A born brute. And what is he truly? An angel in disguise.

"Your master will be well judged in heaven for this, Monsieur Crippus."

"What?"

M. Masselon leaned back in his chair and smiled knowingly. "Monsieur Crippus, the little people of Caen continue to support Monsieur Brummell primarily because they like him. When he had money to be generous with, he was generous. When he had his health, and—your pardon, monsieur—his *full* sanity, he was the first gentleman of the world. It was then a privilege to serve him. Now they consider it a privilege to support him. A man like that! Who talked to kings! I assure you, Monsieur Crippus, none of them, not even the butcher, has been counting on compensation. Now I can tell them that one of Monsieur Brummell's friends has come to his rescue! They shall be recompensed! It will do them all a great deal of good, monsieur, to discover that sometimes virtue has a cash reward." There was suddenly a great peace in M. Masselon's good heart.

"Not so fast, Mr. Masselon. You 'aven't 'eard what I've come to say. You Frenchies like to 'op to conclusions. His Lordship gave me instructions for you. They 'ave nothing to do with paying Mr. Brummell's debts. Quite the opposite end of the stick, Mr. Masselon. I am instructed to order you to foreclose on this 'ere excellent gentleman Mr. Brummell."

It took some time for M. Masselon to find his voice. "I do not understand."

"Then I'll begin at the beginning. Mr. Brummell owes butcher and baker and candlestick maker. Am I correct, Mr. Masselon, in making the wild guess that the butcher and the baker and the candlestick maker all owe money to *you?*"

"Not to me, monsieur. To the bank."

"What I thought. All right. Now it's your job to call in all such persons as Mr. Brummell is indebted to and order them to collect what 'e owes, and right now. 'E's to pay up in three days."

"What!"

"In two words—three days. Mr. Brummell is to pay up everything 'e owes. No fuss. And no 'anky-panky either, I warn you. No secret meetings of the creditors and a nice little subscription fund to shell out and make it up for the old boy. 'E's to pay 'imself. That's 'is Lordship's orders."

M. Masselon met the level gaze of the galley master. "It is a cruel jest," he said.

"No jest. And cruel is not for you or me to judge. 'Is—*His*—Lordship 'as 'is own reasons, and I'd lay 'eavy they're good ones. And don't waste any time, Mr. Masselon. Call 'em in, give 'em the word. Get the money. If you don't, if you don't do it fast, all accordin' to 'Oyle, just the way I'm telling you, there's the matter of the debentures. His Lordship'll 'ave to 'ave the cash, instanter, in bulk, one payment, according to the contract. This is orders."

"Monsieur Brummell will be thrown into the street! He will starve to death!"

"Orders is orders."

Crippus waited until the third day. Give 'im time, he told himself. Let it sink in good.

For two days Mr. Crippus spent the daylight hours sitting at a table at the sidewalk café opposite the Angleterre. He watched them go in and he watched them come out—the doctor, the old washerwoman, the butcher, the baker. They weren't hard to identify. One good thing about doing dirty work in France, you could tell a man's profession from the clothes he wore. They came to the door of the Angleterre, one by one, heavy-footed, shaking their heads; they entered with loathing to do this black business with an insane old man. Crippus sat at his table and played the little game of imagining what was going on in that hole of a room up there. In his mind's eye he could see them breaking the old boy into little pieces. That very polite little doctor with the pointed beard, very shamefaced, saying he was sorry, oh, so sorry, but circumstances beyond his control made it imperative, most imperative, that at this moment, this very day, Mr. Brummell would have to, would simply have to— Then there would be the meeting between Brummell and the owner of the hotel: "I am so sorry, monsieur—I am devastated—but I must have the nine months' arrears—tomorrow at the latest; otherwise—" The French shrug, the palms turned upward, one backward step, then a finger swiping the nose. Very sad, thought Crippus, very sad indeed. On the third day he went in to skin the great cat himself.

The hotel owner sat behind the desk in the lobby. He was a forlorn little man with rheumy eyes. (I'll be blowed! thought Crippus. 'E's been crying!) Crippus walked past him without a nod and took the stairs slowly.

He rapped on Brummell's door with his stick. There was no answer. He walked in.

The old man was standing by the window, silhouetted by the light, bent and dark, his hands behind his back. Crippus slammed the door. Brummell turned.

'E's ten thousand years old, thought Crippus. They've done a job on him these two days.

"Your servant," said Brummell, squinting, bowing with his hands behind his back. He was wearing his wig. It was slightly askew. "Which of my creditors are you?"

"I'm an Englishman, sir. Crippus is my name. I was here to see you a fortnight ago."

"Ah. Do come in. Forgive an old man his eyes and his memory. Come in, sir. Do make yourself comfortable."

Good, thought Crippus. 'E's not loony today. If he talks reason, he'll listen to it.

Crippus took the one rickety chair in the room, removed his black hat, and placed it on the floor beside him. "I'm 'ere—here—on no *official* business, sir. Just passing by. In and out, making for the boat at Calais tonight."

"Calais! Yes. I spent fourteen years turning it into a corner of London. I hope some of my little effects are still in evidence. The English club. I taught them how to improve the cold fowl on the buffet."

For a blighter, thought Crippus, who's being dunned to death, who knows 'e's going to wind up in the street any minute now, 'e's got an uncommon frisky tongue. The true test of the gentleman, I'm told. Never show your bleedin' 'eart to a stranger. Your bleedin', gentleman's 'eart.

"I had 'eard—heard—you were still here, sir, and I thought as how a visit from one Englishman to another might not be amiss, sir. Just paying my respects to a gentleman I've heard of all my life and always wanted to meet. If I'm not intruding, sir."

Brummell nodded. "I have been hoping, sir, and praying, sir, for England to intrude upon me these twenty-one years. Tell me of England, Mr. Crippus." The old man raised a hand to cover his eyes, to speak to an audience unseen. "Catechize me on politics and dogs and poetry. And ladies' hats. They were all in the Grecian phase when I said farewell, Mr. Crippus. My London was full of temples to Hymen and Virtue, Arcadian entertainments, marble columns carefully built and carefully broken, masquerades alfresco—the Mall on a Sunday was a walking frieze. It was the Greek moment, Mr. Crippus. It needed only a real Greek god. I learned my poses from the museum nudes; I indulged in only the classical vices. I became that god."

Now talk sense, thought Crippus. Love-a-duck, talk sense! Don't go balmy on me again. "So I've heard, sir," Crippus said.

"Now, they tell me, the Greek is become the Gothic. No longer does the poet dote on shepherdesses and druids and sylvan glades. He writes prose about haunted castles and monsters. Is this true, sir?"

"I'm not the one to say, sir, not being much of a reader myself."

"No? Well, I'm an old man and I talk too much. An old man who should have quit the stage like his friend Sheridan— 'gone before pity had withered admiration.' You do me honor to visit with me, sir, and I distract you with an old man's nostalgia. I would offer you a cup of something, sir. Unfortunately, I have had visitors today—"

And well I know it, thought Crippus.

"—and the flagons of wine and water are empty. What else is your pleasure, sir?"

"I could take a cup of tea, sir."

"My dear Mr. Crippus. *Crippus?* Yes—Crippus. You take medicine. You take a walk. You take a liberty. You *drink* tea. Or you would, sir, if my mixture had arrived from Paris this week." He was suddenly disturbed. "Something seems to have gone wrong with the post!" He put his hand to his eyes.

"I can do without, sir. Thank you very much. Are you

comfortable, here, sir? I mean, would there be anything I could be sending you from England, sir?"

"No. Thank you. You are kind—" The old man raised an eyebrow over his hand and looked at Crippus through his fingers. His one visible eye was sharp. "It's a poor place, eh?" asked Brummell.

"Not so poor as some I've seen, sir."

"Poor and dirty. Wait until you tell them that! Beau, who made a ceremony of scrubbing himself with a hair cloth two hours every morning of his life—how *dare* he be dirty, eh?" Now he seemed to be growing angry. "Is that what they say in London now, when they talk of Brummell?"

They do not, thought Crippus. They don't talk about you at all. They did, but no longer. "Not necessarily, sir," he said. "Is your health good, sir?"

The old man insisted on worrying the point. "How *dare* he be dirty since he's no longer rich, eh? Filth is still the prerogative of the rich. My friend Lord Gardenstone, who was very rich indeed, kept pigs in his bedroom. That was his inherited right; he was rich. He was simply—ah—eccentric. How are the eccentric rich these days, Mr. Crippus? My Lady Hester Stanhope, does she still dress like an Arab and live on the slopes of Mount Lebanon? Does my Earl of Bridgewater still stock his house with cats and dogs, dress them as ladies and gentlemen, and entertain them at table? Such delightful people, the rich! Such imagination! One wouldn't call them dirty now, would one? One couldn't call them—insane?" He opened his mouth, hollow now but for his nervous tongue.

"You've got a point there, sir."

"Money is their excuse! But they have no advantage over me, Mr. Crippus. I have an excuse too. My age. I blame it for everything. What I am, what I have become, all this I excuse because I am old, Mr. Crippus. How wise my friend Walpole was: 'When dotage can amuse itself, it ceases to be an evil.'"

I'm getting out of here, thought Crippus. Get to the business and get out of here.

He saw the old man's hand make a pathetic gesture. It rose

feebly to the height of his waistcoat pocket—the habit of the habitual snuff user. The trouble was, Crippus quietly noted, the great Mr. Brummell no longer had a waistcoat. (Brummell without a waistcoat!) No waistcoat, no snuffbox pocket, no snuffbox, no snuff.

Crippus dug into his own waistcoat and pulled out his own silver box. "Would you have a pinch, sir?" (Your first, I'd say, in a long, long time.)

The old head bent forward, the old eyes glowed. He was balancing to take a step forward; he had raised a trembling hand; he stopped. "Is it, by any chance," he asked, "the veritable Martinique?"

"No, sir. I'm afraid it's only Bates'."

"Then I thank you, sir, but no."

Well, blast your touchy nostrils! thought Crippus, and proceeded to torture the old man by taking a pinch, sniffing it as slowly as he could, closing his eyes as he inhaled.

"Do you find your rooms—er, your *room*—quite warm enough, sir? Days like this, so raw—don't you *like* a fire, sir?"

"Fire is bad for the complexion, Mr. Crippus! The pink won't last. Fresh cold gives the better flush. Remember that! Only two things good for the human color, sir—cold air, cold water. Never abuse the flesh with anything else, sir—perfumes, or unguents, or heat. Only two things fit to rub on the human skin are clean linen and country washing. And never get too close to the fire."

All right, thought Crippus. I've 'ad me beauty lesson from Beau Brummell 'imself. Let's not waste any more time.

He stood up. "Afraid I must go now, sir. There's a carriage waiting."

"It's been most pleasant of you to call on me, Mr. Crippus. Most pleasant. Tell the hussy, England, I love her. She is heartless, fickle—"

That's right, thought Crippus. Take it out on England. It's the *French* holding you up, squeezing you dry, so take it out on England.

"—she has a coquette's way with old favorites, but I love her. She is warm, sir, *warm*."

The old man shivered.

Crippus put his hat on his head. He started to turn to the door. He made it seem as if something on the mantelpiece caught his eye. He walked over. He took the ormolu dragon in his hand.

"Well, Mr. Brummell, sir—what a fine specimen!"

Brummell smiled absent-mindedly and nodded. "Indeed. Indeed."

Crippus held the dragon up to the light. "I 'ap—happen—to be a collector, Mr. Brummell."

"Do you? *Do* you?" The old man was pleased.

"I've seen few as fine as this in my time."

"If I may be permitted a correction, sir, you've *never* seen a piece as fine as that."

"You may be right."

"It was given me by the Duchess of Bedford."

"Was it now? That's interesting."

"It was given me because I admired it. That was the whole sum of it. I admired it and she gave it to me. And, oh dear—" He dropped his head and covered his eyes with his hand once more.

"Mr. Brummell!" Crippus snapped the words at him. It was like two slaps in the face.

The old man opened his eyes again. "Yes, Mr. Crippus?"

"I'm a businessman, Mr. Brummell. Man of few words. I know what I want when I see it. This is a fine piece of ormolu." And I'd much rather be stealing it, he thought; so much easier than going through this fuss; I wish my fine Lord Trimmeline didn't fancy *himself* a gentleman so much of the time! "I can offer you five hundred pounds for it, sir. Cash on the line. No questions asked. I have the money here."

He placed the dragon back on the mantel and took his wallet out. He dealt the ten-pound notes slowly, like a franc-whist dealer, until they made a gaudy pile on the mantel beside the dragon. He kept his eyes on the money all the time he was counting aloud. Only when his wallet was back in his pocket, when he had squared up the pile of notes, did he look at Brummell.

One look and Mr. Crippus was suddenly aware of the role he was *really* playing in this farce. He was the angel of mercy.

No—blow that—he was playing God! The light in Brummell's face, the *religious* look of gratitude, of unbelieving relief, of prayer answered, of hope reprieved, as it were, on the very gibbet. 'E thinks it's a miracle, thought Crippus, a miracle. And so it is! Take a good look at the lovely manna from heaven, you balmy old windbag! Take a good long look. Pay your debts. Buy some shirts. Buy yourself another of those white cravats I've 'eard so much about, and throw away that black rag that doesn't show the dirt. Get some decent lodgings in a decent place. Sleep on down again. Live like a gentleman for how much longer you've got to live—all it'll cost is 500 pounds, which the Almighty Lord God Thomas Crippus is bringing you from 'eaven, Mr. George Beau Brummell!

Brummell came to the mantelpiece. He was nodding—or was he shaking or quaking? He lifted the dragon in both hands and extended it to Crippus. He bowed low. It was still a bow that would not be forgotten. It hid his eyes. But suddenly from under the brows he looked up at Crippus. Then, only then, for the first time *then!*—pinned to the mantel by the old man's look—did Crippus feel the presence of a force he could not comprehend, nor ever would. This was the power, the spell, they all marveled at whenever they spoke of Brummell; this was the shining thing.

It was there in the gleam in the old man's eye as he pushed the dragon forward. "Mr. Crippus, sir. I do not sell to friends. You admired the dragon. Then it is yours. I pray you accept it. My pleasure, sir. My very great pleasure."

People who can cope with problems in a responsible manner are sometimes victims of those who can't, the alcoholics, the sexually promiscuous, the emotionally unstable. This story explores such a situation with pity, understanding and satiric distaste—and with great skill.

In Greenwich There Are Many Gravelled Walks

|||||||||||||| HORTENSE CALISHER ||||||||||||||

On an afternoon in early August, Peter Birge, just returned from driving his mother to the Greenwich sanitarium she had to frequent at intervals, sat down heavily on a furbelowed sofa in the small apartment he and she had shared ever since his return from the Army a year ago. He was thinking that his usually competent solitude had become more than he could bear. He was a tall, well-built young man of about twenty-three, with a pleasant face whose even, standardized look was the effect of proper food, a good dentist, the best schools, and a brush haircut. The heat, which bored steadily into the room through a Venetian blind lowered over a half-open window, made his white T shirt cling to his chest and arms, which were still brown from a week's sailing in July at a cousin's place on the Sound. The family of cousins, one cut according to the pattern of a two-car-and-country-club suburbia, had always looked with distaste on his precocious childhood with his mother in the Village and, the few times he had been farmed out to them during those early years, had received his healthy normality with ill-concealed surprise, as if they had clearly expected to have to fatten up what they undoubtedly referred to in private as "poor Anne's boy."

He had only gone there at all, this time, when it became certain that the money saved up for a summer abroad, where his Army stint had not sent him, would have to be spent on one of his mother's trips to Greenwich, leaving barely enough, as it was, for his next, and final, year at the School of Journalism. Half out of disheartenment over his collapsed summer, half to provide himself with a credible "out" for the too jovially pressing cousins at Rye, he had registered for some courses at the Columbia summer session. Now these were almost over, too, leaving a gap before the fall semester began. He had cut this morning's classes in order to drive his mother up to the place in Connecticut.

He stepped to the window and looked through the blind at the convertible parked below, on West Tenth Street. He ought to call the garage for the pickup man, or else, until he thought of someplace to go, he ought to hop down and put up the top. Otherwise, baking there in the hot sun, the car would be like a griddle when he went to use it, and the leather seats were cracking badly anyway.

It had been cool when he and his mother started, just after dawn that morning, and the air of the well-ordered countryside had had that almost speaking freshness of early day. With her head bound in a silk scarf and her chubby little chin tucked into the cardigan which he had buttoned on her without forcing her arms into the sleeves, his mother, peering up at him with the near-gaiety born of relief, had had the exhausted charm of a child who has just been promised the thing for which it has nagged. Anyone looking at the shingled hair, the feet in small brogues—anyone not close enough to see how drawn and beakish her nose looked in the middle of her little, round face, which never reddened much with drink but at the worst times took on a sagging, quilted whiteness—might have thought the two of them were a couple, any couple, just off for a day in the country. No one would have thought that only a few hours before, some time after two, he had been awakened, pounded straight up on his feet, by the sharp, familiar cry and then the agonized susurrus of prattling that went on and on and on, that was different from her everyday, artlessly confidential prattle only in that now she could not stop, she could not stop, *she could not stop,* and above the small, working mouth with its eliding, spinning voice, the glazed button eyes opened wider and wider, as if she were trying to breathe through them. Later, after the triple bromide, the warm bath, and the crooning, practiced soothing he administered so well, she had hiccuped into crying, then into stillness at last, and had fallen asleep on his breast. Later still, she had awakened him, for he must have fallen asleep there in the big chair with her, and with the weak, humiliated goodness which always followed these times she had even tried to help him with the preparations for the journey—preparations which, without a word between them, they had set about at once. There'd been no doubt, of course, that she would have to go. There never was.

He left the window and sat down again in the big chair, and smoked one cigarette after another. Actually, for a drunkard—or an alcoholic, as people preferred to say these days—his mother was the least troublesome of any. He had thought of it while he packed the pairs of daintily kept shoes, the sweet-smelling blouses and froufrou underwear, the tiny, perfect dresses—of what a comfort it was that she had never grown raddled or blowzy. Years ago, she had perfected the routine within which she could feel safe for months at a time. It had gone on for longer than he could remember: from before the death of his father, a Swedish engineer, on the income of whose patents they had always been able to live fairly comfortably; probably even during her life with that other long-dead man, the painter whose model and mistress she had been in the years before she married his father. There would be the long, drugged sleep of the morning, then the unsteady hours when she manicured herself back into cleanliness and reality. Then, at about four or five in the afternoon, she and the dog (for there was always a dog) would make their short pilgrimage to the clubby, cozy little hangout where she would be a fixture until far into the morning, where she had been a fixture for the last twenty years.

Once, while he was at boarding school, she had made a supreme effort to get herself out of the routine—for his sake, no doubt—and he had returned at Easter to a new apartment, uptown, on Central Park West. All that this had

resulted in was inordinate taxi fares and the repetitious nightmare evenings when she had gotten lost and he had found
her, a small, untidy heap, in front of their old place. After
a few months, they had moved back to the Village, to those
few important blocks where she felt safe and known and
loved. For they all knew her there, or got to know her—the
aging painters, the newcomer poets, the omniscient news
hacks, the military spinsters who bred dogs, the anomalous,
sandalled young men. And they accepted her, this dainty
hanger-on who neither painted nor wrote but hung their
paintings on her walls, faithfully read their parti-colored
magazines, and knew them all—their shibboleths, their
feuds, the whole vocabulary of their disintegration, and, in
a mild, occasional manner, their beds.

Even this, he could not remember not knowing. At ten,
he had been an expert compounder of remedies for hangover, and of an evening, standing sleepily in his pajamas to
be admired by the friends his mother sometimes brought
home, he could have predicted accurately whether the party
would end in a brawl or in a murmurous coupling in the
dark.

It was curious, he supposed now, stubbing out a final
cigarette, that he had never judged resentfully either his
mother or her world. By the accepted standards, his mother
had done her best; he had been well housed, well schooled,
even better loved than some of the familied boys he had
known. Wisely, too, she had kept out of his other life, so
that he had never had to be embarrassed there except once,
and this when he was grown, when she had visited his Army
camp. Watching her at a post party for visitors, poised there,
so chic, so distinctive, he had suddenly seen it begin: the
fear, the scare, then the compulsive talking, which always
started so innocently that only he would have noticed at first
—that warm, excited, buttery flow of harmless little lies
and pretensions which gathered its dreadful speed and content and ended then, after he had whipped her away, just as
it had ended this morning.

On the way up this morning, he had been too clever to
subject her to a restaurant, but at a drive-in place he was
able to get her to take some coffee. How grateful they had

both been for the coffee, she looking up at him, tremulous, her lips pecking at the cup, he blessing the coffee as it went down her! And afterward, as they flew onward, he could feel her straining like a homing pigeon toward their destination, toward the place where she felt safest of all, where she would gladly have stayed forever if she had just had enough money for it, if they would only let her stay. For there the pretty little woman and her dog—a poodle, this time— would be received like the honored guest that she was, so trusted and docile a guest, who asked only to hide there during the season of her discomfort, who was surely the least troublesome of them all.

He had no complaints, then, he assured himself as he sat on the burning front seat of the convertible trying to think of somewhere to go. It was just that while others of his age still shared a communal wonder at what life might hold, he had long since been solitary in his knowledge of what life was.

Up in a sky as honestly blue as a flag, an airplane droned smartly toward Jersey. Out at Rye, the younger crowd at the club would be commandeering the hot blue day, the sand, and the water, as if these were all extensions of themselves. They would use the evening this way, too, disappearing from the veranda after a dance, exploring each other's rhythm-and-whiskey-whetted appetites in the backs of cars. They all thought themselves a pretty sophisticated bunch, the young men who had graduated not into a war but into its hung-over peace, the young girls attending junior colleges so modern that the deans had to spend all their time declaring that their girls were being trained for the family and the community. But when Peter looked close and saw how academic their sophistication was, how their undamaged eyes were still starry with expectancy, their lips still avidly open for what life would surely bring, then he became envious and awkward with them, like a guest at a party to whose members he carried bad news he had no right to know, no right to tell.

He turned on the ignition and let the humming motor prod him into a decision. He would drop in at Robert Vielum's, where he had dropped in quite often until recently, for the

same reason that others stopped by at Vielum's—because
there was always likely to be somebody there. The door of
Robert's old-fashioned apartment, on Claremont Avenue,
almost always opened on a heartening jangle of conversation
and music, which meant that others had gathered there, too,
to help themselves over the pauses so endemic to university
life—the life of the mind—and there were usually several
members of Robert's large acquaintance among the sub-
literary, quasi-artistic, who had strayed in, ostensibly en
route somewhere, and who lingered on hopefully on the
chance that in each other's company they might find out
what that somewhere was.

Robert was a perennial taker of courses—one of those non-
matriculated students of indefinable age and income, some of
whom pursued, with monkish zeal and no apparent regard for
time, this or that freakishly peripheral research project of
their own conception, and others of whom, like Robert,
seemed to derive a Ponce de León sustenance from the young.
Robert himself, a large man of between forty and fifty, whose
small features were somewhat cramped together in a wide
face, never seemed bothered by his own lack of direction, im-
plying rather that this was really the catholic approach of the
"whole man," alongside of which the serious pursuit of a
degree was somehow foolish, possibly vulgar. Rumor connected him with a rich Boston family that had remittanced
him at least as far as New York, but he never spoke about
himself, although he was extraordinarily alert to gossip.
Whatever income he had he supplemented by renting his
extra room to a series of young men students. The one
opulence among his dun-colored, perhaps consciously Spar-
tan effects was a really fine record-player, which he kept
going at all hours with selections from his massive collection. Occasionally he annotated the music, or the advance-
copy novel that lay on his table, with foreign-language tags
drawn from the wide, if obscure, latitudes of his travels, and
it was his magic talent for assuming that his young friends,
too, had known, had experienced, that, more than anything,
kept them enthralled.

"*Fabelhaft!* Isn't it?" he would say of the Mozart. "Remember how they did it that last time at Salzburg!" and they

would all sit there, included, belonging, headily remembering the Salzburg to which they had never been. Or he would
pick up the novel and lay it down again. "*La plume de mon
oncle*, I'm afraid. *La plume de mon oncle Gide. Eheu, poor
Gide!*"—and they would each make note of the fact that
one need not read that particular book, that even, possibly,
it was no longer necessary to read Gide.

Peter parked the car and walked into the entrance of
Robert's apartment house, smiling to himself, lightened by
the prospect of company. After all, he had been weaned on
the salon talk of such circles; these self-fancying little bo-
hemias at least made him feel at home. And Robert was
cleverer than most—it was amusing to watch him. For
just as soon as his satellites thought themselves secure on the
promontory of some "trend" he had pointed out to them,
they would find that he had deserted them, had gone on to
another trend, another eminence, from which he beckoned,
cocksure and just faintly malicious. He harmed no one
permanently. And if he concealed some skeleton of a weakness, some closeted Difference with the Authorities, he kept
it decently interred.

As Peter stood in the dark, soiled hallway and rang the
bell of Robert's apartment, he found himself as suddenly
depressed again, unaccountably reminded of his mother.
There were so many of them, and they affected you so, these
charmers who, if they could not offer you the large strength,
could still atone for the lack with so many small decencies.
It was admirable, surely, the way they managed this. And
surely, after all, they harmed no one.

Robert opened the door. "Why, hello—Why, hello, Peter!"
He seemed surprised, almost relieved. "Greetings!" he added,
in a voice whose boom was more in the manner than the
substance. "Come in, Pietro, come in!" He wore white linen
shorts, a zebra-striped beach shirt, and huaraches, in which
he moved easily, leading the way down the dark hall of
the apartment, past the two bedrooms, into the living room.
All of the apartment was on a court, but on the top floor,
so it received a medium, dingy light from above. The living
room, long and pleasant, with an old white mantel, a gas
log, and many books, always came as a surprise after the

rest of the place, and at any time of day Robert kept a few
lamps lit, which rouged the room with an evening excitement.

As they entered, Robert reached over in passing and
turned on the record-player. Music filled the room, muted
but insistent, as if he wanted it to patch up some lull he had
left behind. Two young men sat in front of the dead gas log.
Between them was a table littered with maps, an open atlas,
travel folders, glass beer steins. Vince, the current roomer,
had his head on his clenched fists. The other man, a stranger,
indolently raised a dark, handsome head as they entered.

"Vince!" Robert spoke sharply. "You know Peter Birge.
And this is Mario Osti. Peter Birge."

The dark young man nodded and smiled, lounging in
his chair. Vince nodded. His red-rimmed eyes looked beyond Peter into some distance he seemed to prefer.

"God, isn't it but hot!" Robert said. "I'll get you a beer."
He bent over Mario with an inquiring look, a caressing hand
on the empty glass in front of him.

Mario stretched back on the chair, smiled upward at
Robert, and shook his head sleepily. "Only makes me hotter."
He yawned, spread his arms languorously, and let them
fall. He had the animal self-possession of the very handsome;
it was almost a shock to hear him speak.

Robert bustled off to the kitchen.

"Robert!" Vince called, in his light, pouting voice. "Get
me a drink. Not a beer. A drink." He scratched at the blond
stubble on his cheek with a nervous, pointed nail. On his
round head and retroussé face, the stubble produced the
illusion of a desiccated baby, until, looking closer, one imagined that he might never have been one, but might have
been spawned at the age he was, to mummify perhaps but not
to grow. He wore white shorts exactly like Robert's, and his
blue-and-white striped shirt was a smaller version of Robert's
brown-and-white, so that the two of them made an ensemble,
like the twin outfits the children wore on the beach at Rye.

"You know I don't keep whiskey here." Robert held three
steins deftly balanced, his heavy hips neatly avoiding the
small tables which scattered the room. "You've had enough,
wherever you got it." It was true, Peter remembered, that
Robert was fonder of drinks with a flutter of ceremony about

them—*café brûlé* perhaps, or, in the spring, a *Maibowle*, over which he could chant the triumphant details of his pursuit of the necessary woodruff. But actually one tippled here on the exhilarating effect of wearing one's newest façade, in the fit company of others similarly attired.

Peter picked up his stein. "You and Vince all set for Morocco, I gather."

"Morocco?" Robert took a long pull at his beer. "No. No, that's been changed. I forgot you hadn't been around. Mario's been brushing up my Italian. He and I are off for Rome the day after tomorrow."

The last record on the changer ended in an archaic battery of horns. In the silence while Robert slid on a new batch of records, Peter heard Vince's nail scrape, scrape along his cheek. Still leaning back, Mario shaped smoke with his lips. Large and facilely drawn, they looked, more than anything, accessible—to a stream of smoke, of food, to another mouth, to any plum that might drop.

"You going to study over there?" Peter said to him.

"Paint." Mario shaped and let drift another corolla of smoke.

"No," Robert said, clicking on the record arm. "I'm afraid Africa's démodé." A harpsichord began to play, its dwarf notes hollow and perfect. Robert raised his voice a shade above the music. "Full of fashion photographers. And little come-lately writers." He sucked in his cheeks and made a face. "Trying out their passions under the beeg, bad sun."

"*Eheu,* poor Africa?" said Peter.

Robert laughed. Vince stared at him out of wizened eyes. Not drink, so much, after all, Peter decided, looking professionally at the mottled cherub face before he realized that he was comparing it with another face, but lately left. He looked away.

"Weren't you going over, Peter?" Robert leaned against the machine.

"Not this year." Carefully Peter kept out of his voice the knell the words made in his mind. In Greenwich, there were many gravelled walks, unshrubbed except for the nurses who dotted them, silent and attitudinized as trees. "Isn't that Landowska playing?"

"Hmm. Nice and cooling on a hot day. Or a fevered brow."
Robert fiddled with the volume control. The music became
louder, then lowered. "Vince wrote a poem about that once.
About the Mozart, really, wasn't it, Vince? 'A lovely clock
between ourselves and time.'" He enunciated daintily, pushing the words away from him with his tongue.

"Turn it off!" Vince stood up, his small fists clenched,
hanging at his sides.

"No, let her finish." Robert turned deliberately and closed
the lid of the machine, so that the faint hiss of the needle
vanished from the frail, metronomic notes. He smiled. "What
a time-obsessed crowd writers are. Now Mario doesn't have
to bother with that dimension."

"Not unless I paint portraits," Mario said. His parted lips
exposed his teeth, like some white, unexpected flint of intelligence.

"*Dolce far niente,*" Robert said softly. He repeated the
phrase dreamily, so that half-known Italian words—"*log-
gia,*" the "Ponte Vecchio," the "Lungarno"—imprinted themselves one by one on Peter's mind, and he saw the two of
them, Mario and Roberto now, already in the frayed-gold
light of Florence, in the umber dusk of half-imagined towns.

A word, muffled, came out of Vince's throat. He lunged
for the record-player. Robert seized his wrist and held it
down on the lid. They were locked that way, staring at each
other, when the doorbell rang.

"That must be Susan," Robert said. He released Vince and
looked down, watching the blood return to his fingers, flexing
his palm.

With a second choked sound, Vince flung out his fist in
an awkward attempt at a punch. It grazed Robert's cheek,
clawing downward. A thin line of red appeared on Robert's
cheek. Fist to mouth, Vince stood a moment; then he rushed
from the room. They heard the nearer bedroom door slam
and the lock click. The bell rang again, a short, hesitant burr.

Robert clapped his hand to his cheek, shrugged, and left
the room.

Mario got up out of his chair for the first time. "Aren't you
going to ask who Susan is?"

"Should I?" Peter leaned away from the face bent confidentially near, curly with glee.

"His daughter," Mario whispered. "He said he was expecting his *daughter*. Can you imagine? *Robert!*"

Peter moved farther away from the mobile, pressing face and, standing at the window, studied the gritty details of the courtyard. A vertical line of lighted windows, each with a glimpse of stair, marked the hallways on each of the five floors. Most of the other windows were dim and closed, or opened just a few inches above their white ledges, and the yard was quiet. People would be away or out in the sun, or in their brighter front rooms dressing for dinner, all of them avoiding this dark shaft that connected the backs of their lives. Or, here and there, was there someone sitting in the fading light, someone lying on a bed with his face pressed to a pillow? The window a few feet to the right, around the corner of the court, must be the window of the room into which Vince had gone. There was no light in it.

Robert returned, a Kleenex held against his cheek. With him was a pretty, ruffle-headed girl in a navy-blue dress with a red arrow at each shoulder. He switched on another lamp. For the next arrival, Peter thought, surely he will tug back a velvet curtain or break out with a heraldic flourish of drums, recorded by Red Seal. Or perhaps the musty wardrobe was opening at last and this was the skeleton—this girl who had just shaken hands with Mario, and now extended her hand toward Peter, tentatively, timidly, as if she did not habitually shake hands but today would observe every custom she could.

"How do you do?"

"How do you do?" Peter said. The hand he held for a moment was small and childish, the nails unpainted, but the rest of her was very correct for the eye of the beholder, like the young models one sees in magazines, sitting or standing against a column, always in three-quarter view, so that the picture, the ensemble, will not be marred by the human glance. Mario took from her a red dressing case that she held in her free hand, bent to pick up a pair of white gloves that she had dropped, and returned them with an

avid interest which overbalanced, like a waiter's gallantry.
She sat down, brushing at the gloves.

"The train was awfully dusty—and crowded." She smiled
tightly at Robert, looked hastily and obliquely at each of
the other two, and bent over the gloves, brushing earnestly,
stopping as if someone had said something, and, when no
one did, brushing again.

"Well, well, well," Robert said. His manners, always good,
were never so to the point of clichés, which would be for
him what nervous *gaffes* were for other people. He coughed,
rubbed his cheek with the back of his hand, looked at the
hand, and stuffed the Kleenex into the pocket of his shorts.
"How was camp?"

Mario's eyebrows went up. The girl was twenty, surely,
Peter thought.

"All right," she said. She gave Robert the stiff smile again
and looked down into her lap. "I like helping children. They
can use it." Her hands folded on top of the gloves, then
inched under and hid beneath them.

"Susan's been counselling at a camp which broke up early
because of a polio scare," Robert said as he sat down. "She's
going to use Vince's room while I'm away, until college
opens."

"Oh—" She looked up at Peter. "Then you aren't Vince?"

"No. I just dropped in. I'm Peter Birge."

She gave him a neat nod of acknowledgment. "I'm glad,
because I certainly wouldn't want to inconvenience—"

"Did you get hold of your mother in Reno?" Robert asked
quickly.

"Not yet. But she couldn't break up her residence term
anyway. And Arthur must have closed up the house here.
The phone was disconnected."

"Arthur's Susan's stepfather," Robert explained with a
little laugh. "Number three, I think. Or is it *four*, Sue?"

Without moving, she seemed to retreat, so that again
there was nothing left for the observer except the girl
against the column, any one of a dozen with the short,
anonymous nose, the capped hair, the foot arched in the
trim shoe, and half an iris glossed with an expertly aimed
photoflood. "Three," she said. Then one of the hidden hands

stole out from under the gloves, and she began to munch evenly on a fingernail.

"Heavens, you haven't still got that *habit!*" Robert said.

"What a heavy papa you make, Roberto," Mario said.

She flushed, and put the hand back in her lap, tucking the fingers under. She looked from Peter to Mario and back again. "Then you're not Vince," she said. "I didn't think you were."

The darkness increased around the lamps. Behind Peter, the court had become brisk with lights, windows sliding up, and the sound of taps running.

"Guess Vince fell asleep. I'd better get him up and send him on his way." Robert shrugged, and rose.

"Oh, don't! I wouldn't want to be an inconvenience," the girl said, with a polite terror which suggested she might often have been one.

"On the contrary." Robert spread his palms, with a smile, and walked down the hall. They heard him knocking on a door, then his indistinct voice.

In the triangular silence, Mario stepped past Peter and slid the window up softly. He leaned out to listen, peering sidewise at the window to the right. As he was pulling himself back in, he looked down. His hands stiffened on the ledge. Very slowly he pulled himself all the way in and stood up. Behind him a tin ventilator clattered inward and fell to the floor. In the shadowy lamplight his too classic face was like marble which moved numbly. He swayed a little, as if with vertigo.

"I'd better get out of here!"

They heard his heavy breath as he dashed from the room. The slam of the outer door blended with Robert's battering, louder now, on the door down the hall.

"What's down there?" She was beside Peter, otherwise he could not have heard her. They took hands, like strangers met on a narrow footbridge or on one of those steep places where people cling together more for anchorage against their own impulse than for balance. Carefully they leaned out over the sill. Yes—it was down there, the shirt, zebra-striped, just decipherable on the merged shadow of the courtyard below.

Carefully, as if they were made of eggshell, as if by some
guarded movement they could still rescue themselves from
disaster, they drew back and straightened up. Robert, his
face askew with the impossible question, was behind them.

After this, there was the hubbub—the ambulance from
St. Luke's, the prowl car, the two detectives from the precinct
station house, and finally the "super," a vague man with the
grub pallor and shamble of those who live in basements. He
pawed over the keys on the thong around his wrist and, after
several tries, opened the bedroom door. It was a quiet, un-
violent room with a tossed bed and an open window, with a
stagy significance acquired only momentarily in the minds
of those who gathered in a group at its door.

Much later, after midnight, Peter and Susan sat in the
bald glare of an all-night restaurant. With hysterical eager-
ness, Robert had gone on to the station house with the two
detectives to register the salient facts, to help ferret out the
relatives in Ohio, to arrange, in fact, anything that might
still be arrangeable about Vince. Almost without noticing, he
had acquiesced in Peter's proposal to look after Susan. Susan
herself, after silently watching the gratuitous burbling of her
father, as if it were a phenomenon she could neither believe
nor leave, had followed Peter without comment. At his suggestion, they had stopped off at the restaurant on their way to
her stepfather's house, for which she had a key.

"Thanks. I was starved." She leaned back and pushed at
the short bang of hair on her forehead.

"Hadn't you eaten at all?"

"Just those pasty sandwiches they sell on the train. There
wasn't any diner."

"Smoke?"

"I do, but I'm just too tired. I can get into a hotel all
right, don't you think? If I can't get in at Arthur's?"

"I know the manager of a small one near us," Peter said.
"But if you don't mind coming to my place, you can use
my mother's room for tonight. Or for as long as you need,
probably."

"What about your mother?"

"She's away. She'll be away for quite a while."

"Not in Reno, by any chance?" There was a roughness,

almost a coarseness, in her tone, like that in the overdone camaraderie of the shy.

"No. My father died when I was eight. Why?"

"Oh, something in the way you spoke. And then you're so competent. Does she work?"

"No. My father left something. Does yours?"

She stood up and picked up her bedraggled gloves. "No," she said, and her voice was suddenly distant and delicate again. "She marries." She turned and walked out ahead of him.

He paid, rushed out of the restaurant, and caught up with her.

"Thought maybe you'd run out on me," he said.

She got in the car without answering.

They drove through the Park, toward the address in the East Seventies that she had given him. A weak smell of grass underlay the gas-blended air, but the Park seemed limp and worn, as if the strain of the day's effluvia had been too much for it. At the Seventy-second Street stop signal, the blank light of a street lamp invaded the car.

"Thought you might be feeling Mrs. Grundyish at my suggesting the apartment," Peter said.

"Mrs. Grundy wasn't around much when I grew up." The signal changed and they moved ahead.

They stopped in a street which had almost no lights along its smartly converted house fronts. This was one of the streets, still sequestered by money, whose houses came alive only under the accelerated, febrile glitter of winter and would dream through the gross summer days, their interiors deadened with muslin or stirred faintly with the subterranean clinkings of caretakers. No. 4 was dark.

"I would rather stay over at your place, if I have to," the girl said. Her voice was offhand and prim. "I hate hotels. We always stopped at them in between."

"Let's get out and see."

They stepped down into the areaway in front of the entrance, the car door banging hollowly behind them. She fumbled in her purse and took out a key, although it was already obvious that it would not be usable. In his childhood, he had often hung around in the areaways of old

brownstones such as this had been. In the corners there had
always been a soft, decaying smell, and the ironwork, bent
and smeared, always hung loose and broken-toothed. The
areaway of this house had been repaved with slippery flag;
even in the humid night there was no smell. Black-tongued
grillwork, with an oily shine and padlocked, secured the
windows and the smooth door. Fastened on the grillwork
in front of the door was the neat, square proclamation of a
protection agency.

"You don't have a key for the padlocks, do you?"

"No." She stood on the curb, looking up at the house. "It
was a nice room I had there. Nicest one I ever did have,
really." She crossed to the car and got in.

He followed her over to the car and got in beside her.
She had her head in her hands.

"Don't worry. We'll get in touch with somebody in the
morning."

"I don't. I don't care about any of it, really." She sat up,
her face averted. "My parents, or any of the people they
tangle with." She wound the lever on the door slowly, then
reversed it. "Robert, or my mother, or Arthur," she said, "although he was always pleasant enough. Even Vince—even
if I'd known him."

"He was just a screwed-up kid. It could have been anybody's window."

"No." Suddenly she turned and faced him. "I should think
it would be the best privilege there is, though. To care, I
mean."

When he did not immediately reply, she gave him a little
pat on the arm and sat back. "Excuse it, please. I guess I'm
groggy." She turned around and put her head on the crook
of her arm. Her words came faintly through it. "Wake me
when we get there."

She was asleep by the time they reached his street. He
parked the car as quietly as possible beneath his own windows. He himself had never felt more awake in his life. He
could have sat there until morning with her sleep-secured
beside him. He sat thinking of how different it would be at
Rye, or anywhere, with her along, with someone along who
was the same age. For they were the same age, whatever that

was, whatever the age was of people like them. There was nothing he would be unable to tell her.

To the north, above the rooftops, the electric mauve of midtown blanked out any auguries in the sky, but he wasn't looking for anything like that. Tomorrow he would take her for a drive—whatever the weather. There were a lot of good roads around Greenwich.

This deft and charming story marked the first public appearance of one of America's most popular heroines. Whether it is a mite sentimental I am not certain. I am certain that it is likable and marvelously engaging.

The Terrible Miss Dove

IIIIIIIIIIIIIIIII FRANCES GRAY PATTON IIIIIIIIIIIIIIIII

Miss Dove was waiting for the sixth grade to file in for its geography lesson. She stood behind her desk, straight as the long map pointer in her hand. And suddenly she had the feeling of not being really alone. Someone or something was moving about the room. Over there, near the sand table where the first grade's herd of rickety clay caribou grazed at the edge of the second grade's plateau, it paused and looked at her. But even when the presence glided, like the shadow of a drifting cloud, along the wall behind her; even when she heard—or almost heard—a new stick of chalk squeaking on the blackboard, Miss Dove did not turn around. She knew, of course, that nobody was there. Her imagination was playing tricks on her again. It was something, she had to admit, humiliatingly close to nerves. Miss Dove did not believe in nerves.

Through the open door she watched the sixth graders come out of the music room down the hall. They came out with a rush, as if for two minutes of freedom between classroom and classroom they were borne along upon some mass exhilaration. They always left the music room in that fashion, but this morning they managed to be noisier than usual. It was the season, she supposed. The spring day was warm, and the children were restless as the weather. There was a sharp sound among them, as of a plump posterior being spanked with

a book; there was a voice saying, "Double dare, Randy!";
there was a breathless giggling.

But as they approached Miss Dove's room their disorder
began to vanish. They pulled their excitement in, like a proud
but well-broken pony. One by one they stepped sedately
across her doorsill. "Good morning, Miss Dove," they said,
one by one, with the same proper lack of voice inflection, and
went demurely to their places. At a nod from her they took
their seats. Hands folded, eyes to the front, posture correct—
they were ready for direction.

Jincey Webb, Miss Dove noticed without enthusiasm, had
a permanent wave. Yesterday her carrot-colored mane had
been neatly braided and pulled back from her serious,
freckled face. Now it hung to her shoulders, a bushy mop of
undulations and frizzy ringlets. It hung on her mind, too;
that was plain to see. For Jincey's expression was one of utter
and enviable complacency. It seemed doubtful that a long
lifetime of repeated triumphs could again offer her an achievement so sublime with self-satisfaction.

Randy Baker, a pink boy of exceptional daring, wiggled
his ears at Jincey. Miss Dove looked at him. Randy's pinkness
paled. A glaze of innocence came over his round eyes. His
ears grew very still.

Miss Dove kept looking at him, but she had stopped seeing
him. Instead, she was seeing his brother Thomas, who had
sat there at Randy's desk seven years before, with the same
glaze over the mischief in his eyes. And then she saw Thomas
on a raft in the Pacific. She did not see him as they had described him in the papers—skin and bones and haggard young
face overgrown with a rough, wild beard. The Thomas she
saw looked like Randy. He had braces on his teeth and a
dimple in his chin. And he was all alone in the dismal gray
mountains of the sea.

A wave of giddiness swept over her, but she did not sit
down. It was nothing. It had been happening to her off and on
all year, and it always passed. Miss Dove had a poor opinion
of teachers who could not practice self-control.

For thirty years Miss Dove had taught geography in Cedar
Grove Elementary School. She had been there before the
brooding cedars had been chopped down by a city council

that believed in progress and level playgrounds. She had seen
principals and fads and theories come and go. But the school
still squatted there, red brick, ugly, impervious. Inside it still
smelled of wet raincoats and pickle sandwiches. Galahad still
petted his charger on the left wall of the vestibule, and Washington still crossed the Delaware on the right. Every fall
nervous six-year-olds had to be sent home in tears to put on
dry drawers. Every spring there occurred the scandal of
cigarette butts in the boys' basement. The same deplorable,
old-fashioned words sprang up overnight like mushrooms on
the cement walk. And now and then some hitherto graceless
child could still surprise you with an act of loyalty or understanding. The school had not changed much. Neither had
human nature. Neither had Miss Dove.

Each June some forty-odd little girls and boys—transformed
by the magic of organdy ruffles and white duck pants into a
group picture of touching purity—were graduated from Cedar
Grove. They went on to the wider world of junior high and,
beyond that, to further realms of pleasure and pain. In the
course of time they forgot much. They forgot dates and
decimals and how to write business letters.

But they never forgot Miss Dove.

Years afterward the mention of the Euphrates River or the
Arctic Circle or the Argentinian pampas would put them right
back in the geography room. They would see again the big
map with its flat blue ocean and its many-colored countries.
(India was pink, they would recall, and China was orange,
and the Italian boot was purple.) They would see Miss Dove
lifting her long stick to point out the locations of strange
mountains and valleys. And they would feel again the wonder
of a world far-flung and various and, like themselves, entirely
under control. They would also feel a little thirsty.

"Remember Miss Dove?" they would smile.

But this green remembrance and the accident of her name's
rhyming with a tender word should not deceive anybody
about Miss Dove. She was no valentine. Miss Dove was a
terror.

She had been young when she first started teaching. Her
pupils would have hooted at the notion; they would have felt

it more reasonable to believe Miss Dove had been born middle-aged with her mousy hair screwed into a knot at the back of her head and a white handkerchief pinned to her dark, bony bosom. Nevertheless, it is true. She had once been quite young.

Her father had died, leaving her little besides a library of travel books, an anemic violet- scented mother, and two young sisters yet in school. It had been up to Miss Dove. Older people had pitied her. She seemed too thin and pale and untried, they thought, to carry the burden alone. But Miss Dove never pitied herself. She loved responsibility.

The children of each grade came to her forty-five minutes a day, five days a week, six years of their lives. She saw them as a challenge. Their babyish shyness, their lisping pronunciation, their reckless forgetfulness—these evoked no compassion from Miss Dove. They were qualities to be nipped and pruned. Her classes were like a body of raw recruits that she was to toughen and charge with purpose. Miss Dove was the stuff that commanders are made of.

Other teachers had trouble keeping order, but not Miss Dove. Other teachers tried to make a game of their work— they played store and pasted gold stars on foreheads. They threatened and cajoled. Miss Dove never raised her voice. She rarely smiled. She laid before the children the roster of her unalterable laws. And the laws were obeyed. Work was to be done on time. There was to be no whispering, no hair chewing, no wriggling. Coughing, if at all, was to be covered with a clean handkerchief. When one of these laws was chipped, Miss Dove merely looked at the offender. That was all. If a child felt obliged to disturb the class routine by leaving the room for a drink of water (Miss Dove loftily ignored any other necessity), he did so to the accompaniment of dead silence. The whole class would sit, idle and motionless, until he had returned. It was easier—even if you had eaten salt fish for breakfast—to remain and suffer.

Miss Dove managed to introduce a moral quality into the very subject she taught. The first graders, who studied the animals of different lands, repeated after her, "The yak is a very helpful animal." And they knew she expected them all to be yaks. Later they learned a more complicated sentence.

"The camel," they recited in perfect unison, "is not a pretty beast, either in looks or disposition, but he is able to go many days without water." And they knew what was meant. "Above the fiftieth parallel," sixth graders wrote in their notebooks (keeping the margins even), "life requires hardihood."

Occasionally a group of progressive mothers would nearly rebel. "She's been teaching too long," they would cry. "Her pedagogy hasn't changed since we were in the third grade. She rules the children through fear." They would turn to the boldest one among them. "*You* go," they would say. "You go talk to her."

The bold one would go, but somehow she never did much talking. For under the level gaze of Miss Dove she would begin to feel—though she wore her handsomest tweeds and perhaps a gardenia for courage—that she was about ten years old and her petticoat was showing. Her throat would tickle. She would wonder desperately if she had a clean handkerchief to cough into.

And then there was the little matter of the state achievement tests. Cedar Grove always placed first in geography.

Occasionally, too, there would be an independent child who did not yield readily to group discipline. Miss Dove knew how to deal with him.

Once she had overheard two small boys talking about her at the drinking fountain. (They had no business at the fountain; it was their library period. But the librarian was lax.)

"I bet Miss Dove could lick Joe Louis," one of them had said.

"Who? That ole stick?" the other one had jeered. "I could beat her with my little finger."

He had glanced up then to see Miss Dove looking down at him. She had looked at him for a long time. Her light gray eyes were expressionless. Her long nose was pink at the tip, but no pinker than usual. At last she had spoken.

"Thomas Baker," she had said in the tone of one making a pure observation, "you talk too much, don't you?"

"Yes, ma'am," Thomas had said in a tiny voice. He went off without getting any water. Seven years later he sweated when he thought of it. He could not know that Miss Dove also remembered. But she did.

Ever since Pearl Harbor Miss Dove had been troubled. She lived quite alone, for her sisters had married and her mother had departed for a place not on the map. (But decently, with every possible comfort. Miss Dove liked to remind herself of that.) And one evening while she was correcting papers she sensed, with that uncanny perception of the teacher, that something intruded upon her solitude. She turned quickly and looked about the room. A starched white curtain rustled in a puff of wind; her grandmother's rosewood whatnot cast a curious shadow on the polished floor; a finger of lamplight picked out the gilt titles of her father's old brown travel books. There was nothing else. But the red correction pencil was shaking in her fingers; for a moment her throat ached with a spasm of desolate, unaccountable grief, and—less familiar still—with a feeling of her own unworthiness. Miss Dove had never felt unworthy before in her life.

After that the thing happened frequently, until at last she saw who the intruders were. They were the children she had taught long ago.

War had scattered those children. There was a girl—a vain, silly little piece she had been—who was a nurse on Corregidor. At least, when last heard of she had been on Corregidor. One of the boys was dead in Tunisia. Others were on the Anzio beachhead, or in the jungles of New Guinea, or in the flak-brightened skies over Germany. But they came back to Miss Dove. She saw them as they had been at seven, at ten, at twelve. Only they had a beauty she had never seen in them then. They lifted their faces like starry morning flowers. Their limbs quivered with the unreasonable joy of childhood. And as Miss Dove looked at them they grew still. Their faces paled. Their eyes stopped dancing. They folded their little hands. They faded and were gone.

The child who came oftenest was Thomas Baker. The town paper had been full of Thomas. His ship had been bombed, his officers killed, and Thomas had taken over. A hundred men owed their lives to his presence of mind. For days he had floated on a raft with no food and only the water in his canteen. When they picked him up his tongue had protruded from his mouth, black and swollen with thirst. That was what got Miss Dove—he had run out of water.

The Thomas who came to stand before her now was a sturdy boy in knickers. He held his chin at a cocky angle, but the dimple in it trembled. He ran the tip of his tongue over his lips. He looked thirsty.

But they came only at night. When daylight returned Miss Dove could believe she had been imagining things. She would eat her customary boiled egg and her whole-wheat toast; she would take an extra vitamin pill with her orange juice; she would walk forth at her usual measured pace and assume her usual role of unshakable authority. The children at the school would seem plain and ordinary. They would have little in common with those graceful and evanescent figures that haunted her. And no intruders dared come into the geography room. Or they never had until this morning.

A boy on the back row cleared his throat. One by the window followed suit. Soon the whole room was dotted with the sound, a rough "h-hrmph," like frogs in a distant marsh. Miss Dove knew what the sound meant. It was the school's traditional signal—a kind of dare. She had heard other teachers speak of it in exasperation. It had never happened in her room before.

Slowly Randy Baker raised his hand. The sounds stopped. Silence like a caught breath hung on the room. Miss Dove could see a fine dew pop out on Randy's brow; his open palm was damp and gleaming.

"Yes, Randolph?" she said.

Randy stood up. Miss Dove's pupils always stood when they addressed her. He smoothed his round stomach with his hand. "I got a letter from Tom yestiddy," he said.

"*Received,* Randolph," said Miss Dove. "You received a letter from your brother *yesterday*. That was nice."

"Yes, ma'am," said Randy. He paused. He was clearly floundering. "He sent me a dollar he won playing poker in the convalescent hospital."

"I am sorry to hear that Thomas gambles," said Miss Dove, "but we are all very proud of his war record. If you have nothing more interesting to tell us you may take your seat, Randolph."

"H-hr-rmph!" went the boy behind Randy.

"He's been decorated," said Randy, "for bravery beyond

the call of duty." The high words seemed to inspirit him. "He sent a message to the class."

"Did you bring the letter?" asked Miss Dove. "If so, you may read that part aloud."

Randy took an air-mail envelope from his hip pocket. Miss Dove noticed that Thomas' handwriting was as sprawling and untidy as ever. Somehow the observation pleased her.

The class stirred. The ghost of a titter rippled the air.

"Attention, please," said Miss Dove.

Randy opened the letter. The paper was smudged and crumpled. Obviously it had suffered many readings and many hands. Randy cleared his throat. The sound was not a link in the chain signal. Miss Dove could tell the difference. "It's sort of long," Randy demurred hopefully.

Miss Dove knew there was naughtiness afoot. The frog noises as well as Randy's hesitation had told her that. But she did not believe in avoiding an issue. She made a practice of facing impudence in the open—and facing it down.

"We can spare the time," she said.

Randy began to read. His voice was high and clear; it had the girlish sweetness that comes just before the breaking point.

"The funny thing about the world," Randy read, "is that it looks just like you think it does. When they flew me back to Cal. in a hospital plane I looked down and, heck, I might as well have been looking at those diagrams on the geography board back in dear (ha, ha!) ole Cedar Grove. I spotted a peninsula just as plain. A body of land almost entirely surrounded by water. I saw some atolls too. And they really are made in rings like doughnuts, with palm trees sprouting out of the cake part and blue water in the hole in the middle. The water is the color of that blue chalk I swiped once and drew the picture of Miss Dove on the sidewalk with. Remember?"

So it *was* Thomas who had drawn that caricature. She had always suspected him. "Proceed, Randolph," she said.

"You want to know if I was scared when the little yellow insects from"—Randy swallowed and went on—"from hell"— in his embarrassment he brought out the word with unnecessary force—"dive-bombed us. The answer is, you bet. But it came to me in a flash that I wasn't much scareder than I was that time ole lady Dove caught me bragging about how I could beat her up at the drinking fountain. 'I didn't run that time,' I told myself, 'so I won't run now.' Besides, there wasn't any place to run to."

The class laughed nervously.

"And later," read Randy, "when I was bobbing up and down like Crusoe on my raft, what do you guess I thought about? Well, it wasn't any pin-up girl. It was Miss Dove. I thought about that fishy stare she used to give us when we needed a drink of water. So to make my supply hold out I played I was back in the geography room. And even after the water was all gone I kept playing that. I'd think, 'The bell is bound to ring in a few minutes. You can last a little longer.' It took the same kind of guts in the Pacific it did in school. Tell that to the kids in Cedar Grove." Randy stopped abruptly.

"Is that the end?" asked Miss Dove.

Randy looked directly at her. For a fleeting moment she thought he was going to say yes. If he did, the incident would be closed, of course, for Miss Dove never questioned a child's word. That was why they generally told her the truth. He shook his head.

"No, ma'am," he said. "There's a little more." His face turned the color of a nearly ripe tomato. "He says here"—Randy gulped—"he says"—Randy took a deep breath—"he says: 'Give the terrible Miss Dove a kiss for me.'"

"Well, Randolph," said Miss Dove, "I am waiting."

There was an electric stillness that was followed, as the full meaning of her words penetrated the children's consciousness, by a gasp. Randy folded the letter and put it back into his pocket. Then he began to walk toward her. He walked with the deliberate stoicism of a martyr going to the chopping block. Miss Dove inclined her head and turned her cheek in his direction. He did not come any closer than he had to. He leaned forward stiffly from the waist and placed his puckered lips against her cheek. (*He smells like a last year's bird's nest*, thought Miss Dove. It was strange. However frequently a twelve-year-old boy was washed, he always smelled like a bird's nest.) Randy smacked. His kiss resounded, a small explosion in the room.

"Thank you, Randolph," said Miss Dove. "You may give Thomas my regards." She straightened up and faced the class. To her surprise, nobody was grinning.

Jincey Webb spoke. She did not raise her hand first for permission. She just spoke out. "It's like a medal," said Jincey softly. "It's like he pinned a medal on Miss Dove."

For a moment a lamp seemed to burn behind her face. Then over the light swept a shadow, a look of awe. It was as if Jincey had glimpsed some universal beauty—of sorrow, perhaps, or of nobility—too poignant for her youth to bear. She began to cry. She flopped her head down on her desk with her red hair falling forward and spreading out like a crinkly fan.

All the other girls were weeping too. All the boys were trying not to.

For the first time in her teaching career Miss Dove was at a loss. She wanted to make a speech. She wanted to say something beautiful and grateful about what life really meant to her, about the overwhelming generosity of children. No, not generosity. It was something better than that, something much harder to come by. It was justice. And Miss Dove did not know how to say what she felt. She had never thought it dignified to express emotion.

But as she stood there waiting for the words to form in her mind, she realized that she was neglecting her duty. The first duty of a teacher was to preserve order.

She fished a piece of string from a receptacle on her desk. She walked down the aisle to Jincey Webb. She took Jincey's hair, that marvel of art and nature, and bunched it in her hand. She tied it securely at the nape of Jincey's neck with the little bit of grocery string.

"Now it will be out of your way," she said.

At the sound of her voice, cool, precise and natural, the children rallied. They sat erect. They blew their noses on clean handkerchiefs. They folded their hands on their desks.

"Get out your notebooks, class," she said.

A transient mist came over her eyes. Through it, as through a prism, the children glowed. Freckles, cowlicks, pinafores and

polo shirts seemed bathed in a rainbow iridescence. Her love
flowed out to her children—to those opening their notebooks
before her, and to those in the far places she had once helped
them locate on the map. It did not flow tenderly like a
mother's coddling love. It flowed on a fierce rush of pride
and hope, as an old general's heart might follow his men into
battle.

She went to the blackboard and picked up a piece of chalk.
"Above the fiftieth parallel——" wrote the terrible Miss Dove.

Part melodrama and part supernatural fantasy, this
story reads like a legend or fairy tale about Negroes
in the backwoods of Alabama and is pure verbal
magic.

The Black Prince

*"How art thou fallen from heaven,
O Lucifer, son of the morning!"*

SHIRLEY ANN GRAU

Winters are short and very cold; sometimes there is
even a snow like heavy frost on the ground. Summers are
powdery hot; the white ball sun goes rolling around and
around in a sky behind the smoke from the summer fires.
There is always a burning somewhere in summer; the pines
are dry and waiting; the sun itself starts the smoldering. A
pine fire is quiet; there is only a kind of rustle from the
flames inside the trunks until the branches and needles go
up with a whistling. A whole hill often burns that way, its
smoke rising straight up to the white sun, and quiet.

In the plowed patches, green things grow quickly: the
ground is rich and there are underground rivers. But there
are no big farms: only patches of corn, green beans and
a field or two of cotton (grown for a little cash to spend on
Saturdays at Luther's General Store or Willie's Café; these
are the only two places for forty miles in any direction).
There is good pasture: the green places along the hillsides
with pines for shade and sure water in the streams that come
down from the Smokies to the north; even in the burnt-out
land of five seasons back, shrubs are high. But in the whole
county there are only fifty cows, gone wild most of them and
dry because they were never milked. They are afraid of men

and feed in the farthest ridges and the swamps that are the
bottoms of some littlest of the valleys. Their numbers are slowly increasing because no one bothers them. Only once in a
while some man with a hankering for cow meat takes his
rifle and goes after them. But that is not often; the people
prefer pork. Each family keeps enough razorbacks in a run
of bark palings.

It is all colored people here, and it is the poorest part of
the smallest and worst county in the state. The place at the
end of the dirt road leading from the state highway, the place
where Luther's Store and Willie's Café stand, does not even
have a name in the county records.

The only cool time of the summer day is very early, before the mists have shriveled away. There is a breeze then,
a good stiff one out of the Smokies. During the day there
is no sound: it is dead hot. But in the early mornings, when
the breeze from the north is blowing, it is not so lonesomely
quiet: crickets and locusts and the birds that flutter about
hunting them, calling frantically as if they had something
of importance to settle quick before the heat sets in. (By
seven they are quiet again, in the invisible places they have
chosen to wait out the day.)

A pine cone rattled down on Alberta's head and bounced
from her shoulder. She scooped it from the ground and threw
it upward through the branches. "You just keep your cone,
mister birds. I got no cause to want it." With a pumping
of wings the birds were gone, their cries sliding after them,
back down the air. "You just yell your head off. I can hit
you any time I want. Any time I want." There was a small
round piece of granite at her feet and she tossed it, without
particular aim, into the biggest of the bay trees: a gray
squirrel with a thin rattail tumbled from the branches and
peeped at her from behind the trunk with a pointed little rat
face. She jammed her hands in the pockets of her dress and
went on, swaggering slightly, cool and feeling good.

She was a handsome girl, taller than most people in her
part of the county, and light brown—there had been a lot
of white blood in her family, back somewhere, they'd forgot where exactly. She was not graceful—not as a woman

is—but light on her feet and supple as a man. Her dress, which the sun had bleached to a whitish color, leaving only a trace of pink along the seams, had shrunk out of size for her: it pulled tight across her broad, slightly hunched, muscled back, even though she had left all the front buttons open down to the waist.

As she walked along, the birds were making even more of a row, knocking loose cones and dry pine needles and old broad bay leaves, and twice she stopped, threw back her head, and called up to them: "Crazy fool birds. Can't do nothing to me. Fool jackass birds." Up ahead, a couple of minutes' walk, was the field and the cotton, bursting white out of the brown cups and waiting to be picked. And she did not feel like working. She leaned against a tree, stretching so that the bark crumbled in her fingers, listening to the birds.

Something different was in their calling. She listened, her head bent forward, her eyes closed, as she sorted the sounds. One jay was wrong: its long sustained note ended with the cluck of a quail. No bird did that. Alberta opened her eyes and looked slowly around. But the pines were thick and close and full of blue night shadow and wrapped with fog that moved like bits of cloth in the wind. Leaving the other bird calls, the whistle became distinct, high, soaring, mocking, like some rare bird, proudly, insolently.

Alberta moved a few steps out from the tree and turned slowly on her heels. The whistle was going around her now, in slow circles, and she turned with it, keeping her eye on the sound, seeing nothing. The birds were still calling and fluttering in the branches, sending bits of twig and bark tumbling down.

Alberta said: "A fool thing you doing. A crazy fool jackass thing." She sat down on a tumbled pile of bricks that had been the chimney of a sugarhouse burned during the Civil War. She spoke in her best tone, while the whistling went round and round her faster. "I reckon you got nothing better to do than go around messing up folks. You got me so riled up I don't reckon I know what way I'm heading in." The sound went around her and around her, but she held her head steady, talking to the pine directly in front of her. "I don't reckon there's nothing for me but set here till you tires out and goes away." The whistle circled her twice and then abruptly stopped, the last high clear note running off down the breeze. Alberta stood up, pulling down her faded dress. "I am mighty glad you come to stopping. I reckon now I can tell what direction I got to go in."

He was right there, leaning on the same pine she had been staring at, cleaning his front teeth with a little green twig and studying her, and she told him to his face: "That was a crazy mean thing, and you ain't got nothing better to do."

"Reckon not," he said, moving the little green twig in and out of the hole between his lower front teeth.

She pushed her hands in the pockets of her dress and looked him over. "Where you come from?"

"Me?" The little green twig went in and out of his teeth with each breath. "I just come straight out the morning."

She turned and walked away. "I be glad to see you go."

He stood in front of her: he had a way of moving without a sound, of popping up in places. "I be sorry to see you go, Alberta Lacy."

She studied him before she answered: tall, not too big or heavy, and black (no other blood but his own in him, she thought). He was dressed nice—a leather jacket with fringe on the sleeves, a red plaid shirt, and new blue denim pants. "How you know what I'm called?" she asked him politely.

He grinned, and his teeth were white and perfect. "I done seen it in the fire," he said. "I done seen it in the fire and I read it clear: Alberta Lacy."

She frowned. "I don't see as how I understand."

He blew the little green twig out of his mouth. "I might could be seeing you again real soon, Alberta Lacy." Then he slipped around the tree like the last trail of night shadow and disappeared.

Alberta stood listening: only the birds and the insects and the wind. Then everything got quiet, and the sun was shining white all around, and she climbed down the slope to the field.

A little field—just a strip of cotton tucked in between two ridges. Her father and her two biggest brothers had planted it with half a morning's work, and they hadn't gone back to tend it once. They didn't even seem to remember it: whatever work they did was in the older fields closer to home. So Alberta had taken it over. Sometimes she brought along the twins: Sidney and Silvia; they were seven: young enough for her to order around and big enough to be a help. But usually she couldn't find them; they were strange ones, gone out of the house for a couple of days at a time in summer, sleeping out somewhere, always sticking together. They were strange little ones and not worth trouble looking for. So most times Alberta worked with Maggie Mary Evans, who was Josh Evans's daughter and just about the only girl her age she was friendly with. From the field there'd be maybe three bales of real early stuff; and they'd split the profit. They worked all morning, pulling off the bolls and dropping them in the sacks they slung crosswise across their shoulders. They worked very slowly, so slowly that at times their hands seemed hardly to move, dozing in the heat. When it got to be noon, when they had no shadow any more, they slipped off the sacks, leaving them between the furrows, and turned to the shade to eat their lunch.

He was waiting for them there, stretched out along the ground with his head propped up on the slender trunk of a little bay tree. He winked lazily at Alberta; his eyes were big and shiny black as oil. "How you, Miss Alberta Lacy?"

Alberta looked down at him, crooking her lips. "You got nothing to do but pester me?"

"Sure I got something to do, but ain't nothing nice like this."

Alberta looked at him through half-closed lids, then sat down to the lunch.

"You hungry, mister?" Maggie Mary asked. She had stood watching, both hands jammed into the belt of her dress, and her eyes moving from one to the other with the quickness and the color of a sparrow.

The man rolled over and looked up at her. "Reckon I am."

"You can have some of our lunch," Maggie Mary said.

Crazy fool, Alberta thought, standing so close with him on the ground like that. He must can see all the way up her. And from the way he lay there, grinning, he must be enjoying it.

"That real nice," he said to Maggie Mary, and crawled over on his stomach to where the lunch bucket was.

Alberta watched his smooth, black hand reaching into the bucket and suddenly she remembered. "How you called?"

He put a piece of corn bread in his mouth, chewed it briefly, and swallowed it with a gulp. "I got three names."

"No fooling," Maggie Mary said, and giggled in her hand. "I got three names, too."

"Stanley Albert Thompson."

"That a good-sounding name," Alberta said. She began to eat her lunch quickly, her mouth too full to talk. Stanley Albert was staring at her, but she didn't raise her eyes. Then he began to sing, low, pounding time with the flat of his hand against the ground.

> "*Alberta, let you hair hang low,*
> *Alberta, let you hair hang low,*
> *I'll give you more gold than you apron can hold*
> *If you just let you hair hang low.*"

Alberta got up slowly, not looking at him. "We got work to finish."

Stanley Albert turned over so that his face was pressed in the grass and pine needles. "All you get's the muscles in you arm."

"That right." Maggie Mary nodded quickly. "That right."

"Maggie Mary," Alberta said, "iffen you don't come with me I gonna bop you so hard you land in the middle of tomorrow."

"Good-by, Mr. Stanley Albert Thompson," Maggie Mary said, but he had fallen asleep.

By the time they finished work he was gone; there wasn't even a spot in the pine needles and short grass to show where he had been.

"Ain't that the strangest thing?" Maggie Mary said.

Alberta picked up the small bucket they carried their lunch in. "I reckon not."

"Seemed like he was fixing to wait for us."

"He ain't fixing to wait for nobody, that kind." Alberta rubbed one hand across her shoulders, sighing slightly. "I got a pain fit to kill."

Maggie Mary leaned one arm against a tree and looked off across the little field where they had spent the day. "You reckon he was in here most all morning watching us?"

"Maybe." Alberta began to walk home. Maggie Mary followed slowly, her head still turned, watching the field.

"He musta spent all morning just watching."

"Nothing hard about doing that, watching us break our back out in the sun."

Maggie Mary took one long, loping step and came up with Alberta. "You reckon he coming back?"

Alberta stared full at her, head bent, chewing on her lower lip. "Maggie Mary Evans," she said, "you might could get a thought that he might be wanting you and you might could get a thought that you be wanting him—"

Maggie Mary bent down and brushed the dust off her bare feet carefully, not answering.

"You a plain crazy fool." Alberta planted both hands on her hips and bent her body forward slightly. "A plain crazy fool. You wouldn't be forgetting Jay Mastern?" Jay Mastern had gone off to Ramsey to work at the mill and never come back, but left Maggie Mary to have his baby. So one day Maggie Mary took her pa's best mule and put a blanket on it for a saddle and rode over to Blue Goose Lake, where the old woman lived who could tell her what to do. The old woman gave her medicine in a beer can: whisky and calomel and other things that were a secret. Maggie Mary took the medicine in one gulp, because it tasted so bad, waded way out into Blue Goose Lake so that the water came up to her neck, then dripping wet got up on the mule and whipped him up to a good fast pace all the way home. The baby had come off all right: there wasn't one. And Maggie Mary nearly died. It was something on to three months before she was able to do more than walk around, her arms hanging straight down and stiff and her black skin overtinged with gray.

"You wouldn't be forgetting Jay Mastern?"

"Sure," Maggie Mary said, brushing the dust off her bare feet lightly. "I clean forgot about him."

"Don't you be having nothing to do with this here Stanley Albert Thompson."

Maggie Mary began to walk again, slowly, smiling just a little bit with one corner of her mouth. "Sounds like you been thinking about him for yourself."

Alberta jammed both hands down in the pockets of her dress. "I been thinking nothing of the sort."

"Willie'll kill him."

Alberta chewed on one finger. "I reckon he could care for himself."

Maggie Mary smiled to herself softly, remembering. "I reckon he could; he's a real fine-appearing man."

"He was dressed good."

"Where you reckon he come from?" Maggie Mary asked.

Alberta shrugged. "He just come walking out of the morning fog."

That was how he came into this country: he appeared one day whistling a bird call in the woods in high summer. And he stayed on. The very first Saturday night he went down to Willie's and had four fights and won them all.

Willie's was an ordinary house made of pine slabs, older than most of the other houses, but more solid. There were two rooms: a little one where Willie lived (a heavy scrolled ironwork bed, a square oak dresser, a chest, a three-footed table, and on its cracked marble top a blue-painted mandolin without strings). And a big room: the café. Since anybody could remember, the café had been there with Willie's father or his grandfather, as long as there had been people in these parts. And that had been a long while: long before the Civil War even, runaways were settling here, knowing they'd be safe and hidden in the rough, uneven hills and the pines.

Willie had made some changes in the five or six years since his father died. He painted the counter that was the bar with varnish; that had not been a good idea: the whisky took the varnish off in a few weeks. And he painted the walls: bright blue. Then he went over them again, shaking his brush so that the walls were flecked like a mockingbird's eggs. But Willie used red to fleck—red against blue. And the mirror, gilt-edged, and hanging from a thick gold cord: that had been Willie's idea, too. He'd found it one day, lying on the shoulder alongside the state highway; it must have fallen from a truck somehow. So he took it home. It was cracked in maybe two dozen pieces. Anyone who looked into it would see his face split up into a dozen different parts, all separate. But Willie hung it right over the shelves where he kept his whisky and set one of the kerosene lamps in front of it so that the light should reflect yellow-bright from all the pieces. One of them fell out (so that Willie had to glue it back with flour and water) the night Stanley Albert had his fourth fight, which he won like the other three. Not a man in the country would stand up like that, because fighting at Willie's on Saturday night is a rough affair with razors or knives, or bottles.

Not a man in the country could have matched the way Stanley Albert fought that night, his shirt off, and his black body shining with sweat; the muscles along his neck and shoulders twisting like grass snakes. There wasn't a finer-looking man and there wasn't a better: he proved that.

The first three fights were real orderly affairs. Everybody could see what was coming minutes ahead, and Willie got the two of them out in the yard before they got at each other. And everybody who was sober enough to walk went out on the porch and watched Stanley Albert pound first Ran Carey's and then Henry Johnson's head up and down in the dust. Alberta sat on the porch (Willie had brought her a chair from inside) and watched Stanley Albert roll around the dust of the yard and didn't even blink an eye, not even during the third fight when Tim Evans, who was Maggie Mary's brother, pulled a razor. The razor got Stanley Albert all down one cheek, but Tim didn't have any teeth left and one side of his face got punched in so that it looked peculiar always afterward. Maggie Mary went running down into the yard, not bothering with her brother, to press her finger up against the little cut across Stanley Albert's cheek.

The fourth fight came up so suddenly nobody had time
hardly to get out of the way: Joe Turner got one arm
hooked around Stanley Albert's neck from behind. There
wasn't any reason for it, except maybe that Joe was so drunk
he didn't see who he had and that once there's been a couple
of fights there's always more. Stanley Albert swung a bottle
over his shoulder to break the hold and then nobody could
see exactly what was happening: they were trying so hard to
get clear. Willie pulled Alberta over the bar and pushed her
down behind it and crouched alongside her, grinning. "That
some fighter." And when it was all over they stood up again;
first thing they saw was Joe Turner down on the floor and
Stanley Albert leaning on a chair with Maggie dabbing at a
cut on his hand with the edge of her petticoat.

He got a reputation from that Saturday night, and everybody was polite to him, and he could have had just about any
of the girls he wanted. But he didn't seem to want them; at
least he never took to coming to the houses to see them or to
taking them home from Willie's. Maggie Mary Evans swore
up and down that he had got her one day when she was
fishing in Scanos River, but nobody paid her much attention.
She liked to make up stories that way.

He had a little house in a valley to the east. Some boys who
had gone out to shoot a cow for Christmas meat said they saw
it. But they didn't go close even if there was three of them
with a shotgun while Stanley Albert only carried a razor.
Usually people only saw him on Saturday nights, and after
a while they got used to him, though none of the men ever
got to be friendly with him. There wasn't any mistaking the
way the girls watched him. But after four or five Saturdays,
by the time the summer was over, everybody expected him
and waited for him, the way you'd wait for a storm to come or
a freeze: not liking it, but not being able to do anything
either. That's the way it went along: he'd buy his food for the
coming week at Luther's Store, and then he'd come next door
to Willie's.

He never stood up at the counter that was the bar. He'd
take his glass and walk over to a table and sit down, and pull
out a little bottle from his pocket, and add white lightning to
the whisky. There wasn't anything could insult Willie more.

He made the whisky and it was the best stuff in the county. He even had some customers drive clear out from Montgomery to buy some of his corn, and, being good stuff, there wasn't any call to add anything: it had enough kick of its own; raw and stinging to the throat. It was good stuff; nobody added anything to it—except Stanley Albert Thompson, while Willie looked at him and said things under his breath. But nothing ever came of it, because everybody remembered how good a job Stanley Albert had done the first night he came.

Stanley Albert always had money, enough of it to pay for the groceries and all the whisky he wanted. There was always the sound of silver jingling in his trouser pocket. Everybody could hear that. Once when Willie was standing behind the bar, shuffling a pack of cards with a wide fancy twirl—just for amusement—Stanley Albert, who had had a couple of drinks and was feeling especially good, got up and pulled a handful of coins out of his pocket. He began to shuffle them through the air, the way Willie had done with the cards. Stanley Albert's black hands flipped the coins back and forth, faster and faster, until there was a solid silver ring hanging and shining in the air. Then Stanley Albert let one of his hands drop to his side and the silver ring poured back into the other hand and disappeared with a little clinking sound. And he dropped the money into his pocket with a short quick laugh.

That was the way Stanley Albert used his money: he had fun with it. Only thing, one night when Stanley Albert had had maybe a bit too much and sat dozing at his table, Morris Henry slipped a hand into the pocket. He wouldn't have ever dared to do that if Stanley Albert hadn't been dozing, leaning back in his chair, the bottle of white lightning empty in one hand. And Morris Henry slipped his little hand in the pocket and felt all around carefully. Then he turned his head slowly in a circle, looking at everybody in the room. He was a little black monkey Negro and his eyes were shiny and flat as mirrors. He slipped his hand back and scurried out into the yard and hid in the blackberry bushes. He wouldn't move until morning came; he just sat there, chewing on his little black fingers with his wide flaring yellow teeth. Anybody who wanted to know what was happening had to go out there and ask him. And ever afterwards Morris Henry swore that there

hadn't been anything at all in Stanley Albert Thompson's
pocket. But then everybody knew Morris Henry was crazy
because just a few minutes later when Stanley Albert woke
up and walked across to the bar, the change jingled in the
pocket and he laid five quarters on the counter. And the
money was good enough because Willie bounced it on the
counter and it gave the clear ring of new silver.

Stanley Albert had money all right and he spent it; there
wasn't anything short about him. He'd buy drinks for anybody who'd come over to his table; the only ones who came
were the girls. And he didn't seem to care how much they
drank. He'd just sit there, leaning way back in his chair, grinning, his teeth white and big behind his black lips, and matching them drink for drink, and every now and then running his
eye up and down their length just to let them know he was
appreciating their figures. Most often it was Maggie Mary
who would be sitting there, warning all the other girls away
with a little slanting of her eyes when they got near. And
sometimes he'd sing a song: a song about whisky that would
make everyone forget they didn't like him and laugh; or a
song about poor boys who were going to be hanged in the
morning. He had a good voice, strong and clear, and he
pounded time with the flat of his hand on the table. And he'd
always be looking at Alberta when he was singing until she'd
get up, holding her head high and stiff, and march over to
where Willie was and take hold of his arm real sweet and
smile at him. And Willie would give Stanley Albert a quick
mean look and then pour her a drink of his best whisky.

Stanley Albert had a watch, a big heavy gold one, round
almost as a tomato, that would strike the hours. (That was
how you could tell he was around sometimes—hearing his
watch strike.) It was attached to a broad black ribbon and
sometimes he held it up, let it swing before the eyes of whatever girl it happened to be at the time, let it swing slowly
back and forth, up and down, so that her head moved with it.
He had a ring too, on his right little finger: a white-colored
band with a stone big as a chip of second coal and dark green.
And when he fought, the first time he came into Willie's, the
ring cut the same as a razor in his hand; it was maybe a little
more messy, because its edges were jagged.

Those were two things—the watch and the ring—that must have cost more than all the money around here in a year. That was why all the women liked him so; they kept thinking of the nice things he could give them if he got interested. And that was why the men hated him. Things can go as smooth as glass if everybody's got about the same things and the same amount of money knocking around in a jean pocket on Saturday night. But when they don't, things begin happening. It would have been simpler maybe if they could have fought Stanley Albert Thompson, but there wasn't any man keen to fight him. That was how they started fighting each other. A feud that nobody'd paid any mind to for eight or ten years started up again.

It began one Sunday morning along toward dawn when everyone was feeling tired and leaving Willie's. Stanley Albert had gone out first and was sitting aside the porch railing. Jim Mastern was standing on the lowest step not moving, just staring across the fields, not being able to see anything in the dark, except maybe the bright-colored patterns the whisky set shooting starwise before his eyes. And Randall Stevens was standing in the doorway, looking down at his own foot, which he kept moving in a little circle around and around on the floor boards. And Stanley Albert was looking hard at him. Randall Stevens didn't lift his head; he just had his razor out and was across the porch in one minute, bringing down his arm in a sweeping motion to get at Jim Mastern's neck. But he was too drunk to aim very straight and he missed; but he did cut the ear away so that it fell on the steps. Jim Mastern was off like a bat in the daylight, running fast, crashing into things, holding one hand to the side of his head. And Randall Stevens folded up the razor and slipped it back in his pocket and walked off slowly, his head bent over, as if he was sleepy. There wasn't any more sense to it than that; but it started the feud again.

Stanley Albert swung his legs over the railing and stretched himself and yawned. Nobody noticed except Alberta, they were so busy listening to the way Jim Mastern was screaming and running across the fields, and watching Randall Stevens march off, solemnly, like a priest.

And the next night Randall Stevens tumbled down the

steps of his cabin with his head full of scatter shot. It was a
Monday night in November. His mother came out to see and
stepped square on him, and his blood spattered on the hoar-
frost. Randall Stevens had six brothers, and the next night
they rode their lanky burred horses five miles south and tried
to set fire to the Mastern house. That was the beginning; the
fighting kept up, off and on, all through the winter. The
sheriff from Gloverston came down to investigate. He came
driving down the road in the new shiny white state police
patrol car—the only one in the county—stopped in Willie's
Café for a drink and went back taking two gallons of home
brew with him. That wasn't exactly right, maybe, seeing that
he had taken an oath to uphold the law; but he couldn't have
done much, except get killed. And that was certain.

The Stevenses and their friends took to coming to Willie's
on Friday nights; the Masterns kept on coming on Saturday.
That just made two nights Willie had to keep the place open
and the lamps filled with kerosene; the crowd was smaller;
shotguns were leaning against the wall.

That's the way it went all winter. Everybody got on one
side or the other—everybody except Stanley Albert Thompson.
They both wanted him: they had seen what he could do in
a fight. But Stanley Albert took to coming a night all by
himself: Sunday night, and Willie had to light all the lamps
for just him and stand behind the counter and watch him sit
at the table adding lightning to the whisky.

Once along toward the end of February when Cy Mastern
was killed and the roof of his house started burning with pine
knots tossed from the ground, Stanley Albert was standing just
on the rim of the light, watching. He helped the Masterns
carry water, but Ed Stevens, who was hiding up in top of a
pine to watch, swore that the water was like kerosene in his
hands. Wherever he'd toss a bucketful, the fire would shoot
up, brighter and hotter than before.

By March the frosts stopped, and there weren't any more
cold winds. The farmers came out every noon, solemnly, and
laid their hands on the bare ground to see if it was time to
put in their earliest corn and potatoes. But the ground stayed
cold a long time that year so that there wasn't any plowing
until near May. All during that time from March till May

there wasn't anything doing; that was the worst time for the fighting. In the winter your hand shakes so with the cold that you aren't much good with a gun or knife. But by March the air is warmer and you don't have any work to get you tired, so you spend all the time thinking.

That spring things got bad. There wasn't a crowd any more at Willie's though he kept the place open and the lights on for the three nights of the week-end. Neither the Stevenses nor the Masterns would come; they were too easy targets in a house with wall lamps burning. And on Sunday night the only person who ever came was Stanley Albert Thompson. He'd sit and drink his whisky and lightning and maybe sing a song or two for the girls who came over to see him. By the end of April that was changed too. He finally got himself the girl he wanted; the one he'd been waiting around nearly all winter for. And his courting was like this:

Thomas Henry Lacy and his sons, Luke and Tom, had gone for a walk, spoiling for a fight. They hadn't seen anything all evening, just some of the cows that had gone wild and went crashing away through the blueberry bushes. Alberta had taken herself along with them, since she was nearly as good as a man in a fight. They had been on the move all night but keeping in the range of a couple of miles and on the one side of the Scanos River. They were for Stevens and there was no telling what sort of affair the Masterns had rigged up on their ground. They rested for a while on the bluff of the river. Tom had some bread in his pocket and they ate it there, wondering if there was anybody in the laurels across the river just waiting for them to show themselves. Then they walked on again, not saying very much, seeing nothing but the moon flat against the sky and its light shiny on the heavy dew.

Alberta didn't particularly care when they left her behind. She turned her head to listen to the plaintive gargling call of a night quail, and when she looked again her father and the boys were gone. She knew where she was: on the second ridge away from home. There was just the big high ridge there to the left. The house was maybe twenty minutes away, but a hard walk, and Alberta was tired. She'd been washing all day, trying to make the clear brook water carry off the dirt and grease from the clothes, her mother standing behind her, yelling at each spot that remained, her light face black almost as her husband's with temper, and her gray fuzzy hair tied into knots like a pickaninny's. The boys had spent the whole day dozing in the shed while they put a new shoe on the mule.

Alberta listened carefully; there was nothing but night noises; her father and the boys would be halfway home by now, scrambling down the rain-washed sides of the ridge. For a moment she considered following them. "Ain't no raving rush, girl," she told herself aloud. The night was cool, but there wasn't any wind. With her bare feet she felt the dry pine needles, then sat down on them, propping her back against a tree. She slipped the razor from the cord around her neck and held it open loosely in the palm of her hand; then she fell asleep.

She woke when the singing started, opening her eyes but not moving. The moon was right overhead, shining down so that the trunks of the pines stuck straight up out of the white shiny ground. There wasn't a man could hide behind a pine, yet she didn't see him. Only the singing going round and round her.

> *"Alberta, what's on you mind,*
> *Alberta, why you treat me so unkind?*
> *You keep me worried; you keep me blue*
> *All the time,*
> *Alberta, why you treat me so unkind?"*

She pushed herself up to a sitting position, still looking straight ahead, not following the song around and around. She let the hand that held the razor fall in her lap, so that the moon struck on the blade.

> *"Alberta, why you treat me so unkind?"*

Nothing grows under pines, not much grass even, not any bushes big enough to hide a man. Only pine trees, like black matches stuck in the moonlight. Black like matches, and thin like matches. There wasn't a man could hide behind a pine under a bright moon. There wasn't a man could pass a bright open space and not be seen.

> *"Alberta, let you hair hang low,*
> *Alberta, let you hair hang low.*
> *I'll give you more gold*
> *Than you apron can hold."*

"That ain't a very nice song," she said.

> *"I'll give you more gold*
> *Than you apron can hold."*

She lifted her right hand and turned the razor's edge slowly in the light. "I got silver of my own right here," she said. "That enough for me."

The song went round in a circle, round and round, weaving in and out of the pines, passing invisible across the open moon-filled spaces.

> *"Alberta, let you hair hang low,*
> *I'll give you more gold*
> *Than you apron can hold*
> *If you just let you hair hang low."*

There wasn't a man alive could do that. Go round and round.

> *"Alberta, why you treat me so unkind?"*

Round and round, in and out the thin black trees. Alberta stood up, following the sound, turning on her heel.

> *"You keep me worried; you keep me blue*
> *All the time."*

"I plain confused," she said. "I don't reckon I understand."

> *"I'll give you more gold*
> *Than you apron can hold."*

"I ain't got no apron," she said.

> *"Alberta, let you hair hang low,*
> *Just let you hair hang low."*

The song stopped and Stanley Albert Thompson came
right out of a patch of bright moon ground, where there
were only brown pine needles.

Alberta forgot she was tired; the moon-spotted ground
rolled past her feet like the moon in the sky—effortless.
She recognized the country they passed through: Blue
Goose Lake, Scanos River, and the steeper rough ground of
the north part of the country, toward the Tennessee border.
It was a far piece to walk and she wondered at the lightness
of her feet. By moonset they had got there—the cabin that the
boys had seen one day while they were hunting cows. She
hesitated a little then, not afraid, not reluctant, but just not
sure how to go on. Stanley Albert Thompson had been holding her hand all evening; he still held it. Right at the beginning when he had first taken her along with him, she'd shook
her head, no, she could walk; no man needed to lead her. But
he'd grinned at her, and shook his head, imitating her gesture, so that the moon sparkled on his black curly hair, and
his black broad forehead, and he took her hand and led her
so that the miles seemed nothing and the hours like smooth
water.

He showed her the cabin, from the outside first: mustard
color, trimmed with white, like the cabins the railroad company builds. One room with high peaked roof.

"A real fine house," she said. "A real fine house. You work
for the railroad?"

"No."

He took her inside. "You light with candles," she said.

"I ain't ever been able to stand the smell of lamps," he said.

"But it's a real nice house. I might could learn to like it."

"No might could about it." He smoothed the cloth on
the table with his fingers. "You going to like it."

She bent her head and looked at him through her eye-
lashes. "Now I don't rightly know. Seems as how I don't
know you."

"Sure you do," he said. "I'm standing right here."

"Seems as how I don't know nothing. You might could have a dozen girls all over this here state."

"I reckon there's a dozen," he said.

She glared at him, hands on hips. "You old fool jackass," she said. "I reckon you can just keep everything."

He jammed his hands into the back pockets of his denim pants and bent backward staring at the ceiling.

"Ain't you gonna try to stop me?"

"Nuh-uh."

She leaned against the doorjamb and twisted her neck to look at him. "Ain't you sorry I going?"

"Sure." He was still staring upward at the ceiling with its four crossed beams. "Sure, I real sorry."

"I don't see as how I could stay though."

"Sure you could." He did not look at her.

"I don't see as how. You ain't give me none of the things you said."

"You a driving woman," he said, and grinned, his mouth wide and white in the dark of his face.

Then he sat down at the table. There were five candles there, stuck in bottles, but only one was lighted, the one in the center. Wax had run all down the side of the candle and down the bottle in little round blobs, nubby like gravel. He picked one off, dirty white between his black fingers. He rolled it slowly between his flat palms, back and forth. Then he flipped it toward Alberta. It flashed silvery through the circle of lamplight and thudded against her skirt. She bent forward to pick it up: a coin, new silver. As she bent there, another one struck her shoulder, and another. Stanley Albert Thompson sat at the table, grinning and tossing the coins to her, until she had filled both pockets of her dress.

He pushed the candle away from him. "You all right, I reckon, now."

She held one coin in her hands, turning it over and over.

"That ain't what you promised. I remember how you came and sang:

> 'I'll give you more gold
> Than you apron can hold.'"

"Sure," he said and lifted a single eyebrow, very high. "I can do that all right, iffen you want it. I reckon I can do that."

She stood for a moment studying him. And Stanley Albert Thompson, from where he still sat at the table, curled up one corner of his mouth.

And very slowly Alberta began to smile. "I might could like it here," she said. "If you was real nice."

He got up then and rubbed her cheek very gently with his first finger. "I might could do that," he said. "I don't reckon it would be too heavy a thing to do."

The candle was on the table to one side. It caught the brightness of Alberta's eyes as she stood smiling at Stanley Albert Thompson. The steady yellow light threw her shadow over his body, a dark shadow that reached to his chin. His own shadow was on the wall behind. She glanced at it over his shoulder and giggled. "You better do something about your shadow there, Mr. Thompson. That there is a ugly shadow, sure."

He turned his head and glanced at it briefly. "Reckon so," he said.

It was an ugly shadow, sure. Alberta looked at Stanley Albert Thompson and shook her head. "I can't hardly believe it," she said. "You a right pretty man."

He grinned at her and shook himself so that the shadow on the wall spun around in a wild turn.

"I don't reckon you can do anything about it?"

"No," he said briefly. "I can't go changing my shadow." He hunched his back so that the figure on the wall seemed to jump up and down in anger.

She stepped over to him, putting her hands behind her, leaning backward to see his face. "If he don't do any more than dance on a wall, I ain't complaining."

Stanley Albert stood looking down at her, looking down the length of his face at her, and rocking slowly back and forth on his heels. "No," he said. "He ain't gonna do more than wiggle around the wall sometimes. But you can bet I am."

The coins weighed down the pockets of her dress, and

his hands were warm against her skin. "I reckon I'm satisfied," she said.

That was the way it began. That was the courting. The woman was young and attractive and strong. The man could give her whatever she wanted. There were other courtings like that in this country. Every season there were courtings like that.

People would see them around sometimes; or sometimes they'd only hear them when they were still far off. Sometimes it would be Stanley Albert Thompson singing:

> *"Alberta, let you hair hang low,*
> *Alberta, let you hair hang low.*
> *I'll give you more gold*
> *Than you apron can hold*
> *If you just let you hair hang low."*

He had a strong voice. It could carry far in a quiet day or night. And if any of the people heard it, they'd turn and look at each other and nod their heads toward it, not saying anything, but just being sure that everyone was listening. And whenever Willie heard it, he'd close his eyes for a minute, seeing Alberta; and then he'd rub his hands all over his little black kinky head and whistle: "Euuuu," which meant that he was very, very sorry she had left him.

And sometimes all you could hear of them would be the chiming of Stanley Albert's watch every quarter-hour. One night that August, when the moon was heavy and hot and low, Maggie Mary was out walking with Jack Belden. She heard the clear high chime and remembered the nights at Willie's and the dangling gold watch. And she turned to Jack Belden, who had just got her comfortable in one arm, and jammed her fingers in his eyes and ran off after the sound. She didn't find them; and it wouldn't have much mattered if she had. Stanley Albert was much too gone on Alberta to notice any other woman in more than a passing appraising way.

And sometimes people would come on them walking alone, arms around each other's waist; or sitting in a shady spot during the day's heat, his head on her lap and both of them

dozing and smiling a little. And everybody who saw them
would turn around and get out of there fast; but neither of
them turned a head or looked up: there might not have been
anyone there.

And then every night they'd go down to Willie's. The first
night they came—it was on a Thursday—the place was closed
up tight. There wasn't ever anybody came on Thursday.
Stanley Albert went around back to where Willie lived and
pounded on the door, and when Willie didn't answer he went
around to the front again where Alberta was waiting on the
steps and kicked in the front panel of the wood door. Willie
came scuttling out, his eyes round and bewildered like a suck-
ling's and saw them sitting at one of the tables drinking his
home brew, only first putting lightning into it. After that they
came every night, just them. It was all most people could do
to afford a drink on Saturday or the week-end, but some of
them would walk over to Willie's just to look at Stanley
Albert and Alberta sitting there. They'd stand at the windows
and look in, sweating in the hot summer nights and looking.
Maybe a few of them would still be there waiting when
Stanley and Alberta got ready to go, along toward morning.

That's what they did every single night of the year or
so they were together. If they fell asleep, Willie would just
have to stand waiting. They'd go out with their arms around
each other's waist, staggering some, but not falling. And
an hour or so later, people who were going out before dawn
to get a little work done in the cool would see them clear
over on the other side of the county, at Goose Lake, maybe,
a good three hours' walk for a man cold sober. Willie had his
own version of how they got around. They just picked up
their feet, he said, and went sliding off down the winds. Once,
he said, when they were sitting over on the bench against
the wall, Stanley Albert flat on it with his head on her lap,
when the whisky made the man in him come up sudden, so he
couldn't wait, they went straight out the window, up the air,
like a whistle sound. Willie had the broken glass to show
the next morning, if you wanted to believe him.

Willie hated them, the two of them, maybe because they
broke his glass, maybe because they made him stay up late
every single night of the week, so that he had to hold his

eyes open with his fingers, and watch them pour lightning into his very best whisky, maybe because he had wanted Alberta mighty bad himself. He'd been giving her presents— bottles of his best stuff—but he just couldn't match Stanley Albert. Those are three reasons; maybe he had others. And Maggie Mary hated them; and she had only one reason.

Once Pete Stokes shot at Stanley Albert Thompson. He hadn't wanted to: he was scared like everybody else. But Maggie Mary Evans talked him into it. She was a fine-looking girl: she could do things like that. He hid behind the privy and got a perfect bead on Stanley Albert as he came out the door. The bullet just knocked off a piece of Willie's door-frame. When Pete saw what happened he dropped the gun and began to run, jumping the rail fence and crashing face-first through the thick heavy berry bushes. Stanley Albert pursed his lips together and rubbed his hands on his chin, slow, like he was deciding what to do. Then he jumped down from the porch and went after Pete. He ran through the hackberries too; only with him it did not seem difficult: none of the crackling and crashing and waving arms. Stanley Albert just put his head down and moved his legs, and the sprays of the bushes, some of them thick as a rooster's spur, seemed to pull back and make way. Nobody saw the fight: the brave ones were too drunk to travel fast; and the sober ones didn't want to mix with a man like Stanley Albert, drunk and mad. Alberta, she just ran her hand across her mouth and then wiped it along the side of her green satin dress, yawning like she was tired. She stood listening for a while, her head cocked a little, though there wasn't anything to hear, then walked off, pulling down the dress across her hips. And the next night she and Stanley Albert were back at Willie's, and Pete never did turn up again. Willie used to swear that he ended up in the Scanos River and that if the water wasn't so yellow muddy, that if you could see to the bottom, you would see Pete lying there, along with all the others Stanley Albert had killed.

At the last it was Willie who got the idea. For a week, carefully, he put aside the coins Stanley Albert gave him. There were a lot of them, all new silver, because Stanley Albert always paid in silver. Then one morning very early, just after Stanley Albert and Alberta left, Willie melted the coins down, and using the molds he kept for his old outsized pistol, he cast four bullets.

He made a special little shelf for the pistol under the counter so that it would be near at hand. And he waited all evening, sometimes touching the heavy black handle with the tips of his fingers; and he waited, hoping that Stanley Albert would drink enough to pass out. But of course nothing like that happened. So Willie poured himself three or four fingers of his best stuff and swallowed it fast as his throat would stand, then he blinked his little eyes fast for a second or so to clear his vision, and he reached for the gun. He got two shots over the bar, two good ones: the whole front of Stanley Albert's plaid shirt folded together and sank in, after the silver bullets went through. He got up, holding the table edge, unsteady, bending over, looking much smaller, his black skin gray-filmed and dull. His eyes were larger: they reached almost across his face—and they weren't dark any more; they were silver, two polished pieces of silver. Willie was afraid to fire again; the pistol shook where he held it in his two hands.

Then Stanley Albert walked out, not unsteady any more, but bent over the hole in his chest, walked out slowly with his eyes shining like flat metal, Alberta a few steps behind. They passed right in front of Willie, who still hadn't moved; his face was stiff with fear. Quietly, smoothly, in a single motion, almost without interrupting her step, Alberta picked up a bottle (the same one from which he had poured his drink moments before) and swung it against Willie's head. He slipped down in a quiet little heap, his legs folded under him, his black kinky head on top. But his idea had worked: over by Stanley Albert's chair there was a black pool of blood.

All that was maybe eight or ten years ago. People don't see them any more—Stanley and Alberta. They don't think much about them, except when something goes wrong— like weevils getting in the cotton, or Willie's burning down and Willie inside it—then they begin to think that those two had a hand in it. Brad Tedrow swore that he had seen Stanley Albert that night, just for a second, standing on the edge of the circle of light, with a burning faggot in his hand. And the next morning Brad went back to look, knowing that your eyes play tricks at night in firelight; he went back to look for footprints or some sign. All he found was a burnt-out stick of pine wood that anybody could have dropped.

And kids sometimes think they hear the jingle of silver in Stanley Albert's pocket, or the sound of his watch. And when women talk—when there's been a miscarriage or a stillbirth—they remember and whisper together.

And they all wonder if that's not the sort of work they do, the two of them. Maybe so; maybe not. The people themselves are not too sure. They don't see them around any more.

This first story by a very young writer is a savagely
ironic study of character with an original twist. The
true characters of its cast are revealed unintentionally
by its narrator. Miss Rich's people might live next
door, or might have lived next door to your great-
grandparents.

My Sister's Marriage

IIIIIIIIIIIIIII CYNTHIA MARSHALL RICH IIIIIIIIIIIIIII

When my mother died she left just Olive and me to
take care of Father. Yesterday when I burned the package of
Olive's letters that left only me. I know that you'll side with
my sister in all of this because you're only outsiders, and
strangers can afford to sympathize with young love, and with
whatever sounds daring and romantic, without thinking what
it does to all the other people involved. I don't want you to
hate my sister—I don't hate her—but I do want you to see
that we're happier this way, Father and I, and as for Olive,
she made her choice.

But if you weren't strangers, all of you, I wouldn't be able
to tell you about this. "Keep yourself to yourself," my father
has always said. "If you ever have worries, Sarah Ann, you
come to me and don't go sharing your problems around town."
And that's what I've always done. So if I knew you I certainly
wouldn't ever tell you about Olive throwing the hairbrush,
or about finding the letters buried in the back of the drawer.

I don't know what made Olive the way she is. We grew up
together like twins—there were people who thought we were
—and every morning before we went to school she plaited
my hair and I plaited hers before the same mirror, in the same

little twist of ribbons and braids behind our heads. We wore the same dresses and there was never a stain on the hem or a rip in our stockings to say to a stranger that we had lost our mother. And although we have never been well-to-do—my father is a doctor and his patients often can't pay—I know that there are people here in Conkling today who think we're rich, just because of little things like candlelight at dinner and my father's cigarette holder and the piano lessons that Olive and I had and the reproduction of *The Anatomy Lesson* that hangs above the mantelpiece instead of botanical prints. "You don't have to be rich to be a gentleman," my father says, "or to live like one."

My father is a gentleman and he raised Olive and myself as ladies. I can hear you laughing, because people like to make fun of words like "gentleman" and "lady," but they are words with ideals and standards behind them, and I hope that I will always hold to those ideals as my father taught me to. If Olive has renounced them, at least we did all we could.

Perhaps the reason that I can't understand Olive is that I have never been in love. I know that if I had ever fallen in love it would not have been, like Olive, at first sight but only after a long acquaintance. My father knew my mother for seven years before he proposed—it is much the safest way. Nowadays people make fun of that too, and the magazines are full of stories about people meeting in the moonlight and marrying the next morning, but if you read those stories you know that they are not the sort of people you would want to be like.

Even today Olive couldn't deny that we had a happy childhood. She used to be very proud of being the lady of the house, of sitting across the candlelight from my father at dinner like a little wife. Sometimes my father would hold his carving knife poised above the roast to stand smiling at her and say: "Olive, every day you remind me more of your mother."

I think that although she liked the smile, she minded the compliment, because she didn't like to hear about Mother. Once when my father spoke of her she said: "Papa, you're missing Mother again. I can't bear it when you miss Mother. Don't I take care of you all right? Don't I make things happy for you?" It wasn't that she hadn't loved Mother but that she wanted my father to be completely happy.

To tell the truth, it was Olive Father loved best. There was a time when I couldn't have said that, it would have hurt me too much. Taking care of our father was like playing a long game of "let's pretend," and when little girls play family nobody wants to be the children. I thought it wasn't fair, just because Olive was three years older, that she should always be the mother. I wanted to sit opposite my father at dinner and have him smile at me like that.

I was glad when Olive first began walking out with young men in the summer evenings. Then I would make lemonade for my father ("Is it as good as Olive's?") and we would sit out on the screened porch together watching the fireflies. I asked him about the patients he had seen that day, trying to think of questions as intelligent as Olive's. I knew that he was missing her and frowning into the long twilight for the swing of her white skirts. When she came up the steps he said, "I missed my housewife tonight," just as though I hadn't made the lemonade right after all. She knew, too, that it wasn't the same for him in the evenings without her and for a while, instead of going out, she brought the young men to the house. But soon she stopped even that ("I never realized how silly and shallow they were until I saw them with Papa," she said. "I was ashamed to have him talk to them"). I know that he was glad, and when my turn came I didn't want to go out because I hated leaving them alone together. It all seems a very long time ago. I used to hate it when Olive "mothered" me. Now I feel a little like Olive's mother, and she is like my rebellious child.

In spite of everything, I loved Olive. When we were children we used to play together. The other children disliked us because we talked like grownups and didn't like to get dirty, but we were happy playing by ourselves on the front lawn where my father, if he were home, could watch us from his study window. So it wasn't surprising that when we grew older we were still best friends. I loved Olive and I see now how she took advantage of that love. Sometimes I think she felt that if she was to betray my father she wanted me to betray him too.

I still believe that it all began, not really with Mr. Dixon, but with the foreign stamps. She didn't see many of them, those years after high school when she was working in the post office, because not very many people in Conkling have friends abroad, but the ones she saw—and even the postmarks from Chicago or California—made her dream. She told her dreams to Father, and of course he understood and said that perhaps some summer we could take a trip to New England as far as Boston. My father hasn't lived in Conkling all of his life. He went to Harvard, and that is one reason he is different from the other men here. He is a scholar and not bound to provincial ideas. People here respect him and come to him for advice.

Olive wasn't satisfied and she began to rebel. Even she admitted that there wasn't anything for her to rebel against. She told me about it, sitting on the window sill in her long white nightgown, braiding and unbraiding the hair that she had never cut.

"It's not, don't you see, that I don't love Father. And it certainly isn't that I'm not happy here. But what I mean is, how can I ever know whether or not I'm really happy here unless I go somewhere else? When you graduate from school you'll feel the same way. You'll want—you'll want to know."

"I like it here," I said from the darkness of the room, but she didn't hear me.

"You know what I'm going to do, Sarah Ann? Do you know what I'm going to do? I'm going to save some money and go on a little trip—it wouldn't have to be expensive, I could go by bus—and I'll just see things, and then maybe I'll know."

"Father promised he'd take us to New England."

"No," said Olive, "no, you don't understand. Anyhow, I'll save the money."

And still she wasn't satisfied. She began to read. Olive and I always did well in school, and our names were called out for Special Recognition on Class Day. Miss Singleton wanted Olive to go to drama school after she played the part of Miranda in *The Tempest,* but my father talked to her, and when he told her what an actress' life is like she realized it wasn't what she wanted. Aside from books for school, though, we never read very much. We didn't need to because my father has read everything you've heard of, and people in town have said that talking to him about anything is better than reading three books.

Still, Olive decided to read. She would choose a book from my father's library and go into the kitchen, where the air was still heavy and hot from dinner, and sit on the very edge of the tall, hard three-legged stool. She had an idea that if she sat in a comfortable chair in the parlor she would not be attentive or would skip the difficult passages. So she would sit like that for hours, under the hard light of the unshaded bulb that hangs from the ceiling, until her arms ached from holding the book.

"What do you want to find out about?" my father would ask.

"Nothing," Olive said. "I'm just reading."

My father hates evasion.

"Now, Olive, nobody reads without a purpose. If you're interested in something, maybe I can help you. I might even know something about it myself."

When she came into our bedroom she threw the book on the quilt and said: "Why does he have to pry, Sarah Ann? It's so simple—just wanting to read a book. Why does he have to make a fuss about it as though I were trying to hide something from him?"

That was the first time that I felt a little like Olive's mother.

"But he's only taking an interest," I said. "He just wants us to share things with him. Lots of fathers wouldn't even care. You don't know how lucky we are."

"You don't understand, Sarah Ann. You're too young to understand."

"Of course I understand," I said shortly. "Only I've outgrown feeling like that."

It was true. When I was a little girl I wrote something on a piece of paper, something that didn't matter much, but it mattered to me because it was a private thought. My father came into my room and saw me shove the paper under the blotter, and he wanted me to show it to him. So I quickly said, "No, it's private. I wrote it to myself, I didn't write it to be seen," but he said he wanted to see it. And I said, "No, no, no, it was silly anyway," and he said, "Sarah Ann, nothing you have to say would seem silly to me, you never give me credit for understanding, I can understand a great deal," but I said it wasn't just him, really it wasn't, because I hadn't written it for anyone at all to see. Then he was all sad and hurt and said this wasn't a family where we keep things hidden and there I was hiding this from him. I heard his voice, and it went on and on, and he said I had no faith in him and that I shouldn't keep things from him—and I said it wasn't anything big or special, it was just some silly nonsense, but if it was nonsense, he said, why wouldn't I let him read it, since it would make him happy? And I cried and cried, because it was only a very little piece of paper and why did he have to see it anyway, but he was very solemn and said if you held back little things soon you would be holding back bigger things and the gap would grow wider and wider. So I gave him the paper. He read it and said nothing except that I was a good girl and he couldn't see what all the fuss had been about.

Of course now I know that he was only taking an interest and I shouldn't have minded that. But I was a little girl then and minded dreadfully, and that is why I understood how Olive felt, although she was grown-up then and should have known better.

She must have understood that she was being childish, because when my father came in a few minutes later and said, "Olive, you're our little mother. We mustn't quarrel. There should be only love between us," she rose and kissed him. She told him about the book she had been reading, and he said: "Well, as it happens, I do know something about that." They sat for a long time discussing the book, and I think he loved Olive better than ever. The next evening, instead of shutting herself in the bright, hot kitchen, Olive sat with us in the cool of the parlor until bedtime, hemming a slip. And it was just as always.

But I suppose that these things really had made a difference in Olive. For we had always been alike, and I cannot imagine allowing a perfect stranger to ask me personal questions before we had even been introduced. She told me about it afterward, how he had bought a book of three-cent stamps and stayed to chat through the half-open grilled window. Suddenly he said, quite seriously: "Why do you wear your hair like that?"

"Pardon me?" said Olive.

"Why do you wear your hair like that? You ought to shake it loose around your shoulders. It must be yards long."

That is when I would have remembered—if I had forgotten —that I was a lady. I would have closed the grill, not rudely but just firmly enough to show my displeasure, and gone back to my desk. Olive told me she thought of doing that but she looked at him and knew, she said, that he didn't mean to be impolite, that he really wanted to know.

And instead she said: "I only wear it down at night."

That afternoon he walked her home from the post office.

Olive told me everything long before my father knew anything. It was the beginning of an unwholesome deceit in her. And it was nearly a week later that she told even me. By that time he was meeting her every afternoon and they took long walks together, as far as Merton's Pond, before she came home to set the dinner table.

"Only don't tell Father," she said.

"Why not?"

"I think I'm afraid of him. I don't know why. I'm afraid of what he might say."

"He won't say anything," I said. "Unless there's something wrong. And if there's something wrong, wouldn't you want to know?"

Of course, I should have told Father myself right away. But that was how she played upon my love for her.

"I'm telling you," she said, "because I want so much to share it with you. I'm so happy, Sarah Ann, and I feel so free, don't you see. We've always been so close—I've been closer to you than to Father, I think—or at least differently." She had to qualify it, you see, because it wasn't true. But it still made me happy and I promised not to tell, and I was even glad for her because, as I've told you, I've always loved Olive.

I saw them together one day when I was coming home from school. They were walking together in the rain, holding hands like school children, and when Olive saw me from a distance she dropped his hand suddenly and then just as suddenly took it again.

"Hullo!" he said when she introduced us. "She does look like you!"

I want to be fair and honest with you—it is Olive's dishonesty that still shocks me—and so I will say that I liked Mr. Dixon that day. But I thought even then how different he was from my father, and that should have warned me. He was a big man with a square face and sun-bleached hair. I could see a glimpse of his bright, speckled tie under his tan raincoat, and his laugh sounded warm and easy in the rain. I liked him, I suppose, for the very things I should have distrusted in him. I liked his ease and the way that he accepted me immediately, spontaneously and freely, without waiting—waiting for whatever people wait for when they hold themselves back (as I should have done) to find out more about you. I could almost understand what had made Olive, after five minutes, tell him how she wore her hair at night.

I am glad, at least, that I begged Olive to tell my father about him. I couldn't understand why at first she refused. I think now that she was afraid of seeing them together, that she was afraid of seeing the difference. I have told you that my father is a gentleman. Even now you must be able to tell what sort of man Mr. Dixon was. My father knew at once, without even meeting him.

The weeks had passed and Olive told me that Mr. Dixon's business was completed but that his vacation was coming and he planned to spend it in Conkling. She said she would tell my father.

We were sitting on the porch after dinner. The evening had just begun to thicken and some children had wandered down the road, playing a game of pirates at the very edge of our lawn. One of them had a long paper sword and the others were waving tall sticks, and they were screaming. My father had to raise his voice to be heard.

"So this man whom you have been seeing behind my back is a traveling salesman for Miracle-wear soles."

"Surrender in the name of the King."

"I am more than surprised at you, Olive. That hardly

sounds like the kind of man you would want to be associated
with."

"Why not?" said Olive. "Why not?"

"It's notorious, my dear. Men like that have no respect for
a girl. They'll flatter her with slick words but it doesn't mean
anything. Just take my word for it, dear. It may seem hard,
but I know the world."

"Fight to the death! Fight to the death!"

"I can't hear you, my dear. Sarah Ann, ask those children to
play their games somewhere else."

I went down the steps and across the lawn.

"Doctor Landis is trying to rest after a long day," I explained. They nodded and vanished down the dusky road,
brandishing their silent swords.

"I am saying nothing of the extraordinary manner of your
meeting, not even of the deceitful way in which he has carried on this—friendship."

It was dark on the porch. I switched on the yellow overhead light, and the three of us blinked for a moment, redis-
covering each other as the shadows leaped back.

"The cheapness of it is so apparent it amazes me that even
in your innocence of the world——"

My father was fitting a cigarette into its black holder. He
turned it slowly to and fro until it was firm before he struck
a match and lit it. It is beautiful to watch him do even the
most trivial things. He is always in control of himself and he
never makes a useless gesture or thinks a useless thought. If
you met him you might believe at first that he was totally
relaxed, but because I have lived with him so long I know
that there is at all times a tension controlling his body; you
can feel it when you touch his hand. Tension, I think, is the
wrong word. It is rather a self-awareness, as though not a
muscle contracted without his conscious knowledge.

"You know it very well yourself, Olive. Could anything
but shame have kept you from bringing this man to your
home?"

His voice is like the way he moves. It is clear and considered and each word exists by itself. However common it
may be, when he speaks it, it has become his, it has dignity
because he has chosen it.

"Father, all I ask is that you'll have him here—that you will meet him. Surely that's not too much to ask before you—judge him."

Olive sat on the step at my father's feet. Her hands had been moving across her skirt, smoothing the folds over her knees, but when she spoke she clasped them tightly in her lap. She was trying to speak as he spoke, in that calm, certain voice, but it was a poor imitation.

"I'm afraid that it is too much to ask, Olive. I have seen too many of his kind to take any interest in seeing another."

"I think you should see him, Father." She spoke very softly. "I think I am in love with him."

"Olive!" I said. I had known it all along, of course, but when she spoke it, in that voice trying so childishly to sound sure, I knew its absurdity. How could she say it after Father had made it so clear? As soon as he had repeated after her, "A salesman for Miracle-wear soles," even the inflections of his voice showed me that it was ludicrous; I realized what I had known all along, the cheapness of it all for Olive—for Olive with her ideals.

I looked across at my father but he had not stirred. The moths brushed their wings against the light bulb. He flicked a long gray ash.

"Don't use that word lightly, Olive," he said. "That is a sacred word. Love is the word for what I felt for your mother —what I hope you feel for me and for your sister. You mustn't confuse it with innocent infatuation."

"But I do love him—how can you know? How can you know anything about it? I do love him." Her voice was shrill and not pleasant.

"Olive," said my father. "I must ask you not to use that word."

She sat looking up at his face and from his chair he looked back at her. Then she rose and went into the house. He did not follow her, even with his eyes. We sat for a long time before I went over to him and took his hand. I think he had forgotten me. He started and said nothing and his hand did not acknowledge mine. I would rather he had slapped me. I left him and went into the house.

In our bedroom Olive was sitting before the dressing table

in her nightgown, brushing her hair. You mustn't think I don't love her, that I didn't love her then. As I say, we were like twins, and when I saw her reflection in the tall, gilded mirror I might have been seeing my own eyes filled with tears. I tell you, I wanted to put my arms around her, but you must see that it was for her own sake that I didn't. She had done wrong, she had deceived my father and she had made me deceive him. It would have been wicked to give her sympathy then.

"It's hard, of course, Olive," I said gently. "But you know that Father's right."

She didn't answer. She brushed her hair in long strokes and it rose on the air. She did not turn even when the doorknob rattled and my father stood in the doorway and quietly spoke her name.

"Olive," he repeated. "Of course I must ask you not to see this—this man again."

Olive turned suddenly with her dark hair whirling about her head. She hurled the silver hairbrush at my father, and in that single moment when it leaped from her hand I felt an elation I have never known before. Then I heard it clatter to the floor a few feet from where he stood, and I knew that he was unhurt and that it was I, and not Olive, who had for that single moment meant it to strike him. I longed to throw my arms about him and beg his forgiveness.

He went over and picked up the brush and gave it to Olive. Then he left the room.

"How could you, Olive?" I whispered.

She sat with the brush in her hand. Her hair had fallen all about her face and her eyes were dark and bright. The next morning at breakfast she did not speak to my father and he did not speak to her, although he sat looking at her so intensely that if I had been Olive I would have blushed. I thought, He loves her more now, this morning, than when he used to smile and say she was like Mother. I remember thinking, Why couldn't he love me like that? I would never hurt him.

Just before she left for work he went over to her and brushed her arm lightly with his hand.

"We'll talk it all over tonight, Olive," he said. "I know you will understand that this is best."

She looked down at his hand as though it were a strange animal and shook her head and hurried down the porch steps.

That night she called from a little town outside of Richmond to say that she was married. I stood behind my father in the shadowy little hallway as he spoke to her. I could hear her voice, higher-pitched than usual over the static of the wires, and I heard her say that they would come, that very evening, if he would see them.

I almost thought he hadn't understood her, his voice was so calm.

"I suppose you want my blessings. I cannot give them to deceit and cowardice. You will have to find them elsewhere if you can, my dear. If you can."

After he had replaced the receiver he still stood before the mouthpiece, talking into it.

"That she would give up all she has had—that she would stoop to a—for a—physical attraction——"

Then he turned to me. His eyes were dark.

"Why are you crying?" he said suddenly. "What are you crying for? She's made her choice. Am I crying? Do you think I would want to see her—now? If she—when she comes to see what she has done—but it's not a question of forgiveness. Even then it wouldn't be the same. She has made her choice."

He stood looking at me and I thought at first that what he saw was distasteful to him, but his voice was gentle when he spoke.

"Would you have done this to me, Sarah Ann? Would you have done it?"

"No," I said, and I was almost joyful, knowing it was true. "Oh, no."

That was a year ago. We never speak of Olive any more. At first letters used to come from her, long letters from New York and then from Chicago. Always she asked me about Father and whether he would read a letter if she wrote one. I wrote her long letters back and said that I would talk to him. But he wasn't well—even now he has to stay in bed for days at a time—and I knew that he didn't want to hear her name.

One morning he came into my room while I was writing to her. He saw me thrust the package of letters into a cubbyhole and I knew I had betrayed him again.

"Don't ally yourself with deception, Sarah Ann," he said quietly. "You did that once and you see what came of it."

"But if she writes to me—" I said. "What do you want me to do?"

He stood in the doorway in his long bathrobe. He had been in bed and his hair was slightly awry from the pillows and his face was a little pale. I have taken good care of him and he still looks young—not more than forty—but his cheekbones worry me. They are sharp and white.

"I want you to give me her letters," he said. "To burn."

"Won't you read them, Father? I know that what she did was wrong, but she sounds happy——"

I don't know what made me say that except that, you see, I did love Olive.

He stared at me and came into the room.

"And you believe her? Do you think that happiness can come from deception?"

"But she's my sister," I said, and although I knew that he was right I began to cry. "And she's your daughter. And you love her so."

He came and stood beside my chair. This time he didn't ask me why I was crying.

He kneeled suddenly beside me and spoke very softly and quickly.

"We'll keep each other company, Sarah Ann, just the two of us. We can be happy that way, can't we? We'll always have each other, don't you know?" He put his hand on my hair.

I knew then that was the way it should be. I leaned my head on his shoulder, and when I had finished crying I smiled at him and gave him Olive's letters.

"You take them," I said. "I can't——"

He nodded and took them and then took my hand.

I know that when he took them he meant to burn them. I found them by chance yesterday in the back of his desk drawer, under a pile of old medical reports. They lay there like love letters from someone who had died or moved away. They were tied in a slim green hair ribbon—it was one of mine, but I suppose he had found it and thought it was Olive's.

I didn't wonder what to do. It wasn't fair, don't you see? He hadn't any right to keep those letters after he told me I was the only daughter he had left. He would always be secretly reading them and fingering them, and it wouldn't do him any good. I took them to the incinerator in the back yard and burned them carefully, one by one. His bed is by the window and I know that he was watching me, but of course he couldn't say anything.

Maybe you feel sorry for Father, maybe you think I was cruel. But I did it for his sake and I don't care what you think because you're all of you strangers, anyway, and you can't understand that there couldn't be two of us. As I said before, I don't hate Olive. But sometimes I think this is the way it was meant to be. First Mother died and left just the two of us to take care of Father. And yesterday when I burned Olive's letters I thought, Now there is only me.

Irrational violence and the barbarians within the gates of modern civilization who delight in it are the subjects of this grim story, a fine example of the use of topical material for fiction.

Cyclists' Raid

IIIIIIIIIIIIIIIII **FRANK ROONEY** IIIIIIIIIIIIIIIII

Joel Bleeker, owner and operator of the Pendleton Hotel, was adjusting the old redwood clock in the lobby when he heard the sound of the motors. At first he thought it might be one of those four-engine planes on the flights from Los Angeles to San Francisco which occasionally got far enough off course to be heard in the valley. And for a moment, braced against the steadily approaching vibrations of the sound, he had the fantastic notion that the plane was going to strike the hotel. He even glanced at his daughter, Cathy, standing a few feet to his right and staring curiously at the street.

Then with his fingers still on the hour hand of the clock he realized that the sound was not something coming down from the air but the high, sputtering racket of many vehicles moving along the ground. Cathy and Bret Timmons, who owned one of the two drugstores in the town, went out onto the veranda but Bleeker stayed by the clock, consulting the railroad watch he pulled from his vest pocket and moving the hour hand on the clock forward a minute and a half. He stepped back deliberately, shut the glass case and looked at the huge brass numbers and the two ornate brass pointers. It was eight minutes after seven, approximately twenty-two minutes until sundown. He put the railroad watch back in his pocket and walked slowly and incuriously through the open doors of the lobby. He was methodical and orderly

240

and the small things he did every day—like setting the clock —were important to him. He was not to be hurried—especially by something as elusively irritating as a sound, however unusual.

There were only three people on the veranda when Bleeker came out of the lobby—his daughter Cathy, Timmons, and Francis LaSalle, co-owner of LaSalle and Fleet, Hardware. They stood together quietly, looking, without appearing to stare, at a long stern column of red motorcycles coming from the south, filling the single main street of the town with the noise of a multitude of pistons and the crackling of exhaust pipes. They could see now that the column was led by a single white motorcycle which when it came abreast of the hotel turned abruptly right and stopped. They saw too that the column without seeming to slow down or to execute any elaborate movement had divided itself into two single files. At the approximate second, having received a signal from their leader, they also turned right and stopped.

The whole flanking action, singularly neat and quite like the various vehicular formations he remembered in the Army, was distasteful to Bleeker. It recalled a little too readily his tenure as a lieutenant colonel overseas in England, France, and finally Germany.

"Mr. Bleeker?"

Bleeker realized the whole troop—no one in the town either then or after that night was ever agreed on the exact number of men in the troop—had dismounted and that the leader was addressing him.

"I'm Bleeker." Although he hadn't intended to, he stepped forward when he spoke, much as he had stepped forward in the years when he commanded a battalion.

"I'm Gar Simpson and this is Troop B of the Angeleno Motorcycle Club," the leader said. He was a tall, spare man and his voice was coldly courteous to the point of mockery. "We expect to bivouac outside your town tonight and we wondered if we might use the facilities of your hotel. Of course, sir, we'll pay."

"There's a washroom downstairs. If you can put up with that—"

"That will be fine, sir. Is the dining room still open?"

"It is."

"Could you take care of twenty men?"

"What about the others?"

"They can be accommodated elsewhere, sir."

Simpson saluted casually and, turning to the men assembled stiffly in front of the hotel, issued a few quiet orders. Quickly and efficiently, the men in the troop parked their motorcycles at the curb. About a third of the group detached itself and came deferentially but steadily up the hotel steps. They passed Bleeker who found himself maneuvered aside and went into the lobby. As they passed him, Bleeker could see the slight converted movement of their faces—though not their eyes, which were covered by large green goggles—toward his daughter Cathy. Bleeker frowned after them but before he could think of anything to say, Simpson, standing now at his left, touched his arm.

"I've divided the others into two groups," he said quietly. "One group will eat at the diner and the other at the Desert Hotel."

"Very good," Bleeker said. "You evidently know the town like a book. The people too. Have you ever been here before?"

"We have a map of all the towns in this part of California, sir. And of course we know the names of all the principal hotels and their proprietors. Personally, I could use a drink. Would you join me?"

"After you," Bleeker said.

He stood watching Simpson stride into the lobby and without any hesitation go directly to the bar. Then he turned to Cathy, seeing Timmons and LaSalle lounging on the railing behind her, their faces already indistinct in the plummeting California twilight.

"You go help in the kitchen, Cathy," Bleeker said. "I think it'd be better if you didn't wait on tables."

"I wonder what they look like behind those goggles," Cathy said.

"Like anybody else," Timmons said. He was about thirty, somewhat coarse and intolerant and a little embarrassed at being in love with a girl as young as Cathy. "Where did you think they came from? Mars?"

"What did they say the name of their club was?" Cathy said.

"Angeleno," LaSalle said.

"They must be from Los Angeles. Heigh-ho. Shall I wear my very best gingham, citizen colonel?"

"Remember now—you stay in the kitchen," Bleeker said.

He watched her walk into the lobby, a tall slender girl of seventeen, pretty and enigmatic, with something of the brittle independence of her mother. Bleeker remembered suddenly, although he tried not to, the way her mother had walked away from him that frosty January morning two years ago saying, "I'm going for a ride." And then the two-day search in the mountains after the horse had come back alone and the finding of her body—the neck broken—in the stream at the foot of the cliff. During the war he had never really believed that he would live to get back to Cathy's mother and after the war he hadn't really believed he would be separated from her—not again—not twice in so short a time.

Shaking his head—as if by that motion he could shed his memories as easily as a dog sheds water—Bleeker went in to join Gar Simpson who was sitting at a table in the barroom. Simpson stood politely when Bleeker took the opposite chair.

"How long do you fellows plan to stay?" Bleeker asked. He took the first sip of his drink, looked up, and stared at Simpson.

"Tonight and tomorrow morning," Simpson said.

Like all the others he was dressed in a brown windbreaker, khaki shirt, khaki pants, and as Bleeker had previously observed wore dark calf-length boots. A cloth and leather helmet lay on the table beside Simpson's drink, but he hadn't removed his flat green goggles, an accouterment giving him and the men in his troop the appearance of some tropical tribe with enormous semi-precious eyes, lidless and immovable. That was Bleeker's first impression and, absurd as it was, it didn't seem an exaggeration of fancy but of truth.

"Where do you go after this?"

"North." Simpson took a rolled map from a binocular case slung over his shoulder and spread it on the table. "Roughly we're following the arc of an ellipse with its southern tip based on Los Angeles and its northern end touching Fresno."

"Pretty ambitious for a motorcycle club."

"We have a month," Simpson said. "This is our first week but we're in no hurry and we're out to see plenty of country."

"What are you interested in mainly?"

"Roads. Naturally, being a motorcycle club—you'd be surprised at the rate we're expanding—we'd like to have as much of California as possible opened up to us."

"I see."

"Keeps the boys fit too. The youth of America. Our hope for the future." Simpson pulled sternly at his drink and Bleeker had the impression that Simpson was repressing, openly, and with pride, a vast sparkling ecstasy.

Bleeker sat and watched the young men in the troop file upstairs from the public washroom and stroll casually but nevertheless with discipline into the dining room. They had removed their helmets and strapped them to their belts, each helmet in a prescribed position to the left of the belt-buckle but—like Simpson—they had retained their goggles. Bleeker wondered if they ever removed the goggles long enough to wash under them and, if they did, what the flesh under them looked like.

"I think I'd better help out at the tables," Bleeker said. He stood up and Simpson stood with him. "You say you're from Troop B? Is that right?"

"Correct. We're forming Troop G now. Someday—"

"You'll be up to Z," Bleeker said.

"And not only in California."

"Where else for instance?"

"Nevada—Arizona—Colorado—Wyoming."

Simpson smiled and Bleeker, turning away from him abruptly, went into the dining room where he began to help the two waitresses at the tables. He filled water glasses, set out extra forks, and brought steins of beer from the bar. As he served the troop, their polite thank yous, ornate and insincere, irritated him. It reminded him of tricks taught to animals, the animals only being allowed to perform under certain obvious conditions of security. And he didn't like the cool way they stared at the two waitresses, both older women and fixtures in the town and then leaned their heads together as if every individual thought had to be pooled and divided equally among them. He admitted, after some covert study, that the twenty men were really only variations of one, the variations, with few exceptions, being too subtle for him to recognize and differentiate. It was the goggles, he decided, covering that part of the face which is most noteworthy and most needful for identification—the eyes and the mask around the eyes.

Bleeker went into the kitchen, pretending to help but really to be near Cathy. The protective father, he thought ironically, watching his daughter cut pie and lay the various colored wedges on the white blue-bordered plates.

"Well, Daddy, what's the verdict?" Cathy looked extremely grave but he could see that she was amused.

"They're a fine body of men."

"Uh-huh. Have you called the police yet?"

He laughed. "It's a good thing you don't play poker."

"Child's play." She slid the last piece of blueberry pie on a plate. "I saw you through the door. You looked like you were ready to crack the Siegfried line—single-handed."

"That man Simpson."

"What about him?"

"Why don't you go upstairs and read a book or something?"

"Now, Daddy—you're the only professional here. They're just acting like little tin soldiers out on a spree."

"I wish to God they were made of tin."

"All right. I'll keep away from them. I promise." She made a gesture of crossing her throat with the thin edge of a knife. He leaned over and kissed her forehead, his hand feeling awkward and stern on her back.

After dinner the troop went into the bar, moving with a strange co-ordinated fluency that was both casual and military and sat jealously together in one corner of the room. Bleeker served them pitchers of beer and for the most part they talked quietly together, Simpson at their center, their voices guarded and urgent as if they possessed information which couldn't be disseminated safely among the public.

Bleeker left them after a while and went upstairs to his

daughter's room. He wasn't used to being severe with Cathy
and he was a little embarrassed by what he had said to her
in the kitchen. She was turning the collars of some of his old
shirts, using a portable sewing machine he had bought her
as a present on her last birthday. As he came in she held one
of the shirts comically to the floor lamp and he could see
how thin and transparent the material was. Her mother's
economy in small things, almost absurd when compared to her
limitless generosity in matters of importance, had been one
of the family jokes. It gave him an extraordinary sense of
pleasure, so pure it was like a sudden inhalation of oxygen,
to see that his daughter had not only inherited this tradition
but had considered it meaningful enough to carry on. He
went down the hall to his own room without saying anything
further to her. Cathy was what he himself was in terms which
could mean absolutely nothing to anyone else.

He had been in his room for perhaps an hour, working on
the hotel accounts and thinking obliquely of the man Simpson,
when he heard, faintly and apparently coming from no one
direction, the sound of singing. He got up and walked to the
windows overlooking the street. Standing there, he thought
he could fix the sound farther up the block toward Cunningham's bar. Except for something harsh and mature in the
voices it was the kind of singing that might be heard around
a Boy Scout campfire, more rhythmic than melodic and more
stirring than tuneful. And then he could hear it almost under
his feet, coming out of the hotel lobby and making three or
four people on the street turn and smile foolishly toward the
doors of the veranda.

Oppressed by something sternly joyous in the voices,
Bleeker went downstairs to the bar, hearing as he approached
the singing become louder and fuller. Outside of Simpson
and the twenty men in the troop there were only three townsmen—including LaSalle—in the bar. Simpson, seeing Bleeker
in the door, got up and walked over to him, moving him out
into the lobby where they could talk.

"I hope the boys aren't disturbing you," he said.

"It's early," Bleeker said.

"In an organization as large and selective as ours it's absolutely necessary to insist on a measure of discipline. And it's equally necessary to allow a certain amount of relaxation."

"The key word is selective, I suppose."

"We have our standards," Simpson said primly.

"May I ask just what the hell your standards are?"

Simpson smiled. "I don't quite understand your irritation, Mr. Bleeker."

"This is an all-year-round thing, isn't it? This club of yours?"

"Yes."

"And you have an all-year-round job with the club?"

"Of course."

"That's my objection, Simpson. Briefly and simply stated, what you're running is a private army." Bleeker tapped the case slung over Simpson's shoulder. "Complete with maps, all sorts of local information, and of course a lobby in Sacramento."

"For a man who has traveled as widely as you have, Mr. Bleeker, you display an uncommon talent for exaggeration."

"As long as you behave yourselves I don't care what you do. This is a small town and we don't have many means of entertainment. We go to bed at a decent hour and I suggest you take that into consideration. However, have your fun. Nobody here has any objections to that."

"And of course we spend our money."

"Yes," Bleeker said. "You spend your money."

He walked away from Simpson and went out onto the veranda. The singing was now both in front and in back of him. Bleeker stood for a moment on the top steps of the veranda looking at the moon, hung like a slightly soiled but luminous pennant in the sky. He was embarrassed by his outburst to Simpson and he couldn't think why he had said such things. Private army. Perhaps, as Simpson had said, he was exaggerating. He was a small-town man and he had always hated the way men surrendered their individuality to attain perfection as a unit. It had been necessary during the war but it wasn't necessary now. Kid stuff—with an element of growing pains.

He walked down the steps and went up the sidewalk toward Cunningham's bar. They were singing there too and he stood outside the big plate-glass window peering in at them and listening to the harsh, pounding voices colored here and there with the sentimentalism of strong beer. Without thinking further he went into the bar. It was dim and cool and alien to his eyes and at first he didn't notice the boy sitting by himself in a booth near the front. When he did, he was surprised—more than surprised, shocked—to see that the boy wasn't wearing his goggles but had placed them on the table by a bottle of Coca-Cola. Impulsively, he walked over to the booth and sat across from the boy.

"This seat taken?"

He had to shout over the noise of the singing. The boy leaned forward over the table and smiled.

"Hope we're not disturbing you."

Bleeker caught the word "disturbing" and shook his head negatively. He pointed to his mouth, then to the boy and to the rest of the group. The boy too shook his head. Bleeker could see that he was young, possibly twenty-five, and that he had dark straight hair cut short and parted neatly at the side. The face was square but delicate, the nose short, the mouth wide. The best thing about the boy, Bleeker decided, were his eyes, brown perhaps or dark gray, set in two distorted ovals of white flesh which contrasted sharply with the heavily tanned skin on the cheeks, forehead and jaws. With his goggles on he would have looked like the rest. Without them he was a pleasant young man, altogether human and approachable.

Bleeker pointed to the Coca-Cola bottle. "You're not drinking."

"Beer makes me sick."

Bleeker got the word "beer" and the humorous gulping motion the boy made. They sat exchanging words and sometimes phrases, illustrated always with a series of clumsy, groping gestures until the singing became less coherent and spirited and ended finally in a few isolated coughs. The men in the troop were moving about individually now, some leaning over the bar and talking in hoarse whispers to the bartender, others walking unsteadily from group to group and detaching themselves immediately to go over to another group, the groups usually two or three men constantly edging away from themselves and colliding with and being held briefly by others. Some simply stood in the center of the room and brayed dolorously at the ceiling.

Several of the troop walked out of the bar and Bleeker could see them standing on the wide sidewalk looking up and down the street—as contemptuous of one another's company as they had been glad of it earlier. Or not so much contemptuous as unwilling to be coerced too easily by any authority outside themselves. Bleeker smiled as he thought of Simpson and the man's talk of discipline.

"They're looking for women," the boy said.

Bleeker had forgotten the boy temporarily and the sudden words spoken in a normal voice startled and confused him. He thought quickly of Cathy—but then Cathy was safe in her room—probably in bed. He took the watch from his vest pocket and looked at it carefully.

"Five minutes after ten," he said.

"Why do they do that?" the boy demanded. "Why do they have to be damned indecent about things like that? They haven't got the nerve to do anything but stare at waitresses. And then they get a few beers in them and go around pinching and slapping—they—"

Bleeker shivered with embarrassment. He was looking directly into the boy's eyes and seeing the color run under the tears and the jerky pinching movement of the lids as against something injurious and baleful. It was an emotion too rawly infantile to be seen without being hurt by it and he felt both pity and contempt for a man who would allow himself to display such a feeling—without any provocation— so nakedly to a stranger.

"Sorry," the boy said.

He picked up the green goggles and fitted them awkwardly over his eyes. Bleeker stood up and looked toward the center of the room. Several of the men turned their eyes and then moved their heads away without seeming to notice the boy in the booth. Bleeker understood them. This was the one who could be approached. The reason for that was clear too. He didn't belong. Why and wherefore he would probably never know.

He walked out of the bar and started down the street toward the hotel. The night was clear and cool and smelled faintly of the desert, of sand, of heated rock, of the sweetly-sour plants growing without water and even of the sun which burned itself into the earth and never completely withdrew. There were only a few townsmen on the sidewalk wandering up and down, lured by the presence of something unusual in the town and masking, Bleeker thought, a ruthless and menacing curiosity behind a tolerant grin. He shrugged his shoulders distastefully. He was like a cat staring into a shadow the shape of its fears.

He was no more than a hundred feet from the hotel when he heard—or thought he heard—the sound of automatic firing. It was a well-remembered sound but always new and frightening.

Then he saw the motorcycle moving down the middle of the street, the exhaust sputtering loudly against the human resonance of laughter, catcalls, and epithets. He exhaled gently, the pain in his lungs subsiding with his breath. Another motorcycle speeded after the first and he could see four or five machines being wheeled out and the figures of their riders leaping into the air and bringing their weight down on the starting pedals. He was aware too that the lead motorcycles, having traversed the length of the street had turned and were speeding back to the hotel. He had the sensation of moving—even when he stood still—in relation to the objects heading toward each other. He heard the high unendurable sound of metal squeezing metal and saw the front wheel of a motorcycle twist and wobble and its rider roll along the asphalt toward the gutter where he sat up finally and moved his goggled head feebly from side to side.

As Bleeker looked around him he saw the third group of men which had divided earlier from the other two coming out of a bar across the street from Cunningham's, waving their arms in recognizable motions of cheering. The boy who had been thrown from the motorcycle vomited quietly into the gutter. Bleeker walked very fast toward the hotel. When he reached the top step of the veranda, he was caught and jostled by some five or six cyclists running out of the lobby, one of whom fell and was kicked rudely down the steps.

Bleeker staggered against one of the pillars and broke a finger-nail catching it. He stood there for a moment, fighting his temper, and then went into the lobby.

A table had been overthrown and lay on its top, the wooden legs stiffly and foolishly exposed, its magazines scattered around it, some with their pages spread face down so that the bindings rose along the back. He stepped on glass and realized one of the panes in the lobby door had been smashed. One of the troop walked stupidly out of the bar, his body sagging against the impetus propelling him forward until without actually falling he lay stretched on the floor, beer gushing from his mouth and nose and making a green and yellow pool before it sank into the carpet.

As Bleeker walked toward the bar, thinking of Simpson and of what he could say to him, he saw two men going up the stairs toward the second floor. He ran over to intercept them. Recognizing the authority in his voice, they came obediently down the stairs and walked across the lobby to the veranda, one of them saying over his shoulder, "Okay, pop, okay—keep your lid on." The smile they exchanged enraged him. After they were out of sight he ran swiftly up the stairs, panting a little, and along the hall to his daughter's room.

It was quiet and there was no strip of light beneath the door. He stood listening for a moment with his ear to the panels and then turned back toward the stairs.

A man or boy, any of twenty or forty or sixty identical figures, goggled and in khaki, came around the corner of the second-floor corridor and put his hand on the knob of the door nearest the stairs. He squeezed the knob gently and then moved on to the next door, apparently unaware of Bleeker. Bleeker, remembering not to run or shout or knock the man down, walked over to him, took his arm and led him down the stairs, the arm unresisting, even flaccid, in his grip.

Bleeker stood indecisively at the foot of the stairs, watching the man walk automatically away from him. He thought he should go back upstairs and search the hall. And he thought too he had to reach Simpson. Over the noise of the motorcycles moving rapidly up and down the street he heard a crash in the bar, a series of drunken elongated curses, end-

ing abruptly in a small sound like a man's hand laid flatly
and sharply on a table.

His head was beginning to ache badly and his stomach to
sour under the impact of a slow and steady anger. He walked
into the bar and stood staring at Francis LaSalle—LaSalle
and Fleet, Hardware—who lay sprawled on the floor, his
shoulders touching the brass rail under the bar and his head
turned so that his cheek rubbed the black polished wood
above the rail. The bartender had his hands below the top of
the bar and he was watching Simpson and a half a dozen
men arranged in a loose semi-circle above and beyond La-
Salle.

Bleeker lifted LaSalle, who was a little dazed but not really
hurt, and set him on a chair. After he was sure LaSalle was all
right he walked up to Simpson.

"Get your men together," he said. "And get them out of
here."

Simpson took out a long yellow wallet folded like a book
and laid some money on the bar.

"That should take care of the damages," he said. His
tongue was a little thick and his mouth didn't quite shut after
the words were spoken but Bleeker didn't think he was drunk.
Bleeker saw too—or thought he saw—the little cold eyes
behind the glasses as bright and as sterile as a painted floor.
Bleeker raised his arm slightly and lifted his heels off the
floor but Simpson turned abruptly and walked away from him,
the men in the troop swaying at his heels like a pack of lolling
hounds. Bleeker stood looking foolishly after them. He had
expected a fight and his body was still poised for one. He
grunted heavily.

"Who hit him?" Bleeker motioned toward LaSalle.

"Damned if I know," the bartender said. "They all look
alike to me."

That was true of course. He went back into the lobby,
hearing LaSalle say, weakly and tearfully, "Goddam them—
the bastards." He met Campbell, the deputy sheriff, a tall
man with the arms and shoulders of a child beneath a foggy,
bloated face.

"Can you do anything?" Bleeker asked. The motorcycles
were racing up and down the street, alternately whining and

backfiring and one had jumped the curb and was cruising on the sidewalk.

"What do you want me to do?" Campbell demanded. "Put 'em all in jail?"

The motorcycle on the sidewalk speeded up and skidded obliquely into a plate-glass window, the front wheel bucking and climbing the brick base beneath the window. A single large section of glass slipped edge-down to the sidewalk and fell slowly toward the cyclist who, with his feet spread and kicking at the cement, backed clumsily away from it. Bleeker could feel the crash in his teeth.

Now there were other motorcycles on the sidewalk. One of them hit a parked car at the edge of the walk. The rider standing astride his machine beat the window out of the car with his gloved fists. Campbell started down the steps toward him but was driven back by a motorcycle coming from his left. Bleeker could hear the squeal of the tires against the wooden riser at the base of the steps. Campbell's hand was on his gun when Bleeker reached him.

"That's no good," he yelled. "Get the state police. Ask for a half dozen squad cars."

Campbell, angry but somewhat relieved, went up the steps and into the lobby. Bleeker couldn't know how long he stood on the veranda watching the mounting devastation on the street—the cyclist racing past store windows and hurling, presumably, beer bottles at the glass fronts; the two, working as a team, knocking down weighing machines and the signs in front of the motion picture theater; the innumerable mounted men running the angry townspeople, alerted and aroused by the awful sounds of damage to their property, back into their suddenly lighted homes again or up the steps of his hotel or into niches along the main street, into doorways, and occasionally into the ledges and bays of glassless windows.

He saw Simpson—or rather a figure on the white motorcycle, helmeted and goggled—stationed calmly in the middle of the street under a hanging lamp. Presumably, he had been there for some time but Bleeker hadn't seen him, the many rapid movements on the street making any static object unimportant and even, in a sense, invisible. Bleeker saw him now and he felt again that spasm of anger which was like another life inside his body. He could have strangled Simpson then, slowly and with infinite pride. He knew without any effort of reason that Simpson was making no attempt to control his men but waiting rather for that moment when their minds, subdued but never actually helpless, would again take possession of their bodies.

Bleeker turned suddenly and went back into the lobby as if by that gesture of moving away he could pin his thoughts to Simpson, who, hereafter, would be responsible for them. He walked over to the desk where Timmons and Campbell, the deputy, were talking.

"You've got the authority," Timmons was saying angrily. "Fire over their heads. And if that doesn't stop them—"

Campbell looked uneasily at Bleeker. "Maybe if we could get their leader—"

"Did you get the police?" Bleeker asked.

"They're on their way," Campbell said. He avoided looking at Timmons and continued to stare hopefully and miserably at Bleeker.

"You've had your say," Timmons said abruptly. "Now I'll have mine."

He started for the lobby doors but Campbell, suddenly incensed, grabbed his arm.

"You leave this to me," he said. "You start firing a gun—"

Campbell's mouth dropped and Bleeker, turning his head, saw the two motorcycles coming through the lobby doors. They circled leisurely around for a moment and then one of them shot suddenly toward them, the goggled rider looming enormously above the wide handlebars. They scattered, Bleeker diving behind a pillar and Campbell and Timmons jumping behind the desk. The noise of the two machines assaulted them with as much effect as the sight of the speeding metal itself.

Bleeker didn't know why in the course of watching the two riders he looked into the hall toward the foot of the stairway. Nor did it seem at all unreasonable that when he looked he should see Cathy standing there. Deeply, underneath the outward preoccupation of his mind, he must have been thinking of her. Now there she was. She wore the familiar green robe, belted and pulled in at the waist and beneath its hem he could see the white slippers and the pink edge of her night-gown. Her hair was down and he had the impression her eyes were not quite open although, obviously, they were. She looked, he thought, as if she had waked, frowned at the clock, and come downstairs to scold him for staying up too late. He had no idea what time it was.

He saw—and of course Cathy saw—the motorcycle speed-ing toward her. He was aware that he screamed at her too. She did take a slight backward step and raise her arms in a pathetic warding gesture toward the inhuman figure on the motorcycle but neither could have changed—in that dwarfed period of time and in that short, unmaneuverable space—the course of their actions.

She lay finally across the lower steps, her body clinging to and equally arching away from the base of the newel post. And there was the sudden, shocking exposure of her flesh, the robe and the gown torn away from the leg as if pushed aside by the blood welling from her thigh. When he reached her there was blood in her hair too and someone—not Cathy—was screaming into his ears.

After a while the doctor came and Cathy, her head band-aged and her leg in splints, could be carried into his office and laid on the couch. Bleeker sat on the edge of the couch, his hand over Cathy's, watching the still white face whose eyes were closed and would not, he knew, open again. The doctor, after his first examination, had looked up quickly and since Bleeker too had been bent over Cathy, their heads had been very close together for a moment. The doctor had as-sumed, almost immediately, his expression of professional austerity but Bleeker had seen him in that moment when he had been thinking as a man, fortified of course by a doctor's knowledge, and Bleeker had known then that Cathy would die but that there would be also this interval of time.

Bleeker turned from watching Cathy and saw Timmons standing across the room. The man was—or had been—crying but his face wasn't set for it and the tears, points of colorless, sparkling water on his jaws, were unexpectedly delicate

against the coarse texture of his skin. Timmons waved a
bandaged hand awkwardly and Bleeker remembered, abruptly and jarringly, seeing Timmons diving for the motorcycle
which had reversed itself, along with the other, and raced
out of the lobby.

There was no sound now either from the street or the
lobby. It was incredible, thinking of the racket a moment ago,
that there should be this utter quietude, not only the lack of
noise but the lack of the vibration of movement. The doctor
came and went, coming to bend over Cathy and then going
away again. Timmons stayed. Beyond shifting his feet occasionally he didn't move at all but stood patiently across the
room, his face toward Cathy and Bleeker but not, Bleeker
thought once when he looked up, actually seeing them.

"The police," Bleeker said sometime later.

"They're gone," Timmons said in a hoarse whisper. And
then after a while, "They'll get 'em—don't worry."

Bleeker saw that the man blushed helplessly and looked
away from him. The police were no good. They would catch
Simpson. Simpson would pay damages. And that would be
the end of it. Who could identify Cathy's assailant? Not himself, certainly—nor Timmons nor Campbell. They were all
alike. They were standardized figurines, seeking in each other
a willful loss of identity, dividing themselves equally among
one another until there was only a single mythical figure, un-
speakably sterile and furnishing the norm for hundreds of
others. He could not accuse something which didn't actually
exist.

He wasn't sure of the exact moment when Cathy died. It
might have been when he heard the motorcycle, unbelievably
solitary in the quiet night, approaching the town. He knew
only that the doctor came for the last time and that there was
now a coarse, heavy blanket laid mercifully over Cathy. He
stood looking down at the blanket for a moment, whatever
he was feeling repressed and delayed inside him, and then
went back to the lobby and out onto the veranda. There were
a dozen men standing there looking up the street toward the
sound of the motorcycle, steadily but slowly coming nearer.
He saw that when they glanced at each other their faces were

hard and angry but when they looked at him they were respectful and a little abashed.

Bleeker could see from the veranda a number of people moving among the smashed store-fronts, moving, stopping, bending over and then straightening up to move somewhere else, all dressed somewhat extemporaneously and therefore seeming without purpose. What they picked up they put down. What they put down they stared at grimly and then picked up again. They were like a dispossessed minority brutally but lawfully discriminated against. When the motorcycle appeared at the north end of the street they looked at it and then looked away again, dully and seemingly without resentment.

It was only after some moments that they looked up again, this time purposefully, and began to move slowly toward the hotel where the motorcycle had now stopped, the rider standing on the sidewalk, his face raised to the veranda.

No one on the veranda moved until Bleeker, after a visible effort, walked down the steps and stood facing the rider. It was the boy Bleeker had talked to in the bar. The goggles and helmet were hanging at his belt.

"I couldn't stand it any longer," the boy said. "I had to come back."

He looked at Bleeker as if he didn't dare look anywhere else. His face was adolescently shiny and damp, the marks, Bleeker thought, of a proud and articulate fear. He should have been heroic in his willingness to come back to the town after what had been done to it but to Bleeker he was only a dirty little boy returning to a back fence his friends had defaced with pornographic writing and calling attention to the fact that he was afraid to erase the writing but was determined nevertheless to do it. Bleeker was revolted. He hated the boy far more than he could have hated Simpson for bringing this to his attention when he did not want to think of anything or anyone but Cathy.

"I wasn't one of them," the boy said. "You remember, Mr. Bleeker. I wasn't drinking."

This declaration of innocence—this willingness to take blame for acts which he hadn't committed—enraged Bleeker.

"You were one of them," he said.

"Yes. But after tonight—"

"Why didn't you stop them?" Bleeker demanded loudly. He felt the murmur of the townspeople at his back and someone breathed harshly on his neck. "You were one of them. You could have done something. Why in God's name didn't you do it?"

"What could I do?" the boy said. He spread his hands and stepped back as if to appeal to the men beyond Bleeker.

Bleeker couldn't remember, either shortly after or much later, exactly what he did then. If the boy hadn't stepped back like that—if he hadn't raised his hand. . . . Bleeker was in the middle of a group of bodies and he was striking with his fists and being struck. And then he was kneeling on the sidewalk, holding the boy's head in his lap and trying to protect him from the heavy shoes of the men around him. He was crying out, protesting, exhorting, and after a time the men moved away from him and someone helped him carry the boy up the steps and lay him on the veranda. When he looked up finally only Timmons and the doctor were there. Up and down the street there were now only shadows and the diminishing sounds of invisible bodies. The night was still again as abruptly as it had been confounded with noise.

Some time later Timmons and the doctor carried the boy, alive but terribly hurt, into the hotel. Bleeker sat on the top step of the veranda, staring at the moon which had shifted in the sky and was now nearer the mountains in the west. It was not in any sense romantic or inflamed but coldly clear and sane. And the light it sent was cold and sane and lit in himself what he would have liked to hide.

He could have said that having lost Cathy he was not afraid any longer of losing himself. No one would blame him. Cathy's death was his excuse for striking the boy, hammering him to the sidewalk, and stamping on him as he had never believed he could have stamped on any living thing. No one would say he should have lost Cathy lightly—without anger and without that appalling desire to avenge her. It was utterly natural—as natural as a man drinking a few beers and riding a motorcycle insanely through a town like this. Bleeker shuddered. It might have been all right for a man like Timmons who was and would always be incapable of thinking what he—Joel Bleeker—was thinking. It was not—and would never be—all right for him.

Bleeker got up and stood for a moment on the top step of the veranda. He wanted, abruptly and madly, to scream his agony into the night with no more restraint than that of an animal seeing his guts beneath him on the ground. He wanted to smash something—anything—glass, wood, stone—his own body. He could feel his fists going into the boy's flesh. And there was that bloody but living thing on the sidewalk and himself stooping over to shield it.

After a while, aware that he was leaning against one of the wooden pillars supporting the porch and aware too that his flesh was numb from being pressed against it, he straightened up slowly and turned to go back into the hotel.

There would always be time to make his peace with the dead. There was little if any time to make his peace with the living.

In this delightfully comic and yet pathetic story, a
good little girl (well, comparatively good) comes
under the influence of a very bad little girl indeed.
The results are vastly amusing. Miss Stafford never
wrote a better story than this one.

Bad Characters

IIIIIIIIIIIIIIII J E A N   S T A F F O R D IIIIIIIIIIIIIIIII

Up until I learned my lesson in a very bitter way, I
never had more than one friend at a time, and my friendships,
though ardent, were short. When they ended and I was sent
packing in unforgetting indignation, it was always my fault;
I would swear vilely in front of a girl I knew to be pious
and prim (by the time I was eight, the most grandiloquent
gangster could have added nothing to my vocabulary—I had
an awful tongue), or I would call a Tenderfoot Scout a sissy
or make fun of athletics to the daughter of the high-school
coach. These outbursts came without plan; I would simply
one day, in the middle of a game of Russian bank or a hike
or a conversation, be possessed with a passion to be by myself,
and my lips instantly and without warning would accom-
modate me. My friend was never more surprised than I was
when this irrevocable slander, this terrible, talented invective,
came boiling out of my mouth.

Afterward, when I had got the solitude I had wanted, I was
dismayed, for I did not like it. Then I would sadly finish the
game of cards as if someone were still across the table from
me; I would sit down on the mesa and through a glaze of
tears would watch my friend departing with outraged strides;
mournfully, I would talk to myself. Because I had already
alienated everyone I knew, I then had nowhere to turn, so a
famine set in and I would have no companion but Muff, the

cat, who loathed all human beings except, significantly, me—truly. She bit and scratched the hands that fed her, she arched her back like a Halloween cat if someone kindly tried to pet her, she hissed, laid her ears flat to her skull, growled, fluffed up her tail into a great bush and flailed it like a bullwhack. But she purred for me, she patted me with her paws, keeping her claws in their velvet scabbards. She was not only an ill-natured cat, she was also badly dressed. She was a calico, and the distribution of her colors was a mess; she looked as if she had been left out in the rain and her paint had run. She had a Roman nose as the result of some early injury, her tail was skinny, she had a perfectly venomous look in her eye. My family said—my family discriminated against me—that I was much closer kin to Muff than I was to any of them. To tease me into a tantrum, my brother Jack and my sister Stella often called me Kitty instead of Emily. Little Tess did not dare, because she knew I'd chloroform her if she did. Jack, the meanest boy I have ever known in my life, called me Polecat and talked about my mania for fish, which, it so happened, I despised. The name would have been far more appropriate for *him*, since he trapped skunks up in the foothills—we lived in Adams, Colorado—and quite often, because he was careless and foolhardy, his clothes had to be buried, and even when that was done, he sometimes was sent home from school on the complaint of girls sitting next to him.

Along about Christmastime when I was eleven, I was making a snowman with Virgil Meade in his backyard, and all of a sudden, just as we had got around to the right arm, I had to be alone. So I called him a son of a sea cook, said it was common knowledge that his mother had bedbugs and that his father, a dentist and the deputy marshal, was a bootlegger on the side. For a moment, Virgil was too aghast to speak—a little earlier we had agreed to marry someday and become millionaires—and then, with a bellow of fury, he knocked me down and washed my face in snow. I saw stars, and black balls bounced before my eyes. When finally he let me up, we were both crying, and he hollered that if I didn't get off his property that instant, his father would arrest me and send me to Canon City. I trudged slowly home, half frozen, critically sick at heart. So it was old Muff again for me for quite some time. Old Muff, that is, until I met Lottie Jump, although "met" is a euphemism for the way I first encountered her.

I saw Lottie for the first time one afternoon in our own kitchen, stealing a chocolate cake. Stella and Jack had not come home from school yet—not having my difficult disposition, they were popular, and they were at their friends' houses, pulling taffy, I suppose, making popcorn balls, playing casino, having fun—and my mother had taken Tess with her to visit a friend in one of the T.B. sanitariums. I was alone in the house, and making a funny-looking Christmas card, although I had no one to send it to. When I heard someone in the kitchen, I thought it was Mother home early, and I went out to ask her why the green pine tree I had pasted on a square of red paper looked as if it were falling down. And there, instead of Mother and my baby sister, was this pale, conspicuous child in the act of lifting the glass cover from the devil's-food my mother had taken out of the oven an hour before and set on the plant shelf by the window. The child had her back to me, and when she heard my footfall, she wheeled with an amazing look of fear and hatred on her pinched and pasty face. Simultaneously, she put the cover over the cake again, and then she stood motionless as if she were under a spell.

I was scared, for I was not sure what was happening, and anyhow it gives you a turn to find a stranger in the kitchen in the middle of the afternoon, even if the stranger is only a skinny child in a moldy coat and sopping-wet basketball shoes. Between us there was a lengthy silence, but there was a great deal of noise in the room: the alarm clock ticked smugly; the teakettle simmered patiently on the back of the stove; Muff, cross at having been waked up, thumped her tail against the side of the terrarium in the window where she had been sleeping—contrary to orders—among the geraniums. This went on, it seemed to me, for hours and hours while that tall, sickly girl and I confronted each other. When, after a long time, she did open her mouth, it was to tell a prodigious lie. "I came to see if you'd like to play with me," she said. I think she sighed and stole a sidelong and regretful glance at the cake.

Beggars cannot be choosers, and I had been missing Virgil
so sorely, as well as all those other dear friends forever lost to
me, that in spite of her flagrance (she had never clapped eyes
on me before, she had had no way of knowing there was a
creature of my age in the house—she had come in like a hobo
to steal my mother's cake), I was flattered and consoled. I
asked her name and, learning it, believed my ears no better
than my eyes: Lottie Jump. What on earth! What on earth—
you surely will agree with me—and yet when I told her mine,
Emily Vanderpool, she laughed until she coughed and gasped.
"Beg pardon," she said. "Names like them always hit my funny bone. There was this towhead boy in school named Delbert
Saxonfield." I saw no connection and I was insulted (what's
so funny about Vanderpool, I'd like to know), but Lottie
Jump was, technically, my guest and I *was* lonesome, so I
asked her, since she had spoken of playing with me, if she
knew how to play Andy-I-Over. She said "Naw." It turned out
that she did not know how to play any games at all; she
couldn't do anything and didn't want to do anything; her only
recreation and her only gift was, and always had been, stealing. But this I did not know at the time.

As it happened, it was too cold and snowy to play outdoors
that day anyhow, and after I had run through my list of
indoor games and Lottie had shaken her head at all of them
(when I spoke of parcheesi, she went "Ugh!" and pretended
to be sick), she suggested that we look through my mother's
bureau drawers. This did not strike me as strange at all, for
it was one of my favorite things to do, and I led the way to
Mother's bedroom without a moment's hesitation. I loved the
smell of the lavender she kept in gauze bags among her
chamois gloves and linen handkerchiefs and filmy scarves;
there was a pink fascinator knitted of something as fine as
spider's thread, and it made me go quite soft—I wasn't soft as
a rule, I was as hard as nails and I gave my mother a rough
time—to think of her wearing it around her head as she
waltzed on the ice in the bygone days. We examined stockings, nightgowns, camisoles, strings of beads, and mosaic
pins, keepsake buttons from dresses worn on memorial occasions, tortoise-shell combs, and a transformation made from
Aunt Joey's hair when she had racily had it bobbed. Lottie

admired particularly a blue cloisonné perfume flask with ferns and peacocks on it. "Hey," she said, "this sure is cute. I like thing-daddies like this here." But very abruptly she got bored and said, "Let's talk instead. In the front room." I agreed, a little perplexed this time, because I had been about to show her a remarkable powder box that played *The Blue Danube*. We went into the parlor, where Lottie looked at her image in the pier glass for quite a while and with great absorption, as if she had never seen herself before. Then she moved over to the window seat and knelt on it, looking out at the front walk. She kept her hands in the pockets of her thin dark-red coat; once she took out one of her dirty paws to rub her nose for a minute and I saw a bulge in that pocket, like a bunch of jackstones. I know now that it wasn't jackstones, it was my mother's perfume flask; I thought at the time her hands were cold and that that was why she kept them put away, for I had noticed that she had no mittens.

Lottie did most of the talking, and while she talked, she never once looked at me but kept her eyes fixed on the approach to our house. She told me that her family had come to Adams a month before from Muskogee, Oklahoma, where her father, before he got tuberculosis, had been a brakeman on the Frisco. Now they lived down by Arapahoe Creek, on the west side of town, in one of the cottages of a wretched settlement made up of people so poor and so sick—for in nearly every ramshackle house someone was coughing himself to death—that each time I went past I blushed with guilt because my shoes were sound and my coat was warm and I was well. I wished that Lottie had not told me where she lived, but she was not aware of any pathos in her family's situation, and, indeed, it was with a certain boastfulness that she told me her mother was the short-order cook at the Comanche Café (she pronounced this word in one syllable), which I knew was the dirtiest, darkest, smelliest place in town, patronized by coal miners who never washed their faces and sometimes had such dangerous fights after drinking dago red that the sheriff had to come. Laughing, Lottie told me that her mother was half Indian, and, laughing even harder, she said that her brother didn't have any brains and had never been to school. She herself was eleven years old, but she was only in the third grade, because teachers had always had it in for her—making her go to the blackboard and all like that when she was tired. She hated school—she went to Ashton, on North Hill, and that was why I had never seen her, for I went to Carlyle Hill—and she especially hated the teacher, Miss Cudahy, who had a head shaped like a pine cone and who had killed several people with her ruler. Lottie loved the movies ("Not them Western ones or the ones with apes in," she said. "Ones about hugging and kissing. I love it when they die in that big old soft bed with the curtains up top, and he comes in and says 'Don't leave me, Marguerite de la Mar'"), and she loved to ride in cars. She loved Mr. Goodbars, and if there was one thing she despised worse than another it was tapioca. ("Pa calls it fish eyes. He calls floating island horse spit. He's a big piece of cheese. I hate him.") She did not like cats (Muff was now sitting on the mantelpiece, glaring like an owl); she kind of liked snakes—except cottonmouths and rattlers—because she found them kind of funny; she had once seen a goat eat a tin can. She said that one of these days she would take me downtown—it was a slowpoke town, she said, a one-horse burg (I had never heard such gaudy, cynical talk and was trying to memorize it all)—if I would get some money for the trolley fare; she hated to walk, and I ought to be proud that she had walked all the way from Arapahoe Creek today for the sole solitary purpose of seeing me.

Seeing our freshly baked dessert in the window was a more likely story, but I did not care, for I was deeply impressed by this bold, sassy girl from Oklahoma and greatly admired the poise with which she aired her prejudices. Lottie Jump was certainly nothing to look at. She was tall and made of skin and bones; she was evilly ugly, and her clothes were a disgrace, not just ill-fitting and old and ragged but dirty, unmentionably so; clearly she did not wash much or brush her teeth, which were notched like a saw, and small and brown (it crossed my mind that perhaps she chewed tobacco); her long, lank hair looked as if it might have nits. But she had personality. She made me think of one of those self-contained dogs whose home is where his handout is and who travels alone but, if it suits him to, will become the leader of a pack.

She was aloof, never looking at me, but amiable in the way she kept calling me "kid." I liked her enormously, and presently I told her so.

At this, she turned around and smiled at me. Her smile was the smile of a jack-o'-lantern—high, wide, and handsome. When it was over, no trace of it remained. "Well, that's keen, kid, and I like you, too," she said in her downright Muskogee accent. She gave me a long, appraising look. Her eyes were the color of mud. "Listen, kid, how much do you like me?"

"I like you loads, Lottie," I said. "Better than anybody else, and I'm not kidding."

"You want to be pals?"

"Do I!" I cried. So *there*, Virgil Meade, you big fat hootnanny, I thought.

"All right, kid, we'll be pals." And she held out her hand for me to shake. I had to go and get it, for she did not alter her position on the window seat. It was a dry, cold hand, and the grip was severe, with more a feeling of bones in it than friendliness.

Lottie turned and scanned our path and scanned the sidewalk beyond, and then she said, in a lower voice, "Do you know how to lift?"

"Lift?" I wondered if she meant to lift *her*. I was sure I could do it, since she was so skinny, but I couldn't imagine why she would want me to.

"Shoplift, I mean. Like in the five-and-dime."

I did not know the term, and Lottie scowled at my stupidity.

"*Steal*, for crying in the beer!" she said impatiently. This she said so loudly that Muff jumped down from the mantel and left the room in contempt.

I was thrilled to death and shocked to pieces. "Stealing is a sin," I said. "You get put in jail for it."

"Ish ka bibble! I should worry if it's a sin or not," said Lottie, with a shrug. "And they'll never put a smart old whatsis like *me* in jail. It's fun, stealing is—it's a picnic. I'll teach you if you want to learn, kid." Shamelessly she winked at me and grinned again. (That grin! She could have taken it off her face and put it on the table.) And she added, "If you don't, we can't be pals, because lifting is the only kind of playing I like. I hate those dumb games like Statues. Kick-the-Can—phooey!"

I was torn between agitation (I went to Sunday school and knew already about morality; Judge Bay, a crabby old man who loved to punish sinners, was a friend of my father's and once had given Jack a lecture on the criminal mind when he came to call and found Jack looking up an answer in his arithmetic book) and excitement over the daring invitation to misconduct myself in so perilous a way. My life, on reflection, looked deadly prim; all I'd ever done to vary the monotony of it was to swear. I knew that Lottie Jump meant what she said—that I could have her friendship only on her terms (plainly, she had gone it alone for a long time and could go it alone for the rest of her life)—and although I trembled like an aspen and my heart went pitapat, I said, "I want to be pals with you, Lottie."

"All right, Vanderpool," said Lottie, and got off the window seat. "I wouldn't go braggin' about it if I was you. I wouldn't go telling my ma and pa and the next-door neighbor that you and Lottie Jump are going down to the five-and-dime next Saturday aft and lift us some nice rings and garters and things like that. I mean it, kid." And she drew the back of her forefinger across her throat and made a dire face.

"I won't. I promise I won't. My *gosh*, why would I?"

"That's the ticket," said Lottie, with a grin. "I'll meet you at the trolley shelter at two o'clock. You have the money. For both down and up. I ain't going to climb up that ornery hill after I've had my fun."

"Yes, Lottie," I said. Where was I going to get twenty cents? I was going to have to start stealing before she even taught me how. Lottie was facing the center of the room, but she had eyes in the back of her head, and she whirled around back to the window; my mother and Tess were turning in our front path.

"Back way," I whispered, and in a moment Lottie was gone; the swinging door that usually squeaked did not make a sound as she vanished through it. I listened and I never heard the back door open and close. Nor did I hear her, in a split second, lift the glass cover and remove that cake designed to feed six people.

I was restless and snappish between Wednesday afternoon
and Saturday. When Mother found the cake was gone, she
scolded me for not keeping my ears cocked. She assumed, naturally, that a tramp had taken it, for she knew I hadn't eaten
it; I never ate anything if I could help it (except for raw
potatoes, which I loved) and had been known as a problem
feeder from the beginning of my life. At first it occurred to
me to have a tantrum and bring her around to my point of
view: my tantrums scared the living daylights out of her because my veins stood out and I turned blue and couldn't get
my breath. But I rejected this for a more sensible plan. I said,
"It just so happens I didn't hear anything. But if I had, I
suppose you wish I had gone out in the kitchen and let the
robber cut me up into a million little tiny pieces with his
sword. You wouldn't even bury me. You'd just put me on the
dump. *I* know who's wanted in this family and who isn't."
Tears of sorrow, not of anger, came in powerful tides and I
groped blindly to the bedroom I shared with Stella, where I
lay on my bed and shook with big, silent *weltschmerzlich*
sobs. Mother followed me immediately, and so did Tess, and
both of them comforted me and told me how much they
loved me. I said they didn't; they said they did. Presently, I
got a headache, as I always did when I cried, so I got to have
an aspirin and a cold cloth on my head, and when Jack and
Stella came home, they had to be quiet. I heard Jack say,
"Emily Vanderpool is the biggest polecat in the U.S.A.
Whyn't she go in the kitchen and say, 'Hands up'? He woulda
lit out." And Mother said, "Sh-h-h! You don't want your sister
to be sick, do you?" Muff, not realizing that Lottie had replaced her, came in and curled up at my thigh, purring lust-
ily; I found myself glad that she had left the room before
Lottie Jump made her proposition to me, and in gratitude I
stroked her unattractive head.

Other things happened. Mother discovered the loss of her
perfume flask and talked about nothing else at meals for two
whole days. Luckily, it did not occur to her that it had been
stolen—she simply thought she had mislaid it—but her mono-
mania got on my father's nerves and he lashed out at her and
at the rest of us. And because I was the cause of it all and
my conscience was after me with red-hot pokers, I finally *had*

to have a tantrum. I slammed my fork down in the middle of supper on the second day and yelled, "If you don't stop fighting, I'm going to kill myself. Yammer, yammer, nag, nag!" And I put my fingers in my ears and squeezed my eyes tight shut and screamed so the whole county could hear, "Shut *up!*" And then I lost my breath and began to turn blue. Daddy hastily apologized to everyone, and Mother said she was sorry for carrying on so about a trinket that had nothing but sentimental value—she was just vexed with herself for being careless, that was all, and she wasn't going to say another word about it.

I never heard so many references to stealing and cake, and even to Oklahoma (ordinarily no one mentioned Oklahoma once in a month of Sundays) and the ten-cent store as I did throughout those next days. I myself once made a ghastly slip and said something to Stella about "the five-and-dime." "The five-and-*dime!*" she exclaimed. "Where'd you get *that* kind of talk? Do you by any chance have reference to the *ten-cent store?*"

The worst of all was Friday night—the very night before I was to meet Lottie Jump—when Judge Bay came to play two-handed pinochle with Daddy. The Judge, a giant in intimidating haberdashery—for some reason, the white piping on his vest bespoke, for me, handcuffs and prison bars—and with an aura of disapproval for almost everything on earth except what pertained directly to himself, was telling Daddy, before they began their game, about the infamous vandalism that had been going on among the college students. "I have reason to believe that there are girls in this gang as well as boys," he said. "They ransack vacant houses and take everything. In one house on Pleasant Street, up there by the Catholic Church, there wasn't anything to take, so they took the kitchen sink. Wasn't a question of taking everything *but*— they took the kitchen sink."

"What ever would they want with a kitchen sink?" asked my mother.

"Mischief," replied the Judge. "If we ever catch them and if they come within my jurisdiction, I can tell you I will give them no quarter. A thief, in my opinion, is the lowest of the low."

Mother told about the chocolate cake. By now, the fiction
was so factual in my mind that each time I thought of it I
saw a funny-paper bum in baggy pants held up by rope, a
hat with holes through which tufts of hair stuck up, shoes
from which his toes protruded, a disreputable stubble on his
face; he came up beneath the open window where the devil's
food was cooling and he stole it and hotfooted it for the
woods, where his companion was frying a small fish in a
beat-up skillet. It never crossed my mind any longer that
Lottie Jump had hooked that delicious cake.

Judge Bay was properly impressed. "If you will steal a
chocolate cake, if you will steal a kitchen sink, you will steal
diamonds and money. The small child who pilfers a penny
from his mother's pocketbook has started down a path that
may lead him to holding up a bank."

It was a good thing I had no homework that night, for I
could not possibly have concentrated. We were all sent to our
rooms, because the pinochle players had to have absolute
quiet. I spent the evening doing cross-stitch. I was making a
bureau runner for a Christmas present; as in the case of the
Christmas card, I had no one to give it to, but now I decided
to give it to Lottie Jump's mother. Stella was reading *Black
Beauty*, crying. It was an interminable evening. Stella went
to bed first; I saw to that, because I didn't want her lying
there awake listening to me talking in my sleep. Besides, I
didn't want her to see me tearing open the cardboard box—
the one in the shape of a church, which held my Christmas
Sunday-school offering. Over the door of the church was this
shaming legend: "My mite for the poor widow." When Stella
had begun to grind her teeth in her first deep sleep, I took
twenty cents away from the poor widow, whoever she was
(the owner of the kitchen sink, no doubt), for the trolley
fare, and secreted it and the remaining three pennies in the
pocket of my middy. I wrapped the money well in a handkerchief and buttoned the pocket and hung my skirt over the
middy. And then I tore the paper church into bits—the
heavens opened and Judge Bay came toward me with a
double-barreled shotgun—and hid the bits under a pile of
pajamas. I did not sleep one wink. Except that I must have,
because of the stupendous nightmares that kept wrenching

the flesh off my skeleton and caused me to come close to perishing of thirst; once I fell out of bed and hit my head on Stella's ice skates. I would have waked her up and given her a piece of my mind for leaving them in such a lousy place, but then I remembered: I wanted *no* commotion of any kind.

I couldn't eat breakfast and I couldn't eat lunch. Old Johnny-on-the-spot Jack kept saying, *"Poor* Polecat. Polecat wants her fish for dinner." Mother made an abortive attempt to take my temperature. And when all that hullabaloo subsided, I was nearly in the soup because Mother asked me to mind Tess while she went to the sanitarium to see Mrs. Rogers, who, all of a sudden, was too sick to have anyone but grownups near her. Stella couldn't stay with the baby, because she had to go to ballet, and Jack couldn't, because he had to go up to the mesa and empty his traps. ("No, they *can't* wait. You want my skins to rot in this hot-one-day-cold-the-next weather?") I was arguing and whining when the telephone rang. Mother went to answer it and came back with a look of great sadness; Mrs. Rogers, she had learned, had had another hemorrhage. So Mother would not be going to the sanitarium after all and I needn't stay with Tess.

By the time I left the house, I was as cross as a bear. I felt awful about the widow's mite and I felt awful for being mean about staying with Tess, for Mrs. Rogers was a kind old lady, in a cozy blue hug-me-tight and an old-fangled boudoir cap, dying here all alone; she was a friend of Grandma's and had lived just down the street from her in Missouri, and all in the world Mrs. Rogers wanted to do was go back home and lie down in her own big bedroom in her own big, high-ceilinged house and have Grandma and other members of the Eastern Star come in from time to time to say hello. But they wouldn't let her go home; they were going to kill or cure her. I could not help feeling that my hardness of heart and evil of intention had had a good deal to do with her new crisis; right at the very same minute I had been saying "Does that old Mrs. Methuselah *always* have to spoil my fun?" the poor wasted thing was probably coughing up her blood and saying to the nurse, "Tell Emily Vanderpool not to mind me, she can run and play."

I had a bad character, I know that, but my badness never
gave me half the enjoyment Jack and Stella thought it did.
A good deal of the time I wanted to eat lye. I was certainly
having no fun now, thinking of Mrs. Rogers and of depriving
that poor widow of bread and milk; what if this penniless
woman without a husband had a dog to feed, too? Or a baby?
And besides, I didn't want to go downtown to steal anything
from the ten-cent store; I didn't want to see Lottie Jump
again—not really, for I knew in my bones that that girl was
trouble with a capital "T." And still, in our short meeting,
she had mesmerized me; I would think about her style of talking and the expert way she had made off with the perfume
flask and the cake (how had she carried the cake through the
streets without being noticed?) and be bowled over, for the
part of me that did not love God was a black-hearted villain.
And apart from these considerations, I had some sort of idea
that if I did not keep my appointment with Lottie Jump, she
would somehow get revenge; she had seemed a girl of purpose. So, revolted and fascinated, brave and lily-livered, I
plodded along through the snow in my flopping galoshes up
toward the Chautauqua, where the trolley stop was. On my
way, I passed Virgil Meade's house; there was not just a
snowman, there was a whole snow family in the back yard,
and Virgil himself was throwing a stick for his dog. I was
delighted to see that he was alone.

Lottie, who was sitting on a bench in the shelter eating a
Mr. Goodbar, looked the same as she had the other time except that she was wearing an amazing hat. I think I had
expected her to have a black handkerchief over the lower part
of her face or to be wearing a Jesse James waistcoat. But I
had never thought of a hat. It was felt; it was the color of
cooked meat; it had some flowers appliquéd on the front of
it; it had no brim, but rose straight up to a very considerable
height, like a monument. It sat so low on her forehead and it
was so tight that it looked, in a way, like part of her.

"How's every little thing, bub?" she said, licking her candy
wrapper.

"Fine, Lottie," I said, freshly awed.

A silence fell. I drank some water from the drinking fountain, sat down, fastened my galoshes, and unfastened them again.

"My mother's teeth grow wrong way to," said Lottie, and showed me what she meant: the lower teeth were in front of the upper ones. "That so-called trolley car takes its own sweet time. This town is blah."

To save the honor of my home town, the trolley came scraping and groaning up the hill just then, its bell clanging with an idiotic frenzy, and ground to a stop. Its broad, proud cowcatcher was filled with dirty snow, in the middle of which rested a tomato can, put there, probably, by somebody who was bored to death and couldn't think of anything else to do —I did a lot of pointless things like that on lonesome Saturday afternoons. It was the custom of this trolley car, a rather mysterious one, to pause at the shelter for five minutes while the conductor, who was either Mr. Jansen or Mr. Peck, depending on whether it was the A.M. run or the P.M., got out and stretched and smoked and spit. Sometimes the passengers got out, too, acting like sightseers whose destination was this sturdy stucco gazebo instead of, as it really was, the Piggly Wiggly or the Nelson Dry. You expected them to take snapshots of the drinking fountain or of the Chautauqua meeting house up on the hill. And when they all got back in the car, you expected them to exchange intelligent observations on the aborigines and the ruins they had seen.

Today there were no passengers, and as soon as Mr. Peck got out and began staring at the mountains as if he had never seen them before while he made himself a cigarette, Lottie, in her tall hat (was it something like the Inspector's hat in the Katzenjammer Kids?), got into the car, motioning me to follow. I put our nickels in the empty box and joined her on the very last double seat. It was only then that she mapped out the plan for the afternoon, in a low but still insouciant voice. The hat—she did not apologize for it, she simply referred to it as "my hat"—was to be the repository of whatever we stole. In the future, it would be advisable for me to have one like it. (How? Surely it was unique. The flowers, I saw on closer examination, were tulips, but they were blue, and a very unsettling shade of blue.) I was to engage a clerk on one side of the counter, asking her the price of, let's say, a

tube of Daggett & Ramsdell vanishing cream, while Lottie
would lift a round comb or a barrette or a hair net or whatever on the other side. Then, at a signal, I would decide
against the vanishing cream and would move on to the next
counter that she indicated. The signal was interesting; it was
to be the raising of her hat from the rear—"like I've got the
itch and gotta scratch," she said. I was relieved that I was to
have no part in the actual stealing, and I was touched that
Lottie, who was going to do all the work, said we would "go
halvers" on the take. She asked me if there was anything in
particular I wanted—she herself had nothing special in mind
and was going to shop around first—and I said I would like
some rubber gloves. This request was entirely spontaneous;
I had never before in my life thought of rubber gloves in one
way or another, but a psychologist—or Judge Bay—might have
said that this was most significant and that I was planning
at that moment to go on from petty larceny to bigger game,
armed with a weapon on which I wished to leave no finger-
prints.

On the way downtown, quite a few people got on the trolley, and they all gave us such peculiar looks that I was chick-
enhearted until I realized it must be Lottie's hat they were
looking at. No wonder. I kept looking at it myself out of the
corner of my eye; it was like a watermelon standing on end.
No, it was like a tremendous test tube. On this trip—a slow
one, for the trolley pottered through that part of town in a
desultory, neighborly way, even going into areas where no one
lived—Lottie told me some of the things she had stolen in
Muskogee and here in Adams. They included a white satin
prayer book (think of it!), Mr. Goodbars by the thousands
(she had probably never paid for a Mr. Goodbar in her life),
a dinner ring valued at two dollars, a strawberry emery, several cans of corn, some shoelaces, a set of poker chips, countless pencils, four spark plugs ("Pa had this old car, see, and it
was broke, so we took 'er to get fixed; I'll build me a radio
with 'em sometime—you know? Listen in on them ear muffs
to Tulsa?"), a Boy Scout knife, and a Girl Scout folding cup.
She made a regular practice of going through the pockets of
the coats in the cloakroom every day at recess, but she had
never found anything there worth a red cent and was about

to give that up. Once, she had taken a gold pencil from a teacher's desk and had got caught—she was sure that this was one of the reasons she was only in the third grade. Of this unjust experience, she said, "The old hoot owl! If I was drivin' in a car on a lonesome stretch and she was settin' beside me, I'd wait till we got to a pile of gravel and then I'd stop and say, 'Git out, Miss Priss.' She'd git out, all right."

Since Lottie was so frank, I was emboldened at last to ask her what she had done with the cake. She faced me with her grin; this grin, in combination with the hat, gave me a surprise from which I have never recovered. "I ate it up," she said. "I went in your garage and sat on your daddy's old tires and ate it. It was pretty good."

There were two ten-cent stores side by side in our town, Kresge's and Woolworth's, and as we walked down the main street toward them, Lottie played with a Yo-yo. Since the street was thronged with Christmas shoppers and farmers in for Saturday, this was no ordinary accomplishment; all in all, Lottie Jump was someone to be reckoned with. I cannot say that I was proud to be seen with her; the fact is that I hoped I would not meet anyone I knew, and I thanked my lucky stars that Jack was up in the hills with his dead skunks, because if he had seen her with that lid and that Yo-yo, I would never have heard the last of it. But in another way I *was* proud to be with her; in a smaller hemisphere, in one that included only her and me, I was swaggering—I felt like Somebody, marching along beside this lofty Somebody from Oklahoma who was going to hold up the dime store.

There is nothing like Woolworth's at Christmastime. It smells of peanut brittle and terrible chocolate candy, Djer-Kiss talcum powder and Ben Hur perfume—smells sourly of tinsel and waxily of artificial poinsettias. The crowds are made up largely of children and women, with here and there a deliberative old man; the women are buying ribbons and wrappings and Christmas cards, and the children are buying asbestos pot holders for their mothers and, for their fathers, suède bookmarks with a burnt-in design that says "A good book is a good friend" or "Souvenir from the Garden of the Gods." It is very noisy. The salesgirls are forever ringing their

bells and asking the floorwalker to bring them change for a
five; babies in gocarts are screaming as parcels fall on their
heads; the women, waving rolls of red tissue paper, try to at-
tract the attention of the harried girl behind the counter.
("Miss! All I want is this one batch of the red. Can't I just
give you the dime?" And the girl, beside herself, mottled with
vexation, cries back, "Has to be rung up, Moddom, that's the
rule.") There is pandemonium at the toy counter, where
things are being tested by the customers—wound up, set off,
tooted, pounded, made to say "Maaaah-Maaaah!" There is
very little gaiety in the scene and, in fact, those baffled old
men look as if they were walking over their own dead bodies,
but there is an atmosphere of carnival, nevertheless, and as
soon as Lottie and I entered the doors of Woolworth's golden-
and-vermilion bedlam, I grew giddy and hot—not pleasantly
so. The feeling, indeed, was distinctly disagreeable, like the
beginning of a stomach upset.

Lottie gave me a nudge and said softly, "Go look at the
envelopes. I want some rubber bands."

This counter was relatively uncrowded (the seasonal sta-
tionery supplies—the Christmas cards and wrapping paper
and stickers—were at a separate counter), and I went around
to examine some very beautiful letter paper; it was pale pink
and it had a border of roses all around it. The clerk here was
a cheerful middle-aged woman wearing an apron, and she was
giving all her attention to a seedy old man who could not
make up his mind between mucilage and paste. "Take your
time, Dad," she said. "Compared to the rest of the girls, I'm
on my vacation." The old man, holding a tube in one hand
and a bottle in the other, looked at her vaguely and said, "I
want it for stamps. Sometimes I write a letter and stamp it
and then don't mail it and steam the stamp off. Must have
ninety cents' worth of stamps like that." The woman laughed.
"I know what you mean," she said. "I get mad and write a
letter and then I tear it up." The old man gave her a con-
descending look and said, "That so? But I don't suppose yours
are of a political nature." He bent his gaze again to the choice
of adhesives.

This first undertaking was duck soup for Lottie. I did not
even have to exchange a word with the woman; I saw Miss

Fagin lift up *that hat* and give me the high sign, and we moved away, she down one aisle and I down the other, now and again catching a glimpse of each other through the throngs. We met at the foot of the second counter, where notions were sold.

"Fun, huh?" said Lottie, and I nodded, although I felt wholly dreary. "I want some crochet hooks," she said. "Price the rickrack."

This time the clerk was adding up her receipts and did not even look at me or at a woman who was angrily and in vain trying to buy a paper of pins. Out went Lottie's scrawny hand, up went her domed chimney. In this way for some time she bagged sitting birds: a tea strainer (there was no one at all at that counter), a box of Mrs. Carpenter's All Purpose Nails, the rubber gloves I had said I wanted, and four packages of mixed seeds. Now you have some idea of the size of Lottie Jump's hat.

I was nervous, not from being her accomplice but from being in this crowd on an empty stomach, and I was getting tired—we had been in the store for at least an hour—and the whole enterprise seemed pointless. There wasn't a thing in her hat I wanted—not even the rubber gloves. But in exact proportion as my spirits descended, Lottie's rose; clearly she had only been target-practicing and now she was moving in for the kill.

We met beside the books of paper dolls, for reconnaissance. "I'm gonna get me a pair of pearl beads," said Lottie. "You go fuss with the hairpins, hear?"

Luck, combined with her skill, would have stayed with Lottie, and her hat would have been a cornucopia by the end of the afternoon if, at the very moment her hand went out for the string of beads, that idiosyncrasy of mine had not struck me full force. I had never known it to come with so few preliminaries; probably this was so because I was oppressed by all the masses of bodies poking and pushing me, and all the open mouths breathing in my face. Anyhow, right then, at the crucial time, I *had to be alone*.

I stood staring down at the bone hairpins for a moment, and when the girl behind the counter said, "What kind does Mother want, hon? What color is Mother's hair?," I looked past her and across at Lottie and I said, "Your brother isn't the only one in your family that doesn't have any brains." The clerk, astonished, turned to look where I was looking and caught Lottie in the act of lifting up her hat to put the pearls inside. She had unwisely chosen a long strand and was having a little trouble; I had the nasty thought that it looked as if her brains were leaking out.

The clerk, not able to deal with this emergency herself, frantically punched her bell and cried, "Floorwalker! Mr. Bellamy! I've caught a thief!"

Momentarily there was a violent hush—then such a clamor as you have never heard. Bells rang, babies howled, crockery crashed to the floor as people stumbled in their rush to the arena.

Mr. Bellamy, nineteen years old but broad of shoulder and jaw, was instantly standing beside Lottie, holding her arm with one hand while with the other he removed her hat to reveal to the overjoyed audience that incredible array of merchandise. Her hair all wild, her face a mask of innocent bewilderment, Lottie Jump, the scurvy thing, pretended to be deaf and dumb. She pointed at the rubber gloves and then she pointed at me, and Mr. Bellamy, able at last to prove his mettle, said "Aha!" and, still holding Lottie, moved around the counter to me and grabbed *my* arm. He gave the hat to the clerk and asked her kindly to accompany him and his redhanded catch to the manager's office.

I don't know where Lottie is now—whether she is on the stage or in jail. If her performance after our arrest meant anything, the first is quite as likely as the second. (I never saw her again, and for all I know she lit out of town that night on a freight train. Or perhaps her whole family decamped as suddenly as they had arrived; ours was a most transient population. You can be sure I made no attempt to find her again, and for months I avoided going anywhere near Arapahoe Creek or North Hill.) She never said a word but kept making signs with her fingers, ad-libbing the whole thing. They tested her hearing by shooting off a popgun right in her ear and she never batted an eyelid.

They called up my father, and he came over from the Safeway on the double. I heard very little of what he said because I was crying so hard, but one thing I did hear him say was "Well, young lady, I guess you've seen to it that I'll have to part company with my good friend Judge Bay." I tried to defend myself, but it was useless. The manager, Mr. Bellamy, the clerk, and my father patted Lottie on the shoulder, and the clerk said, "Poor, afflicted child." For being a poor, afflicted child, they gave her a bag of hard candy, and she gave them the most fraudulent smile of gratitude, and slobbered a little, and shuffled out, holding her empty hat in front of her like a beggar-man. I hate Lottie Jump to this day, but I have to hand it to her—she was a genius.

The floorwalker would have liked to see me sentenced to the reform school for life, I am sure, but the manager said that considering this was my first offense, he would let my father attend to my punishment. The old-maid clerk, who looked precisely like Emmy Schmalz, clucked her tongue and shook her head at me. My father hustled me out of the office and out of the store and into the car and home, muttering the entire time; now and again I'd hear the words "morals" and "nowadays."

What's the use of telling the rest? You know what happened. Daddy on second thoughts decided not to hang his head in front of Judge Bay but to make use of his friendship in this time of need, and he took me to see the scary old curmudgeon at his house. All I remember of that long declamation, during which the Judge sat behind his desk never taking his eyes off me, was the warning "I want you to give this a great deal of thought, Miss. I want you to search and seek in the innermost corners of your conscience and root out every bit of badness." Oh, *him!* Why, listen, if I'd rooted out all the badness in me, there wouldn't have been anything left of me. My mother cried for days because she had nurtured an outlaw and was ashamed to show her face at the neighborhood store; my father was silent, and he often looked at me. Stella, who was a prig, said, "And to think you did it at *Christmas*-time!" As for Jack—well, Jack a couple of times did not know how close he came to seeing glory when I had a butcher knife in my hand. It was Polecat this and Polecat that until I nearly went off my rocker. Tess, of course, didn't know what was going on, and asked so many questions that finally I told her to go to Helen Hunt Jackson in a savage tone of voice.

Good old Muff.

It is not true that you don't learn by experience. At any rate, I did that time. I began immediately to have two or three friends at a time—to be sure, because of the stigma on me, they were by no means the élite of Carlyle Hill Grade—and never again when that terrible need to be alone arose did I let fly. I would say, instead, "I've got a headache. I'll have to go home and take an aspirin," or "Gosh all hemlocks, I forgot—I've got to go to the dentist."

After the scandal died down, I got into the Campfire Girls. It was through pull, of course, since Stella had been a respected member for two years and my mother was a friend of the leader. But it turned out all right. Even Muff did not miss our periods of companionship, because about that time she grew up and started having literally millions of kittens.

A ludicrous situation, a dead-pan manner of writing and a fine satiric wit make this story a gem of comic writing. Couldn't it happen to any of us?

A Cold Potato

‖‖‖‖‖‖‖‖‖‖ PETER DE VRIES ‖‖‖‖‖‖‖‖‖‖

Sitting in a lawn chair tinkering with a broken bed lamp, Tom Bristol listened with half an ear to an account his wife, Alice, was giving of some neighbors with whom they'd recently become acquainted. "Guess what the Twinings do," she said. She was sitting across a parasol table from him. "When Bob is in the house, say, and Julia's back in that studio barn where she does her clay modelling, they write each other notes. And guess how they get them to one another." She paused, waiting for his response, but he was engrossed in his puttering. He chewed his tongue and pulled faces as he worked. "Do you know what they do?" Alice asked. Tom grunted inquiringly, poking an electric cord through the back of the lamp base. "They give them to Clementine—that cocker they have, you know—and Clementine delivers them. And waits for answers!" Alice laughed aloud. "Isn't that darling?"

"If I'm not mistaken—" Tom murmured abstractedly.

Alice leaned forward and smacked the tabletop with her palm. "I *wish* you'd listen *once* in a while!" she said.

He dropped everything in his lap, including his hands, and grinned guiltily.

"You're getting worse instead of better," she said.

Tom mopped his brow harassedly with his sleeves, as though to plead concentration rather than disregard. "I

281

listen more than you think," he said. "I get more than you think."

"Let's see what you got this time," she said. "In what way do the Twinings communicate with one another?"

"By writing notes," he answered.

"Who delivers these notes?"

"Clytemnestra."

"And who is that?"

"The cook."

"Who trots around with them in her teeth, I suppose." Alice fell back in her chair with a puff of despair. "*Really,* I don't know."

But she knew one thing. She knew that what called forth such a reaction from her was not alone his inattention to the story but his lack of capacity for the kind of matrimonial fun it illustrated. She envied wives whose husbands wrote cute notes and put them in the mouths of dogs, or, failing that, slipped them under doors or the bottoms of cosmetic jars; whose husbands gave presents rich in imagination, such as the swarm of bees Mary Fresenius had received from Fred one birthday, with a sentimental message about his Queen, or presents rich in whim, like the Afghan pup a man she knew of had given his wife, with a note pinned to the collar reading, "If we're ever going to have one, I guess I'll have to buy it"—an allusion to the Afghan rug she had been three years in knitting for their bed.

Alice often rather ornately fancied her own married life as a trellis on which no vine flourished, or, at best, as a vine on which no flowers bloomed. When it came to gags or devised endearments, Tom guessed he wasn't built that way and amiably wrote himself off as an Anglo-Saxon. Now, watching him under the parasol as he resumed his rapt tinkering, Alice formally traced her discontent to this source. He had negotiated his way from first acquaintance to marriage and through four years of that without having said "I love you"—three words the very thought of which admittedly palsied his tongue. Because of this deficiency in structure, he had to be dragged to movies. During the last picture they'd gone to, a mucilaginous love scene had caused him to stop his ears with his fingers in a spasm of protest and shut his eyes. Before marriage, Alice had had him figured for a reserved chap who simply didn't *show* his feelings, and he had seen in her a pretty, electric girl who could be coached away from highball glasses with humorous inscriptions and from whose speech could in time be edited such expressions as "Good-by now."

Abruptly, Alice picked up a newspaper from the grass beside her chair and opened it to a Broadway column. She ran her eye down it till she found a squib she was looking for. "Listen to this," she said. " 'Bruce Pembroke, the producer, has planned a nifty to surprise his wife,' " she read, extracting the utmost in felicity from the item by pitching her voice musically upward. " 'Said Frau, Kay Lillstrom, sailed for Cherbourg yesterday on the *Queen Mary*. He was there to see her off. Well, unknown to her but not to you and me, Pembroke will hop a plane for France and be on hand to greet her when she steps *off* the boat.' " Alice raised her head. "Could you do that?" she inquired.

"If I had the money," said Tom, who was now listening closely.

Alice slapped the paper down on the grass and rose. "You're a cold potato," she said, and crossed the lawn toward the house with great dignity.

One Saturday afternoon several weeks later, the Bristols were sitting on the back porch. Tom was watching a hummingbird cruise among the blooms of a strip of hollyhocks beside the house. "The Twinings are going away for two weeks," Alice said.

"Well." Tom's interest in the Twinings' whereabouts was more than cursory; he had, in the course of several evenings spent with them, seen a foursome crystallizing against his will. He cared for neither of them. Bob was a waitress-kidder whose conversation was studded with phrases like "from where I sit," and Julia was one of those overexpressive women who frown when they laugh. "When are they leaving?" he asked.

"Next week. Julia will visit her mother in New Hampshire, and Bob, of course, has to go to that dental-equipment convention in Chicago. So-o-o, the Twinings take separate vacations for the first time. Tough, the way they are about each other." Alice reached down to pick up a magazine and tossed it onto a chair. "But the thing is what will they do with Clementine?"

"Board him at a kennel." Tom leaned forward to scrutinize the hummingbird more intently.

"Her . . . Board *her* at a kennel! Well, yes, but it's cruel to do that to some pets—if you can possibly find friends to take them," Alice said. "Besides which, it's an ideal opportunity for the friends if they happen to have been debating whether to get a dog and might like to give having one a try. And it's only for two weeks."

Tom became aware of the tapping of Alice's foot, which, depending on how long she had been tapping it, she might at any moment stamp. Fearing another test quiz, he turned and responded heartily, "You're absolutely right!"

Clementine was in the house when Tom got home from work the next Friday. She sat, alert but dubious, in a corner of the living room, watching Tom as he came in. "How come?" asked Tom, whom office vexations had already left in disheveled spirits.

"We talked about it," Alice said. "You remember. Make her feel at home, because she doesn't know what to make of it yet. Julia dropped her off the last thing before she left this afternoon." Alice ran to the kitchen, where she had a tin of cheese puffs in the oven. There were garlic olives in a large bowl on the coffee table, Tom noted as he sat down on the sofa, across from the still wary cocker. Appetizers on that scale usually meant the day was chronologically special. "Today's the anniversary of our first date—remember?" Alice called from the kitchen as he was rummaging his brain to place the occasion. Resenting the guilt her tone imputed, he glared at the dog and said, "Come here!" The cocker twitched attentively, and was still. "Come here!" he repeated.

"Call her by her name," Alice said from the kitchen. "Don't just sit there and bark at her."

Tom got to his feet and stirred up a couple of Martinis, announcing to Alice that he thought he'd like one drink before he ran up for his shower. She bustled in with a few cheese puffs on a tray. They toasted the anniversary and then settled for a moment with their drinks. The dog sniffed open-mindedly at this and that, now and then pausing to regard one or the other of them, her tail wagging deliberately, like a metronome. Alice beamed down at her. "Orientation tour, Clementine?" she said. She drank, and licked her lips. "Different house? Everything strange? And no notes to deliver?" There was a silence. Tom saw a speculative light come into Alice's eye. "Let's us try it," she said.

"Oh, I don't think so," Tom said. "It wouldn't work."

"Well, let's *see*. I think it would be fun." She set her drink on the coffee table. "I'll tell you what. When you go up to shower, why don't you take her with you, write something, and see if she'll bring it down to me? We'll find out how clever she is. And *you* are." Alice laughed, rising. She passed by him on her way to the kitchen. "Break down," she said, tousling his hair.

Tom scooped the dog up and took her upstairs, scratching her ear as he mounted the steps. He set her down on the bedroom floor. She stayed put. He sat down at a writing desk in a corner of the room, drew a sheet of paper to him, and picked up a pencil. He flourished it abortively over the paper, feeling foolish, then annoyed. "What hath God wrought?" came to his mind. He put the pencil down and tugged up a sock. The dog, he saw, had come closer and now was watching him with understanding. He picked up the pencil again and sat gnawing the butt of it. Was he in fact a cold potato? Rapidly he wrote, "Maybe the Twinings haven't anything better to do," scribbled his name, folded the paper once, and held it out. "Take this down," he said, pointing. The dog snapped it in her teeth, turned, and was off down the stairs.

Tom rose and had started to take off his coat when, glancing down the staircase, which was visible from the bedroom, he saw the dog at the front door, trying to nose the screen door open. It didn't catch very well unless you remembered to jerk it shut. "Hey, no!" Tom called, springing down the stairs. He reached the door just as the dog wriggled out. She scrambled down the porch steps, ran diagonally across the lawn, and lit up the road in the direction of home.

For a moment, Tom stood looking after her, swearing in

gentle amazement. Then he recalled what he'd written. A fine
thing for the Twinings to find lying around someplace when
they got back. Not, he reminded himself with a sick swoop
in his stomach, that he was sure Bob had actually left yet.

His car was parked in front of the house, and he ran out
to it, got in, and shot off toward the Twinings', which was
about a thousand feet up the road. He overtook Clementine
at the house, but as he pulled in to the drive, he saw her
streak not for the house itself but across the lawn to the barn,
where Julia had her studio. Tom got out of the car and ran up
in time to see her squirm through a hole under the wall and
disappear.

He tried the door, which was locked. He peered on tiptoe
through a window, seeing nothing but a beam of the ceiling
inside. The window was locked. He was debating whether to
break a pane of glass when he spotted a doormat. He lifted
it. Nothing under it. He looked along the jamb for nails on
which a key might be hung but found none. His eye went
upward to the lintel. He reached up and felt along it. His
fingers knocked a key down. He opened the door and went in.

The inside was a huge single room with a skylight. There
were clay heads about, of the sort used in shop windows to
display hats on. Julia, as she repeatedly said, was not "a
real artist." The dog was watching him from the far side
of the room, her head cocked in what might be sport, mischief, anxiety, or just curiosity. The paper was on the floor
in front of her. With excessive stealth, Tom worked his way
over and, in a sudden move, snatched it up. He put it in his
pocket. "Nice dog," he said, and caught her up and tucked
her under one arm. He had started back toward the door
when something made him pause.

Alongside a writing table near a side window was a wastebasket with a suggestive wad of paper beside it on the floor.
Tom stood looking at the paper, tempted. He glanced at the
open door, hesitated, then, hitching the dog up under his
arm, went over and picked up the wad. Squatting, he
smoothed it out on his knee. "Princess," it ran in a bold, un-
inhibited hand, "you ought to come on over and take a
breather with the Sunday paper. Besides, you always look
good enough for a smack, even in a smock."

"Oh, God!" Tom said aloud. Fascinated, he plunged his hand into the wastebasket and fished up another wad of paper. Two notes were written on it. The first, in a delicate feminine script, went, "None of your lip, mister, except you know when." And the answer followed directly under it: "I guess I like to get in your hair because it's so soft and gold."

"Oh, *God!*" Tom groaned, and, imagining he had heard a footstep outside, popped erect and hurried out. There was no one around, and he hastily dumped the dog in the back seat and drove home.

Tom carted the dog up the walk to his house, toward Alice, waiting on the porch.

"What on earth happened?" she asked, holding the screen door open for him.

"Goddam dog!" he said, dropping her on the vestibule carpet and spanking his hands. "He ran home with the damn note you made me write." Pausing only to make sure the screen door had been clapped securely to, he tramped on upstairs to the bedroom, pulling off his coat. He attacked his shirt and tie. Alice came up the stairs.

"What was in the note?" she asked gingerly, around the corner of the doorway.

"Plenty! I said how damn silly the Twinings are. And I didn't get it back," he called, feeling that some stretching of the facts served a justifiably punitive end. "The dog took it into the studio and left it there."

She subsided on the top step and burst into tears.

"Oh, God!" Tom groaned for the third time, whipping off his undershirt and firing it into an open hamper. He took a step toward the door and called out quickly, "All right— I did get it back. I really did. So now, for God's sake, stop sniffling. This childish business wasn't my idea."

Instantly, he was sorry. There were footsteps running rapidly down the stairs, an object, probably an ashtray, smacked down on top of something in the living room, and fresh wails. He plowed into the hall with his hands in the air. As he paced there, wondering what to do, his eye lit on Clementine, who was churning confusedly around in the vestibule below, looking up at him and then into the living

room and back again. He snapped his fingers and beckoned
her urgently up. "Come here!" he whispered loudly, and,
pausing only long enough to make sure the dog obeyed,
disappeared into the bedroom. He hurried to the desk,
scribbled, "I guess I like to get in your hair because it's so
soft and silky," and flourished it peremptorily at the dog,
who had been standing beside the desk, panting and apparently a little bemused by the sequence of exertions, but
ready. She snapped up the note and scurried down. Tom
watched her push at the screen door for a few moments before Alice came out of the living room and took the note
from her.

Tom went back to the bedroom and finished undressing
with one ear cocked. On his way to the bathroom, he paused
at the head of the stairs and listened. There was a concluding
sniff below, then silence. He stepped back out of sight, hearing footsteps coming toward the vestibule and, immediately
afterward, the sound of a sheet of paper torn from the telephone pad there. He hurried into the bathroom, closed the
door, and turned the shower up full force.

This fine combination of an expert report on the
Navy's war in the South Pacific with a dramatic
study of courage is my favorite of Mr. Michener's
Tales of the South Pacific.

The Cave

|||||||||||||||||||JAMES A. MICHENER|||||||||||||||||||

In those fateful days of 1942 when the Navy held on
to Guadalcanal by faith rather than by reason, there was a PT
Boat detachment stationed on near-by Tulagi. It was my fortune to be attached to this squadron during the weeks when
PT Boats were used as destroyers and destroyers were used
as battleships. I was merely doing paper work for Admiral
Kester, but the urgency of our entire position in the Solomons was so great that I also served as mess officer, complaints officer, and errand boy for Lt. Comdr. Charlesworth,
the Annapolis skipper.

The job of Charlesworth's squadron was to intercept anything that came down The Slot. Barges, destroyers, cruisers,
or battleships. The PT's went out against them all. The Japs
sent something down every night to reinforce their men on
Guadal. The PT's fought every night. For several weeks, terrible, crushing weeks of defeat, the defenses of Guadalcanal
rested upon the PT's. And upon Guadal rested our entire
position in the South Pacific.

I have become damned sick and tired of the eyewash written about PT Boats. I'm not going to add to that foolish
legend. They were rotten, tricky little craft for the immense
jobs they were supposed to do. They were improvised, often
unseaworthy, desperate little boats. They shook the stomachs
out of many men who rode them, made physical wrecks of

others for other reasons. They had no defensive armor. In many instances they were suicide boats. In others they were like human torpedoes. It was a disgrace, a damned disgrace that a naval nation like America should have had to rely upon them.

Yet I can understand their popularity. It was strictly newspaper stuff. A great nation was being pushed around the Atlantic by German submarines. And mauled in the Pacific by a powerful Jap fleet. Its planes were rust on Hickam Field and Clark Field. Its carriers were on the bottom. Americans were desperate. And then some wizard with words went to work on the PT Boat. Pretty soon everybody who had never seen a real Jap ship spitting fire got the idea our wonderful little PT's were slugging it out with Jap battleships. Always of the Kongo Class.

Well, that crowd I served with on Tulagi in 1942 knew different. So far as I ever heard, none of my gang even sank a Jap destroyer. It was just dirty work, thumping, hammering, kidney-wrecking work. Even for strong tough guys from Montana it was rugged living.

The day I started my duty with the PT Boats we were losing the battle of Guadalcanal. Two American warships were sunk north of Savo that night. Eight of our planes were shot down over Guadal, and at least fifteen Jap barges reached Cape Esperance with fresh troops. Toward morning we were bombed both at Tulagi and at Purvis Bay. A concentration of Bettys. At dawn a grim bunch of men rose to survey the wreckage along the shore.

Lt. Comdr. Charlesworth met me at the pier. A stocky, chunky, rugged fellow from Butte, Montana. Stood about five feet nine. Had been an athlete in his day. I found him terribly prosaic, almost dull. He was unsure of himself around other officers, but he was a devil in a PT Boat. Didn't know what fear was. Would take his tub anywhere, against any odds. He won three medals for bravery beyond the call of duty. Yet he was totally modest. He had only one ambition: to be the best possible naval officer. Annapolis could be proud of Charlesworth. We were.

"We got by again," he said as we studied the wreckage of the night before. "Any damage to the gasoline on Gavutu?"

"None," his exec replied.

"Looks like some bombs might have hit right there beside that buoy."

"No, sir. One of the PT's hit that last night. Tying up."

Charlesworth shook his head. "How do they do it?" he asked. "They can hit anything but a Jap barge."

"Sir!" an enlisted man called out from the path almost directly above us on the hillside. "V.I.P. coming ashore!"

"Where?" Charlesworth cried. As an Annapolis man he was terribly attentive when any V.I.P.'s were about. He had long since learned that half his Navy job was to fight Japs. The other half was to please "very important persons" when they chanced to notice him. Like all Annapolis men, he knew that a smile from a V.I.P. was worth a direct hit on a cruiser.

"In that little craft!" the man above us cried. Probably someone aboard the small craft had blinkered to the signal tower. Charlesworth straightened his collar, hitched his belt and gave orders to the men along the shore. "Stand clear and give a snappy salute."

But we were not prepared for what came ashore. It was Tony Fry! He was wearing shorts, only one collar insigne, and a little go-to-hell cap. He grinned at me as he threw his long legs over the side of the boat. "Hello, there!" he said. Extending a sweaty hand to Charlesworth he puffed, "You must be the skipper. Y'get hit last night?"

"No, sir," Charlesworth said stiffly. "I don't believe I know you, sir."

"Name's Fry. Tony Fry. Lieutenant. Just got promoted. They only had one pair of bars, so I'm a little lopsided." He flicked his empty collar point. It was damp. "Holy cow! It's hot over here!"

"What brings you over?" Charlesworth asked.

"Well, sir. It's secret business for the admiral. Nothin' much, of course. You'll get the word about as soon as I do, commander," Fry said. "I hear you have a cave somewhere up there?"

"Yes, we do," Charlesworth said. "Right over those trees." Above us we could see the entrance to the cave Fry sought. Into the highest hill a retreat, shaped like a U, had been dug. One entrance overlooked the harbor and Purvis Bay, where our big ships were hidden. The other entrance, which we could not see, led to a small plateau with a good view of Guadal and Savo, that tragic island. Beyond Savo lay The Slot, the island-studded passage leading to Bougainville, Rabaul, Truk, and Kuralei.

"I understand the cave's about ten feet high," Tony mused.

"That's about right," Charlesworth agreed.

"Just what we want," Tony replied. He motioned to some men who were carrying gear in black boxes. "Let's go, gang!" he called.

Charlesworth led the way. With stocky steps he guided us along a winding path that climbed steeply from the PT anchorage where Fry had landed. Hibiscus, planted by the wife of some British official years ago, bloomed and made the land as lovely as the bay below.

"Let's rest a minute!" Fry panted, the sweat pouring from his face.

"It's a bit of a climb," Charlesworth replied, not even breathing hard.

"Splendid place, this," Fry said as he surveyed the waters leading to Purvis Bay. "Always depend upon the British to cook up fine quarters. We could learn something from them. Must have been great here in the old days."

As we recovered our breath Charlesworth pointed to several small islands in the bay. "That's where the Marines came ashore. A rotten fight. Those ruins used to be a girls' school. Native children from all over the islands came here." I noticed that he spoke in rather stilted sentences, like a Montana farmer not quite certain of his new-found culture.

"It'll be a nice view from the cave," Fry said. "Well, I'm ready again."

We found the cave a cool, moist, dark retreat. In such a gothic place the medieval Japs naturally located their headquarters. With greater humor we Americans had our headquarters along the shore. We reserved the cave for Tony Fry.

For once he saw the quiet interior with its grand view over the waters he said, "This is for me." He turned to Charlesworth and remarked, "Now, commander, I want to be left alone in this cave. If I want any of you PT heroes in here I'll let you know."

Charlesworth, who was already irritated at having a mere lieutenant, a nobody and a reserve at that, listed as a V.I.P., snapped to attention. "Lieut. Fry," he began, "I'm the officer-in-charge . . ."

"All right, commander. All right," Fry said rapidly. "I'm going to give you all the deference due your rank. I know what the score is. But let's not have any of that Annapolis fol-de-rol. There's a war on."

Charlesworth nearly exploded. He was about to grab Fry by the arm and swing him around when Tony turned and grinned that delightfully silly smirk of his. Sunlight from the plateau leaped across his wet face. He grinned at Charlesworth and extended a long hand. "I'm new at this business, commander," he said. "You tell me what to do, and I'm gonna do it. I just don't want any of your eager beavers messing around. They tell me over at Guadal that you guys'd take on the whole fleet if Halsey would let you."

Charlesworth was astounded. He extended his hand in something of a daze. Tony grabbed it warmly. In doing so he engineered Charlesworth and me right out of the cave. "Men bringin' in the stuff," he explained.

This Fry was beyond description, a completely new type of naval officer. He didn't give a damn for anything or anybody. He was about thirty, unmarried. He had some money and although he loved the Navy and its fuddy ways, he ridiculed everything and everybody. He was completely oblivious to rank. Even admirals loved him for it. Nobody was ever quite certain what he was supposed to be doing. In time no one cared. The important thing was that he had unlimited resources for getting whiskey, which he consumed in great quantities. I've been told the Army wouldn't tolerate Fry a week.

We were several days finding out what he was doing on Tulagi. Late that afternoon, for example, we heard a clattering and banging in the cave. We looked up, and Tony had two enlisted men building him a flower box. That evening he was down in the garden of the old British residency digging up some flowers for his new home. A pair of Jap marauders came winging in to shoot the island up. Tony dived for a trench and raised a great howl.

"What's the matter with the air raid system?" he demanded that night at chow. "That's why I like the cave. It's safe! They'd have to lay a bomb in there with a spoon!"

It soon became apparent that Charlesworth and Fry would not get along. Tony delighted in making sly cracks at the "trade-school boys." Charlesworth, who worshipped the stones of Annapolis, had not the ready wit to retaliate. He took no pains to mask his feelings, however.

It was also apparent that Fry was rapidly becoming the unofficial commanding officer of the PT base. Even Charlesworth noticed that wherever Tony propped his field boots, that spot was headquarters. That was the officers' club.

Settled back, Tony would pass his whiskey bottle and urge other men to talk. But if there was anything pompous, or heroic, or ultra-Annapolis in the conversation, Fry would mercilessly ridicule it and puncture the balloons. The PT captains delighted to invite him on their midnight missions.

"Me ride in those death traps? Ha, ha! Not me! I get paid to sit right here and think. That's all I'm in this man's Navy for. You don't get medals for what I do. But you do get back home!" Unashamedly he would voice the fears and cowardice that came close to the surface of all our lives. Men about to throw their wooden PT's at superior targets loved to hear Fry express their doubts. "Those sieves? Those kidney-wreckers? Holy cow! I'd sooner go to sea in a native canoe!"

But when the frail little craft warmed up, and you could hear Packard motors roaring through Tulagi, Tony would pull himself out of his chair in the cave, unkink a drunken knee, and amble off toward the water front. "Better see what the heroes are doing," he would say. Then, borrowing a revolver or picking up a carbine as he went, he would somehow or other get to where Charlesworth's PT was shoving off.

"Room for a passenger?" he would inquire.

"Come aboard, sir," Charlesworth would say primly, as if he were back at San Diego.

Enlisted men were especially glad to see Tony climb aboard. "He's lucky!" they whispered to one another. "Guys like him never get killed."

Tony, or God, brought the PT's luck one night. That was when Charlesworth got his second medal. His prowling squadron ran smack into some Jap AKA's south of Savo. Charlesworth was a little ahead of the other PT's when the Japs were sighted. Without waiting a moment he literally rushed into the formation, sank one and hung onto another, dodging shells, until his mates could close in for the kill.

Tony was on the bridge during the action. "You handle this tub right well, skipper," he said.

"It's a good boat," Charlesworth said. "This is a mighty good boat. A man ought to be willing to take this boat almost anywhere."

"You did!" Fry laughed.

In the bright morning, when Charlesworth led his PT's roaring home through the risky channel between Tulagi and Florida, Tony lay sprawled out forward, watching the spray and the flying fish. "What a tub!" he grunted as he climbed ashore. "There must be an easier way to earn a living!"

And if one of the enlisted men from Charlesworth's PT sneaked up to the cave later in the day, Fry would shout at him, "Stay to hell out of here! If you want a shot of whiskey that bad, go on down to my shack. But for God's sake don't let the commander see you. He'd eat my neck out." Whether you were an enlisted man or an officer, you could drink Fry's whiskey. Just as long as he had any.

We had almost given up guessing what Fry was doing when he woke Charlesworth and me one morning about five. "This is it!" he whispered.

He led us up to the cave but made us stand outside. In a moment an enlisted radio man, Lazars, appeared. "Any further word?" Fry asked.

"None, sir," Lazars said.

"Something big's up," Tony said in a low voice. We moved toward the cave. "No," Fry interrupted. "We had the boys rig a radio for you over in that quonset," he said. Dawn was breaking as he led us to a half-size quonset at the other side of the plateau. When we stepped inside the barren place Lazars started to tune a radio. He got only a faint whine. He kept twirling the dials. It was cool in the hut. The sun wasn't up yet.

"It may be some time," Fry said. The sun rose. The hut became humid. We began to sweat. We could hear the metal

expanding in little crackles. New men always thought it was
rain, but it was the sun. Then you knew it was going to be
a hot day.

Lazars worked his dials back and forth with patient skill.
"No signal yet," he reported. Fry walked up and down nervously. The sweat ran from his eyes and dropped upon his
thin, bare knees. Finally he stopped and wiped the moisture
from his face.

"I think this is it, Charlesworth," he said.

"What?" the commander asked.

"We sneaked a man ashore behind the Jap lines. Somewhere up north. He's going to try to contact us today. Imagine what we can do if he sends us the weather up there.
News about the Jap ships! How'd you like to go out some
night when you knew the Japs were coming down? Just
where they were and how many. How would that be, eh?"
Tony was excited.

Then there came a crackle, a faint crackling sound. It was
different from the expansion of the burning roof. It was a
radio signal! Fry put his finger to his lips.

From far away, from deep in the jungles near Jap sentries,
came a human voice. It was clear, quiet, somewhat high-
pitched. But it never rose to excitement. I was to hear that
voice often, almost every day for two months. Like hundreds
of Americans who went forth to fight aided by that voice, I
can hear it now. It fills the room about me as it filled that
sweating hut. It was always the same. Even on the last day
it was free from nervousness. On this morning it said: "Good
morning, Americans! This is your Remittance Man. I am
speaking from the Upper Solomons. First the weather. There
are rain clouds over Bougainville, the Treasuries, Choiseul,
and New Georgia. I believe it will rain in this region from
about 0900 to 1400. The afternoon will be clear. It is now
94 degrees. There are no indications of violent weather."

The lonely voice paused. In the radio shack we looked at
one another. No one spoke. Lazars did not touch the dials.
Then the voice resumed, still high, still precise and slow:

"Surface craft have been in considerable motion for the
last two days. I think you may expect important attempts at
reinforcement tonight. One battleship, four cruisers, a carrier,

eight destroyers and four oilers have been seen in this region. They are heading, I presume, toward Kolombangara rendezvous. In addition not less than nineteen and possibly twenty-seven troop barges are definitely on their way south. When I saw them they were making approximately eleven knots and were headed right down The Slot. I judge they will pass Banika at 2000 tonight. Landing attempts could be made near Esperance any time after 0200 tomorrow morning. You will be glad to know that the barges appear to be escorted by heavy warships this time. The hunting should be good."

The speaker paused again. Charlesworth rubbed his chin and studied a map pasted on wallboard and hung from the sloping tin. No one spoke.

"And for you birdmen," the voice continued. "Four flights have set out for your territory. They are in rendezvous at present. North of Munda. I cannot see the types of planes at present. I judge them to be about forty bombers. Twenty fighters. If that proportion makes any sense, I'm not very good on aircraft. Ah, yes! This looks like a flight down from Kieta right above me. Perhaps you can hear the motors! Thirty or more fighter planes. Altitude ten thousand feet, but my distances are not too accurate. I'm rather new at this sort of thing, you know."

The Remittance Man paused and then for the first time gave his closing comment which later became a famous rallying cry in the South Pacific: "Cheerio, Americans. Good hunting, lads!"

As soon as the broadcast ended Charlesworth dashed from the quonset and started laying plans for that night's foray. At every subsequent broadcast it was the same way. No sooner would the Remittance Man finish speaking than Charlesworth would bound into action and move imaginary PT's all through the waters between Guadal and the Russells. For him the Remittance Man was an abstract, impersonal command to action.

But to Tony Fry the enigmatic voice from the jungle became an immense intellectual mystery. It began on this first morning. After Charlesworth had dashed down to the PT's Fry asked me, "What do you make of it?"

"Very clever intelligence," I replied.

"Holy cow!" he snorted. "I don't mean that! I mean this chap. This fellow up there in the jungles. Japs all around him. How can he do it?"

"He probably volunteered for it," I replied.

"Of course he did!" Fry agreed with some irritation. "But what I mean is, how does a guy get courage like that? I should think his imagination alone would drive him frantic."

"He's probably some old duffer's been out in the islands all his life."

"I know who he is," Fry said, kicking at pebbles as we walked over to the cave. "Chap named Anderson. Trader from Malaita. An Englishman. But why did he, of all the men out here, volunteer? How can he face that?" Tony gripped my arm. "A single man goes out against an island of Japs? Why?"

We didn't see Tony that day. He ate canned soup and beer in the cave. That night the PT's went out without him. They did all right, thanks to the Remittance Man. The Japs came down exactly as he said. Charlesworth slipped in and chopped them up. The black year of 1942, the terrible year was dying. But as it died, hope was being born on Guadalcanal and Tulagi.

Next morning at 0700 all those who were not in sickbay getting wounds and burns from the night before patched up were in the steaming quonset. Promptly on time the Remittance Man spoke. Fry stood close to the radio listening to the high-pitched voice extend its cheery greeting: "Good morning, Americans! I have good news for you today. But first the weather." He told us about conditions over Bougainville, Choiseul, and New Georgia. Flying weather was excellent.

"In fact," he said, "flying looks so good that you shall probably have visitors. Very heavy concentrations of bombers overhead at 1100 this morning. If I can judge aircraft, not less than ninety bombers and fighters are getting ready for a strike this morning. Some are in the air ready to leave. They appear to be at 12,000 feet. Don't bet on that, though. I can't say I've learned to use the estimating devices too well yet. Let's say not less than 10,000. Some fighters have moved in from Bougainville. Look at them! Rolling about, doing loops and all sorts of crazy things. There they go! It's quite a circus. This will be a fine day. Cheerio, Americans! Good hunting!" The radio clicked. There was silence.

Immediately, Charlesworth called his men together. "They'll want some PT's for rescue work!" he snapped. "If that man is right, this may be a big day. A very big day. We'll put B Squadron out. Shove. And don't come home till you comb every shore about here. Pick them all up. Get them all!" He hurried his men down to the shore.

A phone jangled. It was headquarters. "Admiral Kester wants the PT's out for rescue," intelligence said.

"They've already left," I reported.

"This Remittance Man," Tony said when the others had gone. "Commander, where do you suppose he is?"

"I thought Bougainville," I said.

"No. I was studying a map. He's on some peak from which he can see Munda."

"Maybe you're right," I said. "He confuses his broadcasts nicely."

"Don't be surprised if he was on Sant' Ysabel all the time," Fry said.

But not then, nor at any other time, did he or any of us say what was in our minds: *How desperately the Japs must be searching for that man! How fitful his sleep must be! How he must peer into every black face he sees in the jungle, wondering, "Is this my Judas?"*

Tony and I went out into the brilliant sunlight to watch the miracle below us. From the unbroken shoreline of Tulagi bits of green shrubbery pulled into the channel. Then camouflage was discarded. The PT's roared around the north end of the island. Off toward Savo. The PT's were out again.

"I've been trying to find out something about the man," Tony continued. "Just a man named Anderson. Nobody knows much about him. He came out here from England. Does a little trading for Burns Philp. Went into hiding when the Japs took Tulagi. Came over to Guadal and volunteered for whatever duty was available. Medium-sized chap. You've heard his voice."

At 1100 the first Jap plane came into view. It was a Zero

spinning wildly somewhere near the Russells. It flamed and lurched into the sea. The battle was on!

For an hour and ten minutes the sky above Guadal and Tulagi was a beautiful misery of streaming fire, retching planes, and pyres flaming out of the sea. The Japanese broke through. Nothing could stop them. We heard loud thunder from Purvis Bay. Saw high fires on Guadal. Eight times Jap fighters roared low over Tulagi. Killed two mechanics at the garage. But still we watched the breathless spectacle overhead.

Yes, the Japs broke through that day. Some of them broke through, that is. And if they had unlimited planes and courage, they could break through whenever they wished. But we grinned! God, we even laughed out loud. Because we didn't think the Japs had planes to waste! Or pilots either. And mark this! When Jap pilots plunged into the sea, The Slot captured them and they were seen no more. But when ours went down, PT Boats sped here and there to pick them up.

So, we were happy that night. Not silly happy, you understand, because we lost a PT Boat to strafers. And we could count. We knew how many Yank planes crashed and blew up and dove into the sea. But nevertheless we were happy. Even when Tony Fry came in slightly drunk and said, "That guy up there in the jungles. How long can he keep going? You radio men. How long would it take American equipment to track down a broadcasting station?"

There was no reply. "How long?" Fry demanded.

"Two days. At the most."

"That's what I thought," he said.

Next morning at seven the Remittance Man was happy, too. "The Japanese Armada limped home," he reported in subdued exultation as if he knew that he had shared in the victory. "I myself saw seven planes go into the sea near here. I honestly believe that not more than forty got back. And now good news for one squadron. My little book tells me the plane with that funny nose is the P-40. One P-40 followed two crippled Jap bombers right into New Georgia waters. They were flying very low. He destroyed each one. Then the Nips jumped him and he went into the water himself. But I believe I saw him climb out of his plane and swim to an island. I think he made it safely."

The distant speaker cleared his throat and apparently took a drink of water. "Thank you, Basil," he said. "There will be something in The Slot tonight, I think. Four destroyers have been steaming about near Vella Lavella. Something's on! You can expect another landing attempt tonight. If you chappies only had more bombers you could do some pretty work up here today. Cheerio, Americans! Good hunting!"

Charlesworth was more excited than I had ever seen him before. Jap DD's on the move! His eyes flashed as he spread maps about the baking quonset. At 1500 Fry came down the winding path, dragging a carbine and a raincoat along the trail. "Might as well see if you trade-school boys can run this thing," he said as he climbed aboard.

At 2300 that night they made contact. But it was disappointing. The big stuff was missing. Only some Jap barges and picket boats. There was a long confused fight. Most of the Japs got through to Guadal. The PT's stayed out two more nights. On the last night they got in among some empty barges heading back to Munda. Got five of them. Fry shot up one with a Thompson when the torpedoes were used up. But the kill, the crushing blow from which the Japs would shudder back, that eluded them.

On the dreary trip home Fry asked Charlesworth if he thought the Remittance Man moved from one island to another in a canoe. "Oh, damn it all," Charlesworth said. "Stop talking about the man. He's just a fellow doing a job."

Tony started to reply but thought better of it. He went forward to watch the spray and the flying fish. As the boats straggled into Tulagi he noticed great activity along the shore.

A PT blinkered to Charlesworth: "The coastwatcher says tonight's the night. Big stuff coming down!"

"What's he say?" Fry asked.

"We're going right out again," Charlesworth said, his nostrils quivering.

Tony barely had time to rush up to the cave. He dragged me in after him. It was my first trip inside since he had taken charge. I was surprised. It looked much better than any of

the quonsets. Spring mattresses, too. "I told the men to fix
it up," Fry said, waving a tired hand about the place. "Commander," he asked quietly. "What did the . . ." He nodded
his head toward Bougainville.

"He was off the air yesterday," I said. "This morning just
a sentence. 'Destroyers definitely heading south.' That was
all."

Tony leaned forward. He was sleepy. The phone rang.
"Holy cow!" Fry protested. "You been out three nights run-
nin', skipper. You're takin' this war too hard." There was a
long pause. Then Fry added, "Well, if you think you can't
run it without me, OK. But those Jap destroyers have guns,
damn it. Holy cow, those guys'd shoot at you in a minute!"

They left in mid-morning sunlight, with great shafts of
gold dancing across the waters of Tulagi Bay. They slipped
north of Savo in the night. They found nothing. The Japs
had slipped through again. Halsey would be splitting a gut.
But shortly after dawn there was violent firing over the hori-
zon toward the Russells. Charlesworth raced over. He was
too late. His exec had sighted a Jap destroyer! Full morning
light. Didn't wait a second. Threw the PT around and blazed
right at the DD. On the second salvo the Jap blew him to
pieces. Little pieces all over The Slot. The exec was a dumb
guy, as naval officers go. A big Slav from Montana.

Charlesworth was a madman. Wanted to sail right into
Banika channel and slug it out. He turned back finally. Kept
his teeth clenched all the way home. When Fry monkeyed
with the radio, trying to intercept the Remittance Man,
Charlesworth wanted to scream at him. He kept his teeth
clenched. A big thing was in his heart. His lips moved over
his very white teeth. "Some day," he muttered to himself,
"we'll get us a DD. That big Slav. He was all right. He was
a good exec. My God, the fools can't handle these boats.
They haven't had the training. Damn it, if the fool would
only stop monkeying with that radio!"

Tony couldn't make contact. That was not his fault, because the Remittance Man didn't broadcast. Fry clicked the
radio off and went forward to lie in the sun. When the PT
hove to at its mooring he started to speak to Charlesworth,
but the skipper suddenly was overwhelmed with that burn-

ing, impotent rage that sneaks upon the living when the dead were loved. "By God, Fry. Strike me dead on this spot, but I'll get those Japs. You wait!"

Fry grinned. "I ain't gonna be around, skipper. Not for stuff like that. No need for me to wait!" The tension snapped. Charlesworth blinked his eyes. The sun was high overhead. The day was glorious, and hot, and bright against the jungle. But against the shore another PT was missing.

Back in the quonset Tony studied his maps, half sleeping, half drunk. In the morning the cool voice of the Remittance Man reported the weather and the diminishing number of Jap aircraft visible these days. Fry strained for any hint that would tell him what the man was doing, where he was, what his own estimates of success were. Charlesworth sat morosely silent. There was no news of surface movements. It was a dull day for him, and he gruffly left to catch some extra sleep.

Tony, of course, stayed behind in the hot quonset, talking about the Remittance Man. "This Basil he mentioned the other day? Who is he?" We leaned forward. For by this time Tony's preoccupation with the Englishman affected all of us. We saw in that lonely watcher something of the complexity of man, something of the contradictory character of ourselves. We had followed Tony's inquiries with interest. We were convinced that Anderson was an ordinary nobody. Like ourselves. We became utterly convinced that under similar circumstances we ordinary people would have to act in the same way.

Fry might ask, "What makes him do that?" but we knew there was a deeper question haunting each of us. And we would look at one another. At Charlesworth, for example, who went out night after night in the PT's and never raised his voice or showed fear. We would ask ourselves: "What makes him do it? We know all about him. Married a society girl. Has two kids. Very stuffy, but one of the best men ever to come from Annapolis. We know that. But what we don't know is how he can go out night after night."

Tony might ask, in the morning, "Where do you suppose he is now?" And we would ponder, not that question, but another: "Last night. We knew Jap DD's were on the loose. But young Clipperton broke out of infirmary so he could take his PT against them. Why?" And Clipperton, whose torpedo-man was killed, would think, not of the Remittance Man, but of Fry himself: "Why does a character like that come down to the pier each night, dragging that fool carbine in the coral?"

And so, arguing about the Remittance Man we studied ourselves and found no answers. The coastwatcher did nothing to help us, either. Each morning, in a high-pitched, cheerful voice he gave us the weather, told us what the Japs were going to do, and ended, "Cheerio, Americans! Good hunting!"

I noticed that Charlesworth was becoming irritated at Fry's constant speculation about the coastwatcher. Even Anderson's high voice began to grate upon the skipper's ears. We were all sick at the time. Malaria. Running sores from heavy sweating. Arm pits gouged with little blisters that broke and left small holes. Some had open sores on their wrists. The jungle rot. Most of us scratched all the time. It was no wonder that Charlesworth was becoming touchy.

"Damn it all, Fry," he snapped one day. "Knock off this chatter about the Remittance Man. You're getting the whole gang agitated."

"Is that an order?" Fry said very quietly, his feet on the table.

"Yes, it is. You're bad for morale."

"You don't know what morale is," Fry grunted, reaching for the whiskey bottle and getting to his feet. Charlesworth pushed a chair aside and rushed up to Tony, who ignored him and slumped lazily toward the door of the quonset.

"You're under quarters arrest, Fry! You think you can get away with murder around here. Well, you're in the Navy now." The skipper didn't shout. His voice quivered. Sweat was on his forehead.

Fry turned and laughed at him. "If I didn't know I was in the Navy, you'd remind me." He chuckled and shuffled off toward the cave. We didn't see him in the quonset ever again.

But it was strange. As the tenseness on Tulagi grew, as word seeped down the line that the Japs were going to have one last mighty effort at driving us out of the Solomons, more and more of the PT skippers started to slip quietly into the cave. They went to talk with Tony. Behind Charlesworth's back. They would sit with their feet on an old soap box. And they would talk and talk.

"Tony," one of them said, "that damn fool Charlesworth is going to kill us all. Eight PT's blown up since he took over."

"He's a good man," Tony said.

"The enlisted men wish you'd come along tonight, Tony. They say you're good luck."

"OK. Wait for me at the Chinaman's wharf." And at dusk Fry would slip out of the cave, grab a revolver, and shuffle off as if he were going to war. Next morning the gang would quietly meet in the cave. As an officer accredited directly to Charlesworth I felt it my duty to remain loyal to him, but even I found solace of rare quality in slipping away for a chat with Tony. He was the only man I knew in the Pacific who spoke always as if the destiny of the human soul were a matter of great moment. We were all deeply concerned with why we voyagers ended our travels in a cave on Tulagi. Only Fry had the courage to explore that question.

As the great year ended he said, "The Remittance Man is right. The Japs have got to make one more effort. You heard what he said this morning. Ships and aircraft massing."

"What you think's gonna happen, Tony?" a young ensign asked.

"They'll throw everything they have at us one of these days."

"How you bettin'?"

"Five nights later they'll withdraw from Guadal!"

The men in the cave whistled. "You mean . . ."

"It's in the bag, fellows. In the bag."

You know what happened! The Remittance Man tipped us off one boiling morning. "Planes seem to be massing for some kind of action. It seems incredible, but I count more than two hundred."

It was incredible. It was sickening. Warned in advance, our fighters were aloft and swept into the Jap formations like sharks among a school of lazy fish. Our Negro cook alone counted forty Zeros taking the big drink. I remember one glance up The Slot. Three planes plunging in the sea. Two Japs exploding madly over Guadal.

This was the high tide! This was to be the knockout blow at Purvis Bay and Guadal. This was to be the Jap revenge against Tulagi. But from Guadal wave after wave of American fighters tore and slashed and crucified the Japs. From Purvis our heavy ships threw up a wall of steel into which the heavy bombers stumbled and beat their brains out in the bay.

In the waters around Savo our PT's picked up twenty American pilots. Charlesworth would have saved a couple of Japs, too, but they fired at him from their sinking bomber. So he blasted it and them to pieces.

He came in at dusk that night. His face was lined with dirt, as if the ocean had been dusty. I met him at the wharf. "Was it what it seemed like?" he asked. "Out there it looked as if we . . ."

"Skipper," I began. But one of the airmen Charlesworth had picked up had broken both legs in landing. The fact that he had been rescued at all was a miracle. Charlesworth had given him some morphine. The silly galoot was so happy to see land he kept singing the Marine song:

> Oh we asked for the Army at Guadalcanal
> But Douglas MacArthur said, "No!"
> He gave as his reason,
> "It's now the hot season,
> Besides there is no USO."

"Take him up to sickbay," Charlesworth said, wiping his face.

The injured pilot grinned at us. "That's a mighty nice little rowboat you got there, skipper!" he shouted. He sang all the way to sickbay.

At dinner Charlesworth was as jumpy as an embezzler about to take a vacation during the check-up season. He tried to piece together what had happened, how many Japs had gone down. We got a secret dispatch that said a hundred and twelve. "Pilots always lie," he said gruffly. "They're worse than young PT men." He walked up and down his hut for a few minutes and then motioned me to follow him. We walked out into the warm night. Lights were flashing over Guadal. "The Japs have got to pull out of that island," Charlesworth insisted as we walked up the hill behind his hut. When we were on the plateau he stopped to study the grim and silent Slot. "They'll be coming down some night." To my surprise he led me to the cave. At the entrance we could hear excited voices of young PT skippers. They were telling Tony of the air battles they had watched.

We stepped into the cave. The PT men were embarrassed and stood at attention. Tony didn't move, but with his foot he shoved a whiskey bottle our way. "It's cool in here," Charlesworth said. "Carry on, fellows." The men sat down uneasily. "Fry," the commander blurted out, "I heard the most astonishing thing this morning."

"What was it?" Tony asked.

"This Remittance Man," Charlesworth said. "I met an old English trader down along the water front. He told me Anderson was married to a native girl. The girl broke her leg and Anderson fixed it for her. Then he married her, priest and all. A real marriage. And the girl is as black . . . as black as that wall."

"Well, I'll be damned!" Fry said, bending forward. "Where'd you meet this fellow? What was he like? Holy cow! We ought to look him up!"

"He said a funny thing. I asked him what Anderson was like and he said, 'Oh, Andy? He was born to marry the landlady's daughter!' I asked him what this meant and he said, 'Some fellows are born just to slip into things. When it comes time to take a wife, they marry the landlady's daughter. She happens to be there. That's all.'"

The cave grew silent. We did not think of Jap planes crashing into The Slot, but of the Remittance Man, married to a savage, slipping at night from island to island, from village to hillside to treetop.

At 0700 next morning all of us but Fry were in the steaming quonset listening to the Remittance Man. We heard his quavering voice sending us good cheer. "Good morning, Americans!" he began. "I don't have to tell you the news. Where did they go? So many went south and so few came back! During the last hour I have tried and tried to avoid optimism. But I can't hide the news. I sincerely believe the

Nips are planning to pull out! Yes. I have watched a considerable piling up of surface craft. And observe this. I don't think they have troops up here to fill those craft. It can mean only one thing. I can't tell if there will be moves tonight. My guess, for what it is worth, is this: Numerous surface craft will attempt to evacuate troops from Guadalcanal tonight. Some time after 0200." There was a pause. Our men looked at one another. By means of various facial expressions they telegraphed a combined: "Oh boy!" Then the voice continued:

"You may not hear from me for several days. I find a little trip is necessary. Planes are overhead. Not the hundreds that used to fly your way. Two only. They are looking for me, I think."

From that time on the Remittance Man never again broadcast at 0700. He did, however, broadcast to us once more. One very hot afternoon. But by then he had nothing of importance to tell us. The Japanese on Guadal were knocked out by then. They were licking their wounds in Munda. They didn't know it at the time, but they were getting ready to be knocked out of Munda, too.

The Remittance Man guessed wrong as to when the Japs would evacuate Guadal. It came much later than he thought. When the attempt was made, we were waiting for them with everything we had. This time the PT boats were fortified by airplanes and heavy ships. We weren't fighting on a shoestring this time.

I suppose you know it was a pretty bloody affair. Great lights flashed through the dark waters. Japs and their ships were destroyed without mercy. Our men did not lust after the killing. But when you've been through the mud of Guadal and been shelled by the Japs night after night until your teeth ached; when you've seen the dead from your cruisers piled up on Savo, and your planes shot down, and your men dying from foes they've never seen; when you see good men wracked with malaria but still slugging it out in the jungle . . .

A young PT skipper told me about the fight. He said, "Lots of them got away. Don't be surprised if Admiral Halsey gives everybody hell. Too many got away. But we'll get them sometime later. Let me tell you. It was pitch black. We knew there were Japs about. My squadron was waiting. We were all set. Then a destroyer flashed by. From the wrong way! 'Holy God!' I cried. 'Did they slip through us after all?' But the destroyer flashed on its searchlights. Oh, man! It was one of ours! If I live to be a million I'll never see another sight like that. You know what I thought? I thought, 'Oh, baby! What a difference! Just a couple of weeks ago, if you saw a destroyer, you knew it was a Jap!' " The ensign looked at us and tried to say something else. His throat choked up. He opened his mouth a couple of times, but no words came out. He was grinning and laughing and twisting a glass around on the table.

Of course, one Jap destroyer did get through. As luck would have it, the DD came right at Charlesworth. That was when he got his third ribbon. It happened this way. We got a false scent and had our PT's out on patrol two days early. All of them. On the day the little boats ripped out of Hutchinson Creek and Tulagi Harbor Charlesworth stopped by the cave. "The boys say you're good luck, Tony. Want to go hunting?"

"Not me!" Fry shuddered. "There's going to be shooting tonight. Somebody's going to get killed."

"We're shoving off at 1630."

"Well, best of luck, skipper."

Tony was there, of course, lugging that silly carbine. They say he and Charlesworth spent most of the first day arguing. Fry wanted to close Annapolis as an undergraduate school. Keep it open only as a professional school for training regular college graduates. You can imagine the reception this got from the skipper. The second day was hot and dull. On the third afternoon word passed that the Nips were coming down. Fourteen or more big transports.

"Those big transports have guns, don't they?" Tony asked at chow.

"Big ones."

"Then what the hell are we doin' out here?"

"We'll stick around to show the others where the Japs are. Then we'll hightail it for home," Charlesworth laughed.

"Skipper, that's the first sensible thing you've said in three days."

That night the PT's were in the thick of the scramble. It was their last pitched battle in the Solomons. After that night their work was finished. There were forays, sure. And isolated actions. But the grand job, that hellish job of climbing into a ply-wood tug, waving your arms and shouting, "Hey fellows! Look at me! I'm a destroyer!" That job was over. We had steel destroyers, now.

You know how Charlesworth got two transports that night. Laid them wide open. He had one torpedo left at 0340. Just cruising back and forth over toward Esperance. With that nose which true Navy men seem to have he said to Fry and his crew, "I think there's something over there toward Savo."

"What are we waiting for?" his ensign asked. The PT heeled over and headed cautiously toward Savo. At 0355 the lookout sighted this Jap destroyer. You know that one we fished up from the rocks of Iron Bottom Bay for the boys to study? The one that's on the beach of that little cove near Tulagi? Well, the DD they sighted that night was the same class.

Tensely Charlesworth said, "There she is, Tony."

"Holy cow!" Fry grunted. "That thing's got cannons!"

This remark was what the skipper needed. Something in the way Tony drew back as if mortally afraid, or the quaver in his voice, or the look of mock horror on his thin face was the encouragement Charlesworth wanted.

"Pull in those guts!" he cried. The PT jumped forward, heading directly at the destroyer.

At 2000 yards the first Jap salvo landed to port. "Holy cow!" Fry screamed. "They're shooting at us!"

At 1800 yards three shells splashed directly ahead of the PT. One ricocheted off the water and went moaning madly overhead. At 1500 yards the PT lay over on its side in a hard turn to starboard. Jap shells landed in the wake. The PT resumed course. The final 500 yards was a grim race. Jap searchlights were on the PT all the time, but at about 950 Charlesworth nosed straight at the port side of the destroyer and let fly with his last torpedo.

I wish that torpedo had smacked the Jap in the engine-room. Then we might have some truth to support all the nonsense they write about the PT's sinking capital ships. A little truth, at any rate. But the damned torpedo didn't run true. You'd think after all this time BuOrd could rig up a torpedo that would run true. This one porpoised. The Jap skipper heeled his tug way over, and the torpedo merely grazed it. There was an explosion, of course, and a couple of the enlisted men were certain the Jap ship went down. But Charlesworth knew different. "Minor damage," he reported. "Send bombing planes in search immediately." So far as we knew, our planes never found the Jap. We think it hid in some cove in the Russells and then beat it on up to Truk.

Back at Tulagi our officers and men tried to hide their feelings but couldn't. Nobody wanted to come right out and say, "Well, we've licked the yellow bastards." But we were all thinking it. Tulagi was exactly like a very nice Sunday School about to go on a picnic. Everybody behaved properly, but if you looked at a friend too long he was likely to break out into a tremendous grin. Fellows played pranks on one another. They sang! Oh, Lord! How they sang. Men who a few days before were petty enemies now flopped their arms around each other's necks and made the night air hideous. Even the cooks celebrated and turned out a couple of almost decent meals. Of course, we starved for the next week, but who cared? The closest anyone came to argument was when Charlesworth's ensign ribbed a pilot we had fished from The Slot. "If you boys had been on the job, you could have knocked over a Jap DD." A week earlier this would have started a fight. But this time the aviator looked at the red-cheeked ensign and started laughing. He rumpled the ensign's hair and cooed, "I love you! I love you! You ugly little son-of-a-bitch!"

But there was a grim guest at all of our celebrations. Fry saw to that. He would come out of the cave at mealtime, or when we were drinking. And he would bring the Remittance Man with him. He dragged that ghostly figure into every bottle of beer. The coastwatcher ate every meal with us. Officers would laugh, and Fry would trail the ghost of that lonely voice across the table. The aviator would tell a joke, and Tony would have the silent broadcaster laughing at his side. He never mentioned the man, his name, or his duties. Yet by the look on Fry's face, we all knew that he was constantly wondering why the morning broadcasts had not been resumed.

One night Charlesworth and I followed Tony to the cave. "Fry, goddam it," the skipper began. "You've got me doing it, too!"

"What?"

"This coastwatcher. Damn it all, Fry. I wish we knew what had happened to that chap." The men sat on boxes in the end of the cave toward the bay.

"I don't know," Tony said. "But the courage of the man fascinates me. Up there. Alone. Hunted. Japs getting closer every day. God, Charlesworth, it gets under my skin."

"Same way with me," the skipper said. "His name comes up at the damnedest times. Take yesterday. I was down at the water front showing some of the bushboys how to store empty gas drums. One of them was from Malaita. I got to talking with him. Found out who this Basil is that Anderson referred to one morning."

"You did?" Fry asked eagerly.

"Yes, he's a murderer of some sort. There was a German trader over on his island. Fellow named Kesperson. Apparently quite a character. Used to beat the boys up a good deal. This chap Basil killed him one day. Then hid in the bush. Well, you know how natives are. Always know things first. When word got around that Anderson was to be a coastwatcher this Basil appears out of the jungle and wants to go along. Anderson took him."

"That's what I don't understand, skipper," Fry commented. "The things Anderson does don't add up to an ordinary man. Why would a good man like that come out here in the first place? How does he have the courage?"

Fry's insidious questions haunted me that night. Why do good men do anything? How does any man have the courage to go to war? I thought of the dead Japs bobbing upon the shorelines of The Slot. Even some of them had been good men. And might be again, if they could be left alone on their farms. And there was bloody Savo with its good men. All the men rotting in Iron Bottom Bay were good men, too.

The young men from the *Vincennes*, the lean Australians from the *Canberra*, the cooks from the *Astoria*, and those four pilots I knew so well . . . they were good men. How did they have the courage to prowl off strange islands at night and die without cursing and whimpers? How did they have the courage?

And I hated Tony Fry for having raised such questions. I wanted to shout at him, "Damn it all! Why don't you get out of the cave? Why don't you take your whiskey bottles and your lazy ways and go back to Noumea?"

But as these words sprang to my lips I looked across the cave at Tony and Charlesworth. Only a small light was burning. It threw shadows about the faces of the two men. They leaned toward one another in the semi-darkness. They were talking of the coastwatcher. Tony was speaking: "I think of him up there pursued by Japs. And us safe in the cave."

And then I understood. Each man I knew had a cave somewhere, a hidden refuge from war. For some it was love for wives and kids back home. That was the unassailable retreat. When bad food and Jap shells and the awful tropic diseases attacked, there was the cave of love. There a man found refuge. For others the cave consisted of jobs waiting, a farm to run, a business to establish, a tavern on the corner of Eighth and Vine. For still others the cave was whiskey, or wild nights in the Pink House at Noumea, or heroism beyond the call of valor. When war became too terrible or too lonely or too bitter, men fled into their caves, sweated it out, and came back ready for another day or another battle.

For Tony and Charlesworth their cave was the contemplation of another man's courage. They dared not look at one another and say, "Hell! Our luck isn't going to hold out much longer." They couldn't say, "Even PT Boats get it sooner or later." They dared not acknowledge, "I don't think I could handle another trip like that one, fellow."

No, they couldn't talk like that. Instead they sat in the cave and wondered about the Remittance Man. Why was he silent? Had the Japs got him? And every word they said was directed inward at themselves. The Englishman's great courage in those critical days of The Slot buoyed their equal courage. Like all of us on Tulagi, Tony and Charlesworth knew that if the coastwatcher could keep going on Bougainville, they could keep going in the PT's.

Then one morning, while Tony sat in the cave twisting the silent dials, orders came transferring him to Noumea. He packed one parachute bag. "An old sea captain once told me," he said at lunch, "to travel light. Never more than twenty-five pieces of luggage. A clean shirt and twenty-four bottles of whiskey!"

At this moment there was a peremptory interruption. It was Lazars. "Come right away!" he shouted. "The Remittance Man."

The coastwatcher was already speaking when we reached the cave. ". . . and I judge it has been a great victory because only a few ships straggled back. Congratulations, Americans. I am sorry I failed you during the critical days. I trust you know why. The Nips are upon us. This time they have us trapped. My wife is here. A few faithful boys have stayed with us. I wish to record the names of these brave friends. Basil and Lenato from Malaita. Jerome from Choiseul. Morris and his wife Ngana from Bougainville. I could not wish for a stancher crew. I do not think I could have had a better . . ."

There was a shattering sound. It could have been a rifle. Then another and another. The Remittance Man spoke no more. In his place came the hissing voice of one horrible in frustration: "American peoper! You die!"

For a moment it was quiet in the cave. Then Fry leaped to his feet and looked distractedly at Charlesworth. "No! No!" he cried. He returned to the silent radio. "No!" he insisted, hammering it with his fist. He swung around and grabbed Charlesworth by the arm. "I'm going over to see Kester," he said in mumbling words.

"Fry! There's nothing you can do," the skipper assured him.

"Do? We can get that man out of Bougainville!"

"Don't be carried away by this thing, Fry," Charlesworth reasoned quietly. "The man's dead and that's that."

"Dead?" Tony shouted. "Don't you believe it!" He ran out of the cave and started down the hill.

"Fry!" Charlesworth cried. "You can't go over to Guadal. You have no orders for that." Tony stopped amid the flowers of the old English garden. He looked back at Charlesworth in disgust and then ran on down the hill.

We were unprepared for what happened next. Months later Admiral Kester explained about the submarine. He said, "When Fry broke into my shack I didn't know what to think. He was like a madman. But as I listened to him I said, 'This boy's talking my language.' A brave man was in trouble. Up in the jungle. Some damn fools wanted to try to help him. I thought, 'That's what keeps the Navy young. What's it matter if this fool gets himself killed. He's got the right idea.' So there was a sub headed north on routine relief. The skipper would try anything. I told him to take Fry and the Fiji volunteer along." The admiral knocked the ashes out of his pipe as he told me about it. "It's that go-to-hell spirit you like about Tony Fry. He has it."

The sub rolled into Tulagi Bay that afternoon. The giant Fiji scout stayed close to Tony as they came ashore. Whenever we asked the Fiji questions about the trip into the jungle he would pat his kinky hair and say in Oxford accents, "Ah, yes! Ah, yes!" He was shy and afraid of us, even though he stood six-feet-seven.

I dragged my gear down to the shore and saw the submariners, the way they stood aloof and silent, watching their pigboat with loving eyes. They are alone in the Navy. I admired the PT boys. And I often wondered how the aviators had the courage to go out day after day, and I forgave their boasting. But the submariners! In the entire fleet they stand apart.

Charlesworth joined us, too. About dusk he and Fry went to the PT line and hauled out a few carbines. They gave me one. We boarded the sub and headed north. In the pigboat Tony was like the mainspring of a watch when the release is jammed. Tense, tight-packed, he sweated. Salt perspiration dripped from his eyebrows. He was lost in his own perplexing thoughts.

We submerged before dawn. This was my first trip down into the compressed, clicking, bee-hive world of the submariners. I never got used to the strange noises. A head of steam pounding through the pipes above my face would make me shudder and gasp for air. Even Charlesworth had trouble with his collar, which wasn't buttoned.

At midnight we put into a twisting cove south of Kieta on the north shore of Bougainville. I expected a grim silence, ominous with overhanging trees along the dark shore. Instead men clanked about the pigboat, dropped a small rubber boat overboard, and swore at one another. "Ah, yes!" the Fiji mused. "This is the place. We were here four weeks ago. No danger here." He went ashore in the first boatload.

While we waited for the rubber boat to return, the submariners argued as to who would go along with us as riflemen. This critical question had not been discussed on the way north. Inured to greater dangers than any jungle could hold, the submariners gathered in the blue light of a passageway and matched coins. Three groups of three played odd-man-out. Losers couldn't go.

"Good hunting," one of the unlucky submariners called as we climbed into the boat. "Sounds like a damned fool business to me. The guy's dead, ain't he?" He went below.

Ashore the Fiji had found his path. We went inland half a mile and waited for the dawn. It came quietly, like a purposeful cat stealing home after a night's adventure. Great trees with vine-ropes woven between them fought the sun to keep it out of the jungle. Stray birds, distant and lonely, shot through the trees, darting from one ray of light to another. In time a dim haze seeped through the vast canopy above us. The gloomy twilight of daytime filled the jungle.

As we struggled toward the hills we could see no more than a few feet into the dense growth. No man who has not seen the twisting lianas, the drooping parasites, the orchids, and the dim passages can know what the jungle is like, how oppressive and foreboding. A submariner dropped back to help me with my pack. "How do guys from Kansas and Iowa fight in this crap?" he asked. He went eight steps ahead of me, and I could not see him, nor hear him, nor find any trace that a human had ever stood where I then stood. The men from Kansas and Iowa, I don't know how they cleaned up one jungle after another.

The path became steeper. I grew more tired, but Tony

hurried on. We were dripping. Sweat ran down the bones at the base of my wrist and trickled off my fingers. My face was wet with small rivulets rising from the springs of sweat in my hair. No breath of air moved in the sweltering jungle, and I kept saying to myself, "For a man already dead!"

The Fiji leaned his great shoulders forward and listened. "We are almost there," he said softly, like an English actor in a murder mystery. The pigboat boys grinned and fingered their carbines. The jungle path became a trail. The lianas were cut away. Some coconut husks lay by the side of a charred fire. We knew we were near a village of pretensions.

Fry pushed ahead of the Fiji. He relaxed his grip upon the carbine and dragged it along by the strap. He hurried forward.

"There it is!" he cried in a hoarse whisper. He started to run. The Fiji reached forward and grabbed him, like a mother saving an eager child. The giant Negro crept ahead to study the low huts. Inch by inch we edged into the village square. We could see no one. Only the hot sun was there. A submariner, nineteen years old, started to laugh.

"Gosh!" he cried. "Nobody here!" We all began to laugh.

And then I saw it! The line of skulls! I could not speak. I raised my arm to point, but my hand froze in half-raised position. One by one the laughing men saw the grim palisades, each pole with a human head on top. I was first to turn away and saw that Fry was poking his carbine into an empty hut.

"Hey!" he shouted. "Here's where he was. This was his hut!"

"Tony!" I cried. My voice burst from me as if it had a will of its own.

"What do you know?" Tony called out from the hut. "Here's the guy's stuff! I wouldn't be surprised if he . . ."

Fry rejoined us, carrying part of a radio set. The bright sun blinded him for a moment. Then he saw my face, and the row of skulls. He dropped his carbine and the rheostat. "No!" he roared. "God! No!" He rushed across the sun-drenched square. He rushed to the fifteen poles and clutched each one in turn. The middle, thickest and most prominent, bore the sign: "Amerrican Marine You Die."

Charlesworth and I crossed to the skull-crowned palisades.
I remember two things. Fry's face was composed, even relaxed. He studied the middle pole with complete detachment. Then I saw why! Up the pole, across the Jap sign, and
on up to the withering head streamed a line of jungle ants.
They were giving the Remittance Man their ancient jungle
burial.

Charlesworth's jaw grew tense. I knew he was thinking,
"When I get a Jap . . ." I can't remember what I thought,
something about, "This is the end of war . . ." At any rate,
my soliloquy was blasted by an astonished cry from a submariner.

The skulls had shocked us. What we now saw left us hor-
rified and shaken. For moving from the jungle was a native
with elephantiasis. He was so crippled that he, of all the
natives, could not flee at our approach.

I say he moved. It would be more proper to say that he
crawled, pushing a rude wheelbarrow before him. In the
barrow rested his scrotum, a monstrous growth that otherwise would drag along the ground. His glands were diseased.
In a few years his scrotum had grown until it weighed more
than seventy pounds and tied him a prisoner to his barrow.

We stepped back in horror as he approached. For not only
did he have this monstrous affliction, but over the rest of
his body growths the size of golf balls protruded. There must
have been fifty of them. He, knowing of old our apprehen-
sions, smiled. Tony Fry, alone among us, went forward to
greet him and help him into the shade. The man dropped
his barrow handles and shook hands with Tony. Fry felt the
knobs and inwardly winced. To the man he made no sign.
"You talk-talk 'long me?" Tony asked. The man spoke a few
words of Pidgin.

Fry gave the man cigarettes and candy. He broke out some
cloth, too, and threw it across the wheelbarrow. Without
thinking, he placed his right foot on the barrow, too, and
talked earnestly with the crippled native.

All that steaming midday, with the sun blazing overhead,
Tony asked questions, questions, and got back fragments of
answers in Pidgin. "Japoni come many time. Take Maries.
Take banan'. Take young girls. Kill missi. One day white

man come. Two bockis. Black string. There! There! There! Chief want to kill white man like Japoni say. Now chief he pinis. That one. That he skull.

"White man got 'long one Mary. Black allasame me. She say, 'No killim.' White man live in hut 'long me." We were revolted at the thought of the Remittance Man and his wife living with the scrofulous man and his wheelbarrow. The dismal account droned on. "One day Japoni come. Fin' white man. Break bockis. Tear down string. Shoot white man. White man he not die."

Tony reached out and grabbed the man by his bumpy arm. The man recoiled. Fry turned to us and called in triumph, "He isn't dead! They didn't kill him, did they?"

"Not killim," the diseased man replied. "Jus' here!" The man indicated his shoulder and tried to simulate blood running from a wound.

"Where did they take him?" Tony pressed, his voice low and quick.

"Bringim out here. Tie him to stick. Big fella b'long sword cut him many time." With his cigarette the native made lunging motions. Finally he swished it across his own neck. "Cut 'im head off."

Tony wiped his long hand across his sweating forehead. He looked about him. The sun was slanting westward and shone in his eyes. He turned his back on the barrow and studied the ants at their work. "We'll bury the guy," he said.

Immediately the native started to wail. "Japoni say he killim all fella b'long village we stop 'im 'long ground. All fella b'long here run away you come, like Japoni say." It was apparent the Japs had terrified the jungle villages. "No takem skull. Please!"

We looked up at the whitening remnants. The ants, impervious to our wonder, hurried on. Fry raised his right hand to his waist and flicked a salute at the middle skull. He shook hands with the thankful native and gave him four packages of cigarettes. He gave him his knife, a penknife, his handkerchief, the last of his candy and two ends of cloth. Again he shook the knobby hand. "Listen, Joe," he said sharply, his eyes afire. "We'll be back to get you one of these days. Won't be long. We fix you up. American doctors. They can cut that away. No pain. Good job. All those bumps. All gone. Joe! I've seen it done in Santo. We'll fix you up, good. All you got to do, Joe. Watch that one. Don't let it get lost. We'll be back. Not long now."

In a kind of ecstasy Fry motioned us into the jungle. When we were halfway back to the submarine he stopped suddenly. He was excited. "You heard what I told that guy. If any of you are around when we take Bougainville, come up here and get him. Haul him down to a hospital. A good doctor can fix that guy up in one afternoon. Remember. And when you're up here bury that skull."

We plunged into the deepest part of the jungle and waited for the submarine to take us to whatever caves of refuge we had fashioned for ourselves. Fry hid in his atop Tulagi for the better part of a week, drunk and unapproachable. On the seventh day he appeared unshaven, gaunt, and surly.

"I'm gettin' to hell out of here," he said. He went down to the bay and caught a small boat for Guadal.

I can't say he left us, though, for his fixation on the Remittance Man remained. We used to say, "Who do you suppose that guy actually was?" We never found out. We found no shred of evidence that pointed to anything but a thoroughly prosaic Englishman. As I recall, we added only one fact that Fry himself hadn't previously uncovered. On the day that Charlesworth received notice of his third medal he rushed into the mess all excited. "What do you know?" he cried. "That fellow up in the jungle. At least I found out where he came from! A little town near London."